Tomb Divers

Robyn Bee

Book Cover by ZeD, Miblart

ISBN: 978-1-0689295-1-9

To the love that's made these stories possible and to the life we share.

Chapter One

My father hit me the first time he caught me reading a book. Then, he hit me again when I told him that it was an account of Grand Necrophant Marduss and his arrival at the great walls of Uruq.

History, my father said, was as worthless as the dust it was buried under.

But I couldn't get enough of it. I loved those old stories, and our town's vizier was a drunk old elf who never locked his meager collection of books. Through them, I lived hundreds of different lives.

I marched with the lamians—humans whose bottom half was a long serpent's tail—as they led their armies of dog-soldiers out of the desert to make war on the elven kings of Ashur. I followed behind the chariots of those first necrophants and warrior-viziers as they rolled over fields of the slain. I deliberated with them in their campaign tents and shared in their triumph as the great elven cities burned.

And then, when the ashes were swept away by a legion of newly risen dead, I saw the birth of an empire that has lasted for more than three millennia.

My father beat me more than once in the years before my sixteenth birthday. Although, I admit that many of those bruises were well deserved. I wasn't a very good worker, often sneaking out of the copper mines that were the source of my village's scant wealth to stare out over the horizon.

The world was so much bigger, so much older and grander than the little collection of mountain cabins in which I'd been born. I wanted to walk in the footsteps of those ancient figures, to step back into the annals of history and into the stories that had shaped us.

The more I read, however, the more I realized how incomplete those stories were. Time, and the ever-blowing winds of the desert, had rubbed away at our past. Details were lost. Entire chapters were fragmented, buried, and forgotten. So much of our history, the tale of all that we were, was a mystery.

It was frustrating, infuriating, and irresistible.

For the answers were out there. The truth of our past existed and was hinted at in a thousand ancient fragments. There were clues to be gathered, studied, and slotted into place. Those stories could be completed, and somewhere, between the pages of those books I, ahem—*borrowed* from the vizier, I decided that I would be the one to do it.

"How are you going to eat, Naroh?" My father had asked me on the day I'd left my home. *"There's no worse foolishness than looking at the past while you starve in the present."*

And while the man who'd raised me may have been an illiterate miner and a bit of a bastard, he was, unfortunately, not completely wrong. A passion for everything that may be called 'ancient' may have been good for my soul, but it didn't do much to nourish my body.

In those first few months after escaping my natal mountains, I don't think that there was a single night where I didn't go to bed hungry. There weren't many who cared about archaic stones and battlefields as much as I did. No one was out there ready to give gold to a skinny young man so he could peer at worn tablets or chase millennia-old mysteries across the sands of the Great Desert.

The truth was that there was no money in the study of history. Not unless one got a little... creative.

"Come on, Balasi," I said, waving a little statuette beneath the other man's nose. "Look at this! This is a representation of the God Tel'aman from the middle of the Nabonassaran Dynasty. It's more than two thousand years old!"

Balasi scoffed, flicking his ears. "A god nobody worships from a dynasty that nobody cares about. My clients are looking for gold, Naroh, not old rock."

We were in the man's little dry goods shop, the space around us filled with bags of flour, dried food, leather, cloth, and a hundred other things. Sweat trickled down my back, the rising heat of the morning already filling the cramped, stuffy place.

The shopkeeper watched me swallow my initial surge of indignation with an amused quirk. He leaned both forearms on the counter between us, not reacting as I placed the statuette down beside the mask I'd brought out earlier.

"It's got rubies set in its eyes," I said at last. "And this copper funeral mask here belonged to the second wife of Pharon Nabonassara IV. This stuff is rare, maybe one of a kind. I'm sure that you can find a buyer for it."

"I already told you," he said, folding his arms. "I'll give you five silver for the rubies, but I'm not paying more than a bit of bronze for the mask. You know as well as I do that the snakes like gold, not junk from a dynasty that accomplished nothing. Did you bring any of that for me?"

"They did not accomplish 'nothing,'" I said through gritted teeth. "And you know as well as I that it wasn't common for lamians to have their gold buried with them until about three centuries after the end of the Nabonassaran Dynasty."

"Exactly," Balasi growled. His ears stiffened, and I heard his irritation in the swish of his tail. "I don't understand you, Naroh. You're not some stupid sand grub who can't tell the difference between a necropolis and a mausoleum. There's a million fucking tombs in Ashura and you're the only diver I've met who wastes my time with this shit."

"It's not a waste," I said, matching his glare. "The things I'm learning down in those tombs are things you can't find in any book! It's—"

"Pointless," Balasi interrupted. "I need artifacts I can sell."

"And I need more than five and a bit silver!"

"You're lucky I'm even giving you that much."

"This is worth more than that," I insisted. "You can't fuck me on this."

"Fuck you?" The shopkeeper said, baring his sharp teeth in a wide grin. "What does a little runt like you know about fucking?"

My face twisted into a frown, and Balasi's grin dissolved into that high scavenger's cackle for which his people were known. I felt the hairs on my neck stand up and had to consciously suppress a cringe.

Gods of fucking death, I hated that laugh.

I was ready to snap out a reply when the door behind me opened. My heart lurched as I swept the relics off the counter and into a fold of my loose robe. Balasi choked on the rest of his mirth and straightened from the hunch he'd fallen into.

Our lamian rulers did not appreciate the pillaging of their ancestral tombs, and the practice was *very* illegal. Never mind that they were the ones who bought most of the artifacts that tomb divers like me plundered.

I turned, trying not to let too much of my relief show when I saw that it was a hyenaling woman that had entered and not a squad of noble house guards. Balasi stepped out from behind the counter, his own spotted, hyena ears flat against his head. He rushed over to the woman, greeting her with an obsequious tone and a downward curl of his tail.

Hyenalings looked like a cross between a human and a hyena, though they were as intelligent as any other race of the Ashuran Empire. They had large, rounded ears on top of their heads and tails curling out from their lower backs. Their hair grew long and thick, and though it varied in color, was always speckled like the fur of their ears and tail.

I drifted over to an out-of-the-way corner of Balasi's shop, watching her take my place at the counter and send the shopkeeper scurrying back and forth with a few impatient commands.

She must be of his clan.

Much like their distant, four-legged ancestors, hyenaling women were generally quite a bit larger and more powerful than their men. And, unfortunately for Balasi, they tended to rule their familial clans with an iron fist.

"You know, Naroh," the hyenaling said when we were once again alone in his little shop. "Maybe it's your shaggy, black hair or dark eyes, or the fact that you look like a half-starved cub, but I like you."

"Alright," I cautiously replied. "I like you too."

I moved back to the counter, conscious of the sling that was coiled beneath the wide sleeve of my robe, as well as the pouch of stones and knife at my belt. Sifters, people like Balasi who bought and sold looted artifacts, could be ... unpredictable.

The lamians were always hunting crypt desecrators, even as they built larger and more fortified tombs for themselves. Balasi may be smart and good at keeping his head down, but a sifter's career usually ended with a swing of the headman's axe.

And seeing as our demi-serpent lords were masters of death magic, punishment didn't typically stop with the removal of one's head.

"I'm happy to hear that," the hyenaling said, planting his hands on the surface of his counter. "Now, let me take another look at what you've brought me."

Indeed, it took a special sort to gamble one's life on so thin a chance at wealth. Sifters were crazy, I thought, once again pulling out the artifacts that I'd plundered.

Almost as crazy as tomb divers.

I left the hyenaling's little shop a while later with an extra seven silver coins in my pocket. It wasn't much, especially considering that I'd had to spend four days navigating that crypt's ancient traps and corridors to get it.

But I had to admit that, in the end, Balasi hadn't ripped me off too badly.

I turned out of the dusty alley where the sifter had his shop, breathing deeply of the morning air. It was late in spring, yet so close to the Northern Mountains, there was still a tinge of freshness to the breeze that blew past me.

This was a fairly typical northern town. It was medium-sized, dry, and dusty. The streets were narrow, and the houses were built of gray stone quarried from the nearby mountains. That stone, I figured, was probably the entire reason the town existed. The Nazlun River and the great city of Ikkad were only a few days to the south and they were no doubt always hungry for good stone down in that fertile plain.

I came upon what looked like a market and stepped into the swirl of color and sound. The air was heavy with the scent of bodies, spiced meat, and the competing calls of merchants, craftsmen, farmers, and ranchers. The townsfolk moved amongst them; men shouted and called to each other, women chattered, and children ran about and laughed. I saw hyenalings speaking with elves, the latter being easy to spot with their long robes and colorful headscarves. There were even a few humans in the crowd. We were by no means an uncommon sight within the Ashuran Empire, though the elves and hyenalings far outnumbered us.

A worn obelisk in the center of the square caught my attention. The stone was worn by time and wind, its surface festooned with chips, gouges and faded markings. I saw a mix of cuneiform lettering and hieroglyphic symbols, a strangely blended form of writing that had really only ever been used in the century following the development of our alphabet.

"The wise ... of the stork," I murmured to myself. *"To nest ...?"*

I frowned, though I wasn't able to make out much else no matter how much I shifted and squinted. I brushed my fingers against the worn stone, tracing the faded hieroglyphics.

"The wise," I started, sliding my fingers over that symbol and past the two that had been chipped away. *"Fly on the wings of the stork, to nest immortal in wisdom's source."*

This was a guess, but a good one. The first Nabonassaran pharons had had an important effect on this region, and this was the motto of their now extinct house. I'd seen these same markings carved all over the tomb from which I'd just surfaced.

After a few moments, I straightened and glared at the crowd swirling around me. Why hadn't they taken better care of this?

I hated this sort of waste, this wanton destruction of history. I—I was no different.

Guilt washed over me as I let out a long breath. The statuette I'd sold to Basali was likely older than this entire damned town. I was sure that he was smashing it even now, eager only for the precious stones set within it.

I'd condemned another piece of history to destruction, all for a few pieces of silver.

I shook myself before pushing my way out through the rest of the market. It was a sacrifice, one of hundreds I'd made over the years. These coins would get me to Ikkad... and to whatever lay beyond.

I set my feet onto the road out of town, feeling my guilt trickle away with every step. A tingling excitement rose to take its place.

I'd done it. Finally, after ten and more years of searching, I'd—

"You!" A voice called, pulling me from my thoughts. "Human! Is that massive beast yours?"

I was a dozen steps beyond the bounds of the town, moving down a dusty road and towards the river that was the lifeblood of this area. I raised my head to find an elf hurrying up the path. He was tall, with the weathered, sun-darkened skin of a man who was well used to the brutal Ashuran sun. He was dressed in a loose, flowing robe in the same style as my own; although his was a pale gray while mine was a dirty-looking ochre.

"Is something wrong?" I asked.

The elf's face was twisted in a glower beneath his headscarf, and I paused to let him close the space between us. Despite his sour expression, I wasn't truly worried. We weren't far from where I'd left my mount.

And there'd be a lot more screaming if Asu had decided to cause trouble.

"Yes," the elf snapped. "Your beast is blocking access to the river. My beetles are thirsty and they can't get to the water!"

"Ah," I said, starting back down the road. "Sorry about that. We just got in after several days in the foothills and he was pretty thirsty. I'll get him out of the way."

The elf made a harumphing sound, falling in beside me. The sun was growing hot, so I pulled the large hood of my robe over my shaggy hair.

"Where are you in from?" I asked.

"Ikkad," he said tersely.

"By way of the Storkling Road?"

He jerked his head up and down in a nod.

"How was the road?"

"Fine."

"Did you stop at the caravansary along the Storkling River?" The elf glowered at me, but I kept my tone pleasant as I continued. "I'm heading that way now. I'm hoping to stop there tonight if it's not too busy."

He snorted. "It's a full night of travel to that caravansary. Your bug is big, but the sun's already too high for you to make it today."

I smiled. "What Asu brings in trouble he makes up for with speed."

I could see the caravaner wrestling with his desire to hold on to his annoyance. But I kept the smile on my face, and eventually, he let out a breath.

"You'll be fine. It's still a bit early for the fig trains to be passing through, so the road is fairly quiet."

"Thanks," I said. "I'm sorry again about Asu. He ate just a few days ago, so your beetles aren't in any danger."

The elf surprised me by giving me a wry smile. "Trust me, I'd be a lot less polite if he'd killed one of my bugs."

"Fair enough," I grinned.

At that point, the trail rounded a high boulder and we came upon the river. It cut through the dry, rocky landscape, a shock of greenery blooming on either side of it.

In truth, being but a handful of paces wide, this river was hardly worthy of the name. But outside of the central floodplains where the great cities could be found, Ashura was dominated by rock and desert. And here on the outskirts of the empire, water was treated with all the reverence it was due.

"Ah," I said. "I see the problem."

We were just past the foothills of the Northern Mountains, and the banks were often steep and rocky. There weren't many places where the river could be easily accessed and, sunning itself right beside the water, ignoring the fearful milling of a dozen carrier beetles, was a colossal, bone-white scorpion.

"Yeah," the elf said as we continued down. "I'm not too proud to say that I started to sweat a little when I first saw him there. I've never seen a white one before, though, I thought they were mostly black."

"They are," I acknowledged. "But Asu is pretty special. We travel mostly by day, and so, his pallor has its advantages."

"Might I ask where you came across him? I heard that an egg can cost as much as a small estate."

"More," I said.

Like the smaller carrier beetles, the great scorpions were native to the Great Desert. Though the creatures had been first tamed by the elves, the lamians had taken a keen interest in them once Grand Necrophant Marduss had completed his conquest. In the following millennia, generations of selective breeding by the lamian noble houses had made Asu and his kind into weapons of war. They were far larger and fiercer than the great insects that could still be found in the wild and took to the battlefields of the Ashuran Empire as unstoppable titans of claw and armored chitin.

War-scorpions were breakers of armies, and Asu himself was large even for his breed. His body was as long as five camels while his head was of a height with one. His segmented body was thickly armored in chitinous plates, and his eight legs were powerful enough to propel him at speeds to match a charging horse. He could rip a man apart with his pincers, and his stinger, curved like a crescent sword, was nearly as long as a man was tall. Even at rest, Asu's tail curled up behind him, rising to the height of a small tree.

"Well," the merchant said. "I suppose that makes you a lucky man."

The elf was too polite to say it, but it was clear he thought I had stolen Asu's egg. Technically, that wasn't true, but he was right in thinking that there was no way I could ever have afforded to buy it.

There'd been a few attempts to separate me from Asu in the six years that we'd been together, but they'd been perfunctory at best. Unlike the large, placid carrier beetles favored by most caravaners, war-scorpions were notoriously difficult to manage. They were known to imprint on whoever fed them in the first few days after their hatching, and once that bond was formed, it was impossible to break.

If I died, Asu would kill whoever tried to ride him again.

"I am lucky," I said, giving the elf another smile. "Although, on some days more than others."

The caravaner snorted, though his farewell was polite when we parted a few paces later. He moved off to ready his carrier beetles, and I continued to where my scorpion basked in the morning's heat.

"Asu," I called. "What are you doing here, you lazy bug?"

Water cascaded as the scorpion pushed itself up at the sound of my voice. He skittered over to me, rolling over the ground like an avalanche of happily chittering muscle. I wasn't a particularly tall man, and Asu loomed over me. He stopped when I was in the circle of his colossal pincers and I reached up to scratch the underside of his hairy mouth.

"You were hogging the best spot for yourself, eh big boy," I crooned, digging my fingers in between the segments of his body. "I can't believe what a lazy bug you are."

Asu let his forearm-length mouth pincers hang open. He dropped his head lower, letting out a pleased chitter. I scratched vigorously at his favorite spots, seeing a happy haze roll over his large eyes.

I laughed, feeling a surge of affection for the dopey-looking insect. Asu and I had gone through a lot together. And though he could be difficult to care for, there was no better companion for roaming the dry, desert lands of the Ashuran Empire.

"We've got a long day ahead of us, Asu-boy," I said, ducking under his arm to reach his side. "I hope that you got all that sleepiness out of your system."

Attached to the war-scorpion's body was a large saddle that I'd nearly died a dozen times trying to pay for. It was a large platform that ran the length of his back with a lowered bench for me right behind Asu's head. I went around checking each of the straps, taking the time to wipe away every grain of sand I could find beneath them before cinching the leather tight.

"I wish I could take this saddle off you, big boy," I said, speaking to him while I worked. The scorpion kept carefully still, remaining in place even while I filled a bucket with water to properly wash the grit from him. "But this saddle is just too big. Though, when we finally become the most famous historians in the empire, I'll be able to get an entire team to care for you. Those will be the days, eh Asu-boy?"

I scrambled up his body when I was finally done, my lean frame handling the task with ease. I knelt on the wooden platform, checking the sacks that I had piled atop it and hanging from its sides. Everything I owned in the world was up here; from spare clothes, food, and survival supplies, to my tomb diving tools, equipment, and the dozens of treasures and knick-knacks that I'd never quite been able to bring myself to sell.

There was the bounty of several tombs up here, enough for me to be executed a hundred times over. But I wasn't worried about any sort of casual discovery. War-scorpions were intensely territorial and Asu wouldn't tolerate anyone, or anything, coming too close if I wasn't there.

I made sure the cargo net holding it all down was strapped tightly and that everything else was secure before I allowed myself to open the pouch that my eyes kept straying to. My fingers shook as I teased apart the hemp drawstrings, pulling open the pouch and revealing the gleam of gold.

For you see, I hadn't been entirely honest with the sifter this morning. I had found something in that tomb, a thing that I had spent a decade and more searching for.

A clue.

My face stretched into a wide grin, an excited wave of tingling energy rolling through my limbs as I tied the pouch shut once more. I stuffed it into a fold of my robe, conscious of the eyes that might find me.

"Alright, Asu-boy," I said, sliding myself into the seat right behind the war-scorpion's head. "Are you ready to go?"

I drew a long wooden stick from a special holder. I tapped it on the right side of Asu's head, getting him moving and using it to steer him towards the road that led away from the Northern Mountains.

I settled in as the scorpion flowed down the path, pulling my wide hood lower over my eyes. We'd be travelling all day and the heat was already uncomfortable. Despite that, a smile still pulled at my lips.

I was moving.

This artifact, pulled from the very sarcophagus of the last pharon of the Nabonassaran Dynasty, had changed everything. I tapped the stick twice in the center of Asu's head, and obediently, the giant scorpion lurched forward into a sprint.

I laughed, gripping the edge of my bench as we flew down the road. The wind ripped the hood from my head, and I tilted my face up towards the sun's glare.

I was finally moving.

And although I had yet to take the first real step, I had found the path. It would no doubt be long, dangerously curved, and deadly should I falter, but I wouldn't be pushed from it. I would follow it to its end.

Because that was where I would solve the greatest mystery of all. I would find the lost tomb of the empire's legendary founder and the treasure buried within.

Chapter Two

LAMIANS WERE BORN NECROMANCERS. They were masters of death magic, their power flowing through their serpentine bodies like the warm blood in their veins. They were each of them gifted, though, of course, not all were created equal. The greatest of them rose to the rank of necrophant, ruling below the pharon from their seats within the empire's greatest cities.

It was they who led Ashura's armies, each of them powerful enough to chain a veritable legion of corpses to their will. Yet, such power, it was said, came with a price. They were steeped in death, suffused with the chill of the grave. Their bodies remained cold to the touch, even at the height of summer, and the earth withered in the wake of their slithering tails.

Now, I'd never met a necrophant, nor did I have the barest spark of magic within me. But what I, and every other child born within the sands of Ashura knew, was that there existed magic that was beyond even them.

You see, if magic was a mountain, then in the more than three thousand years of our empire, only one had ever reached the pinnacle. Grand Necrophant Marduss, the conqueror of the elves; one whose might had been such that even the gods had taken notice.

His was the tomb I had sworn to find; the mystery that I had dedicated my life to solving.

I was startled from my thoughts by the clatter of something on my table. I looked up from my supper, surprised to see that a woman was lowering herself into the empty seat before me.

She was a hyenaling of about my age, her large, spotted ears poking up through the mass of hair that was a paler blonde than I was used to seeing. It was spotted with brown and tumbled down in thick, curling waves. Her shoulders and arms were covered in a long, dust-covered garment. It was a robe, hooded like my own, though she wore hers open at the front to reveal a naked midriff and a chest bound by a long, winding strip of cloth. She was lean and tight strings of muscle played beneath her tanned flesh as she settled into the chair.

"You shouldn't stare." The hyenaling reached for her tray of food. "It's not polite."

"I—ahem," I cleared my throat, heat curling up the back of my neck. "Sorry. I hadn't expected ..."

The woman's eyes had yet to leave the tray before her. As I trailed off, I watched her inhale deeply before spearing her fork into the thick, spice-crusted cut of meat that was her supper.

The Storkling River caravansary, like most others, typically had a variety of food available to serve the myriad of races that stayed as guests within its wings. Hyenalings, for example, preferred meat over just about any sort of food. They weren't purely carnivores, of course, though I've never met one that wasn't ready to spurn a fruit or vegetable for something bloodier and more thickly spiced.

My mouth watered as I watched her chew her first bite, imagining the searing heat of the meat's flavor. Suddenly, I regretted my decision to not pay for something other than the thin stew I was eating.

"What hadn't you expected?" She asked.

"You?" I said, trying to swallow my hunger. "Who are you? Why are you sitting here?"

The hyenaling finally raised her gaze to mine. Her features were angular, the lines of her face sharp and distinct. Her skin was smooth, her nose and cheeks dusted with freckles. Yet, it was her eyes that really drew my gaze. They were yellow, an amber color that deepened to a honeyed gold at their center. Something within them shone, and I wondered if I had ever seen anything so striking.

"Why shouldn't I sit here? Do I stink, or something?"

"No, no, the opposite, actually."

She flicked her ears, the movement accompanied by a raised eyebrow. I felt my cheeks burn a shade hotter as I hurriedly added; "Your supper, I mean. Your supper smells really good."

The corner of her lip quirked upward, and I had to bite back on another nonsensical stream of babble. I was off balance, more than I should be. I'd been too focused on my own thoughts, not watching my surroundings.

This woman had surprised me, and for a tomb diver, surprises were, more often than not, lethal.

"Then, what's the problem?"

"The problem," I said, finally managing to haul my thoughts into some sort of order. "Is that compared to yours, my supper tastes like thickened piss."

The hyenaling grinned, revealing two bright canines. "That's your own fault. Why end a long day of travel with something bad?"

"Good point," I said, leaning back in my seat. "Is that why you came to sit with a stranger?"

Caravansaries were, essentially, inns that were set along the routes that were popular with caravaners. This particular one was large; a sprawling complex of rooms, wings, and courtyards where dozens of people lived and serviced the passing merchants. It was built at a crossroads, on the banks of a river larger than the one Asu and I had followed out from Balasi's hometown.

We were in the taproom now, the space filled with dozens of tables. Most were empty, though a few groups were scattered about.

The hyenaling shrugged. "We spend the day travelling alone. Why end the day like that, as well?"

It was my turn to raise an eyebrow. "How do you know I arrived alone?"

Her ears twitched, and I saw two spots of red bloom high on her cheeks. Her eyes flicked down long enough to cut away another sliver of her supper.

"I watched you come in on that scorpion," she admitted. "You were hard to miss."

"Asu's hardly subtle," I acknowledged.

I watched the hyenaling pop the meat into her mouth and chew. I bent over my supper as well, the wide sleeves of my robe sliding down my forearms as I brought my bowl of stew to my lips.

I saw her eyes flick to the sling I kept coiled around my arm, but she did not comment. We ate in silence for a time, examining each other. I wondered what she saw in my black hair, dark eyes, and sun-weathered skin.

"I'm Naroh," I said once I'd set my bowl back down. I extended my hand. "Most recently from Rapiq."

"Eshi." The hyenaling took my hand. Her grip was strong and her palm was heavily callused. "I came from Anat."

"Anat?" I said, perking up. "I've heard that there's a particularly intact example of a Nabonassaran library there. Did you see it?"

She blinked, a little taken aback. "You mean that old pile of rocks on the edge of town?"

"Yes!" I said, leaning forward. "You saw it then? Did you notice the stork statue?"

"I didn't really..." she started, trailing off as her brows creased into a frown. "Actually, you know what, I think I did. There was one big one, but its head was missing."

I laughed, clapping my hands together. "That's it! You saw a storkling! Ah, I'm so jealous. The Nabonassarans built hundreds, but there aren't too many of them around anymore."

"Who?" Eshi said. "And do you mean the Storkling *River*? The one right outside?"

"The Nabonassarans," I explained, "Are a lamian noble house that doesn't exist anymore. They were the empire's fifth ruling dynasty, coming into power about twenty-seven hundred years ago. Nabonassara I was actually from around here and he was the Necrophant of Ikkad before becoming Pharon."

The hyenaling crossed her arms, her features still curled into a frown. "What does that have to do with the river? Or libraries?"

"Well, you see, the Nabonassarans were special because they venerated Tel'aman, the stork-headed god of knowledge and writing, more than Djed or Eanna. They saw themselves as keepers of knowledge and history, and they made the stork the symbol of their house."

I was warming to the subject, speaking past my excited smile.

"The first Nabonassaran pharon was the one who reformed our writing, you know. Because of him, we don't use hieroglyphics anymore, and his entire dynasty spread literacy by building hundreds of public libraries. They were called storklings because of the statues out front, and since this is one of the important rivers in the region, there were probably quite a few built along it. People likely named the river after them."

"How do you know all this?" Eshi asked. "Or are you just pulling my tail?"

"I read a lot," I said. "And Asu and I make our living digging up and selling historical artifacts. It's my job to know this stuff."

The hyenaling's ears stiffened, her attention suddenly a touch sharper. "Isn't that illegal?"

"Only going into old tombs is illegal," I said, speaking this truth before the lie that came after. "Asu and I focus on old cities and temples. There are plenty of those scattered about."

Eshi made a sound with her throat, relaxing her ears somewhat. "Alright, but I still think that you're just making up stories."

I grinned. "In the end, that's all that history is—a story we never stop telling."

The hyenaling considered me for a time before shaking her head. She leaned forward onto her elbows, something too small to be called a smile tugging at her lips. "This wasn't what I expected when I decided to sit with the scorpion rider. You're pretty strange, Naroh."

I chuckled somewhat sheepishly, rubbing at the back of my neck. "I've heard worse. And sorry, I know that I tend to babble about this sort of stuff."

"Don't apologize." Eshi rested her cheek in the palm of her hand and something shifted within her amber eyes. "Real passion isn't something that I've come across too often. It makes you... interesting, as well as strange."

Then, she smiled, and I felt my throat go dry. I'd thought her beautiful when she first sat down, intensely so, albeit in a fierce, predatory sort of way. This smile, however, transformed her features, softening her and smoothing the sharp lines of her face. Eshi could never be called delicate, though that smile hinted at the warmth buried within her.

"Interesting..." I started, trailing off into a cough. Gods of fucking death, my cheeks were on fire. "Interesting sounds better than strange."

Eshi's ears twitched in a gesture of amusement and I heard her tail swish through the air behind her.

"Interesting is good," she confirmed. "And passionate is even better."

I coughed again, my stomach suddenly buzzing with a hundred motes of heat. I wasn't exactly inexperienced with women, though I'd be the first to admit that I hadn't known many. Eshi's ferocious beauty, the light in her eyes, and her easy confidence were affecting me more than any other woman had in a long time.

"Thank you... ahem, yeah. So... you're a merchant, then?"

The hyenaling's ears perked up and I heard her tail actually thump against the chair. She lifted her head off her palm, her smile growing wider beneath. "Yes! I'm bringing a load of figs down to sell in Ikkad. If everything goes well, I'm hoping to be able to come back with more than just one blind old camel."

"You only have one camel?"

"This is my first run as a merchant," she admitted. "I was... somewhere else before coming up here. I've spent all the money I've been able to save up on this. You got any tips?"

"I do actually." I leaned forward, flicking my eyes about and gesturing for her to come in. "I know the secret to making coin. Do you want to hear it?"

Eshi narrowed her eyes but leaned closer after a heartbeat.

"The secret," I said in a low, conspiratorial tone. "Is to sell your figs for more than you bought them."

She blinked once, twice, and then burst into laughter. I grinned, my cheeks flushing with delight as her high-pitched hyena's cackle washed over me.

"Thank you." Her amber eyes were bright and merry. "That is a valuable secret."

I nodded. "It's how I've survived this long."

We spoke for a while longer, though it was growing late and soon I was pushing myself to my feet.

"Good luck, Eshi," I said, holding my hand out to her. "I really hope that it goes well for you in Ikkad. I'll look for you when I'm there."

"Are you heading there as well?" She asked, rising to grip my hand.

She was shorter than a lot of hyenaling women I've met, which is to say that her eyes were just below mine. I noticed the two knives on her belt as well.

"Asu and I are leaving tomorrow morning." I smiled as I released her hand. "And you were right, it was much more fun to spend the evening talking."

"You sure did a lot of it." She grinned, letting out another stream of her scavenger's cackle.

We bade each other farewell not long after, though her laughter still drifted through my mind when I lay down to sleep in my rented room. It was strange, I thought, shutting my eyes.

I normally couldn't stand a hyenaling's laughter, but Eshi's hadn't been horrible at all.

I awoke to a scream of raw, unfiltered rage.

I tumbled out of bed, blinking in the light spilling in through the single window.

The scream came again, and this time, I was lucid enough to realize it had come from outside. I stuck my head out the window, hearing more shouts and loud curses. My room was at the rear of the caravansary, and before me, I saw nothing but empty scrubland. It sounded like whatever was going on was taking place at the front. The animals were over that way, and I had a sinking feeling that Asu was involved.

Somewhere, I heard the crash of splintering wood.

I jerked into motion, wrapping my sling—a well-cared-for length of braided cord with a split at its center—around my forearm. I threw my robe on afterward, tightening my belt with a quick flex of my hands. I was pulling on my boots when I heard that furious voice cry out again.

"Where is he!?"

Footsteps pounded through the hallway beyond my door, and my heart leaped into my throat when I heard someone shriek in pain. A dozen men were yelling now, a chorus to accompany the unending howl of fury.

Then, something heavy slammed into my door and the whole thing rattled.

"Naroh!" There was another crash against my door, followed by a loud crack. "Come out here, you bastard!"

I backed away, having no intention of obeying. There was a third crash and the door splintered. A fourth crash and it exploded inward, a woman stumbling in after it.

"Eshi!" I shouted, recognizing the hyenaling. "What are you doing!?"

She was without her robe, appearing only in her loose pants and chest wrap. She fell into a ready crouch over the ruins of the door, her teeth bared, her spotted ears and tail stiff with fury.

My eyes flicked down, catching the wicked glint of the knives she held in each hand. When I raised my gaze to hers an instant later, I saw that her amber eyes were alight with the same red anger that burned beneath her flesh.

"You killed him!" Eshi roared, launching herself towards me. "Fucking die!"

Confused, terrified, my head spinning with a rising swirl of fear and adrenaline, I did what many men before me have done when faced with an angry hyenaling woman.

I threw myself out of the window.

I flew for a single, gut-wrenching instant before hitting the ground. My room was on the ground floor, and so there was nothing painful about the fall. I heard Eshi thump into the dirt behind me, but I was already sprinting away.

She screamed at me to stop, but I didn't look back.

I raced along the inn's stone wall, my eyes frantically searching for anything that might help me. Eshi was on my heels, too far for her knives to reach me and too close for me to use my sling. She was fast; her anger, hyenaling athleticism, and long legs giving her the speed of a charging jackal.

Would she kill me if she caught me? I didn't know but thought it was possible. Despite that, I felt my panic subside. My fear and confusion drained away, my mind slowing into a familiar, focused stillness.

I was a tomb diver, and fleeing death was something I'd long grown used to. Right now, I just had to get to Asu.

I stretched my legs and smoothed out the pumping of my arms as walls and windows blurred past. This caravansary was built at an important crossroads. It saw a lot of visitors, and in the light of the morning, I finally got a real sense of the size of the place. Wings and courtyards flashed by, the windows of hundreds of rooms on two floors blurring as I ran past.

After a turn, I burst into some sort of courtyard and a crowd of people froze at the sight of us. Some called out, but they were easy to ignore as I raced towards the boxes I spied piled against one wall. There was a gallery lining the second floor, elves and other hyenalings peering down at us from over the wooden railing that kept them from falling.

That was my target.

I leaped onto the first box, vaulting over another one and clawing my way up the pile. The boxes shifted and tilted beneath me, but I trusted my agility and launched myself toward the second-story gallery when I could climb no higher.

My hands found the top of the wooden railing, and with a heave, I rolled over it to land on all fours on the second floor. I heard the crash of crates and looked up in time to see Eshi slam into the railing.

"Wha—" I started but cut myself off an instant later.

Her eyes were murderous, and I didn't waste my breath. She'd lost one of her knives, I noticed, but had the other one wedged between her teeth. Muscles bunched beneath the bare flesh of her shoulders to heave herself up. I was on my feet and racing away when I heard her roll onto the second floor.

I threw myself into a random hallway, hearing Eshi's boots pound the floor behind me. The air burned in my chest, but I didn't slow. I cut around a corner, closed doors flashing by. I had no idea where I was going, and I cursed myself for not having explored when I'd arrived the night before. I'd gotten lazy, and I prayed that I wasn't racing towards a dead end.

Turns out that I was.

I was running towards a wall of flat stone and Eshi was too close to try and backtrack. Before the spike of my fear had time to stab too deeply into me, however, I saw one of the last doors open. An elf peeked out, just in time for me to slam into him. He let out a startled squawk, falling to the floor as I bulled past him and into his room.

It was identical to the one I'd slept in, nothing more than a bed tucked against one wall and an open window. I raced towards that hole in the wall, sticking my upper body through it to see.

We were on the second floor and the hard ground was far below. I twisted to look upward, noting with relief that the roof's edge did not hang too far out. I scrambled onto the narrow ledge of the window, straightening to grip onto a roof beam. I leaned my body out, reaching as far along the beam as I could before swinging my feet out over the open air.

I didn't look down, using my momentum to swing myself to the end. The motion was smooth, my body moving with a tomb diver's ease. Within moments, I was dangling from the edge of the roof, my fingers wedged beneath the clay shingles.

I was facing the open window, and so I saw the moment that Eshi appeared in the doorway. Her knife was in one hand, her lips were pulled back in a vicious snarl. I heaved myself upward as she came towards me and kicked the elf whose room we'd invaded back to the floor.

She hurled her knife, but I got lucky. She'd aimed low and I'd curled my legs up, already halfway onto the roof. The blade cut through the air beneath me and I was clawing my way up the slanted roof a heartbeat later.

I ripped shingles away as I scrambled up the slanted surface. I got to my feet when I could, catching my breath and shaking blood into my aching arms and fingers. I took a moment to sweep my gaze around, looking for the line of trees that would mark the banks of the Storkling River.

That's where Asu would be.

I let out a loud curse when I spotted it. I'd been running the wrong fucking way!

Then, I heard a shout, followed by a thump. When I looked over, I saw Eshi's fingers digging into the roof's edge. She'd be up here in moments.

I felt a trickle of admiration, despite the situation. Not very many people could keep up with me.

I took one final moment to plot out my route to the river, and then I was running. I suppose that I could have used the time it would take her to climb to ready my sling, but I wasn't much for fighting. I had a giant scorpion to do that for me, after all.

I didn't look back to see when the hyenaling gained the heights. The footing was treacherous; the clay roofing tiles were slippery and uneven. When I heard her shout, however, I knew that she wasn't far behind.

We raced over the caravansary's roof, startling flocks of roosting birds and leaping what gaps we could. My blood pounded in my ears. Sweat dripped from my forehead and coated my back, the rising sun already hot against my shoulders.

I could hear her gaining, but I didn't adjust my pace. I focused on where I placed my feet, glancing up periodically to see the building's final edge looming larger with every passing moment. I spared a brief moment to lament the fact that I didn't have my diving tools, knowing that this next part was about to hurt.

"Asu!" I roared, closing in on the roof's end. "Guard!"

Then, when I was only a few paces from the edge, I threw myself into a slide. The clay shingles tore at my legs and side, my feet careening towards the open void. I twisted onto my stomach, slowing myself further by clawing at the tiles with stiffened fingers. The roof ripped away the flesh of my fingertips and tore at my nails. I gritted my teeth against the pain, venting what speed I could before my feet plunged into the open air.

My legs flew off next, then it was my hips and stomach. I screamed as my torso passed the roof's edge, catching a glimpse of Eshi's wide, disbelieving stare as the air reached up to yank me back toward the earth.

But I caught myself on the edge, ignoring the shriek of my abused fingers and focusing on the rest of my body. My momentum was enough to swing me back towards the inn's stone wall, though I was, I saw with a twist of my stomach, between two windows. I tried to adjust myself as I released the roof, managing to snag the nearest window-ledge with one hand. The rest of me slammed into the wall a moment later, stunning me and causing me to lose my grip.

I clawed at the stone as I fell, my blood roaring in my ears. I crashed to the earth a few moments later, retaining just enough presence of mind to throw my body into a backward roll. It was a difficult, sloppily executed maneuver, but I managed it.

And when I lay on my back blinking up at the distant roof, I felt the mad urge to laugh.

That feeling vanished as Eshi's head popped out over the edge. She glared down at me, her ears stiff over her speckled mane of blonde hair. She lay on her stomach and spun to dangle her feet out into the open air.

By all the gods, she was stubborn.

My body felt like one great, throbbing mass of pain. I forced myself up and into a slow run, ignoring the confused, indignant shouts of the people around me.

Asu stood at one end of the large courtyard, still as only an ambush predator could be. War-scorpions were surprisingly intelligent, able to follow commands of relative complexity. The 'guard' order was one that we'd practiced often and had Asu waiting for me with raised pincers and tail.

He looked for all the world like a great, eight-legged statue. Though should I give the command, he would attack with a viper's speed and ruthlessness.

I was most of the way to him by the time I heard Eshi slam onto the ground behind me.

Hyenalings were the empire's famed dog-soldiers. They were ferocious warriors and agile hunters. They were naturally hardy, being generally stronger and faster than most humans and elves.

And though I didn't doubt that she could survive a straight fall like that, it would still have hurt.

My frame was drenched with sweat and my breath was ragged and torn by the time I reached the giant insect. I slipped between two of his legs, taking shelter beneath his armored body.

The hyenaling limped towards us, the exposed flesh of her arms and stomach scraped red and raw. She'd lost both of her knives. Her pants were torn, and her face was twisted into a pained snarl beneath the cloud of her hair.

I tensed as she approached, a shout of warning ready on my lips. I didn't want to see her die, but whether I commanded it or not, Asu would kill her if she came too close.

To my relief, she seemed to realize it too. Eshi slowed, meeting my gaze as she came to a stop a dozen and more paces away. Her amber eyes were bright, her fists and body clenched against the helpless rage coursing through her.

We stared at each other, and as my rapidly beating heart started to slow, her shoulders slumped. Despair bubbled up to the surface of her features. The bright anger drained away from her eyes, leaving behind a crystalline knot of denial that shattered into a thousand shards of pain. Beyond that was a dark, yawning pit of hopelessness deep enough to drown in.

Then, she crumpled to her knees and began to weep.

I let out a long, long breath, my mind empty but for the rising sound of Eshi's grief. "Down, Asu," I said, the tension flowing out of my body. "It's over. Down."

The war-scorpion chittered, and I felt his body relax above me. He shifted nervously on his eight legs, and I moved out from beneath his unarmored belly. He didn't much like it when I was there.

It was only then that I noticed the blood.

Red streaked my scorpion's pincers and mouth, bright against the white of his chitin. I saw puddles of it on the ground around us, finding a large, half-devoured lump of flesh in the middle of it all. Scattered around the corpse was the debris of broken crates, with smashed, blood-stained fruit spilling out of them.

My heart sank as I realized what I was looking at. It was a camel, a single, old, blind camel; the one that Eshi had spent everything on. My eyes drifted back to her, remembering the despair on her face.

It was rare to see a hyenaling alone. They lived close to one another, fiercely loyal to their familial clans. That bond was important to them, central to many of their beings and identities.

Eshi, I suspected, had been severed from that family. She was an exile, thrust away from the warmth of all she knew into a world that would give her nothing. This camel had been her chance at something better, and Asu had ripped it away from her and ground it into the dust at our feet.

I lay a hand on one of the scorpion's legs.

He hadn't done it with any sense of malice, of course, neither had it been for any reason of hunger. Asu was simply territorial, and in my mind, I had this vision of the animal ambling over to the sound of the babbling river. He would have been focused on his thirst, deaf to any warning chitter and too blind to see the looming shadow of his death.

"Fuck," I swore, softly.

I ran my fingers through my hair, hissing as the sweat stung my torn fingers. Guilt gnawed at my stomach, though I knew there was nothing I could do. I didn't have the money to replace what had been lost.

There were laws in our empire, of course. But we were far from any major city and Asu was very big. Might still made right out here on the open road. It wasn't fair, but that's what it was.

The world was hard, especially for those of us that were alone.

I tried to force myself to turn away, to get onto Asu's back and drive the both of us out of her life for good. But I couldn't move, unable to take my eyes off the lonely, weeping girl.

In my mind, I heard her laugh as she had the night before. I felt that scavenger's cackle thrum through me, so different than any I had heard before. I saw again the happy wag of her tail and the way the light had danced within her amber eyes.

Finally, I remembered her smile, and how soft it had made the lines of her face. I didn't have a plan as my body jerked into motion and I was still searching for what words I could possibly say when I sat down beside her.

Eshi didn't scream at my presence; she didn't try and shove me away or even acknowledge me. She merely wept with her head cradled in her hands.

I watched without uttering any words of comfort. Neither did I shift myself closer or try and soothe her with my touch.

I simply sat beside her; a lonely soul who knew the pain of losing everything you had.

The sun rose higher, and soon, Eshi's tears ran dry. She stared down at the pain-soaked earth, silent.

"I can't give back what you've lost," I said, at last. "But I can take you to Ikkad. I know some people there, merchants and traders. It won't be glamorous, but one or two might be able to give you a job."

And because she had nowhere else to go, she nodded. "Okay."

Chapter Three

I STIRRED AT THE sound of a voice, blinking my eyes back into focus beneath the darkness of my hood. I shifted and stretched, wincing at the cramped stiffness of my limbs.

"Wha—" I croaked, the rest of the word getting lodged in my too-dry throat.

My hand found the waterskin beside me. The hide felt rough, and hot, even through the strips of cloth with which I'd bandaged my fingers. The water, thankfully, was blessedly cool. There were few spots of shade on the back of a traveling war-scorpion, but the ones I had were reserved for water.

"What did you say?" I managed a few moments later, turning to look behind me.

Eshi was there, seated further down Asu's back. She was leaning against the netted pile of packs, her eyes gleaming from beneath her drawn-up hood.

"How much further were you planning on going today?"

I shrugged, turning to squint ahead of me once more. The sun was low in the sky, hanging fat and orange over the empty wilderness. We were in the space between cities, surrounded by nothing but rock, parched earth, and the tough, scraggly plants that grew within it.

"Not much more," I decided. "We might as well stop before it gets too dark."

"Then turn this bug around. We passed a good campsite not far back."

She hadn't said a word since I'd coaxed her onto Asu's back that morning. She'd spent much of the day in a daze, her eyes distant and listless.

It was perfectly understandable, of course, especially while beneath the crushing weight of the sun.

"Alright, then. Come up here and show me."

Beneath us, Asu flowed over the rocky earth at the speed of a running man. Eshi's eyes flashed and, after a short moment of hesitation, she began to crawl cautiously over the netted supplies.

I stiffened as I heard her settle in behind me, feeling the back of my neck prickle.

"Relax," Eshi said. "I'm not going to hurt you."

"You did try to stick a knife in me this morning," I reminded her, resisting the urge to look back.

"That was hours ago. And you deserved it."

"Yeah, maybe." A silence settled back over us, heavier than it had been a few minutes before. I let out a breath and pulled down my hood. "I am sorry about that. I'd have stopped Asu if I could."

She snorted.

"I'm serious."

"He's the size of a house. You can't stop a predator that big from eating."

"He wasn't eating, he was just—" I cut myself off and shook my head. "Anyway, it doesn't matter. I'm sorry that we're the reason you lost everything. You didn't deserve that."

Eshi's gaze drifted from my face to stare out over the empty horizon. After a while, she pulled down her hood and shook out her mane of pale, speckled hair. The setting sun warmed her freckled cheeks, making them glow with a burnished depth.

"I'd do more for you if I could," I continued, "whatever that's worth. But I'm pretty broke. There's not a lot of money in history."

She brought her amber eyes back to mine and, within her, I saw nothing of that earlier despair. The hyenaling was a survivor, a woman with an iron endurance that was no stranger to the harshness of the world. "Only broken bits of clay and lumps of old rock?"

I frowned at her.

"I went through a few of your packs. You have a lot of junk."

"Junk? Some of that stuff is thousands of years old! And what the hell were you doing going through my stuff?"

Eshi shrugged and flicked her ears, showing not one bit of shame. "I was looking for something valuable."

"You were going to fucking steal from me, after I've—"

"After you what, Naroh." She bared her teeth, her canines long and bright. "After you destroyed everything I had, shredded what I'd made of my life, and cost me years of work?"

I glared at her, though I was unable to hold her stare for very long. "You don't have to accept my apology, but I still wanted to say it. We're a few days from Ikkad and we can spend that in silence if you want."

"No," Eshi said, folding her ears back. "At least you're doing something."

I nodded, swallowing the rest of my anger. Bitterness still twisted her features but, as I said, Eshi was a survivor. Though I'd wronged her, she would take whatever kindness I had to give.

"Anyway," she continued with a quick huff. "It was partly my fault. I didn't think that stupid camel would wander off so quickly. I'd loaded him up and figured that I didn't need to tie him back up for the few minutes I needed to go get breakfast. I got back as he was being torn apart." She shifted, her eyes flicking to Asu's colossal pincers. "Something this big shouldn't be able to move so fast."

"Asu-boy is impressive, that's for sure. Although, the females are supposed to be even deadlier."

"As it should be." She gave me a wide, toothy grin. "I'd have shown you if you'd fought me this morning."

I bared my teeth in a smile of my own. "Why do you think I ran?"

Eshi chuckled, though it was forced. Nevertheless, it helped to thaw the air between us, and I felt myself start to relax. I hefted my guiding stick and spoke.

"So, where's this camping spot you saw?"

We ended up in a sheltered hollow which, by some trick of the land, was just humid enough to support the existence of a few gnarled trees.

I whistled a nonsensical song as I wandered beneath them, chopping at whatever branches I found scattered about with a small hatchet.

Trees weren't always easy to find so far from the empire's rivers, and it would be nice to burn wood instead of dung tonight.

"How did you know that this was here?" I asked Eshi when I returned with an armful of wood. "We didn't pass too close to it on Asu."

"It's simple to see if you're paying attention," the hyenaling answered. She stood from where she'd been arranging rocks into a tight circle and wiped her hands on her robe. "I saw half a dozen other places like this before I spoke up."

"Ah, well, I'm glad you said something. This place is great."

Eshi gave me a look that reminded me of my father. Heat crawled up my neck and I felt the childish urge to justify myself. "We'll be in Ikkad in a few days, and I don't typically worry too much about where I'm going to sleep when the journey is that short."

"Mmhmm," the hyenaling said, her tone carefully neutral. "I guess you don't have to worry about bandits too much when traveling with a war-scorpion. Do you want to hunt or should I?"

"Hunt?" I asked.

"You were planning on eating tonight, right?"

"Obviously. I have some dried meat and stuff in a pack somewhere. I was..." I trailed off at the expression on Eshi's face. I tried changing tack. "Is there even anything to eat out here?"

"No wonder you don't have any money to pay me back," the hyenaling said. She gave an exasperated shake of her head before gesturing to the world around us. "Look at this place, it's full of buffalo grass. There will be hares around to eat it, with foxes and maybe even a few jackals around to eat them. Why waste your supplies when you could have something fresh?"

I stared down at the plant she was pointing at, unable to tell it apart from the rest of the scraggly vegetation no matter how hard I squinted.

"Well," I said, at last, "fresh meat definitely sounds better."

"Give me your sling, then. I'll take care of it."

"My sling?" I frowned at her. "Do you know how to use one?"

"Better than you can."

I raised an eyebrow at that. "You've never seen me use it."

"I don't need to," Eshi said with a dismissive flick of her ears. "The sling is a hyenaling weapon, and I've been hunting with one since I was old enough to pick up a rock. You might be able to hit a man at two-dozen paces but hitting a moving rabbit is something else entirely."

My expression must have betrayed something of my amusement because annoyance flashed through her eyes.

"Well," she demanded, her tail stiff. "Am I wrong?"

"No," I answered. "Those two things are certainly very different."

Eshi narrowed her eyes. She was about to speak, but the sound of rustling vegetation caused her ears to perk up. Her gaze darted towards it for a few moments before she turned her head to squint at the rapidly setting sun.

"It's starting to get dark, and the rabbits are emerging from their dens now. I need to go while I can still see."

Even as she spoke, Eshi untied her robe and let it slip off her shoulders. She stretched, the movement pulling at her naked shoulders and stomach.

"I thought hyenalings had pretty good night vision?" I asked, losing myself for a beat in the strings of muscle rippling beneath her bronzed flesh.

"We do," she said, letting her arms flop downward with a loud exhalation. "But I'm not a lamia, so, it's not perfect. Now come on, give me your sling."

I didn't move, causing Eshi to frown. "Naroh, come on. I'm just going hunting." She tapped a hand on the hilt of one of her weapons. "All I have are my knives and it'll be a lot harder with just these."

I swept one hand through my hair, unsure. She had a point, but if I gave up my sling, all I'd have was my own knife. She'd tried to kill me that very morning and judging from the blade scars I could see going up her forearms, she was much more experienced with the weapon than I was.

She could also, I supposed, just take my sling and disappear into the wilderness. She seemed comfortable out here, and I did not doubt that she could survive long enough to reach civilization.

I'd be stranded, then, weaponless and alone.

After another moment of indecision, I tossed her the pouch of stones from my belt and reached up to unwind the braided weapon from around my forearm. Asu was here; I'd be safe no matter what she decided to do.

I turned to the war-scorpion once she had stalked away, working to loosen his saddle amidst a rising chorus of nocturnal birds and insects. I got the fire going once I'd made him comfortable, settling down onto the ground when the wood was properly burning. It was dark now, and Eshi still hadn't returned. I was hungry, but I decided to wait a while longer before I surrendered the faith that I'd extended her and dug into my stores.

After a moment's hesitation, I reached within the folds of my robe for the pouch I kept hidden there. I stared at it for a few moments by the fire's orange glow. I shouldn't open it, the hyenaling could be back at any moment and this urge I had to check on the artifact was idiotic.

Nothing about it had changed. It hadn't suddenly shifted into something different, and I sure as hell hadn't missed any crucial detail in my hundreds of other examinations.

Right?

I swore, took a moment to sweep my eyes over the still-empty campsite, and drew out the artifact I'd pulled from the tomb of Nabonassara IV. My heart beat faster as I examined it by the light of the fire.

It was a medallion, a palm-sized disc of beaten gold that was engraved on both sides. Those etchings were still visible, although time, and the fingers of ancient hands, had rubbed away much of the detail.

On one side was the symbol of the Nabonassarans; a stork clutching a tablet in one foot with the pharon's hooded crown resting atop its gracefully curved head. Around it, the words of their house had been carved: *The wise fly on the wings of the stork, to nest, immortal in wisdom's source.*

And while I would normally love nothing more than to spend hours poring over every detail of a long-extinct dynasty's heraldry, I barely glanced at it before turning it over in my bandaged palm.

Here, I found an image of Grand Necrophant Marduss. The lamian necromancer-king was shown in profile, his powerful serpent's tail holding up the muscled body of a man. In his hands, he held the Black Scythe, a weapon said to have been granted to him by Djet, the god of death.

It was an image that every child of the empire knew.

More than three millennia ago, the lamians and dozens of hyenaling clans had followed Marduss across the Great Desert. It had been the grand necrophant who had led the conquest of the elven city-states. One by one, he'd broken their armies, using his magic to raise their fallen and sending them marching towards Uruq, their capital. Once there, he'd pulled down Uruq's impregnable walls, flooding the streets with the dead to force the final elven surrender.

Tragically, he never got to witness the empire that he had fought to create. He disappeared in the aftermath of the battle at Uruq, slain by an elite order of elven assassins when he was at his weakest. And though the grand necrophant's successor, Ramesh the Great, had exterminated the Order of the Broken Mountain and burned out their home, neither Marduss's body nor his Black Scythe were ever seen again.

I tilted the medallion in my hands so it better caught the firelight and traced my fingers along the curved blade of the scythe.

The legend of this artifact was woven tightly within the fabric of Marduss's own. It was a weapon of awesome power, said to have been the key to the ancient lamian's ascension to grand necrophant.

And in the millennia since, entire lamian dynasties have gone extinct in the search for it. Necrophants have bribed, seduced, and killed. They've waged war on each other, bankrupting themselves and driving their houses to ruin in the pursuit of the faintest rumor. Foreign kingdoms have been invaded, their people slaughtered, and corpses used in grand, and ultimately fruitless, projects of excavation.

Untold wealth, fame, and power would come to whoever first found Marduss's tomb, and the pages of our history were soaked in the blood of the millions who had died for the ambition.

"And for all that," I murmured to myself. "I'm going to be the one to find it."

Because there was something different to this depiction of Marduss. For while he was normally shown bearing the pharon's crown, he instead had—

"What's that?" A voice said from right behind me.

I reacted without thought, my body moving while surprise paralyzed my mind. I pushed forward, got my feet under me, and threw myself away in one, smooth motion. The fire was in front of me, but I dove over it too high and too fast for the flames to touch me. I caught myself on the other side with one hand, tucking my shoulder in to turn my fall into a tight roll. I was on my feet an instant later, my legs propelling me forward as I sprinted away from whoever had spoken.

I was a dozen paces from the fire before my thoughts finally juddered into motion. I slowed, my heart pounding, seeing next to nothing in the darkness. It was a miracle I hadn't tripped over anything. I turned back to see Eshi standing by the fire, right where I'd been sitting. She was watching me, a little smile pulling at the corner of her mouth.

Heat blazed through me as I stomped back towards the campsite. "Eshi! What the fuck was that?!"

The hyenaling's eyes were bright in the flickering light of the flames. "You didn't scream. I was hoping you would."

"What the fuck does that mean?" I growled. "Why did you sneak up on me?"

"Screaming is the natural reaction," she said. "But you just ran without making any sort of sound."

"Obviously! Of all the stupid fucking things to do in a—" I cut myself off, snapping my teeth shut around the rest of my words.

Eshi cocked her head to the side, her ears perked above the tangle of her blonde, speckled hair. "In a what?"

In a fucking tomb! I wanted to roar. Divers who screamed drew guardians that they might have avoided and died with their fucking limbs hacked from their bodies! I ground my jaw, trapping those words within me. My fists shook with how tightly they were clenched. I focused on my breathing, needing several long moments before I was finally able to begin to relax.

Throughout it all, Eshi's eyes were on me, watchful and curious.

"Don't do that again," I said with a final exhalation. "You might startle Asu into attacking."

The hyenaling snorted. Her body relaxed as well, though her ears remained raised. "I wasn't trying to hide. The big bug is smart enough to keep his ears open and he heard me coming."

I flicked my eyes to the side and saw that Asu was still right where I'd left him. The giant scorpion was resting, his tail curled high while his pincers and belly lay low to the ground. He hadn't so much as shifted during my mad flight.

"Some help you were," I grumbled.

Eshi nodded her head towards one of my hands. "So what is that?"

I raised my hand to find the medallion still clutched between my fingers. The gold shone in the firelight, and I hurriedly tucked it back within a fold of my robe.

"It's nothing."

"It's gold," Eshi said, baring her teeth. "Enough for me to get a half-dozen camels."

She shifted, folding her knees to bend ever so slightly forward. The firelight danced over her skin, sharpening her and emphasizing the predatory leanness of her face and muscled limbs. It darkened her hair and I saw a dozen and more silvery lines appear on her forearms and biceps; scars from knife and claw.

"It's nothing," I said again, not looking away.

Eshi didn't move. Her eyes shone brightly and her lips curled into a wide, scavenger's grin.

The air grew thick between us, but my body was loose, and my mind focused and without fear. I met her gaze without flinching. She may have my sling, but I trusted in my ability to dodge the first stone she launched my way.

And with Asu's kill command on my lips, she wouldn't get another.

After a moment, Eshi's ears relaxed. She straightened and the tension flowed out of the lines of her body. "Fine. Then, I guess it's nothing. Here, I got you supper."

Two rabbits appeared in her hands, their bodies lean and stringy. She tossed one over the fire towards me, but I didn't look away from her as it thumped into the ground at my feet.

"My sling," I said. "I'd like it back."

She laughed that high, hyena's cackle. "You shouldn't be scared around me, Naroh," she said through her scavenger's grin. "You've got that big bug with you, remember?"

I crossed my arms. Eshi chuckled once again before untying my sling and rock pouch from her belt and tossing both my way. Afterward, she sat by the fire with her rabbit, pulling one of her knives from its sheath.

I watched her get to work, blood darkening her blade as she expertly skinned and quartered her meal. I was regretting my decision to bring her along.

Her scavenger's grin flashed through my mind, and I resolved to sleep on Asu's back that night.

Chapter Four

I SLEPT POORLY THAT night, my dreams stalked by a bright-eyed demon with a wide, murderous smile. I was awake long before sunrise and watched the sun appear through gritty, bloodshot eyes. I pushed myself up, my breath steaming in the frigid morning air.

Asu chittered as I climbed down from his back. The giant scorpion shifted on his eight legs, clacking his pincers energetically as I walked around him. Despite my foul mood, I smiled, reaching up beneath his mouth to scratch at the joint he liked.

"You had a good sleep then, Asu-boy?" I said, scratching vigorously. It hurt my bandaged fingers, but seeing the happy fog roll over the scorpion's eyes made it worth it. "Eh, big boy? You all ready to go then?"

"That bug isn't really what I expected," Eshi said from behind me. I turned to find her pushing herself up from where she'd been curled up beside the fire pit. Her robe was wrapped tightly around her, her hood down so she could catch the first rays of sunlight on her face. "I don't know if that makes him scarier or not."

She stretched, raising her hands high above her speckled ears. Something in her back popped, causing her to shiver and make a small sound of pleasure. Her robe fell open, drawing my attention to the knives sheathed at her waist. My smile faded into a glower.

"What's that look mean?" Eshi said, frowning. "Did I kill something of yours?"

"I slept like shit," I told her. "Unlike you, I guess."

"And that's my fault?"

I opened my mouth, closed it, and then settled for redoubling the force of my glare. Eshi perked her ears and cocked her head to the side. I noticed her fingers tap the hilt of one of her knives, and she noticed me notice. A moment later, her mouth stretched into her wide, scavenger's grin.

"Bad dreams?"

I turned and stomped away, her high-pitched cackle ringing in my ears as I went to relieve myself. Eshi was squatting over the firepit when I returned, feeding kindling to the tiny curls of flame she'd coaxed into life. She looked up at the sound of my approach.

"The fires started," she said, her eyes twinkling. "It was hours before it died out last night, so I'm fine. But you look a little cold."

My glower returned, but I was fucking freezing so I didn't let that stop me from squatting down before the flickering heat of the flames.

"Are you sure it's safe here?" Eshi asked from beside me. "I wouldn't want you to feel... threatened."

"How am I the idiot for being careful?" I could hear the whine in my voice, but I didn't care. I was cold, sore, exhausted, and hungry. "Gods of fucking death, you've already tried to stab me!"

"You're an idiot, Naroh," she said, grinning through falling strands of her blonde hair. "Because the chances of this job you promised me being worthless are lower than those of that scorpion eating me if I do anything to you."

"Then stop—"

I wasn't able to finish, interrupted by the high, joyful sound of Eshi's laughter. It escaped her in short, breathy bursts, thrumming through me and somehow loosening some of the tightness of my anger. She reached over and gripped my shoulder for balance, using me to push herself to her feet a handful of heartbeats later.

"You really know how to make a girl feel better," she said, looking down at me with a brilliant smile. "Should I get us some breakfast?"

Eshi was golden in the light of dawn. Her hair was like a river of liquid honey and her amber eyes were full and bright. There was a softness to her face now, and a happy flush spreading over the freckled curve of her cheeks. I felt the rest of me relax, what remained of my temper draining away beneath the glow of her smile and slow swish of her tail.

I let out a breath and managed a smile of my own when I said, "Sure."

We made good time once we got onto Asu's back, continuing on through the empty wilderness towards Ikkad. The air thickened as the sun climbed steadily overhead, the heat making it harder to breathe. Eshi and I stopped trying to speak as the day wore on and I spent the hours huddled in my robe, my back hunched and eyes gritty from dust and lack of sleep.

By the time we were into the afternoon, I'd just about forgotten that the hyenaling was with me. Until the sound of a knife being drawn caused me to straighten.

"We're going east," Eshi said from directly behind me.

"For almost two hours now," I confirmed. Shifting in my seat behind Asu's head, I peered back to find the hyenaling crouched with a blade held ready in one hand. Gods, I hadn't even heard her approach. "Is knifing people the only way you solve your problems?"

"Usually. Now, tell me where you're taking me."

Eshi's amber eyes were bright beneath her hood. She balanced easily on Asu's back as the war-scorpion flowed smoothly over the barren landscape.

"Relax." I didn't fault her suspicion, even as I wished she weren't so quick to act on it. "There's something out here that I want to see. We'll be there soon and then we'll keep going towards Ikkad."

She didn't put away her blade. "Where are you taking me, Naroh?"

I pushed my hood back to squint out into the wilderness. This stretch of the empire was empty, and a land so devoid of any distinct features could be hard to navigate. I'd been to this particular site before, however, and judging by the shape of the Northern Mountains rising in the distance, I thought that we were getting close.

"We'll be seeing it soon, and it's not dangerous." A buzzing sort of anticipation rolled through me and I tapped Asu on the side of his head, starting him up a long, gentle slope. "Well, it might be, but we're not going to get too close."

"I'd feel a lot less like sticking a knife into you if you just told me where we were going."

"That would ruin the surprise." I grinned back at her. "Besides, it's not my fault that it took you so long to notice we'd changed directions."

Eshi bared her teeth, though two spots of heat bloomed beneath her freckled cheeks.

"You were taking a nap," I guessed, grinning wider. "Did you also sleep badly last night?"

"You're annoying," she growled, her ears shifting beneath her hood. Finally, she settled down more comfortably behind me and sheathed her knife. "And I got tired of digging through all the garbage in your packs."

"I told you to stop going through my stuff," I said, my good mood evaporating. "And be careful when you crawl over them, the things in there are precious."

"Precious?" Eshi snorted, reaching into the fold of her robe and producing a brightly colored shard of pottery with a little flourish. "This is the literal definition of garbage."

"Gods of fuckin—" I swore, snatching the artifact from her hand. "Be careful! This shard is from the Syksos Dynasty! It's thousands of years old!"

"It's worthless." Eshi leaned towards me, her eyes flicking to where I'd tucked the artifact within the fold of my robe. "But lucky for me, I already know where you keep your gold."

I very deliberately turned my back to her, though her cackle told me that she noticed the sudden stiffness of my frame.

Gods of death, I couldn't wait to get rid of her. Throughout the day, I'd debated long and hard over whether or not to extend our time together with this detour. It added about half a day of travel, and in the end, wasn't at all necessary for my search of the grand necrophant's tomb.

But I was curious and that was a feeling that I'd never really learned how to deny.

Asu's eight churning legs made quick work of the long slope we were ascending. I tapped him to a stop at the crest of the hill, my earlier irritation swallowed by the sight of the monumental, half-built pyramid rising from the empty wilderness below us.

It was huge, growing into a mountain to rival those of the Northern range. The square base of pale rock was larger than some towns, and the whole of it was surrounded by a sprawling complex of low temples, statues, and obelisks.

And swarming over the vast worksite were thousands of corpses.

"What is this?" Eshi asked, her voice low. "Naroh..."

"We're fine," I assured her. "Keep your knives away."

Hordes of fleshless skeletons, powered by lamian magic rather than muscle and sinew, worked to build the great monument. They worked with a weird, mechanical precision, their movements stiff and synchronized. Great blocks of stone were hauled from the nearby mountains to where others waited to cut them into shape and push them up massive ramps of earth to then shove them into place. Still more assembled wooden scaffolds decorated the stone with chisels or dug into the earth with picks and shovels.

The hyenaling snorted, though, I felt some of the tension leave her body. "Is this some new temple, then?"

"Not quite," I said. "This is the tomb of Ballasu Malash, or, well, it will be once he dies."

"You brought me to the tomb of Ikkad's necrophant?" Eshi hissed. "Are you insane?"

I laughed and a fresh wave of energy tingled through my limbs. "Don't worry. I was here three years ago when they started and I just want to check on their progress. Can you grab my spyglass for me? It's in one of my packs back there."

"I'm not getting your fucking spyglass," Eshi growled, her tail lashing the air behind her. "We have to go!"

Beneath us, Asu stiffened. His tail curled low and he flexed his pincers, sensing the rising tension. I took a few moments to scratch between two of his armored plates, a task made painful by my still-healing fingers, before I turned back to frown at the hyenaling. "We're fine."

"This is the necrophant's tomb, Naroh! What if they see us and think we're divers?"

I opened my mouth, hesitated, then closed it again. Eshi's eyes narrowed and I fought to keep the wince from my features.

"Naroh..."

"They've probably already seen us," I admitted. "Asu isn't very subtle."

She drew her knives.

"It's okay!" I said, lifting my hands. "We're allowed to be here, it's fine!"

"I'm going to cut you."

"Look at this!" I spoke quickly, gesturing to the construction site with my guiding stick. "This place is huge and we're only a handful of days from Ikkad. It's impossible to keep something like this a secret, so, they don't even try. We're fine as long as we don't try and get too close."

"That doesn't mean they want us spying on them!"

"They don't care! Eshi, I'm telling you, people from Ikkad or the nearby villages come here every day to watch them work. House Malash isn't going to send their guardians after us because we're doing the same thing. And look—" I pointed to a string of carrier beetles winding its way toward the site. "Do you see those merchants there?"

The hyenaling's ears were still beneath her hood and her fingers flexed around the hilts of her knives. After a moment, she nodded.

"They're going to that area with the tents and houses," I said, shifting my pointing stick. "Unless the necrophant himself is here, it takes dozens of lamians to control this many undead. The overseers live there, along with their families, servants, and a large contingent of House Malash dog-soldiers. That's hundreds of people, and it takes a lot of merchants traveling back and forth to keep them fed. That's not even mentioning those that come with tools and other building supplies."

"So, you're telling me that the lamians don't care about security at all," Eshi said. "For a necrophant's fucking tomb."

I shook my head. "Oh, they'll kill us if we get too close. Those soldiers, merchants, and even some of the lamian overseers are usually only allowed in very specific areas. The architect will be the only one allowed to do any work inside the tomb itself."

Her eyes narrowed. "How do you know all this? I thought that you dug up old temples and cities."

"I'm a historian. All history interests me."

"This isn't history."

"But one day it will be," I said, suddenly smiling. I didn't even have to lie to her, well, not fully. "Lamians tend to decorate their tombs with tales of their deeds and grandeur. In a thousand or two thousand years, when all of us are dead and gone, the stories carved into the stone of this tomb might be the only record of this time that survives. Don't you want to know what they're writing?"

Eshi's expression was disbelieving. She stared at me for several moments before slowly shaking her head. "I'm more interested in getting to Ikkad and off this bug for good."

I nodded past her. "Get my spyglass for me, then."

Her eyes flashed, her features sharper than the blades in her hands. "I'm not your servant."

"The sooner I start, the sooner we get moving again."

"You are the most fucking infuriating—" She bit off the rest of her words, letting out a low growl. "Fine."

Then, she let out a quick breath and put away her knives. Pushing her hood back, Eshi closed her eyes as the sun painted her freckled cheeks. She reached up to run a hand through her mane of pale, speckled hair, causing shadows to dance and play across her features.

I watched her let out a long breath, her shoulders finally unknotting. A flush was already spreading over her sun-warmed flesh, softening the fierce lines of her face. Something unfamiliar fluttered deep within me, though, before I could think to examine it, Eshi had opened her eyes.

"What?" She scowled.

Heat, that had nothing to do with the near summer sun, burned through me. I coughed and looked away. "Nothing, sorry. Are you going to grab my spyglass?"

"First, get us to that big outcropping of rock," she said, gesturing with one hand. "I don't know if it will make us a bit harder to see, but it will get us out of the sun, at least."

I nodded and turned Asu with a few taps to his head. Not long after, I was seated on a flat section of rock with my hood down. It was comfortable in the shade and I was able to fully concentrate on staring through my spyglass.

I started by examining what I could of the design, conscious that I might one day decide to dive this tomb. The architect, and the lamian overseers working beneath him, knew their business, however. The outer walls were going up first, and I could see nothing of the traps or layout being set up within.

Eventually, after moving on to spying on the emerging decorative carvings, I heard Eshi settle down beside me. "Anything interesting?"

"Mmm," I said, not lowering my glass. "It's hard to see from up here, but I think I can see something about the locust plague from ten years ago and the skirmish with the centaurs to the east."

"This isn't an act, isn't it?"

"Huh?" I was watching a team of skeletons carve the rough outline of a statue from a large block of stone. "What was that?"

"This thing with history. I could see your passion for it when we first met, but after everything that happened, I think that I started to tell myself that I'd imagined it. Obviously, I was wrong."

I frowned, having no clue what she was talking about. I lowered my spyglass and then paused when I noticed the sun. Instead of being high in the sky, it was down low enough to be nearly touching the horizon.

"...Fuck."

"You really didn't notice, did you?" Eshi propped her chin on the palm of one hand. She'd discarded her robe, letting the sun soak the bare flesh of her shoulders and stomach. "You haven't moved in four hours, Naroh."

"Fuck," I said again, then groaned as I tried to shift my stiffened limbs. "Gods, is it really this late?"

"Mmm," Eshi confirmed. "We're not going to get much further before it's dark."

"Why didn't you..." I trailed off, running a hand through my hair. Then, I closed my spyglass with a sigh. "Never mind. It's my fault."

I expected Eshi to say something cutting, to bare her teeth and berate me for wasting an entire afternoon of her time.

I certainly would've deserved a bit of a haranguing.

But instead, the hyenaling turned to look out over the rising tomb. "You said they only started building this three years ago?"

"Yeah," I answered, a little hesitantly. "They were still putting up the overseer dwellings last time I was here."

"That's amazing," Eshi said with a shake of her head. "I can't believe they did all this in just three years."

"You can get a lot done with a legion of workers that don't eat, sleep, or feel pain." I let out another breath. "Look, I'm sorry about this, Eshi. I know you wanted to get to Ikkad as fast as possible and I swear that I didn't mean to spend so long here."

"That's okay, Naroh." She turned, and the smile she gave me sent sparks cascading through me. "I find real passion fascinating to see."

"Uh, yeah—" I coughed past my suddenly dry throat. "Still, I shouldn't have stayed here so long."

"Don't worry." Light sparkled in her amber eyes and her smile curled wider. "It gave me the time to dig this up."

Something thumped into my lap and I looked down to find that she'd tossed an ancient bronze bracelet at me. I snatched at it before it could roll onto the ground.

"Stop going through my bags!"

Eshi laughed and her high, joyful cackle filled the air around us. The sound rolled through me, loosening the lines of my face and easing something within me. It was a sort of stiffness, a tightness in my body that I hadn't even realized was there.

I smiled.

That stiffness returned, unfortunately, when a voice cut through the cloud of Eshi's laughter.

"Naroh! There you are!" Turning to the side, I saw another grinning, female hyenaling moving up the rocky ground towards us. "You owe me some money, you slippery bastard!"

"Rishka!" I said, scrambling to my feet. "What the hell are you doing here?"

The other hyenaling stopped a handful of paces away, far enough back that, though Asu's attention was on her, he didn't otherwise react.

"I don't know, boy," she said, her scavenger's grin growing wider. "I bet I'm here for the same reason you are."

Rishka was a tall, broad-shouldered hyenaling woman about fifteen years my senior. Her eyes were dark beneath a short-cropped tangle of speckled hair and her furry ears were loose and relaxed. A tight, hide vest showed off muscled arms, and her feet were encased in heavy boots. Two hatchets hung from a thick belt around her waist, and I'd personally seen her bury one in an undead guardian's skull from two-dozen paces away.

Rishka was as tough and gnarled a tomb diver as they come.

"Naroh," Eshi growled. She'd gotten to her feet at the same time I had and was facing the other hyenaling with her daggers ready. "Who's this?"

"Rishka's a historian, like me," I lied easily. "We've worked together once or twice."

"Aye," Rishka responded, not missing a beat. "And I ended up with nothing but debts and a pile of dirt after the last job he talked me into."

"That's too bad." The stiffness of Eshi's tail and ears was in sharp contrast to the other hyenaling's almost indolent pose. "But Naroh cost me gold. His money is mine."

Rishka laughed, a high, yelping sound that grated my ears. "I don't know who you are, pup, but there's a long line of us who were here first."

"I don't care. I'm here now."

Rishka's grin widened. She didn't respond, but the slow stiffening of her ears and the way her hands slid down to grip the weapon-laden belt at her waist said all that she needed to.

"Rishka." I stepped forward, but very deliberately did not put myself between the two hyenalings. "Money's a bit tight right now, but we were about to make camp. Would you like to join us for supper?"

Chapter Five

THE SHADOWS WERE GROWING long and the air was finally starting to cool by the time we started to make our way down from the hill overlooking the tomb. We were making our way toward a camping spot, following Eshi over the dry ground and through a rising chorus of insect calls.

"I like her." Rishka grinned, nodding to the other hyenaling leading from a few dozen paces away. "She looks like trouble."

"You have no idea."

The hyenaling cackled and I hid my wince by turning to peer behind me. Asu was watching us from the top of the hill, his body still and unmoving. The lazy bug didn't like to move much once the sun started going down, though I'd call him over once we made camp.

"Trouble's a good thing," Rishka said, pulling my attention back to her. "She try to stick you with those knives, yet?"

"A dozen times already."

"Aye," Rishka said, light dancing in her dark eyes. "She likes you."

I snorted. "She tried to kill me."

"Don't be dramatic. I bet she never even cut you."

"Only because I ran away!"

"Come on, Naroh." She flicked her ears dismissively. "If she'd wanted to, I'm sure that girl had a thousand opportunities to actually hurt you. And besides," Rishka tapped one of the hatchets on her belt, "I play the same way with those I like."

"Yeah?" I said, coming to a stop. "Then why haven't you ever threatened me with your axes?"

"Oh, Naroh." The older hyenaling stopped beside me on the dry slope. "You're smart enough to know what that means."

We stared at each other for a moment before I broke into a laugh. Rishka's tail started to wag and she bared her teeth in another wide grin.

"Ah, my boy," she said, slinging a muscled arm around my shoulder and pulling me into a rough embrace. "I've missed you. It's been too many years."

"Aye," I coughed, my bones creaking as the hyenaling squeezed me to her chest. "I've missed you too."

And it was true. Trust was in short supply in a line of work as deadly as ours, but Rishka was a woman to whom I quite literally owed my life. She'd found me, bumbling around outside the entrance to the second tomb I was attempting to dive. I'd been seventeen years old, a stupid, mouthy little shit who was feeling cocky after surviving my very first dive. Instead of chasing me away, the hyenaling had brought me along with her team. She'd shown me what sort of gear to bring with me into the dark and had taught me how to spot and disarm traps. I learned how to avoid the guardians, when to sneak, and when to sprint for the exit. And when the dive was done, she'd taught me how to sell what we'd brought out.

I'd have likely died down there without her, and though I'd learned a lot on my own in the following years, those first lessons and the contacts I'd made had been invaluable.

"I'm happy to hear that," the gruff woman said, finally releasing me from her hug. "But don't think I was joking about the money you owe me. That Thopep Dynasty tomb you talked me into helping you crack didn't net me a damned thing."

"I know, I know." I shot the hyenaling a grin. "Why do you think I've been avoiding you?"

Rishka cackled and reached out to cuff me. We started back down after Eshi, our boots crunching through the dirt and rock of the hill.

"I didn't expect to see you around here," I said. "You're serious about scouting this tomb?"

"Eh," the hyenaling said. "I'm not sure. The overseer I'm bribing is an idiot, but if even half of what he's telling me is true, then this is going to be a tough one to get into. That old snake from House Malash is putting a lot of gold into this."

"Who's the architect?"

"Imassna."

I whistled.

"Aye," Rishka agreed. "We'll see what comes of it. But what about you? When we split last year, you were planning on diving around the Valley of Kings."

I shrugged. "I went, but I didn't stay long. There wasn't anything too interesting for me."

"But there is up here?"

"The Northern Province isn't as empty as people think," I said. "There are the tombs of Ikkad's necrophants and the Ahmosses are mostly buried up here as well. There's also the Nabonassarans."

"The Nabonassarans," Rishka deadpanned. "Really?"

"Nabonassara the first created our system of writing! He built the first libraries and revolutionized the way we gather and pass on knowledge."

"Alright, so you dove his tomb. What did you pull out of it?"

"Well, I'm still looking for his tomb," I admitted. "But Nabonassara IV's is up in the mountains, not far from Rapiq."

Rishka pulled me to a stop with a grip on my shoulder. "How much did you pull out of there?"

"It's not all about gold, Rishka. The things I'm learning in these old tombs are—"

"How much? The hyenaling interrupted, her dark eyes hard. "How much did you pull out of there, Naroh?"

"Seven silver."

"Seven fucking sil—!" Rishka shoved me, sending me stumbling back. "Do you have a fucking death wish, boy? Seven fucking silver, how the fuck do you ever plan on retiring? We roll with our lives every time we dive into the dark and one of these days—"

"One of these days, I'm going to fuck up and die!" I stepped back up to the furious hyenaling, my pounding heart sending waves of tingling energy through me. "I know that, Rishka! But Marduss's tomb—"

"That's what you're looking for!? Still!? Naroh, I fucking swear," Rishka's tail lashed the air behind her and she stabbed a finger into my chest. "When are you going to grow the fuck up? Do you think that we haven't all dreamed of finding that place? Do you think that you're the only one who believed they'll be the lucky idiot to stumble on a legend? We all do. We all want to be rich and famous and remembered for fucking ever. But then, our stomachs start to cramp and we stop risking our lives digging through empty old tombs. You need gold, boy. Cold, hard fucking metal."

I glared back at her, blood surging through my ears. Gods of fucking death, I was tired of hearing the same damn thing over and over again.

"That tomb is out there," I said, fighting to remain calm. "I'm going to find it, and I don't care how many more fucking clues it takes."

"You found something?" Rishka's ears flicked back, her anger vanishing as surprise rippled over her features. "You found a clue to Marduss's tomb?"

"I—fuck." I snapped my mouth shut, taking several long moments to silently curse myself. "No."

The older hyenaling didn't dignify that with a response. She crossed her muscled arms, waiting, her ears stiff above her short mop of speckled hair.

Eventually, I ran a hand through my hair and let out a long breath. "Maybe."

"Show me."

The medallion's weight pulled at the fold in my robe, but I didn't look or move toward it. "I can't."

"You won't," Rishka corrected. Then, she let out a sigh, uncrossed her arms, and shook her head. "Sorry, that's smart of you to do. I take it that's why you're headed to Ikkad?"

I nodded. "I'm going to show it to Kashir."

"Kashir?" She frowned. "Is that a good idea? That old elf is Broken Mountain."

"Name a sifter in Ikkad who isn't Broken Mountain," I said. "Kashir knows his history and has been doing this longer than I've been alive."

"He's dangerous."

It was my turn to frown. "What the hell, Rishka? You've introduced me to sifters that are way loonier than Kashir. Why are you so worried?"

"I just want to be sure you know what you're getting into, my boy. Marduss's fucking tomb..." The hyenaling slid a palm down her face, suddenly looking like every one of her four decades. "Look, I doubt that whatever you found is anything special, but shit tends to get blown way past serious when that tomb is involved. Every generation, some handful of lamians get obsessed with finding it and start throwing gold and bodies at whatever rumor they can dig up."

"I wouldn't have made it this long if I didn't know how to stay away from the snakes."

"I know, my boy, but old women tend to worry."

"Old?" I smiled, feeling the tension drain from the air. "You'd break me in two if I ever called you that."

"Aye, and don't you forget it," Rishka growled. Then, she cuffed me on the shoulder. "Now, come on, your girl is starting to look angry down there."

Sure enough, Eshi had stopped to stare at us from a spot at the base of the hill. She was too far for me to see the expression on her face, but her hands were near the hilts of her knives and her back was stiff and unhappy.

"Gods, I can't wait to get to Ikkad and be done with her."

"I don't know. You were laughing together when I showed up."

"That was..." I shook my head. "It doesn't matter. I'm bringing her to Ikkad and introducing her to some merchants I know."

"Mmm, you're not thinking of making her a partner?"

I gave Rishka an incredulous look. "Are you trying to get me killed?"

"I told you to stop being dramatic." She flicked her ears and we started down the hill. "She's a proper hyenaling woman— fierce, strong, and I'll bet you she's real good in a scrap too. A girl like that doesn't quit when shit gets hard."

I didn't doubt any of that, but still, I shook my head. "I've always worked better alone, Rishka. You know that."

"That's the kind of person you want with you in a tomb, is all I'm saying."

"She'd just slow me down."

"I think she might surprise you on that, boy," Rishka said. "Come on, are you telling me that no part of you likes having her around?"

Unbidden, a scene from the night in the caravansary flashed through my mind. I remembered the way Eshi had smiled at me from across the table. I saw again the warmth in her amber eyes and the candlelit softness of her cheeks. And then, when she'd laughed, the whole of me had—

I shook my head, scowling even as heat curled beneath my cheeks. "I'm done talking about this."

Rishka cackled.

"Gods of fucking death," I said, with an exaggerated roll of my eyes. "Save me from pushy hyenaling women."

"Mouthy pup," Rishka growled, checking me with her hip. "Do I need to remind you how to show some damned respect?"

We bickered good-naturedly the rest of the way down the hill. Eshi had stopped in a hollow sheltered by large boulders. Water pooled within a shallow hole that she'd dug with her hands and the hyenaling glared suspiciously at us.

"You two going to kill each other? It sounded like things were getting pretty heated."

"Aye, well, Naroh often makes me feel like screaming." Rishka's hands were on her hips and she looked approvingly around the site Eshi had chosen. "You'll know what I mean if you decide to stick around."

The younger hyenaling snorted. I gave Rishka a flat stare before turning and calling to Asu. The lazy bug lifted himself slowly off the ground, coming down the hill even more sedately than I had.

"You can sit," I told Rishka. "We'll be able to eat once Asu gets here with all my supplies."

"Eh, I'm actually going to head back to my crew. We're down in the overseer's town."

"You sure?"

"Yes," Rishka smirked. "I haven't forgotten what a shit cook you are."

I chuckled. "Fair enough. Say hi to Shireen and Fashri for me, then."

The older hyenaling arched an eyebrow. "Not Raza?"

"He's a lot better at cards than I am," I said. "I don't want to remind him that I owe him money."

Rishka laughed and pulled me into another tight hug. "Take care of yourself, my boy. Remember what I said."

"Aye," I coughed. "I will."

"And you too, girl." The hyenaling grinned at Eshi. "Keep your knives sharp and your circle tight."

Eshi's ears folded back. She didn't speak but nodded once. Rishka turned away with one last wave and started back up the hill. The evening was quiet in the wake of her departure, Rishka's loud exuberance replaced by the calls of birds and overeager insects. The silence was not uncomfortable, and I spent what daylight we had left working on the straps of Asu's saddle and pulling supplies off his back.

Eshi had a fire lit by the time night fell. She didn't go hunting, so we ate some of the dried meat and cheese I had in my packs.

"Naroh?" Eshi was looking at me from across the fire, her expression unreadable. Her fingers pulled absentmindedly at the cloth of her pants. "How long have you known that hyenaling?"

"Rishka?" I settled back on the rock beneath me. "Almost nine years, I think. Why?"

"Was she..." Her ears flicked back and she chewed on her lip for a moment before continuing. "Was she an outcast back then?"

"Do you mean, was she exiled from her clan?" At her quick nod, I went on. "I think so."

"And her crew, are they all hyenalings?"

"Uh, Fashri is, but Raza and Shireen are both elves. Other people have come and gone over time."

"And she just..." Eshi trailed off, her expression strangely helpless. "She just has people with her?"

"Rishka's like that," I smiled. "She just sort of gathers people around her. I doubt she's been alone for a day in her life."

"Huh," Eshi murmured, staring into the fire. "Imagine that."

Ikkad was the northernmost of the empire's great cities and the furthest from the fertile floodplains between the two great rivers of the heartland. It was dry, and the comparatively near peaks of the Northern Mountains made the surrounding landscape rougher and rockier than what could be found further south.

That wasn't to say, however, that the land was barren.

Ikkad was built on the banks of the Nazlun, and that great river ensured that nobody would ever starve or be without water. The people who lived here had adapted to the more rugged soil by focusing their energy less on the growth of barley and more on the cultivation of fruit and livestock.

Ikkad was thus known for the stone from its quarries, the sweetness of its fruit, and the quality of its horseflesh.

Eshi and I arrived at the city gates late in the morning. We were on foot, standing in a line of farmers, merchants, and travelers that was slowly moving forward as guards inspected each person in turn. Nothing larger than a camel was permitted into the city, and though there were corrals designed for carrier beetles and war-scorpions, I'd left Asu in the shade of an out-of-the-way grove instead.

That was technically against the law but, to me, the exorbitant stabling fees were a much greater danger. I'd be gone before anyone with any authority noticed Asu.

Hopefully.

"I don't care." Eshi's voice was loud and angry. "I'm not going to wait in some tavern while you run off. I don't trust you."

I glowered at her. The air smelled of apricots and cherries, and though it was hard to feel sour surrounded by such sweetness, the hyenaling was doing an admirable job of curdling my mood. "I'm not going to break my promise to you. I know some caravaners that are based here, and I won't leave before introducing you."

"You won't," Eshi said, baring her teeth. "Because I'm going to make sure of it."

"Eshi," I said, changing tack. "The person I need to see is pretty particular. He won't let me in if you're there."

The hyenaling folded her arms over her cloth-wrapped chest and her ears were stiff above her blonde, speckled hair. "Then let's go talk to your merchant friend first. The sooner I can start working, the better."

"We can't," I said, trying to keep the exasperation from my voice. "I already told you that Kashir usually leaves his house in the late afternoon. If I miss him, I won't be able to see him until tomorrow."

"And I told you," she said, her eyes on mine. "I don't trust you, and until then, I'm not letting you out of my sight. Tomorrow, I'll be out of your hair. Just see him then."

"I can't! What I have to show him can't wait!"

"Well," Eshi flicked her ears. "I guess that you'd better convince him to let me in."

Gods of fucking death she was stubborn. I gritted my teeth, but before we could launch back into the same argument that we'd been having all morning, there was a disturbance at the gate.

A hyenaling man emerged, his broad frame armored in leather and bronze. He swept hard eyes over the mass of us, his blade-notched ears high and alert.

"Is that a house guard?" Eshi asked. "What the hell is he doing out here?"

The men and women that the lamians hired to guard their necropolises and crypt-manors were typically a cut above the rest. They were better paid, better trained, and better equipped; and this hyenaling appeared to be no exception. He was large, with broad shoulders and arms scarred by war.

He stalked over to speak to the handful of common guards, one hand resting on the hilt of a khopesh. The curved, sickle-shaped sword hung from a sheath at his side.

"I don't know," I answered, peering through the crowd. "Can you tell which house he belongs to?"

Before Eshi could answer, the guards at the gate had finished their conversation. They turned and bellowed to clear the road. Moving amongst us, they yelled, argued with, and eventually pushed at and threatened the waiting farmers and merchants. Traffic snarled as dozens of carts were made to turn around, but the guards insisted that every camel, cart, mule, and horse had to be off the road.

"Good thing that you didn't bring the bug," Eshi remarked as we were pressed between two farmers' carts. They were both piled high with various fruits and vegetables, their respective drivers keeping a close eye on all who were pushed too close.

"Asu would have done great," I said, eyeing a basket of particularly tasty-looking apricots. "He's a good boy."

"As long as nobody's entire livelihood wanders too close," Eshi said.

I winced but didn't answer.

It took about twenty minutes to clear the road. The hyenaling house guard disappeared back through the gate and emerged not long after, marching in front of a palanquin. It was a large, open-sided box carved from a rich, dark wood. Layers of thin, blue cloth curtained off the interior, and though the occupant was hidden from our sight, everyone in line knew that a lamian lounged within.

For the shrouded palanquin was borne on the backs of a dozen corpses.

Eshi hissed and I felt my own body stiffen. A nervous tremor rippled through the crowd and many bowed their heads or even kneeled in the dirt as the necromancer was carried past us. To see the bodies of the slain get up and walk was novel to no one born within the Ashuran Empire. Corpses did a lot of the drudge work within cities as large as Ikkad, and it was common to see the dead toiling in the fields, or hauling waste and heavy debris through the city streets.

These, however, were no simple shambling corpses.

They were massive, jackal-headed creations of flesh and bone. They were humanoid in shape, their organs removed, and the flesh stripped from everything save the ferocious, canid heads. Purple fire burned within their eyes and the pale bone of their skeletal bodies gleamed in the sunlight. Thick, golden shackles were clamped around each wrist. Their fingers ended in wicked claws and each had twin, bronze khopeshes of monstrous proportions crossed along their backs.

Lamian magic touches on every part of death, and these *constructs* would have started as a normal body. The necromancer would have suffused each corpse with magic; sculpting, stretching, and strengthening the bones into this new, monstrous form.

Making undead servants such as these took a lot of time, energy, and magical might. They were the hallmark of the greatest lamian magic-wielders and though every noble house had its own preferred constructs, only one used the heads of jackals.

House Malash—Ikkad's ruling family.

The palanquin swayed past us with the strange, rhythmic steps of the dead. The whole crowd was silent and through the thin, layered curtains, I saw the shadow of a long, coiled tail and the lounging form of a distinctly feminine curved upper body. The cloth shifted with a breeze and I caught the flash of burnished gold and deep, dark eyes.

Then, the palanquin was past, and everyone breathed a sigh of relief. I frowned as it disappeared down the road, staying still as, around me, traffic rippled back into motion. The lamia was heading towards Asu, and I hoped that she did nothing to aggravate the big scorpion.

After a moment, I shook my head and turned towards the gates. It was no use worrying over; the whims of the nobility were as destructive and unpredictable as the desert storms.

I'd deal with whatever might come of it when it arrived.

Chapter Six

Ashur meant home in the dead language of the elves. It was the name they'd given to the land between the two great rivers, the floodplains upon which history itself had begun.

Those first elves, desert nomads and wanderers, had been the first to plunge their hands into this dark, rich soil. They'd settled and spent generations taming the world around them. Wild seeds were gathered and sowed into neat rows, the native beasts were lured into fenced paddocks, and they'd cut channels into the earth to draw away the waters of the Nazlun and Gibris to irrigate their fields and animals.

Great cities of stone, brick, and wood arose upon that fertile plain. The elves grew stronger and more numerous. They cut precious gems, melted down ore from the mountains, and worked with fur, leather, flax, and wool. They traded with one another, spreading out into the wide world in search of distant wealth. They built monuments; temples, statues, and grand walls of stone. Great works of infrastructure were made to better their lives and a vast network of roads, bridges, and canals bloomed in the spaces between their cities.

The elves made their *Ashur* into a blooming paradise. And it was from this gentle cradle that the wonder of civilization was born.

Ikkad, like most of the other elven metropolises, was ancient. Nowadays, it was a city of old stone and new brick. A patchwork of narrow streets wove past modern industry and forgotten monuments, through bustling squares and past stepped temples.

I did my best to keep my mind from wandering as Eshi and I were let through the gate and into the city. We'd entered on the northern side of the sprawling river docks and into an area that was dominated by blocky warehouses, mudbrick tenements, cheap taverns, slaughterhouses, and foul-smelling tanneries.

The trader's road, which would lead us into the city's center, was busy despite the late morning heat. The air was thick with the smell of smoke, dust, and unwashed bodies. We passed broad-shouldered bargemen, elven laborers and artisans with soiled headscarves, and swaggering hyenaling women. There were merchants and farmers, mothers with their children, and peddlers with their carts. Thugs and thieves prowled along the edges and the alleys were populated by drunks and beggars. Prostitutes called down from brothel balconies and gangs of poor, hard-eyed elven youths watched with empty bellies and minds full of anger.

And then, of course, there were the dead.

Corpses moved amongst us, skeletons whose eye sockets burned with purple, necromantic fire. Ikkad's worker constructs were much less impressive than the jackal-headed guardians of House Malash. Raised from the remains of criminals and the claimed, these unmodified skeletons were infused with just enough magic to sweep the streets or haul waste to the pits beyond the walls.

"Where are we going?" Eshi asked. "Is your merchant somewhere in the trade quarter?"

"Have you been to Ikkad before?"

She shrugged. "A few times."

I made to speak but hesitated when I caught sight of a brightly colored claimer. This one was an elf, though the guards surrounding him were mostly hyenalings. His robe was rich, and his hands were wrapped around pouches of coin he loudly promised to the crowd. The lamian noble houses were always hungry for bodies, and their agents were a fixture of the poorer parts of every city. One could sell their bodies to the necromancers if one was desperate enough, and the claimers prowled the worst sort of streets to prey on just those people.

A line of undead shambled past in their strange, rhythmic gait, and I couldn't help but wonder how many of the living people around me would one day join their ranks. How many people had had their flesh inked by the claimers? How many had traded the dignity of death for a meager handful of coins?

I'd almost done it.

In that first year since leaving my village, when hunger had been my constant companion, I'd stood before a claimer. I'd turned away before taking his coin, but it had been a very near thing.

I let out a breath and tried to push the thought from my head. I watched the constructs walk past. They held picks and hammers slung over their shoulders, and their bones were cracked and stained. No golden shackles gleamed around their wrists.

Corpses were cheap in Ashura, but gold was not.

"Naroh," Eshi growled, nudging me with her elbow. "Come on."

"Right, sorry." I shook my head to finish clearing it. "We're going into Pharon's Square first."

Eshi pulled an apricot from within her robe and took a bite, speaking around a mouthful of fruit. "And after that?

"You stole that," I accused. "From that farmer's cart."

She shrugged her shoulders, a casual gesture at odds with the sudden stiffness in her ears. Her amber eyes were on mine as she took a second, even larger bite.

"Do you have another one?"

She blinked.

"I didn't think that I could get away with grabbing one," I continued. "And they looked really good."

The corner of her mouth quirked upward. "They taste good too."

"So, are you going to share?"

"Are you going to actually answer my question?"

"Gods of fucking death you're stubborn."

"Maybe." Eshi's amber eyes sparkled, and she raised the apricot back to her lips. "But at least I'm not hungry."

I chuckled, despite myself. The hyenaling took a third bite of the stolen fruit, her expression curling into one of satisfaction. Behind her, her tail started to swish through the air.

"We'll go up towards the Grand Ziggurat when we get to the square," I said, once she'd swallowed. "The elf I'm meeting has a house in the Shadow Quarter."

Eshi whistled. "No wonder you've been trying so hard to get rid of me."

"Speaking of which," I said, pointing to a tavern that we were even now walking past. "Why don't you—"

"No," she interrupted. "I'm not going to wait for you anywhere. Stop trying."

I glowered at her. "Stubborn."

She sniffed, flicking her ears dismissively. Her tail, I noticed, had not yet stilled.

"So," I said after another handful of steps. "Do you have another apricot, or..."

She considered me for a moment before, then she reached into her open robe and pulled out a large onion.

I blinked.

"The guy in the fruit cart was getting vigilant," Eshi said, laughter tugging at the edge of her voice. "I had to turn to the vegetable one."

I gave her a flat stare. She grinned and an unexplainable warmth bloomed in me as I noticed the sparkle in her amber eyes and the delighted flush of her freckled cheeks. Abruptly, I decided to play along.

"This is perfect," I said, plucking the bulb from her hand. "Thanks!"

Then, without giving myself time to reconsider, I brought it to my lips and took a bite. My teeth crunched through the papery peel and the onion's raw, overwhelming flavor exploded in my mouth.

Eshi gaped and I took another bite before holding it out to her. I spoke through a mouthful of the vegetable. "Want some?"

"Do I..." Then, she threw her head back and howled.

Laughter poured from her, a high, breathless cackle that seemed to take the very air from her chest. It was loud and filled the street around us, drawing the eye of all who passed. Eshi seemed not the least bit self-conscious, however, doubling over herself as her entire frame heaved with the hiccupping gasp of her laughter.

I stopped along with her, my chest buzzing with the sound of her pure, unfiltered joy. My face split into a wide grin and I waved the onion in front of her. "You sure you don't want any?"

"Stop!" She gasped, leaning away from it. "Get away!"

The words disappeared into another breathless stream of cackles as her body was wracked with another gleeful convulsion. The warmth that had boomed within me spread, until the whole of me was alight with the sound of her laughter.

"Naroh, you—" Eshi started, interrupted by a final hiccupping laugh. She smiled and pushed strands of sun-colored hair away from her reddened, freckle-dusted face. "You just get more and more interesting."

"Interesting is good," I said, not losing my smile. "Way better than stubborn."

She snorted and pushed me with her shoulder. "Stubbornness is a quality."

"Really?" I said, starting back down the street. "How so?"

"Well," Eshi said, falling in beside me. "When I find something I want, I don't let go."

Pharon's Square was large, and its proximity to the river docks meant that it hosted the city's largest market. Merchants, farmers, and artisans competed for space and customers atop the square's dusty cobbles.

Goods from all over the empire and beyond could be found here. Eshi and I passed by potters selling plates and vases set up beside traders from Basri with baskets full of olives. There were smiths and wine merchants, finely woven carpets and bolts of cloth from the looms of Niveh. Elves were clustered around sellers of spices and bartered with artisans selling combs and other objects carved from fragrant wood, while hyenalings considered carts full of caged chickens and bloody cuts of goat and mutton. Humans wandered through the crowd as well, some sporting the wild beards and furred cloaks that marked them as natives of the kingdoms beyond the Northern Mountains.

As Eshi and I pushed our way through the crowd of people, we even saw a pair of lamians at a gem merchant's stall. The two men were surrounded by constructs encased in heavy armor, the distinct guardians marking them as members of House Ussar.

We made our way towards the center of the square, where a large statue of Ramesh the Great, first pharon of the Ashuran Empire, dominated the area.

Three millennia ago, when the elven swordmasters of the Broken Mountain had murdered Marduss on the cusp of his final victory at Uruq, it had been Ramesh, then a necrophant and general, who had rallied the legions. He had led them in the final storming of the capital and had been the one to accept the surrender of the last elven kings.

Ramesh, now crowned pharon of what he would make into the Ashuran Empire, was not kind to the elves. Following their capitulation, he tracked what remained of the Broken Mountain swordmasters to their fortress across the desert to the south and cracked their walls after a protracted siege. He put every elven man, woman, and child he found within to death and, upon his return to Uruq, decreed that the elven race was not finished atoning for the sin of their resistance. He condemned them all to slavery, breaking them with whip and chain and using their bodies to rebuild the ruin brought on by years of war.

The statue of the lamian necromancer-king was of a size with the surrounding buildings and was carved from a dark stone that had admirably weathered the passing millennia. I could still see the pointed beard at his chin and the proud set of his features. He was depicted wearing a set of long, flowing robes. His head, held high, was covered with the Hooded Crown, and in one outstretched hand, he held a snake-headed scepter.

Ramesh the Great had avenged Marduss and wiped out the elves of the Broken Mountain. Although, as was evident when we reached the base of his statue, death, in Ashura, was not always permanent.

"Gods of fucking death," I swore, staring up at the statue. "What in the hells is the point of this?"

Eshi shrugged. "Who knows why elves do anything."

"Yeah, but this," I gestured with my hands. Covering the bottom portion of the statue was the symbol of the Broken Mountain; a triangle with a notch cut into one side, was splashed onto the stone in bright white paint. "What does this even accomplish? Do you know how old this statue is?"

"No." A little smirk curled her lips. "But I'm sure that you're about to tell me."

I glowered at her before turning back to the symbol. What had risen to become the Order of the Broken Mountain was something that those ancient elven swordmasters wouldn't recognize. In the centuries following their extinction, slaves escaping the lamian lash had crossed the desert and rediscovered the mountain stronghold. They'd rebuilt it, turning it into a base for rebels and freedom fighters.

After emancipation, the Order had become less militant. They'd moved back into the cities of the empire, dedicating themselves to preserving what remained of elven culture and securing a future for themselves as citizens. Yet, so humble an ambition did not last long. The lamian grip on the upper echelons of power was absolute and the elves of the Broken Mountain chaffed under these restrictions.

Ashur had once been theirs, they said. It was only right that they should have a say in its governance.

Elven power and elven supremacy became the foundation of their Order. They made themselves into warriors once again, becoming rebels, bandits, and violent revolutionaries who swore themselves to the liberation of their people. Elven gangs set themselves up in every major city, using the money they gained from running brothels, gambling dens, and smuggling rings to fund their struggle.

And yet, they could never truly face the lamians.

In the past thousand years, the same cycle would repeat itself over and over again. The Broken Mountain would grow in wealth and power, burning and killing and pillaging until the lamians cracked down. There'd be purges and wars fought in the streets. What existed of the Order would be wiped out. For a century or two, it would be gone, then, a new generation of elves would be born, hungry for what their ancestors had lost. The young would swear themselves anew to the cause of elven supremacy and the Broken Mountain would rise once more.

"Whatever," I said, letting out a breath. "We need to get going."

"Come on." Eshi bumped me with her shoulder. "Are you really not going to tell me?"

"No, I—" Next to me, the hyenaling's expression was open. Her ears were perked and I didn't see a hint of mockery in the lines of her face. "Do you really want to know?"

"I already told you, Naroh. I like your passion." She smiled and bumped me again with her shoulder. "Now, come on, you can tell me while we walk."

Something in me fluttered at that smile, but I pushed it aside. I *really* wanted to talk about this and I was deep into my retelling of Ramesh the Great's siege of the Broken Mountain by the time we emerged from Pharon's Square.

The surrounding buildings became nicer the further we got from the docks; adobe tenements and open-air workshops were replaced by windowed shops of plaster and stone. Restaurants and wine houses started to appear as we left brothels and smoky taverns behind. We passed airy elven homes and many-floored hyenaling compounds, as well as the blocky, solidly built houses that my own kind preferred.

The crowds became cleaner and better dressed, and as we moved into the wealthy Shadow Quarter, we even began to see a few lamians on the street. They moved between pyramid-roofed palaces and gathered before the great temples, necropolises and crypt-manors of the noble houses.

I hardly noticed any of it, however, focused as I was on recounting the elven slave revolts that Ramesh the Great had spent the final years of his rule putting down. Then, we stepped into the shadow of a massive edifice and my mind finally stuttered back into awareness.

Ikkad had doubtless changed much in the ages since it had been built. A brutal war of conquest and three millennia of progress had ground away much of what those ancient elves had created.

And yet, some things time simply could not erase.

Eshi and I had reached the heart of the city, and before us was a wonder whose very grandeur defied destruction.

"I've never been this close to it before," Eshi said, craning her neck upward. We were in the shadow of Ikkad's Grand Ziggurat, the great edifice rising high above us. "It's a monster."

Monster was a good word to describe it. Ikkad's Ziggurat was immense, a great, blocky, many-tiered complex of carved stone, wide staircases, and hanging gardens. It dominated the center of the city, towering over even the most lavish necropolis-palaces that surrounded it. There was a mountain's worth of stone here, and its very size made it into a fortress.

The elven kings of Ikkad had once ruled from this great monument, though it now served as the seat of the province's necrophant. Guards in the colors of House Malash were everywhere, patrolling along the higher tiers and standing at attention before the entrance and at the base of wide staircases. I even noticed a pair of jackal-headed constructs, the undead guardians waiting silent and still in shadowed nooks by the main gate.

"I've read that it took the elves more than five hundred years to build," I said, leading her along the Ziggurat's outer edge. "And I read somewhere else that it was the first building they ever built here. The author claimed they just lived around it in their tents until it was done, but I don't think I believe that."

I craned my head upward as the hyenaling had, squinting to peer at the building's highest tier. It seemed to scrape the bottom of the very sky.

"It's pretty much a city in itself," I continued. "There are supposed to be more than ten thousand rooms in there. It was designed to be able to hold the city's entire population if they were ever attacked.

"I'm surprised the snakes didn't rip it apart when they invaded."

I shook my head. "Ikkad was never touched during the conquest. It's a bit out of the way, so all the elves ever did was send their army to join the unified one after Niveh fell. They surrendered along with the other city-states once Marduss smashed the army and pulled down the walls of Uruq."

"Must have stung that old elf king's pride to just give up a house like this."

"It probably hurt less than seeing the army he sent out come back as a legion of corpses."

Eshi cackled, and we didn't speak again until we reached a stone manse built in the Ziggurat's shadow. It was large and decorated with ornately carved stone and patterned tilework. The inner corridors, I knew, were large and airy, kept cool by a half-dozen fountained courtyards.

The hyenaling narrowed her eyes as we stopped before a door of polished wood. She stared at me a moment before she said, "This is the house of the man you're supposed to meet?"

"Elf," I corrected. "And yeah, this is Kashir's house."

Kashir was an elf that I'd known for many years. He was rich, obviously, and well-known by the city's noble houses. He was an elf from an old merchant family who, unlike many a wealthy scion, had actually added to the fortune he'd inherited instead of just pissing it away.

"See this," Eshi said, waving between me and the house, "is why I don't trust you."

I rolled my eyes. "Stop sniffing for secrets where there are none. Kashir and I both love history and we sometimes do business together. That's it."

"There's no way that you," she made a show of looking me up and down, "have anything legitimate to do with the type of person that lives in this sort of house."

"What's wrong with..." I looked down at myself and grimaced. My ochre robe did look rather more rumpled and dirt-stained than I remembered. The bandages that still wrapped my hands were soiled and bloody, and my black hair was longer than it ought to be. Although I had, at least, shaved that morning. "...whatever. Come on."

As we made our way to the entrance, I briefly considered attempting a final bid to keep Eshi outside. One glance at the stubborn set of her jaw dissuaded me of that notion. Instead, I spent those minutes between my knocking and the servant appearing in the doorway trying to figure out exactly how the hell I was going to talk the both of us in.

"Master Naroh," the sharply dressed elf who opened the door said. "What a... pleasure it is to see you again."

"Hey, Emran," I answered. "Is your master in? I've got something to show him."

"Do you now?" Emran's expression was carefully neutral beneath his fine, white headwrap. "So good of you to... dress for the occasion."

Eshi stifled a laugh, and I felt the heat crawl up my neck. "Yeah, sorry, I just arrived from the foothills."

"Where you picked up a stray, I see." Beside me, Eshi choked on her mirth. "Master Kashir doesn't run a charity, and as you know, does not let just anyone into his private dwelling. Tell me where you are staying and I will inform him that you have called. Although," he flicked his eyes over me, "he will doubtless suspect once he sees the fresh dirt staining his stoop."

"Come on, Emran," I said, spreading my hands, "You know me. When have I ever wasted Kashir's time?"

The elf quirked an eyebrow, but I held up a hand before he could speak. "Don't answer that. I have some big news to share with him and trust me when I say that he doesn't want to miss what I have to tell him. I need to see him now, before he leaves for court at the Ziggurat."

The manservant folded his arms. "I hardly believe that what you have to say is that urgent. I'll tell him you stopped by. You may try coming back in a few days if you haven't heard from him. Though, leave this mutt at home when you do."

I threw an arm out in front of Eshi, keeping her from snapping out a reply. I met Emran's satisfied smirk with a steady gaze, took a deep breath, and then started talking.

Chapter Seven

I WAS A FAST talker, but even still, it took nearly an hour of pleading, arguing, and negotiating before Emran let us into the manor.

Kashir's home was as luxurious as I remembered. The hallways were open and airy, and I marveled anew at the burbling fountains set within finely tiled courtyards. There were richly appointed sitting rooms and busts of serious-looking elves. The kitchen was large and hummed with energy. It was connected to a dining room that looked large enough to feed an army, the centerpiece of which was a massive table made from a beautiful, dark-red wood that could only be found beyond the Northern Mountains.

Kashir liked to conduct much of his business here, and so, the place was busy. We passed throngs of servants, as well as pairs of armored, blade-scarred elves patrolling the hallways. Scribes bearing sheaves of parchment in ink-stained fingers hurried by, and there were merchants with boots still dusty from the road.

Emran eventually tucked us into a small, out-of-the-way antechamber. He left us alone for another hour before escorting me into his master's presence.

Eshi, I was relieved to see, drew the line at demanding to be let into this meeting.

"Naroh," Kashir said, looking up from his desk. He leaned back in his chair, and away from the abacus he'd been working with. "Emran here tells me that you've caused him quite a bit of trouble. And that you've brought a stranger into my home, no less."

Kashir was a thin elf with dark eyes and a lined face. He was in his fifth decade, and while an elf's skin tended to remain smooth until the day they died, Kashir's was marked by the stress of guiding a trading family through the shifting dunes of the necrophant's court. He was dressed in a robe like my own, though infinitely finer. It was dyed a rich shade of blue, the fabric matching the cloth he wore wrapped around his head. I imagined his hair to be liberally streaked with gray, though, of course, I could see nothing but his dagger-shaped ears.

"Yeah," I said, scratching at the back of my head. "Sorry about that. Eshi is... anyway, I've got something for you."

The elf frowned. He dismissed his servant with a wave while I sat in the opposite chair without prompting. His frown deepened, though he waited until Emran had shut the door behind him before he spoke.

"I'm used to being treated with more respect in my own home, Naroh."

Kashir's rebuke was mild, though there was a very real threat beneath his words. I wasn't worried, though, I knew the value of what I'd brought him.

Besides, it had been a long day.

"Too bad," I said, leaning forward. "Emran made me work way too fucking hard to get in here."

"He is good at keeping my home free of trash," Kashir said, matching my forward lean. "Tread carefully, Naroh. My patience is not limitless."

I grinned into his anger, reaching a hand into the fold of my robe. "I'm a tomb diver, Kashir. I know when to tiptoe, and when to sprint."

I punctuated my last word by tossing a pouch onto the desk between us. It landed with a heavy thunk, pulling the elf's eyes down to it. He didn't reach for it, moving instead to steeple his fingers. He raised his gaze back up to mine after a few heartbeats.

"Your clever wordplay is doing little to improve my mood."

My grin widened. I was playing a dangerous game, but I couldn't help it. Some forms of authority just rubbed me the wrong way. I could blame that on my father, I supposed.

"Just open it."

He wanted to hold onto his anger, to sate his pride and toss me out on my ears. But I had my hooks in him. He was curious, and my apparent disregard for my own well-being had only served to deepen that feeling.

And so, it was just a few moments later before he reached for the pouch and pulled out the golden medallion.

"Nabonassaran, if the heraldry is any indication. And the words: *The wise fly on the wings of the stork, to nest, immortal in wisdom's source.* Yes, indeed, the motto of their house." Kashir turned it over in his hands. His voice was carefully neutral as he examined it. "It is lamian made and the gold bears the slight discoloration of heavy magical use. The detail is poor, but that is to be expected for a piece of such apparent antiquity. What decoration there was along the edges has been rubbed smooth."

I relaxed, listening to the drone of the elf's voice. I enjoyed the novelty of not worrying about prying eyes or ears. Kashir was the sort of sifter that small-timers like Balasi dreamed of becoming. He was at the pinnacle of this particular illicit trade, protected from the viziers and their laws by his friendship with the necrophant and the no doubt meticulously kept list of the lamians he sold to.

"A depiction of the grand necrophant," Kashir continued. "Bearing the Black Scythe of Djed and the Hooded Crown..."

He trailed off, his features falling back into a slight frown. Tilting it to catch the light from an open window, the elf examined it more closely.

"... Is absent," I finished, drawing his eyes back to me. My heart was pounding in my chest, sending blood vibrating through my limbs. "He's got an elven headwrap on, instead."

Covering one's head in cloth was a distinctly elven custom. It was easily recognizable, an aspect of their culture that set them apart from all the others. It was a tradition from deep into antiquity, from a time when the elves had wandered the desert in nomadic tribes. It had supposedly been a way to show respect to the spirits of the land and to keep their minds safe from wicked *djinn.* And though the lamian pantheon had generally replaced those older beliefs, the elven headscarf remained practical. The summer sun could be brutal and the cloth shielded their heads from its burning glare.

For Grand Necrophant Marduss, the conqueror of the elves and their greatest enemy to be *dressed* as one of them was... noteworthy, to say the least.

Beneath his own cloth winding, Kashir's face was slack. He was stunned, speechless in a way I don't think he'd ever been before.

"This ..." he said, at last. "Naroh, do you know what this is?"

"It's something different," I answered. "Something that we've never seen before."

"Marduss in a headwrap," Kashir said, reaching up to touch his own. "Why? What does it mean?"

I settled back with a grin, waiting for the elf's thoughts to stutter back into motion.

Kashir was Broken Mountain to his very core, though on the surface, he appeared much different than the hard-eyed, gutter-born elves that made up most of their rank and file. He did not deal with the underworld and even as a sifter, he sold only to the wealthiest clients.

Kashir would never be hungry. He'll never suffer the deprivations of poverty or sleep in dank alleys. He was rich, absurdly so, and commanded more power and respect than even many lamians within the necrophant's court.

Yet, it wasn't enough.

He'd risen as high as he could go, and when his gaze sharpened, I saw a flicker of the rage that burned within him.

Ashur, he believed, belonged to the elves.

"I want this."

"I'll sell it to you," I told him. "For a pouchful of gold and the whereabouts of Nabonassara I's tomb."

Kashir's face fell back into his merchant's mask. He set the medallion down between us and once more steepled his fingers. "The gold can perhaps be negotiated. The location of that tomb, however, is lost. You know this as well as I, Naroh."

"Sure," I said. "But you're better connected than most, Kashir. If anyone knows something, it's you."

"You overestimate my influence." The elf's expression didn't flicker beneath his tightly wound headwrap. "Even I can't dig up something hidden beneath three thousand years of sand."

"I need something," I said, leaning forward once again. "I'm on the path to the big one, Kashir, the grandest mystery in the whole fucking empire!" I laughed. This conversation was dangerous, but I couldn't help it. I was dying to finally *talk* to someone about this. "Gods of death, Marduss is in a fucking headwrap! I don't know when, or how, but this will lead me to his—"

"Be quiet!" Kashir interrupted, his body suddenly tight. "Don't finish that sentence. Nowhere is safe for this sort of talk, not even here. If word of this gets to the lamians... The snakes have gone to *war* for less. Rest assured that I understand the significance of what you've brought me."

The elf glared at me until I nodded. "Good. Now, tell me again what you need."

I let out a breath, trying to calm myself down. I failed, and when I spoke, it was in a stream of excited babble.

"I need to go diving, Kashir. The Nabonassarans were historians and worshippers of Tel'aman. They were academics who saw themselves as the guardians of knowledge and truth. That might have faded as their house declined, but Nabonassara I was a ferocious scholar who lived mere centuries after the conquest. I don't know what this artifact means, but the answer to this is down in his tomb. I fucking know it is! So, I need you to tell me where it is, and I need gold to fund my search."

"The gold is easy, but the tomb... that is a problem that has no simple solution."

I opened my mouth, but Kashir held up his hand to forestall me. "That doesn't mean that I don't have anything to offer. What this might represent... I don't know where Nabonassara I is buried, but I do know the location of his granddaughter's tomb."

"Nabonassara III?" I swept a hand through my hair, considering. "Has it been looted?"

"Millennia ago," Kashir answered. "Nothing of value remains, as far as I know. But you might find clues that earlier divers have missed."

I scowled. "That's not much."

"It's all I have. Do we have a deal?"

I met the elf's stare for a few heartbeats. In truth, I hadn't come here really expecting to get the exact answer I was looking for. Nothing about this had been easy so far, and there was no reason for that to change now.

Kashir wasn't offering me much, but it was still a possible way forward, something I'd lacked before coming in here.

"Fine, but this isn't what I was after. You're going to need to throw in some more gold."

"That can be negotiated," Kashir said.

His hands once more reached down for the medallion, his eyes gleaming with something between hope and desperation. The expression unsettled me, but I pushed my unease away.

"Alright, then," I started. "Let's—"

I was interrupted by a shout from outside Kashir's office. Another one came right after, followed by the sound of breaking clay and running feet.

I was out of my seat in an instant, tearing the medallion from Kashir's hand and stuffing it back into my robe.

"What the fuck is this," I hissed to the elf. "Did you call the lamians?"

"N—No!" The elf stuttered, half out of his own chair. "I don't..."

There came a scream of pain, and I was turning to sprint toward the room's only window when the door burst open and Emran stumbled in. The servant's eyes were wide and his headwrap was in disarray. His fine tunic was slashed open, blood oozing from the cut flesh beneath.

"Naroh," Eshi said, striding in an instant later. She sheathed her bloody knives, meeting my astonished gaze with her scavenger's grin. "We need to talk."

There was a lot of shouting following Eshi's declaration. A *lot* of shouting.

Kashir was not happy at the interruption, screaming for his guards and going on a tirade about guests and betraying trust. Blade-scarred elves piled into the room and restrained us none too gently. He took the medallion and none of my pleading and fast-talking could ease the thunder of his expression.

Nevertheless, I managed to convince him to actually tell me where to find the tomb of Nabonassara III before we were thrown out onto our faces.

Though, he just laughed in my face when I asked him for my gold.

I was heading back toward Grand Ziggurat now, my mood significantly worse and my body in more pain than when I was last here. Eshi followed a few paces back.

"Why the fuck are you still following me?!" I said, rounding on her. "Haven't you done enough?"

The hyenaling blinked slowly and flicked her ears. "I want to talk with you."

I sneered. "And I wanted to get fucking paid. Goodbye, Eshi."

I turned and stomped away. Gods of fucking death, what was I going to do now? I really needed some of Kashir's money. Finding Marduss's tomb was everything I'd ever wanted, and now that I finally had a real fucking lead I was down to a mere handful of silver coins? How was I going to stretch that for the week-long trip to this first tomb?

It wasn't until I was back on the road to Pharon's Square that I noticed that Eshi was still following me.

"What are you doing?" I asked, lengthening my stride.

She matched my pace. "I want to talk."

"I'm not talking with you."

"I'm not leaving until you do."

"I'm not fucking talking with you!"

She let out an exasperated breath. "Will you stop being so dramatic?"

"Dramatic!" I roared, whirling on her. "I bring you all the way to Ikkad and this is how you repay me?! You've just pissed on ten years of my fucking life!"

There were people on the street around us, elves and other hyenalings. I felt their eyes on me, but I didn't care. I took a half step towards Eshi, my flesh burning with angry heat.

"Ten fucking years I've been looking for this! Ten years of hunger, pain, and searching. I was always fucking searching and now, because of you, I can't move on!"

I loomed above her, my lips curled back into a snarl. Shock rippled across her features, followed by incredulity, disbelief, and a dozen other things. But she didn't see. She didn't fucking understand what she'd done to me.

"I'm stuck here," I roared, "you stupid fucking dog! I'm stuck here while Marduss's tomb rots!"

My words rang through the street, followed by a beat of absolute, perfect silence. Then, Eshi's face twisted, and a giggle slipped out of her. She caught another one by clapping a hand over her mouth. A shiver ran through her, and when her gaze met my wide, astonished eyes, she could hold it back no longer.

Laughter burst out of her, a breathless, hiccupping cackle that filled the space around us. She tried to speak, but couldn't, waving her hands in denial even as she hunched over in a fit of mirth. Around us, I heard others chuckle. People shook their heads and went on with their business.

But I didn't move.

I was frozen, my vision seared white by a rage unlike any I've ever felt before. She was laughing at me. She didn't get it, she'd ruined everything and she *didn't fucking get it!* I raised one clenched fist, unseen by Eshi as peals of laughter continued to rip through her.

No. She didn't understand. But she would.

"*Do you think I want to do this?*" A voice drifted through my mind, faint, yet impossible to ignore. "*Do you think that this makes me happy? I'm trying to teach you, but you don't fucking listen!*"

"I'm sorry!" Eshi managed to gasp between breaths and bouts of laughter. "It's not—I'm sorry!"

"*Why don't you get it!?*"

My father had yelled that after he'd caught me sneaking into the vizier's library. I heard the words so clearly now, along with the meaty thump of his fists against my flesh.

At once, all the anger drained from me. I lowered my fist, feeling it pull my shoulders into a slump, and my head into a bow. I was so tired, and my legs trembled as if they could barely support my weight.

I let out a long breath, turned, and walked away.

"Naroh!" Eshi called, still laughing. "Naroh!"

But I ignored her. My path stretched before me, and though the going was rougher than it had been before, I would walk it until its end.

Chapter Eight

Eshi, of course, caught me within moments.

"Naroh, I'm sorry," she said, grabbing my arm. "I didn't mean to laugh like that."

"It's fine," I said, tugging myself loose. "I don't care."

"It's just that you got *so* angry, and it looked so unfamiliar on your face that... well, I'm sorry. It took me by surprise but I shouldn't have laughed."

"It's fine."

Eshi skipped ahead of me and spun around, forcing me to stop. Her pale, tangle of speckled hair blazed in the light of the afternoon sun.

"I didn't think that you had that in you, Naroh." Eshi rested her hands on her hips. Her amber eyes were bright and she gave me her scavenger's grin. "I like it."

I shook my head. "Whatever, Eshi. Come on, the merchants I know are closer to the river."

"I don't want to see your merchant friends," Eshi said, falling in beside me. "I want to talk with you."

"There's nothing to talk about. We're going to go see the people I know, get you a job, and then go our separate ways."

"I think we can help each other." Eshi's tone and tail were both stiff with annoyance. "I just want to talk."

"The sooner we split up, the sooner we can stop ruining each other's lives."

She didn't answer, simply looping her arm around mine and yanking me to the side. I let out a surprised squawk, stumbling after her as she pulled me towards the curtained entrance of a cheap-looking alehouse of sun-baked brick.

"We're going to talk," she growled.

"Fine! Fine!" I said, too tired butt heads with the stubborn hyenaling. "But you're buying the beer."

The curtain parted and we walked in right as a group of hyenalings seated nearby burst into laughter. The sound was like a series of claws scraping at my mind, and I cringed away from the headache I felt coming on. Eshi didn't slow, pulling me deeper into the dark, smoky interior to a small, knife-scarred table far away from the cackling hyenalings. I sat with my back to the main entrance, crossing my arms as Eshi settled into a seat across from me.

Then, she let out a quick breath and met my gaze. "I want to come with you."

"Absolutely not."

She gritted her teeth. "You haven't even heard what I have to say."

"There's nothing you can say." I held up one hand and counted on my fingers. "You spied on me, cost me a sackful of gold, and burned a valuable contact. And you already tried to kill me!"

"You killed my camel and destroyed my cargo!"

"I don't owe you anything, Eshi," I said, shaking my head. "Especially not now."

"No." Her amber eyes shifted. "But a part of you still thinks you do. You're a good man, Naroh."

I snorted. "You don't know anything about me."

"What I know," Eshi said, planting her elbow on the table to rest her chin in her palm, "is that you brought me to Ikkad to try and help me. You didn't hit me back there, even though you *really* wanted to. And you're still here with me, even after everything."

I blinked, suddenly having a weirdly difficult time holding her gaze. The smile she gave me was so soft and the light in her eyes was so warm. She leaned forward to speak, her breath slipping through parted lips. "Can you just... listen, Naroh? Please."

I sighed, uncrossing my arms to sweep a hand through my hair. "Eshi, diving t—"

The hyenaling's ears stiffened and she lunged across the table at me. She silenced me by shoving her palm into my lips and, a moment later, a woman appeared at our table.

"What do you want?"

Her voice was impatient, and she seemed not at all interested in why Eshi had her hand over my mouth. She was a human with a lined face and stringy hair that was pulled back into a tight bun. She wore a soiled apron over a rough dress, marking her out as one of the barmaids.

"Beer," Eshi said, turning her head without removing her hand. "Two of them."

The barmaid disappeared with a grunt, and the hyenaling's ears relaxed. She removed her hand.

"You know," she said, settling back in her seat. "For a criminal, you're not very observant."

"I'm a historian," I said. "And your palm tastes like Emran's blood."

Her ears twitched in amusement before her face twisted into a scowl. "That stupid elf. Kashir would never have learned I was listening at the door if the fucking servant hadn't decided to show up with a jug of wine. I hate rich people."

"Yeah, well..." I let out a breath, not sure how to finish that sentence. "How much of our conversation did you hear?"

"Enough." Her lips quirked into a small smile. "And, well, you also just screamed your mission to a street full of people."

I winced.

"In any case," Eshi continued. "Back to what I was saying, tell me how many doors there are to this room."

I raised an eyebrow. "What?"

"How many entrances are there in this room?" She repeated, "No looking!"

I opened my mouth to argue, but then just decided to humor her. I thought about it for a moment before I said. "Two?"

"And how many men are sitting at the nearest table?"

"Also, two?"

The hyenaling shook her head. "There are three *women* at the nearest table and there are four exits to this taproom if you count the trap door."

I scowled, the expression deepening when I swept my gaze about and confirmed that she was right. "Does this have a point?"

"The point is exactly what I said— you're not very observant." Eshi rolled on, not letting me speak. "I've been watching you these past couple of days, Naroh. You get lost in your own head. Constantly. You're distracted, painfully oblivious to the world around you and it's honestly a miracle that you're still alive."

Heat rose beneath my cheeks. I planted my hands on the table and made to push myself to my feet. "I don't need to listen to this."

Eshi's hand once again flashed out, though it was my hand she now gripped. Her fingers were strong, I noted, and warm.

"Let me finish." Her voice was low. "Please."

I hesitated, holding myself halfway out of my seat.

"You going somewhere?" The barmaid said, arriving with our mugs of beer. "You still gotta pay if you go."

"No," I sighed, settling back down. "I'm not going."

Eshi flashed me a quick smile. She pulled her hand from mine and used it to sweep back her mane of blonde hair. Straightening in her seat, she let out a long breath.

"I'm not trying to insult you, Naroh. I know you well enough by now to know that you're smart. You're decisive and cautious, though you're not afraid to stand up for yourself. You're a fast runner, more agile than even a lot of hyenalings I know, and you have this *passion* that I really—ahem."

Eshi cut herself off, red blooming beneath her freckled cheeks.

I shifted, my cheeks growing a little hotter. "Yeah, well, slow idiots don't live long in my line of work."

The hyenaling's ears twitched, and she took a moment to clear her throat before continuing. "You've survived this far, but this job is bigger than anything you've done before."

"I still can't believe you spied on me," I grumbled, lifting my tankard.

"Oh, I'd already figured out what sort of work you do." Eshi waved her hand dismissively. At my disbelieving snort, she continued. "I'm not an idiot, Naroh, and you're really not very good at hiding it. I found a lot of your gear after that first day on Asu's back. Going to see the tomb and that Rishka woman were also both suspicious as hell."

I scowled, my face twisting further as I took a sip of the cheap, sour beer.

"You need a partner. Someone practical, who can take care of the real world while you keep your nose buried in your artifacts."

"And that partner is you?"

"Why not?" Eshi retorted. She held up one hand and counted on her fingers. "I'm a warrior, and you're not. I'm a better huntress and know more about the wild. I've got better senses and I don't forget to use them. I'm good with merchants and, most importantly, I'm a faster runner than you."

I shook my head, latching onto the only real objection I could make. "You couldn't catch me when you wanted to."

"I was blind with rage, Naroh. And I came close."

"Maybe so," I answered. "But I have Asu for everything else."

"That bug can't do everything."

I shrugged, lifted my beer for another sip but then set it down when I thought better of it. Eshi considered me for several long moments, her ears shifting in thought. Around us, the tavern was starting to fill up and the air grew thicker with the hum of conversation and the scent of bodies.

"When you go into one of these... *places*," the hyenaling said. "How long does it usually take?"

"Depends on the size of it." I pushed my beer away. Eshi hadn't touched hers. "A few days or a week, sometimes more. Going down there isn't something you want to rush."

"More than a week," she repeated. "Naroh, what I've heard about these places; the death, the darkness... You go in by yourself?"

"Yeah," I nodded. "I didn't even have Asu for the first few years."

"Naroh, you—" Eshi swallowed and something shifted deep within her amber eyes. "Aren't you just so tired of being alone?"

The way her voice became smaller and the naked emotion I could see splashed across her face tightened my throat. Whatever flippant answer I might have given stayed lodged there.

"I don't know. I—I've been alone for a long time."

"That can change, for both of us." She leaned forward and her hands, resting on the table, were close to mine. "I can keep up, Naroh. I can watch your back."

"Until you put a knife in it."

Eshi's fingers tightened into fists and her ears stiffened into angry stillness. "I followed a strange man onto the back of his war-scorpion after that same bug destroyed everything I had. Are you really going to blame me for being a little fucking cautious?"

"No," I answered, not looking away. "But trust is important."

"Then, trust me on this fucking thing—if I wanted to kill you, I would have."

"Yeah, Rishka said the same thing."

Eshi narrowed her eyes, but didn't otherwise let herself get distracted. "Then, what? Do you think I'll panic at the first sign of danger?"

"No," I admitted. "You don't look like the type."

"Then, what the fuck is it, Naroh? Is it me? Do you just not like being around me?"

"Eshi—"

"No," she interrupted, pushing herself to her feet. Her freckled cheeks were flushed scarlet and her eyes blazed with something very like hurt. "Naroh, if you don't like spending any time with me, then this won't work at all. I thought that we were starting to—" She shook her head angrily before refocusing her gaze on me. "It doesn't matter. Tell me right now. Tell me that you hate the thought of being around me and that you'd rather be alone and I'll leave. I'll walk out of here and you'll never have to see me again."

I opened my mouth to speak but then closed it as a strange weight settled over my chest. I let out a breath and forced myself to slow down, to take a moment and really consider her words.

Did I want to never see her again?

The ache in my chest grew. The feeling surprised me, and I peered into myself, examining that discomfort. I thought about returning to my old routine, to going back to spending my days alone with Asu. But it felt... strange. It was uncomfortable, somehow, like waking up to find that your favorite pair of boots had grown just a little too small.

My tongue once again tasted like onion and the ache within me eased as I remembered how joyfully she'd laughed in the middle of the street.

I blinked, unsure of what to make of the warmth that was now rising through me. The feeling was unfamiliar and a large part of me cautioned against trusting it. Although, that too faded when I looked up at the fiercely beautiful hyenaling, at the fire burning in her eyes and the sharp rise and fall of her chest.

Whatever came next, I couldn't just send her away. My days would be much too quiet without the sound of her laughter.

"Can you sit back down, Eshi?" I said, at last. "Please?"

She hesitated, searching my face for several moments before lowering herself into her seat. There was a shout, followed by a loud chorus of laughter. The barmaid brushed past our table but I hardly noticed, my eyes on Eshi as I worked to gather my thoughts.

"I ruined your life," I said, at last. "Asu tore it up and smashed it into a million pieces. You asked if I hated you, but why would you want to spend any more time with me?"

"I told you—I think that you're a good man." Her ears folded back, and twin spots of color bloomed beneath her cheeks. Then, she straightened and forced the air out of herself in a short huff. "Listen, Naroh, I know that we started off weirdly, but these past few days have been strangely good. I want to do this."

"But why?" I pressed. "I wasn't lying about the merchants I know. You can get a real job. This is dangerous, Eshi, really fucking dangerous."

"It's also got a chance to make me more gold than I could if I worked another fifty years."

"That chance is barely above zero." I shook my head. "I don't think you understand, for three thousand years, people a lot richer and smarter than me have been hunting this thing. I'm no closer to actually finding it than any of them were."

"Maybe, but I've seen your passion." Eshi's lips curled into a small smile. "I think that it's something worth gambling on."

My chair creaked beneath me as I leaned back. I let out a breath. "I still don't know about this."

"I won't slow you down, Naroh."

"You don't know anything about this sort of work."

"I'm a fast learner!" Her eyes were intent. "And I don't want any fame, glory, or whatever else you males long for. I want to be a merchant. It's all I've wanted to be for... well, for a few years now. All I need is a fair share of the gold, enough that I can start my life over again."

I opened my mouth to speak but Eshi forestalled me by holding up a hand.

"Think of it this way, Naroh, you need help. Maybe I won't be able to do much with the tombs at first, but there's one other huge thing that we haven't even talked about yet."

I crossed my arms, waiting.

"Kashir," she said. "And the Broken Mountain."

"How do you—"

"Because I'm not an idiot, Naroh. It's obvious, just as it's obvious that he's going to tell someone about this."

I shook my head. "There's a reason I went to Kashir. He's deep in this world and he won't talk."

"To the snakes, maybe, but what about to other divers? Or the other elves of the Broken Mountain?"

I frowned.

It had been decades since the last lamian purge and today, the Order of the Broken Mountain was the largest criminal organization in Ashura. Hard-eyed, angry young elves were in the streets of every major city, acting as killers and thieves, smugglers and pimps. They controlled entire districts and neighborhoods, taxing those who made their lives there and using them as bases of operation. A fortune of illicit gold flowed into the coffers of the Broken Mountain, protected by soldiers made remorseless by the knowledge that every atrocity they committed was in service to a cause greater than themselves.

Ashura belonged to the elves and revolution had to be paid for with blood and gold.

"You saw better than I did how excited he was about what you showed him," Eshi continued. Her eyes never left mine. "Do you really think he'll just wait around and trust that you'll bring something back to him? You're not an elf, and I guarantee you that he already regrets telling you where to go. He's got the gold to send an entire team to wait for us there."

"Asu's faster," I protested weakly. "We'll get there first."

"Then, they'll just kill us once we've found what he needs. Kashir wants this thing for the elves, and you're not under his control. You're dead as soon as you find anything."

She was right. Gods of fucking death, she was right and I'd been in this game long enough to know that.

"Focus on the past, Naroh." She leaned forward, her voice growing soft. "Let me worry about the present."

I let out a breath and chuckled ruefully. "You're good at this. You're going to make one hell of a trader, Eshi."

The hyenaling bared her teeth in a scavenger's grin and her tail thumped against her chair. "With the gold we get from this, I'll take over the world."

"I believe it."

"So, what do you say?" At my uncertain expression, Eshi's eyes flashed. "Stop being stupid, Naroh. You need help. Because word of what you're doing will get out, and people..."

She trailed off, her ears perking up and her eyes drawn to something over my shoulder. I turned around in my chair, in time to see the curtains of the main entrance settle behind an armored hyenaling. It was the hyenaling guardsman from House Malash, the one we'd last seen at the gates. His spotted ears perked as he swept his gaze over the taproom.

"...are already here," Eshi finished.

"Well," I muttered, as the guard's hard eyes settled on us. "That timing is certainly unfortunate."

"You two," he growled. "Come with me. My mistress would like a word."

"We can't go with him," Eshi hissed, her ears stiff and straight. "If that snake knows about this, we're fucked."

"You said there's a way out back?" I asked, before rising out of my seat and more loudly addressing the other hyenaling. "Who's your mistress? Why does she want to talk to us?"

His eyes narrowed. "I know you saw me at the gates of the city, boy. You know who I work for."

I shrugged, my heart beating faster. Behind me, Eshi rose to her feet as well. "Let's say that I'm new here."

Something glimmered in the guard's narrow-eyed stare. He took a step towards us, his hand drifting down to the hilt of his khopesh. "You're new, eh? Well, in Ikkad, when Mistress Issia Malash calls, you come running."

I blanched, feeling, more than hearing, the collective intake of breath. I'd expected not to recognize the name, figuring that this lamia lordling would be some distant cousin far from the main trunk of the family tree.

But Issia... that was a name all in the Northern Province knew. She was the necrophant's daughter; a sinfully beautiful lamia of ruthless intelligence whose necromantic power was said to be nearing that of her father.

Fuck.

Sweat prickled my scalp, and my heartbeat quickened. The room was deathly quiet, the silence settling on my shoulders like a cloak of bricks. Had she been the lamia I'd seen in the palanquin? Had I somehow insulted her?

"Naroh," Eshi said, her voice deafening in the heavy silence.

I looked towards her. Her body was loose, her ears had lost their stiffness and her hands rested on the table between us. "If I get us out of here. Am I in?"

The words hung in the air, crystallizing into a moment of perfect stillness. I stared into the burnished depths of Eshi's amber eyes, and there, in that single space between the beats of our hearts, she opened herself to me.

I saw her ferocity and strength, her passion and iron-willpower. There was a desperate wanting at the center of her, a burning fire of yearning that spread to the whole of her. Eshi was a survivor, a woman who refused to surrender to a world that was cruel to those of us who walked alone. That fire fueled her, and though I didn't yet know what she burned for, the wonder of those flames took my breath away.

Despite Rishka's constant pestering over the years, I'd never really considered finding a partner before. I had never met anyone with the right mix of desperate ambition, stubbornness, and crazed will that it took to dedicate themselves to this path.

Yet, in that moment, I knew, without a shadow of a doubt, that what Eshi had offered me was real. *"A girl like that doesn't quit when shit gets hard,"* Rishka had said, and the older hyenaling had been right. No matter where this path led, Eshi would follow. If I let her, she would walk this with me until the end.

I suppose that was it, then. Gods of fucking death, I could already hear Rishka's cackle.

The world rushed back over me. I blinked my eyes back into focus and my heart lurched into an eager gallop. Waves of energy rolled from my chest, making my limbs tingle and buzz.

I gave Eshi a wild grin. "Lead the way, partner."

The room exploded into motion. Eshi pushed herself back, letting out a stream of her scavenger's cackle as she spun away. I vaulted over the table, sending our mugs of beer crashing to the floor. People shouted and the guard roared.

He drew his sword and threw himself towards us.

I dashed after Eshi, weaving around the chairs and tables knocked over by people scrambling to their feet. We were racing towards the back of the room, where a door set behind a bar separated us from what I figured was probably a kitchen. The door shattered before we were halfway there and a jackal-headed horror shackled in gold burst in.

The fat barman squealed, yanked to the side by the still sour-faced barmaid. She pulled them both to the floor, the man's blubbering joined by a chorus of shrieks from the nearest patrons. The skeletal monster, however, made not a sound as its burning eyes settled on us.

"Roof!" Eshi shouted, veering sharply to the side and heading towards a flight of stairs that I was only now noticing.

We tore up the stairs two at a time, the screams behind us growing in pitch as the undead guardian charged after us. We were on the second floor by the time I heard the guard's heavy boots slam into the stairs. They were slow, having had to crash through the crowd that Eshi and I had been quick enough to get ahead of.

We pounded up towards the rooftop, ripping through the ratty old sheet of hanging cloth that separated it from the stairs and spilled out into the sunlight. Ikkad stretched out before us, baking in the afternoon heat. The great Nazlun River and the Ziggurat rose in opposite directions, a landscape of closely packed walls and roofs covering the space in between.

"Asu?" Eshi asked. "There's probably more of them waiting for us around him."

"We have to," I said. "Hiding in the city just gives them more time to gather. Go!"

This roof, like most other low, mudbrick buildings in the city, was flat. Eshi took a moment to plot her route, then, she sprinted towards the edge and leaped. Her open robe streamed behind her as she soared over the alley and onto the nearest roof. She landed easily, ducking beneath lines of drying clothes as she continued running.

I moved right after her and was just landing on the next roof when I heard the hyenaling from House Malash reach the top of the alehouse. The jackal-headed construct would be just behind him. I didn't look back, focusing on the path ahead, slipping between the lines of hanging cloth and launching myself after Eshi.

This third roof was longer and free of any sort of obstacles, allowing the two of us to really stretch our legs and gather speed. I was a bare few paces behind Eshi, following her as she charged towards the far edge of the building. The gap to the next building was larger, a full street instead of a mere alley. But the hyenaling didn't hesitate. She leaped onto the low, guarding wall and launched herself into the air without losing a drop of speed.

I was there a moment later, using that low wall as a step to catapult myself into the gap. I let out an excited whoop, feeling my stomach lurch as I soared over the chasm between these two houses. The wind tore at me, and I barely saw the approaching roof through my tear-blurred vision.

I landed hard on the other side, slapping the adobe flooring and tucking my body into a tight roll. I was back on my feet a few moments later, laughing madly as I pushed myself back into a run. I was only a bare step behind Eshi's tail now, my heart thundering in time to the pounding of our feet.

This gap ahead was narrow, and once forded, I risked a backward glance. The house guard was stopped on the edge of the third roof, watching us from the other side of the wide street. The huge, jackal-headed skeleton was there as well; neither of them was able, or willing, to continue the pursuit.

"We're free!" I shouted over the roaring of my blood. "But don't slow down!"

Eshi flashed me a quick grin, her face flushed with heat and exertion. She veered to the left, speckled hair streaming behind her as she vaulted over a dividing wall to continue towards the city gates looming in the distance. We ran for several long minutes, crossing Ikkad's rooftops as fast as we were able. Long gaps disappeared beneath us and we ran through rooftop gardens, kitchens, and workshops. We sprinted past smoking chimneys, through groups of shouting locals and flocks of startled birds.

We raced and we jumped, we climbed and we soared, never stopping, hardly slowing.

At a certain point, I ended up alongside Eshi. I tried to pass her. I wanted to take the lead, but I couldn't. I gave up after a few minutes, and somehow, as if we'd been doing this together for years, we fell into a rhythm. We jumped at the same instant, air escaping us in the same measured breaths. Our boots hammering an identical beat on the mud and stone, and when I glanced over, it was to find her bright, amber eyes flicking to meet my own.

Gods of fucking death, she really could keep up.

Eshi cackled, then howled as we soared, together, over another wide street. We only slowed down when we neared the gate, dropping down to the ground below using a series of window ledges and conveniently piled barrels. The gate guards shouted at us as we raced through the wide entrance, but didn't pursue us as we left the city behind.

Sweat soaked my skin and my muscles ached by the time Asu came back into sight. The great scorpion chittered happily at my return. He flexed his pincers, though the lazy bug didn't get up from the shade of the little grove. We slowed to a walk as it became clear that nobody from the city was waiting for us.

"Well," Eshi said from beside me. "Didn't I tell you I could keep up?"

"You did," I laughed, filling my lungs with the sweet air of the fruit trees. We stopped a dozen or so paces from Asu, my body strangely light. "I guess I got lucky that morning by the Storkling."

"Mmm," she said, a light gleaming in her amber eyes. "You have no idea."

Eshi's expression was pleased, her tail swishing through the air behind her. Sweat darkened her hair, moisture beading along the curve of her neck to trickle down her heaving chest to soak into the cloth binding her breasts. She had let her robe fall from her shoulders, holding it at her wrists and letting it puddle by her waist. Her exposed flesh gleamed and the muscles of her shoulders and arms were taut against her heated skin.

"So," she said. "We're partners, then?"

I held out my hand for her to shake. She stepped closer to take my hand and I caught a whiff of her scent; an intoxicating swirl of sour sweat and sun-warmed flesh.

"Partners," I grinned and I saw the same expression bloom over Eshi's face. "Let's go find Marduss's tomb."

Eshi's palm was warm, her skin soft beneath her calluses. She tightened her grip. "I'm right beside you."

Interlude

Issia Malash was a woman who was well used to getting what she wanted.

"And right now," she told the figure lying before her, "what I want is for you to be perfect."

Perfection was important to Issia, even if it was something of a bore. But as the daughter of Ikkad's necrophant, she had long ago learned that being without reproach was the best form of protection within her father's viperous court.

"Will you be perfect for me?" she asked, slithering around the elevated slab of stone. "Will you be strong?"

The unmoving corpse before her did not answer, of course, but Issia wasn't bothered by that. She continued to speak to it as the powerful muscles of her serpentine lower body carried her around the table. She examined every inch of the gleaming skeleton, looking for flaws.

The slow pace chafed her, but perfection could not be rushed.

"Ah," she said. "What's this?"

Issia flexed her serpent's tail, rearing up to lean far over the table. She placed a hand on the stone for balance, ignoring the golden, scorpion-shaped pendant that spilled out from between her large breasts. The metal pinged against bone as she brought her face down to squint at the slight bit of discoloration she'd spotted on the third rib.

It was a little splotch of darkness amidst the gleaming white. She pursed her lips and scratched at the imperfection with a single nail.

She'd have been able to tell that these bones had belonged to a hyenaling, even if she hadn't been the one to strip them of flesh and muscle.

Hyenaling bones were dense, though still, this skeleton had suffered the ravages of time. The man had been old when he'd died, and his bones were worn at the joints. They were frail in places and even sported a couple of hair-thin cracks that pointed to a life hard-lived.

But those problems didn't preoccupy her.

Issia's magic was powerful. Once she was done elongating, thickening, and strengthening these bones, not one of those structural flaws would remain. She could shape this skeleton into a creature without flaw or equal; a being that was stronger, faster, and tougher than almost any other.

Gold bracelets jangled at her wrist as she scratched harder at the stubborn little spot.

With her magic, she could make this skeleton into something that would watch millennia trickle by. A guardian that would never falter or tire, one that would still be standing when time had reduced the stone of her tomb into powder. And yet, for all that, her magic could do nothing about this little blemish.

Issia could acknowledge the humor in that fact, though, at this particular moment, she did not find it very funny.

"I need the scraper," she said, letting out a sigh. She pulled her hand away, holding it out behind her without shifting the rest of her body. "The small one."

Issia's stomach and the underside of her serpent's body were, by necessity, tightly corded with muscle. A lamia's movement was controlled by her core, and Issia didn't feel the slightest bit of discomfort as she waited with her upper body almost perfectly horizontal.

"Thank you, darling," she said, feeling the smooth haft of the tool slide into her hand. "Have the little brush ready, as well."

Her drudge, a many-armed servitor skeleton, silently turned to obey. The animated corpse certainly did not require her thanks, but Issia believed in remaining polite.

Besides, it was nice to talk to someone other than herself for a change.

Clearing the blemish took a few more minutes of careful work, and once done, Issia straightened to survey the totality of the skeleton. She hummed in satisfaction. Each bone gleamed a bright, pristine white and was perfectly set in its proper place.

She liked skeletons. They were so much neater than the fleshier forms of undead.

"Not much left now," she said, settling back down onto her coiled tail. "You'll be up and walking in no time, my sweet."

She took a moment to stretch her back and turn her neck, letting out another satisfied sound when she felt something pop. It was a lot of work to build a proper construct. She wasn't, after all, simply shoving magic into a pile of corpses and forcing them to their feet. That sort of working had its place, of course, but those sorts of undead were weaker and lost most of their usefulness once the organs had rotted away within them.

"Please set the jackal head in place," she told her servitor. "And then be ready with the spool of gold wire."

The servitor moved silently away, and Issia, in another rare moment of indulgence, moved towards one of her workshop's two open balconies. She slithered out into the light of the setting sun, the marble floor smooth and warm against the soft scales of her underbelly. The view of the city was spectacular from so high in the Grand Ziggurat, and the air was free of the stench from below.

Issia rested her palms on the balustrade and closed her eyes. She breathed deeply, relishing the way the sunlight enveloped and caressed her exposed skin. She loved the heat on her scales and the way sweat started to prickle beneath her thick layers of golden hair.

Unfortunately, now that she wasn't busying herself with work, Issia's thoughts turned back to the events of that day. Through her closed eyelids, she saw again the shaggy-haired man in the dust-stained robe. At first glance, there had been nothing to really distinguish him from the crowd. He was young, of an age with her if she had to guess. She liked the shape of his nose and she supposed that he could be called handsome, though not enough to truly stand out. There was nothing of the warrior in him, nor did he appear rich or particularly successful.

He looked perfectly average, until, through the shifting curtains of her palanquin, Issia had caught a glimpse of his dark eyes. Even now, the memory made her flesh prickle and her serpentine coils flex and shift. There had been… something within them, a watchful intensity or the flicker of his will, or… something. Lamians had been predators in the more savage epochs of the distant past, their muscled tails giving them an advantage in size and power that few others could match. It was that half-forgotten instinct that spoke to her now; he wasn't prey but rather a hunter. No, that wasn't quite right. He was a challenge, perhaps, a man worth hunting. Or—

Issia let out a breath and had to consciously will her tightening coils until stillness. Something in him had caught her attention and the fact that she could not pin down exactly what it had been frustrated her to no end.

She had felt his gaze on her as her palanquin had been carried down the road, and only the thought of how little time she'd had to enjoy her outing before returning to the palace had kept her from calling for a halt. That had been a mistake, one she'd only learned when coming across the pale war-scorpion lounging beneath a grove of cherry trees.

Blinking her eyes open, Issia became aware of a burning sensation. It was her pendant; the scorpion-shaped bit of jewelry was resting atop the soft, light-drenched flesh of her chest. She'd forgotten about it and the sun was making the gold uncomfortably hot. She reached up, cradling it in her palm for a few moments as she stared into its burnished depths.

"Naroh," she murmured, tucking the gold between her breasts. "You're a different man than what I'd pictured."

The human with the white war-scorpion. Issia had known about him for a few years now. A creature that distinct was hardly subtle and she'd been tracking his movements since he'd last passed through Ikkad. And as she'd learned more about the sort of places he visited, her interest in him had only grown.

Tomb divers weren't nearly as hidden from the eye of the lamian houses as many no doubt liked to believe, and Naroh wasn't the first one of his kind that had piqued Issia's interest. Most were little more than thugs; men and women who were as greedy and destructive as they were empty-headed. Gold drew them like flies to shit and they died in droves to the traps and guardians they were too weak and stupid to avoid.

Yet, Naroh... Naroh was searching for something more. She'd had that feeling ever since she'd heard of him emerging from the tomb of Khufu II, a pharon who'd reigned a bare four centuries after the death of Grand Necrophant Marduss. That feeling had grown into certainty as, over the next few years, he'd continued to dive almost exclusively into the oldest, long-plundered tombs.

He was on the trail of something, and Issia—

Her thoughts were interrupted by a heavy knock on the door, and she turned her head much too quickly. There was only one person that her guardian constructs would have let come this far, and her heartbeat quickened in anticipation of the news he brought.

"Get the door for me, would you, darling?" She told her servitor as she made her way back into the room.

In the time it took the construct to carry out her orders, Issia looked herself over. The ink-black, diamond-patterned scales of her serpent half were polished and clean, as was the deeply tanned flesh of her upper body. She wore no gloves or ugly protective layers within her workshop. Her dress was instead woven from silk that was pale to the point of translucence. It clung deliciously to her body's every luscious slope and curve, the plunging neckline exposing a generous slice of her chest. The garment was cut without any thought for utility or practicality, and such was the perfect skill with which she practiced her craft that not a drop of corpse filth stained the pale silk.

Issia positioned herself in a beam of sunlight, carefully sculpting her appearance. She adjusted the gold banding her wrists and arms before raising both of her hands to her thick, golden waves of hair. She didn't change the way it tumbled down over her bare shoulders, merely using that as an excuse to stretch her body so that the silk of her dress stretched over the taut flesh of her stomach and hips.

This was the way that her visitor would find her; a vision of golden beauty wrapped in the light of the setting sun. Issia was the perfect daughter of the necrophant, she shone even here, surrounded by death and corpses.

"Sarach," she said, as the door was opened. "Do come in."

Sarach was her personal guardsman, a member of House Malash's guard whose duties were restricted to her alone. The older hyenaling had been with Issia since she was a child, and she'd even given him some authority over her constructs. Though, that authority was nothing she couldn't rip away with a snap of her fingers.

She trusted him implicitly, but there were limits.

"Mistress," the scarred hyenaling said, snapping out a salute. "I'm here to report."

Issia made a small sound in her throat, extending her arms high in one last, undulating stretch. Her lip quirked as she noticed Sarach's normally hard eyes soften. She liked it when people looked and she held her pose for a beat longer than was natural, letting him roam his gaze over the curves of her body.

Beauty was something Issia had learned to wield as both a weapon and shield in her father's viperous court. It was one of the facets of the perfection that she continuously worked to cultivate; for beauty, more than almost anything else, was admired. To be beautiful was to be set above, and she gained a measure of power over all those who gazed upon her with envy or desire. Over time, the minds of those who beheld her made her into something beyond reach, something perfect and deserving of instant obedience.

And most importantly, one did not typically think to harm, or even defend themselves, against what they thought of as beautiful.

"Excellent," she said, lowering her arms. "Did you find them, Naroh and that hyenaling?"

Sarach blinked once before clearing his throat. "I did, Mistress. I found them seated in some trade district tavern and approached them with your summons. They ran as soon as they heard your name."

"They ran?" Issia frowned. "I lent you one of my palanquin bearers for this very situation, Sarach. Should I take this as an admission of failure?"

The hyenaling fell onto one knee and bowed his head. "It is as you say, Mistress. I accept whatever punishment my failure deserves."

Issia didn't answer, raising herself high while she turned to look out of the open balcony. She lifted one hand to chew on her fingernails but tapped on her lip instead when she noticed herself about to indulge in that ugly habit.

The gesture did little to quell the frustration roiling within her.

"Tell me what happened," she said, at last.

Her guard began to speak, and as she listened, she made her way back to her corpse-laden bier. Her servitor was in place, a spoil of gold wire, and her tools held ready in its many arms. Her future construct's bones had been cleaned of flesh, its heart burned and the other important organs properly stored within their canopic jars.

All was ready.

"So the divers are gone," she said, settling back on her coils and turning to face her guard. "They strolled through the gate and disappeared on the back of their scorpion."

"Yes, Mistress," the hyenaling said.

"I am quite disappointed, Sarach."

The guard lifted his eyes back to hers. "Allow me to completely wipe away this failure, Mistress. Let me take a contingent of the city guard. If I go after them now, I can have them back before the end of the week."

"No," she said, after a few moments of thought. "Something so blatant would catch my father's attention and he mustn't learn of this. You will take a squad of the house guard, instead, ones that you can trust to be silent."

"Your will, Mistress," he said, bowing his head once more.

Issia lifted herself off of her coils and slithered over to him. Once there, she reached down and gripped Sarach below the chin. She lifted his face to hers and let him see what burned behind her eyes. "Do not fail me again, Sarach."

Her guard nodded. Issia released him and turned away without ceremony. She slithered back to where her work awaited her, hearing him climb back to his feet. The door closed and she pushed away what remained of her frustration and anger as best she could.

Patience did not come easily to Issia, but that too, was something that she had worked to perfect.

"Alright, darling." She clapped her hands. "Let's get to work."

Her servitor followed as Issia shifted around to the jackal head that was waiting above the skeleton's bony shoulders. She suppressed a grimace as she pulled the first of the gold wire from the spool. She hated the jackal heads and thought them horrid and ugly. Her father loved the vile creatures, however, and she could only be grateful that necromancy didn't work on the remains of beasts. The Ziggurat would otherwise be crawling with them.

Issia shook her head and got back to work. These were her father's favorite constructs and she was nothing if not dutiful.

To be the perfect daughter required no less.

Chapter Nine

"Jars?" Eshi said, from somewhere behind me. "What the hell are you talking about?"

I blinked, clicking my mouth shut over the middle of my explanation. I was seated in my place behind Asu's head, sheltering from the late morning sun beneath the wide sleeves and hood of my robe.

"Canopic jars," I said, tapping my guiding stick on the right side of Asu's head to keep him on this dusty road. "Weren't you listening?"

We'd spent our first afternoon from Ikkad getting as much distance between us and the city as possible, dashing north along the banks of the Nazlun, and spending that first night in some unknown farmer's orchard. It had not been a comfortable night, neither of us sleeping much as we took turns watching for any pursuit that might have come from the city.

When the dawn had found us free and unbothered, we'd decided to get back on track. We'd forded the Nazlun, moving west and south, leaving behind the green fields and orchards of the river's banks. We were heading towards the distant Gibris River, and this far north, the two great rivers that enclosed the empire's heartlands were still quite far apart. Without that proximity, the ground here was as dry and rocky as the mountain foothills I'd left behind.

"Yes, yes." Eshi scrambled over the stuff lashed to Asu's back. "You see that smoke ahead of us, right? Let's stop in that town."

"Eshi, this is serious! Lamians spend their entire lives getting their tombs ready. The traps and guardians they leave behind are deadly. You're going to get us killed if you don't know this stuff."

I heard the shuffle of packs over the drum of Asu's legs, followed by an explosive sigh. "Of course I've been listening, Norah. I just missed the last part. You were talking about skeletons and why they're more dangerous than zombies."

"That's not what I said."

"Yes, it is," Eshi insisted, and I heard the creak of the cargo net being shifted. "You said that skeletons are stronger because the snakes take the organs out instead of just letting them rot."

"Canopic jars are what they put those organs in." We were indeed approaching a town, and I kept an eye out for a good spot for Asu while I continued to speak. "Magic keeps the organs connected to their original bodies, and more magic is used to seal the jars so that what's in them doesn't rot. A man without a brain can't do much, and the undead are no different."

"There you go," Eshi said. "I got it right."

"No, you didn't! I told you that skeletons are more clearly dangerous because you can see that the organs have been removed. Zombies are often inferior, but not always! The fleshsmiths of Sorgan, for example, are known for—"

"Stop here!" Eshi exclaimed, interrupting me. "This is a good spot for the bug."

"Don't interrupt me!"

"You were going to move right past it," she said. "It's over here, on the right. In the shade of that big boulder."

I scowled and was about to snap back at her when my eyes found the spot she'd been talking about. It was perfect for Asu, damn her.

"Fine," I said, tapping the scorpion on the head. "But you need to know this stuff, Eshi."

"I already know most of it." I heard more shuffling. "And besides, the tomb is still a week away, right?"

"Yes, but—what are you even doing back there?"

"I'm looking through your supplies to see what we need," Eshi said. "You've a lot of rope, but not much else."

I tapped Asu to a stop in the shade and stretched my limbs, happy to take a moment out of the sun. "Don't you already know everything I have?"

"Don't be an ass. I couldn't properly look through everything before."

I chuckled. "Well, I still don't know why you're bothering to look. We don't have any money, remember?"

"Oh, don't worry," Eshi said. "I stole some of Kashir's silverware before he kicked us out."

I coughed, choking on a bit of spit I'd sucked back into my throat. I twisted in my seat to find the hyenaling woman on all fours over the netted packs. Her side was to me, her robe cinched tight around her lean frame.

"When did you do that?" I eventually managed.

"Before finding the door to Kashir's office." She tilted her head towards me, grinning through the falling locks of her blonde, speckled hair. "I helped myself to some stuff from his larder, as well."

I shook my head, but couldn't keep the smile from my face. "I'm surprised you were able to escape the city at all with your pockets loaded like that."

She flicked her ears and her grin widened. "I told you I was fast. Now, get up and help me take a proper look through this stuff."

It took us about an hour to go through and properly look at everything I had. I'll admit to not being the most organized, and so, some of the stuff we found was a surprise even for me. I had a lot of artifacts from old dives, and Eshi was vocal in her scorn every time she pulled out another bit of 'useless weight.' She was blind to any of the historical value and bickered against me when I tried to educate her. It was tiring and was putting me in a bad mood. There was a moment, however, when I was in the middle of a particularly vigorous defense of a brightly painted pottery shard, that I thought I caught a glimpse of the light dancing in her amber eyes.

I took it all a lot less seriously after that.

Otherwise, I had a lot of diving gear. This consisted mostly of rope, hooks, harnesses, prying bars, glowstones, as well as specialized climbing claws and spikes. A lot of that stuff, especially the metal tools, were difficult enough to get that I'd had them made in duplicates. Eshi wouldn't be lacking that sort of equipment, at least.

"Alright," she said. We were still on the war-scorpion's back, though Asu had long ago made himself comfortable. "I'm going to need a bedroll, waterskins, soap, needle and thread, my own pack, extra food..."

She rattled off several other things, my eyebrows raising with every item she added to the list.

"You sure that you're going to be able to get all that for a couple of nice forks?"

"I've got more than a couple." She flashed me her scavenger's grin. "And I'm good, Naroh."

I frowned. Eshi, like me, had pulled her hood down once we'd taken shelter in the shade. She was resting atop the packs, stretched out as if on a divan. Her robe was completely open at the front, with the wide collar having slipped down one arm to expose much of her neck and the bronze flesh of one shoulder. The pose emphasized the tightly bound swell of her chest and the angle at which she lay made the muscles of her stomach stand out. Her hips bloomed beneath the loop of leather at her waist, the thin linen of her pants clinging to the shape of her legs.

More than a couple of forks? I thought, running my eyes up and down the lean curves of her body. Where was she hiding them?

Eshi cleared her throat, her stomach rippling as she shifted in her seat. I blinked, flicking my gaze up to find her watching me. The amber of her eyes was deeper than I had ever seen it, and there were two spots of red beneath the freckled skin of her cheeks.

"I—" Heat seared up my neck. "I wasn't—I was looking for where you were keeping the forks!"

"Well," Eshi drew the word out and gestured at her torso. "You're not going to find them here."

I ran a hand through my hair. Gods of death, I was an idiot. "Yeah, sorry."

"No, it's ok." She shifted, sitting a bit straighter and the flush on her face deepened. She reached up to slide the top of her robe back over her shoulder, though left the rest of it open. The gesture, and her voice, were both strangely hesitant. "Don't worry, I... I don't mind."

I coughed, my throat suddenly dry. I had no idea what to say, but luckily, Eshi didn't wait for a response. "Anyway, it's getting late. Help me get down from here and I'll go into town."

"Yeah," I coughed again. "Yeah, let's get you down." I moved toward Asu's head. "We're really going to have to do something about him if you're sticking around."

"Shopping first," Eshi said. "Hurry up!"

"Fair enough." I settled in behind Asu's head and the great scorpion's pincers scraped against the earth as he shifted. Eshi had not been with us long enough to make much of an impression on him. He still saw her as an intruder, and he'd kill her if she ever tried to approach him alone. He tolerated her well enough when she was out of sight atop his armored back, but getting close to his softer belly by scrambling up and down his body was something else entirely.

"Ok, my Asu-boy," I cooed, rubbing my palms along his chitinous head. "Eshi is going to get off now, ok? You'll be alright, my big boy. She's a friend, okay? A friend."

The scorpion chittered as I started to scratch at one of the seams between his armored plates. His body relaxed, though I never stopped speaking and scratching.

"We don't hurt our friends, right, Asu-boy? I know you like having friends, so we have to keep them safe, ok? That's a good boy. Eshi's a friend, Asu. Go now, slowly."

That last was directed at the hyenaling. I never looked her way but could track her progress in the slow stiffening of Asu's body.

"Friend, Asu," I said, seeing his pincers flex and imagining the slow uncurling of his tail. "She's a friend."

A few moments later, I heard the scuff of boots in dirt and, after another handful of heartbeats, Asu relaxed.

"Alright!" Eshi called from a dozen paces away. "I'm clear. Are you coming into town?"

"Good boy, Asu," I said. "You're such a good boy. And, uh, yeah, I'll meet you in the main square! I'm going to fill our water barrels in the stream by the road here."

"Don't take too long." She was standing in the sun, with her hands on her hips and a grin on her lips. "Or I'll have cleaned out the entire town."

I never made it into town.

When I was filling the last of our water barrels at the stream, I spotted a broken pile of stone through the band of leafy vegetation. It turned out to be the ruins of a small tower, one that, after a bit of poking around, I was excited to discover an eye-topped cross carved into one of the stones.

This tower was nearly five hundred years old!

This watchtower must have been made to keep watch on the remnants of the traitorous clans of hyenaling dog-soldiers that had fled north after the defeat of House Menkasse during the last civil war!

I was crouched down amongst the stones of the tower's foundation, scraping dirt aside and squinting to try and find some more graffiti, when a voice from directly behind me said, "Naroh."

I leaped to my feet, my heart surging up into my throat as I launched myself away. I was a dozen paces from the last of the leafy trees when Eshi's wild laughter reached me through the wild galloping of my heart.

"Eshi, what the hell!" I roared, stomping back to her. "Stop doing that!"

That, unfortunately, only made her hunch over herself and laugh harder. Her ears flopped as her cackle turned breathless and, despite my embarrassment, her obvious delight eased whatever anger had flared up in me.

"You can't keep doing that," I said, returning to the ruin. "Seriously."

"You make it so easy." She raised a hand to wipe her tear-bright eyes. "Besides, I waited in town for you."

I had no real response to that, so instead, I moved over to a different part of the ruined tower. I wanted to see what else I could learn before we left.

"Did you get everything you needed?" I asked, crouching down.

"Oh yeah," Eshi said, coming over to lean against a nearby section of wall. "A caravan happened to be passing through, so I got rid of the silver pretty easily. They had everything else I needed, too, and I even found a few extra surprises."

"Hmm." I got down on my hands and knees. There was a mass of shrubbery growing through this part of the ruin, and I had to push aside a few scraggly bushes to get to the stone.

"Did you get the water barrels filled?"

There wasn't much of interest on these particular stones, just a few meaningless scrapes here and there. Still, I made sure to look each over carefully. Something caught my gaze, and I narrowed my eyes.

"Naroh, did you hear me?"

There were a few shards of clay poking out of the ground here, and I reached out to gather a few.

"Naroh!"

"What?" I settled back onto my knees with several pieces of broken pottery in my lap. I held the first one up to my face, twisting it about and searching the plain clay for any sort of sign or symbol.

"Were you even listening?"

"Did you say something?"

"Did I—yes! Naroh, this is why it's so easy to creep up on you! Do you love to be laughed at, or something?"

"I don't love it," I said, squinting at the second bit of clay I'd gathered. "But I like it when you laugh. It's nice..."

I trailed off, seeing something on the edge of the clay piece. Unfortunately, it turned out to just be a bit of dried mud. I let out a breath, only then realizing that Eshi hadn't spoken again. She hadn't moved away and when I turned my head, I saw her watching me with eyes that were wider than I'd ever seen them.

"Eshi," I said, slowly regaining my feet. "Are you ok?"

She started, then flushed a deep red. Shock rippled across her features, followed by confusion, disbelief, and embarrassment before settling on anger. "What did you mean by that?"

"What?" I said, taken aback. "Eshi—"

"What did you mean!?" She stepped towards me, her ears stiff and eyes blazing. "Tell me!"

Unbalanced and with my arms hanging stupidly at my sides, I stared at her with wide-eyed confusion. "I don't know what you're talking about!"

"My laugh, Naroh!" She was close enough that I swore I could feel the heat from her reddened flesh. "Why did you lie about my laugh?"

"Lie!? What are you—?"

"Nobody likes hyenaling laughter!"

"Well, I like yours!"

"No, you don't!" She shook her head. "You don't like hyenaling laughter! I've seen you cringe at it."

"Not at yours!" I should step back, put some space between us, and try to speak rationally. But something, some emotion rising through me, kept me from backing away. "Why is it so hard to believe that I like it when you fucking laugh?"

Eshi didn't answer, her ears stiff and body tight. She searched my face and I didn't look away, staring into the fire blazing within her amber eyes. The silence stretched between us, time passing with the measured beating of our hearts.

Finally, she blinked. "You really like my laugh?"

"Yes!" I let out an explosive breath. "What the fuck, Eshi?!"

"Don't be dramatic, Naroh." She flicked her ears and turned away. "There are some things you can't lie to a girl about, Naroh. I had to make sure."

I followed her as she made her way back towards the road. "Make sure of what?"

She didn't answer, and I pushed it from my mind when we got to where she'd piled her new supplies. She'd gotten quite a variety of things, including several packs for herself, a bedroll, and quite a bit of food. It didn't take more than a few minutes to load everything, including the freshly filled water barrels, onto Asu's back. We were moving again not long after that, Eshi settling back in the netted pile while I guided the scorpion from my place behind his head.

"So," the hyenaling said. "What was so special about that old ruin, anyway?"

"The tower?" I tilted my head back, but I'd drawn my hood up once more and couldn't see her. "It was from the Menkasse civil war."

"I've never heard of that." I heard the creak of rope and leather. "Were any of the Nabonassarans involved in it?"

I chuckled, guiding Asu in a wide circle around the town. "No, the civil war happened about five hundred years ago. The Nabonassarans were—"

Eshi's hand fell on my shoulder and I just about leaped from my skin.

"Stop that," she said. "It's just me. Move over."

I twisted my head around in time to see her slide down onto the seat beside me. My driver's bench was small and I scooted over without thinking. She squeezed herself in to fit, her body pressed tightly against me.

"What are you doing?" I pushed against her hip to try and keep one of my buttcheeks from hanging uncomfortably off the side. "There's no space here!"

"Sure, there is." She wormed into me, sliding one shoulder behind mine so that we weren't wedged quite so painfully together. "See?"

"No!"

"Well, I'm comfortable. And I couldn't hear you from back there."

I blinked at her in disbelief. She met my gaze with a small smile, her eyes bright beneath the hood she'd also pulled up. She'd closed her robe up to protect herself from the sun, but I could still clearly feel the shape of her with how tight she was against me.

"I need to steer Asu, and look," I pointed to where the giant scorpion's pincers were opening and closing. "You're stressing him out by being so close to his head."

"Asu and I need to get used to each other, right?" Then, she shifted slightly, and I felt the soft squish of her breasts pressing against my arm. "But if you're not comfortable...?" She trailed off, raising an expectant brow.

I coughed, her nearness making my limbs tingle. Her scent; heavy, sour, and heart-poundingly feminine, filled the air I breathed. It was sand and sun, heat and sweat clinging to warm flesh. It was intoxicating, and I was suddenly having a hard time focusing on anything but the soft press of her body.

"Well?" Eshi's eyes danced and there was a delighted flush to her freckled cheeks. She slid her thigh against mine and squeezed my arm harder against her tightly bound, yet surprisingly soft, breasts. "Am I making you uncomfortable? Should I go back to where I was?"

"No," I said, deciding all at once that I really wasn't that uncomfortable with her so close. "You can stay."

"Good." She settled herself in a slightly different way on the bench, and suddenly I heard the swish of her tail wagging against the saddle behind us. "Now come on, I want to hear about the rest of this civil war."

I had turned back to guiding Asu, holding my tapping stick in my left hand now. "What do you want to know?"

"All of it."

My face was hidden from her by the depth of my hood, but I was sure that she'd be able to hear the astonishment in my voice. "All of it? Don't you find this kind of thing boring?"

"I like listening to you talk about this sort of stuff. It's interesting."

"Really?"

"Yes!" I heard the laughter on the edge of her voice. "Just start already, from the beginning."

"Well, to really understand the civil war, you have to know who the players were. No! Actually, before that, we have to talk about the death of the necrophant of Lussa. Or should I start at about the weevil infestation in the fields around Nippur? You know what, that's important, so I think I will start there."

Eshi laughed, high and without reservation. "I'm all ears."

I smiled and a warm glow spread through my chest.

Chapter Ten

It took us a little less than a week of travel to find the tomb of Nabonassara III. It was tucked away in a remote bend of the Gibris River, not far from the western edge of the empire. The terrain here was rough, and the great river flowed through a canyon carved deep into the sandy rock.

Eshi and I stood at the edge of that canyon, looking down at a rocky stretch of beach far below. The tomb was supposedly carved into the cliff directly beneath us. We couldn't see it from here, though the shattered remains of statuary I could see scattered about the riverbank told me we were likely in the right place.

"Are you sure this is it?" The hyenaling asked, standing beside me. "This doesn't look like anything."

"Kashir knows his business." I scanned the beach below for any other sort of clue. There wasn't much, and with the sun already tickling the top of the mountains to the west, we were running out of daylight. I turned away with a sigh. "Anyway, we'll know for sure when we climb down tomorrow morning."

"Is there even a path?" Eshi asked, turning with me.

"There's supposed to be one up that way." I gestured upstream. "But Kashir said it was a good half a day's walk from the tomb. We'll just climb down a rope."

We made our way back to where Asu waited. Like most of the areas outside the ever-blooming heartland, this part of the empire was dry, rocky, and sparsely vegetated. It wasn't a desert, but with the Gibris trapped between canyon walls, the only moisture the area received was the infrequent bout of rain that came over the nearby mountains.

"How did that elf even know this was here?" Eshi said, sweeping her eyes over the empty wilderness. "We're in the middle of nowhere."

"He does a lot of business with the kingdoms on the other side of these mountains. This isn't the main trade route, but caravans do sometimes pass this way."

"Traders," Eshi scoffed. "Smugglers, more like."

"Maybe," I shrugged. "It's not any of my business."

"It will be if we come out and find that all of our supplies have been stolen," Eshi said. "The bug won't be around, right?"

Asu clacked his pincers at our approach but otherwise didn't move. He was tired and hadn't eaten anything since tearing into Eshi's camel. That was fairly normal for Asu, who typically only needed to feed two or three times a month. But we'd been moving almost constantly, crossing in a week what would have taken a camel caravan more than two and draining even the war-scorpion's considerable reserves.

"He needs to hunt," I agreed. "And he needs to rest. He'll go up into the foothills looking for goats while we're gone."

"Sure," Eshi said, her expression bland. "It's the part where you want to take all of our supplies off his back and just pile them somewhere that I don't understand."

"I mean, I was going to hide them."

"Where?" Eshi said, her ears flicking to the surrounding barren landscape. "In that pile of rocks over there?"

"What's wrong with that? Those rocks are big enough to hide most of what we have."

"They're also right on the edge of the river, which, I'm assuming, is a common landmark that any passing group of smugglers or bandits would use to navigate."

"I'm sure we'll be fine."

Eshi's stare was flat. "It's stupid, Naroh."

I sighed, pushing my hood off my head and rubbing at my eyes. "I'm guessing that you have a better idea?"

"Obviously. Let's get back onto Asu and head away from the river. I'm sure that I'll be able to find us a good spot."

I frowned. "Remember that we have to walk back here tomorrow morning. With all of our gear."

"Don't worry, Naroh," she said with a teasing smile. "I'll carry you if you want."

Rolling my eyes, but otherwise not dignifying that with a response, I kept Asu distracted while Eshi scrambled onto his back. I almost needn't have bothered; the scorpion was *tired* and didn't so much as twitch.

"You're such a strong boy, Asu," I said, scratching him in his favorite spot beneath his head. "Just a little further, ok? I promise."

The scorpion only flexed his pincers, though shifted a bit when he felt me climbing onto his back. Eshi, I noticed, was already seated on the bench directly behind Asu's head. Her eyes followed me as I picked my way over and her smile was pleased when I squished in beside her without complaint.

The hyenaling had wormed her way into this seat every day during the past week, and by now, I had given up on trying to get her to move to the back. In truth, despite the somewhat awkward position, I'd grown to enjoy having her there. The sun-warmed scent of her hair was comforting, and I couldn't deny how pleasant it was to feel her body pressed tightly against mine.

"Ready?" I asked, taking up my guiding stick.

"Mmhm," Eshi answered, sliding one leg below mine and shifting her body so that it was more comfortably tangled up with my own. "Let's go."

We ended up choosing to camp in a little dip of land sheltered by a few massive boulders and hardy-looking pine trees. It was only around half an hour from the entrance to the tomb, though walking that on our own two feet in the morning would take quite a bit longer.

"I need to get everything off of Asu," I said, once my feet had touched the ground. "And then we have to get our packs organized. We still have a few days worth of dried meat, right?"

"Yup," Eshi said, with her back to me. "There's lots of that left."

She let her robe slide off her shoulders to puddle on the ground at her feet. A small sound of pleasure slipped from her as she lifted her arms into a long, luxurious stretch. The fading sunlight shone in her thick mane of straw-colored hair and played across the naked flesh of her back. My eyes drifted down from the bright, clean cloth of her chest wrap. I followed the smooth arch of her back, past the leather belt looped above her waist to the blooming swell of her hips. Her linen pants, despite being loose around her knees and calves, were tight around the curve of her behind. The cloth clung to the shape of her, and as Eshi twisted through her stretch, I watched, hypnotized, as the soft flesh of her ass bounced and shifted.

Then, her tail, poking through a specially cut hole in her trousers, cut through my vision in a slow wag.

I blinked and, looking up, found the hyenaling peering back at me through the falling strands of her speckled hair. A small smile curled her lips and there were two spots of pink high on her freckled cheeks.

Heat seared the back of my neck as I tore my gaze away.

"Alright," Eshi said, letting out a breath and settling back from her stretch. Then, she clapped her hands together and her smile widened as she half-skipped towards me. "I'll take care of supper tonight. Give me your sling."

I coughed, reaching to unwind it from my forearm. "Okay, I'll... ahem, I'll just get started here, then."

"Perfect! Bring my packs down but don't look inside. I've got a surprise for tonight."

That, for some reason, made my face burn even hotter and the knowing sparkle in Eshi's amber eyes didn't help. She turned away with a low cackle, the sound staying with me as I watched her stalk off into the fading sunlight.

I let out a long breath when she was out of sight, running both my hands through my shaggy hair. What the hell was I doing? As much as my father, or any one of my brothers, might think otherwise, I wasn't a total fool. I could feel something growing between Eshi and me.

There was so much about her to admire.

She was a ruthless negotiator, a warrior, and a gifted huntress who was infinitely practical. In the short time we'd been partnered, her presence had already made my life easier in a dozen little ways. She was also ferociously beautiful, wickedly clever, stubborn as a field full of goats, and the fire of her emotions blazed hot enough for everyone to see. She was a joy to be around, and when she listened to me speak, her face softened into that smile that I—

I blew out another breath, shaking my head to clear it. I slapped my palms to my cheeks a few times for good measure, shoving thoughts of the hyenaling woman from my mind.

She was my partner, I told myself, and I had a tomb dive to get ready for.

I spent the hour Eshi was gone taking care of Asu. I unloaded everything from his back, removing every pack, bag, and netted pouch. Then, I used some of our water to clean the grit from beneath his saddle straps. I wasn't sparing with it as we'd be able to fill our skins up at the river tomorrow. Until he got more tolerant of Eshi, his saddle was still too much for me to remove and this was the best I could do.

"Alright, my hungry boy," I said, once I'd finished. I was scratching him below the head. "We'll be fine without you, ok, Asu-boy? You were so good this week. Such a good, strong boy. Go and fill yourself up and we'll meet you back here. Hunt, Asu."

The scorpion stilled at the sound of my command. His mouth pincers slid shut and his eyes focused on me.

"Hunt," I said again. "Go hunt."

The scorpion backed away from me without a sound, turned, and flowed away. He moved towards the mountains, his ghost-pale body quickly disappearing into the rising darkness. Asu was an effective hunter, even if the ground was too rocky for his preferred tactic of burying himself and waiting for something to wander close. He was smart enough to adapt, and in a few days, when his belly was full, he'd return and wait for us here.

I shook myself back into motion, using what was left of the daylight to unpack my diving gear. Darkness had fallen by the time Eshi returned with a brace of dead hares.

"Where's my pack?" She asked, setting the limp bodies down. "I need to start cooking."

"Cooking?" I asked, squinting at her through the darkness. "You're not just going to roast them over the fire?"

I saw her cock a hip and her canines flashed as she grinned. "Oh, no. I already told you; this is the night before our first tomb dive and I'm doing something special."

"Alright," I answered, a bit bemusedly. "Your stuff is over there. Empty your pack for me when you take what you need, I have to get the gear organized tonight."

"You have a lot to do, then?" Eshi hauled her pack a few steps away and crouched before it. She started pulling things free and setting them aside, the darkness keeping me from seeing anything but vague shapes. "Because this will take me a while."

I raised an eyebrow. "Well, I can't see anything, so I need to get a fire going. And then I have to go over every bit of the gear. If there's any sort of split in the rope or warp in the metal, I'd rather know now than when I'm hanging above a spiked pit-trap."

"Makes sense." Eshi pushed herself to her feet and tossed me her empty pack. "I'll take care of the fire, though. I need to set it up in a certain way and I can still see well enough not to hit myself with the axe."

"Fair enough," I said, with a chuckle. "I've got to say, you're definitely making me curious about this."

"Mmm, good." She grinned down at me, her bound breasts and the naked, muscled flesh of her stomach were still clear, despite the surrounding darkness. "I wouldn't want you to lose interest."

I swallowed, feeling my heartbeat quicken. Eshi's grin widened, and I heard the swish of her tail moving through the air.

She turned away and scooped up my hatchet. "How spicy can I make this rabbit, by the way?"

"Hot as you can. I like it spicy."

"Careful," Eshi purred, glancing back as she walked away. "Some people don't know what to do with that much heat."

"Trust me," I said, admiring the rolling sway of her hips. "I can handle it."

The hyenaling spent nearly half an hour gathering wood and rock for the fire, taking the time to find a wide, flat piece of stone. After that, she skinned and quartered the hares, cutting the meat into slivers which she tossed into a pot of ready water. She made a thick, meaty stew, to which she added onions, garlic, chickpeas, and several pinches from various pouches of spice.

"Did you get all that stuff in town?" I was seated across the fire from her, wrapping a length of rope back into a tight coil. "It must have cost a fortune."

"The spices were a bit much," Eshi admitted, her hands kneading a ball of dough in a wooden bowl wedged between her knees. "But I got a lot of them."

"Did you spend all of our money?"

"I still have a bit left." She blew a few strands of hair away from her face and grinned her scavenger's smile. "That elf had a great eye for cutlery."

The pot was starting to bubble, filling the air around us with a fragrant steam. My stomach rumbled, twisting itself into a hungry knot. It was incredibly distracting, and I often caught myself looking up from what I was supposed to be doing to stare into it. But I pushed on, checking over every single piece of equipment and packing it away with days' worth of dry food. I had flint and tinder, pouches of glowstone powder, hooks, coils of rope, hammers, and a dozen other types of tools that I was happy to be able to spread through two different packs for a change.

Preparedness was key when stepping into a tomb. I never knew what I would find or how long it would take me to return.

The lamians believed that, upon their deaths, their souls were judged and then welcomed into the realm of the gods. An eternity in paradise awaited them and they believed that everything buried with them would follow their souls into the afterlife. And so, they filled their sarcophagus chambers with all the gold, jewelry, weaponry, and luxury they would need.

To guard that wealth, lamian necromancer-lords had their tombs made into vast, maze-like complexes of stone and darkness. The corridors twisted like writhing serpents, splitting and coiling back onto each other in impossible snarls. Traps of wicked ingenuity were scattered through the darkness and the whole of it was watched over by the undying guardians of flesh and bone that the entombed lamians spent their lives creating.

The stars twinkled high above us by the time Eshi declared that supper was ready.

"Hunter's stew and garlic flatbread." She handed me a bowl, settling on the ground beside me close enough for our knees to almost touch. "Tell me what you think."

The stew was thick with slivers of meat and chunks of vegetables. A little curl of steam rose from it, making my eyes water and nose prickle when I inhaled it.

"Smells spicy," I said.

"You like it hot, right?" Eshi's head was turned towards me and was watching me with a strange sort of intensity. "Try it."

"Alright," I said, digging a wooden spoon into the bowl. "Thanks for cooking."

I brought the spoon to my lips, conscious of the weight of her eyes. But then, I took that first bite and lost myself in an explosive blend of richness and heat. It was delicious and full of flavor, most of which I didn't have a name for. It was spicy, but not overwhelmingly so. It worked to enhance the savory tenderness of the stewed meat and vegetables. The flatbread was a perfect addition, adding a welcome thickness to the whole.

I swallowed that first bite, and another one after that. I took a third, and pretty soon I was scraping the last of it off the inside of my bowl. Eshi's eyes had grown wider and there was a slight softness to her features as she watched me finish. She hadn't touched her own bowl, which lay full and forgotten in her lap.

"Is there enough for seconds?" I asked.

A smile bloomed across her face, one that made her cheeks glow and her eyes shine with a thousand points of light. Her tail shook hard enough to wiggle her hips, the whole of it an expression of such pure, unbridled joy that I felt it reach into my chest and squeeze.

I swallowed past an unexplainable lump in my throat, feeling this vision of her weave itself into the fabric of my memory.

"You like it? It's good?"

"Eshi, this is incredible. This is really, really incredible." I shook my bowl. "Now, can I have some more, or—"

"Yes!" She laughed.

"Fuck," I groaned, once I'd finished my third and final bowl "I can't remember the last time I ate this well."

"Aren't you happy you brought me along?" Her hands cradled her second bowl. The night was cool despite being so near to summer, and Eshi had thrown her robe back on.

"Absolutely," I said, letting myself flop down onto the ground on my back. The ground was hard and rocky beneath me, but I was too full to be anything but comfortable. "Where did you learn to cook like that?"

I wove my fingers beneath my head. Above me, the stars were painted across the sky in a thousand sparkling shapes. I could recognize very few of the constellations, though one, hanging above the mountains to the north, drew my gaze.

Tel'aman's flight, named after the stork-headed god of wisdom and knowledge, was spread across the sky. It was one of the largest constellations, and was made of five stars in a line that looked like a sort of shallow 'm.' The shape was similar to the silhouette of a bird soaring far away. In the center of its 'body' was the north star, the brightest point of light in that twinkling ocean.

"My dad taught me," she said. "He always made this when we were out hunting. He said that every day away from home had to end with something good, or else you miss it too much."

"I like that," I said, still staring into the star-streaked sky. "Although, I've never had to do much to keep from missing my home."

"Yeah," Eshi said. "Me neither."

Silence settled over us and I turned my head, finding her staring down into the bowl she cradled in her lap. Her features were soft in the orange glow of the fire and her spotted ears were folded back in an expression of uncertainty.

"My dad loved to hunt," she eventually said. "He was the best in our clan and went whenever he could. He took me whenever my mother allowed, and sometimes we would be gone for weeks at a time. He taught me everything I know, and I..."

She trailed off, blinking a few times. I turned back to the endless black of the sky, waiting for her to speak.

"My mother was the matriarch of our clan. My father was her fourth mate, and I was the only child they had together. I was the youngest of all her daughters, and the clan kept my mother busy. She never had much time for my dad and me. And with my sisters... it was better to be away."

"Me too," I said, my eyes following a few rising sparks. "Although, I only had brothers and my da was a bastard."

"You left?"

"As soon as I turned sixteen."

"Well," Eshi said, and I could hear the grimace in her voice. "You're better than me."

"I don't know about that. It sounds like you just had more to lose."

The hyenaling let out a breath. I heard the crunch of dirt as she shifted, and glanced over in time to see her lie down beside me. She stared up into the sky, close enough that I could reach out and touch her if I wanted.

"Do you... do you ever think of going back to them?"

"To my family?" I shook my head. "Never."

"You're not lonely without them?"

"I told you, they were bastards."

"So was mine," Eshi said. "But all families have problems."

"Mine won't." At her snort of disbelief, I continued. "Seriously! Someday, I'm going to make my own family. We'll have problems, sure, but in the end, we're going to be happier than everyone else."

"That's not how it works. You can't just decide to be happy."

"Why not? A family can be happy as long as we all actually love each other and want to be together."

"It's still not that simple."

"Sure it is." I stretched my legs out and let out a contented sigh. "It'll be my family, so I get to decide if that's how it works or not."

Eshi laughed softly. "Just like that?"

"Just like that."

I heard her shift and turned to find her lying on her side. She was facing me, her eyes dark in the flickering shadows of the fire.

"So, how do you think you'll get this happy family of yours?"

"I don't know," I said, suddenly very aware of how near she was to me. "But I guess that finding the right woman comes first."

"Mmm," she smiled. "That's true. The right woman makes all the difference."

We didn't speak much more that night, settling down to sleep not long after cleaning the bowls and the pot. I lay down on one side of the fire and was surprised when Eshi curled up beside me. She normally slept on the other side of the fire, but now, her back was hardly more than an arm's length away.

I wondered about that for a few moments before letting out a breath and closing my eyes. It was nice having her so close and I didn't let myself think about it anymore. I was asleep in another handful of heartbeats.

The rising sun found Eshi and me trooping back to the canyon's rim. The dawn was cool and loud with the sounds of the life that thrived in the hours before the furnace heat of the day. We arrived right as it became bright enough to see, and I didn't waste any time in dropping my pack and detaching my longest coil of rope.

"You sure that you don't need to practice?" I glanced over to where Eshi was stretching. "Going down a rope isn't as easy as it looks."

The hyenaling grunted, coming out of her stretch with a loud exhalation. She flicked her ears dismissively. “I’ve gone down lots of ropes, Naroh. I don’t need to practice.”

“Are you sure?” I asked, looping the rope around the trunk of a convenient pine and tying it tight. “This isn’t like climbing out of a window. There will be wind and this cliff is pretty high.”

“That’s cute of you to worry.” Eshi met my gaze with a quirking smile. “I’ll be fine.”

That smile sent sparks cascading through me, but I forced myself to turn away. I moved back to the canyon’s edge with what was left of the rope, tossing the coil into the air and watching it unravel as it fell.

“Looks like it’s long enough,” I said when the end of the rope hit the rocky beach below. “Can you pull this back up? We’ll lower my pack down first and then I’ll go so that you can see how I do it.”

The hyenaling rolled her eyes. Her robe was strapped to the outside of her pack and she wore her usual pants and chest wrap. Muscles shifted beneath golden skin as she reached up with her hands. I couldn’t help sliding my gaze down the length of her as she swept her speckled mane back.

“You’re not going to help me?” She asked, her amber eyes bright and cheeks kissed by pink.

I coughed, releasing the tied length of rope. “I need to change out of this robe. I’ll come to help once I’m done.”

Eshi’s ears perked, and then, she nodded. I moved back towards my pack. Inside, I had a tunic and a pair of pants. They were made of light wool, dyed a coal gray, and were short enough to leave my movements unrestricted.

Once I found them, I stripped down to my loincloth, shivering in the cool morning air. I had my pants laced around my waist after a few moments and was reaching for my tunic when I felt the prickle of something on my naked back. I looked up to find Eshi’s eyes on me. She’d turned completely away from the canyon edge, watching me with her head cocked and the rope held limply in one hand.

"You need to get that rope up, Eshi," I said, nodding to her hand. "Come on."

"Hmm." She didn't turn away, running her eyes along my naked chest. My heart quickened as something shifted in the amber depths of her eyes. "I could feel some of that sitting next to you, but it wasn't... There's a lot more of you than I thought there was."

I glanced down at the lean cords of muscle shifting beneath my flesh. I'd always considered myself a scholar, though my study of history had always pulled me towards the more... tangible. As much as I would have liked, I'd never had the wealth to spend my days hunched over old books. Instead, I did a lot of running, a lot of climbing, and a lot of digging. Diving tombs was physical work, and my body reflected that.

"Your skin is so pale," Eshi said, and I felt my limbs tingle at the throaty edge of her voice. "Leave it out in the sun for a while."

"Is that what you're doing?" I asked, pointedly looking up and down her mostly bare torso. "Getting a tan?"

"A bit of sun is good for your skin." She rested her empty hand on one hip, her stomach rippling as she shifted her weight. "Are you telling me to cover up?"

"Well," I said, drawing out the word. "I wouldn't want you to be unhealthy."

"There you go." She grinned wickedly, her tail sweeping the air behind her. "Be healthy with me, Naroh."

"Come on," I laughed, pulling on my tunic. "We have a lot of work to do."

Moving back towards her, I wondered why I was so unembarrassed by her attention. Perhaps it was the openness with which she accepted my gaze? Or, maybe it had something to do with the warmth of her smile and the way it made the whole of me tingle? Either way, I felt not a bit of discomfort as her eyes slid over me while we worked. I couldn't remember the last time a beautiful woman had looked at me with such frank appreciation. It was... nice.

It took only a few minutes to pull the rope up, fasten my pack to it, and lower it back down. Once it hit the rocky beach, it was my turn. I sat on the edge of the cliff, wrapping my legs in the rope and making sure my hold on it was tight. I turned back to Eshi before beginning my descent.

"I'll shout when I untie my pack. Pull the rope back up and send yours down after."

"Yes, yes, I remember."

"I'll see you down there, then." I gave her a mocking grin as I lowered myself off the edge. "Sorry for taking away your view."

She cackled, the sound following me as I disappeared from her line of sight. My chest was warm as I lowered myself down the rope. When I finally did manage to push Eshi's dawn-softened smile from my mind, it wasn't through any sort of mental discipline.

Rather, it was the sudden emergence of the Nabanossaran tomb that resharpened my focus. I slowed to a snail's crawl, my eyes wide with the wonder of what I found before me.

As Kashir had described, the entrance was set into the sandstone wall of the canyon. It wasn't, however, a simple rectangular doorway dug into the stone. Lamians were nothing if not grandiose, and this ancient Nabonassaran pharon, no, *pharona*, had had an entire facade chiseled out of the cliff face. Two enormous lamians were sculpted from the rock on either side of a dark entrance that was set about a quarter of the way up the cliff. The lamians were female, their sinuously curved bodies depicted wearing the same hooded crown and flowing dress. Their features were beautifully detailed, their faces set in identical expressions of imperial serenity.

I was climbing down between the two sculptures, moving past the series of carved arches that stretched between them. These were decorated with statues of roosting storks, ankh-wielding figures, and grinning skulls.

"Storks of Tel'aman," I muttered to myself, hardly noticing the burn in my shoulders or the coarse grind of the rope. "Prayers carved into columns; Djed, the death god, and appeals to the Judge. Pyramids of Eanna, the Life-Mother, and ankhs to symbolize a necromancer's power."

I was halfway down when the human bodies of the twin lamia, which I suspected had been done in the image of Nabonassara III herself, flowed into their serpent halves. Their long tails twisted downward before coiling and curving up and around each other so that each tip ended above the door. The stairs up from the beach followed those tails.

My feet touched down on the rocky ground a bare dozen paces from the first set of stairs. The Gibris River flowed behind me but I hardly noticed it. No other civilization could match the sheer, monumental majesty of the Ashuran Empire, and I wondered if I would ever become jaded by the marvels that the lamians were able to create.

"Naroh!" Eshi shouted, her voice echoing all around me. "Stop gaping and untie your damned pack!"

I squinted up, noting with amazement that a bare few camel lengths separated the top of the stone lamian's head from where the hyenaling stood at the top of the cliff. It was incredible how invisible this had all been from up above. I moved to unfasten my pack and the rope zipped back up the cliff as Eshi hauled it back upward. She lowered her pack and was soon climbing down herself. Within a surprisingly short amount of time, the two of us stood together on the rocky beach.

"This is more what I had in mind," Eshi said, gazing up at the tomb. "But it looks a lot smaller than the Malash one we stopped at."

"Smaller tombs were more the custom back then," I said, crouching down by my pack and taking out my sling, a pouch of stones, and another of glowstone powder. "The empire was younger and more unstable. The lamians had more to do than just sitting around dreaming up their crypts. Tie the rope down, and then we'll fill up our water skins."

"Sure." She flicked her ears in acknowledgment and moved to secure our way back up the cliff. "You'd still think this dusty pharona could have come up with something better than this crack in the middle of nowhere."

"That part was purposeful as well. Smaller tombs have less space for traps and guardians, so they tried to tuck them away and make them hard to reach. I bet," I continued, sweeping my gaze around. "That this canyon is actually flooded for a large part of the year. It's a good spot."

"That's a good sign, right? Do you think there'll be any gold left in there?"

"Not a chance," I said, pushing myself up to my feet. "Even if this place hadn't already been raided, lamians didn't start burying themselves with gold until a few hundred years after this one died. The living needed it more than the dead, in those days."

"No gold..." Eshi looked up from where she was pulling empty water skins from her pack, giving me a flat stare. "You didn't feel like telling me this before I signed up for this crazy venture?"

"I tried telling you," I grunted, winding my sling around my forearm. "It's not my fault you didn't listen."

Eshi snorted and straightened with a dozen empty water skins dangling from her arm. "How is this even going to help us find Marduss's tomb?"

"I told you that as well."

The hyenaling scowled as we started towards the water. The rounded rocks of the riverbank shifted and clacked beneath our boots. "Just tell me again, Naroh."

"Are you actually going to listen this time?"

"Naroh, can you just—" She checked me with her hip, causing me to stumble. "I see what Rishka meant about making her want to scream."

I glared at her but she just stared back. We reached the edge of the flowing river and I let out a sigh.

"Fine," I said, crouching down to fill my first waterskin. "But listen this time."

"I'm going to knife you."

I chuckled, though I still flicked my gaze over to her as she crouched beside me just in case. "Alright, well, do you remember that medallion I brought to Kashir's?"

"I remember you worrying I'd take it from you." Eshi grinned her scavenger's smile and bumped me with her shoulder. "That was fun."

"I'm not going to tell you if you don't listen."

She wiped away her grin but her eyes didn't lose their sparkle. "I'm listening, Naroh. That artifact was your first clue, right?"

I nodded, plunging the first of my waterskins into the flowing water. "I pulled it out of the tomb of Nabonassara IV. It had an image of Marduss wearing an elven headscarf instead of the Hooded Crown."

"What does that mean?"

"I have no idea, but I think that it's important. I told you that the Nabonassarans were strange because they worshipped Tel'aman, god of wisdom, above the other gods?"

"Hmm," Eshi acknowledged. "That's why there are all these stork statues everywhere, right?"

"Exactly. The Nabonassarans were ferocious scholars and some of their works survive to this day. They saw knowledge as the most important thing and were committed to guarding as much of it as they possibly could. If Nabonassara IV decided to have a medallion with that specific depiction of Marduss buried with him, it means that there's some sort of truth to it."

Eshi and I were onto our second waterskins now. She'd shifted closer while I'd been speaking, near enough for our arms to brush against each other's as we worked. Her skin was warm, despite the chill of the morning. "So, why aren't we going back to that tomb, then?"

"Because that medallion is the only clue I found. That dynasty was pretty short-lived and, out of all of them, Nabonassara I was the most accomplished. He's the one who actually changed our system of writing and—"

"The storkling libraries," Eshi interrupted. "I remember, Naroh. You're hoping that his tomb will have another clue like that medallion?"

"Yeah. He lived only a few centuries after the conquest and with the reputation he has..." I shrugged, my arm sliding along hers. "If anyone recorded anything from that era, it would be him. Or, Ramesh the Great, I suppose, but his tomb is beneath the Imperial Palace in Uruq and there's no way we'd survive trying to sneak into there."

"And, the reason that we're not going to this Nabo... whatever, tomb now is because you don't know where it is?"

"Nobody does," I confirmed. "But I'm hoping that there's a clue in here that will help me find it."

"And if there isn't?"

"Then, we'll have to try something else."

"That's not much to go on." Eshi shook her head, and my nose was filled with the sunny scent of her hair. "I almost wish you hadn't told me."

"It's not," I admitted. "But maybe we'll get lucky."

"Or, maybe we'll come out with nothing."

"That too."

A few minutes later we had the waterskins filled and packed away. The two of us hefted our packs and made our way up the zigzagging staircase.

"Why all this?" The hyenaling asked, holding onto the lamian's stone tail. "If they wanted to hide this tomb, why not just dig a little door in the cliff?"

"Because snakes are vain."

Eshi laughed, but I didn't join in. My attention was on the steps ahead, my heart beating a slow, ready rhythm. I stopped when we reached the dais before the tomb's dark opening, turning to watch Eshi make the final few steps.

There was a discussion that we needed to have, and now, with the grave-cold air of the crypt blowing out past us, it was time.

"Before we go in," I said, meeting her quizzical gaze. "We have to set down a few rules."

"Rules?" She quirked her lip. "This should be interesting."

I didn't react to her teasing tone, staring silently at her until her smile faded away.

"When we're in there, you stay quiet unless I speak. You don't wander, or explore, or go off on your own. And most importantly, you will follow my every order the instant that I give it."

Eshi bristled, her spotted ears going stiff. But I wasn't done.

"You don't know this world, Eshi. If I tell you to jump into a pit of spiders, you jump. If I need you to slice your hair away and leave it scattered in the hall, you reach for your knife. And if I tell you to ditch your pack and run, you fucking run."

Eshi hissed and bared her sharp canines. "I can take care of myself."

"Not here. In there, you're a babe in a fucking nappy." The hyenaling's eyes flashed, but I continued, shouting over whatever she was opening her mouth to say. "Shut up and listen! In there—" I raised my arm to point at the rectangle of blackness, "is nothing you've ever seen. This is a tomb, Eshi, an endless fucking maze of death and silence that wants nothing more to keep you trapped within it. There are a thousand ways to die in there, and somewhere within all that madness is a clue to something that I've given ten years of my life to find."

I lowered my arm, taking a half step forward so that I loomed over her. I never took my eyes off hers, letting her see the truth burning behind them.

"I am not giving this up, or dying, because my partner can't follow a simple command. You'll swear to this, or you can climb up that rope and leave."

Eshi's face had settled into a mask of dangerous neutrality. Her voice, when she spoke, was cold. "We had a deal."

"Am I backing out of it?" I asked, leaning back and spreading my hands. "No. I said that I'd take you with me into these tombs, and I will. But you're going to follow my rules. If not, I'll leave you to impale yourself on the first fucking trap you set off."

I expected her to snarl and go for her knives; it was why I'd leaned away, in fact. But instead, Eshi remained silent. She stared into my eyes, her own bright and clear. She searched me for several long moments before she eventually nodded.

"Alright. I swear by my name and cl—" She cut herself off, closed her eyes, and let out a quick breath. When she opened them, her voice was steady. "I swear by my name and everything I am to obey these rules, and any others you might give me. Anything else?"

"Uh..." I blinked, somewhat taken aback. "Yeah, okay. Good."

Eshi rolled her eyes, stepping back from me. I felt the tension within me drain, and only then did I realize that my hands had been clenched into fists. "Don't look so surprised, Naroh. I'm not an idiot, I know I'd be completely out of my depth in there."

I settled back on my heels, frowning. "Then why didn't you just agree right away?"

"Because I wanted to hear how you'd say it."

"How I'd say it?"

"Yup," she said, flicking her ears. "It's important."

"How I'd...?" I stared at her for a few more seconds before giving up on trying to decipher her meaning. I let out a breath, feeling the pull of my pack while I ran one hand through my shaggy hair. "Are you ready to head inside, then?"

Light flickered through Eshi's eyes, and a ghost of a smile played across her face. "Lead the way."

Chapter Eleven

DJED, THE SERPENT-HEADED GOD of death, held dominion over all. He was King of the Gods, ruling at the side of his beloved Queen Eanna, the Goddess of all Life. Together, they spun the world from the nothingness of chaos, shaping it around an endless cycle of birth and death.

From Eanna's womb came the hundreds of gods; Sekna of nature, Osirin the Judge, and Imhopta of rainfall, to name but a few. This world was for them and, watched over by their parents, they molded it. Together, they pulled mountains from the earth, carving out lakes and rivers, and making a paradise for themselves and all the beasts that were born from their various unions.

Yet, one god did not participate.

Sek, the locust god, was the first and mightiest child of life and death. He was the first to walk the paradise his parents created and the only one of the gods that hungered for something more. And so, he left the world, venturing out into the blackness between the stars where demons lurked. For uncountable ages, Sek fought them. He ripped and tore and devoured them, keeping the endless demonic hosts in check and ensuring that the world he'd left behind remained the Eden it had been created to be.

But as time passed, his hunger, once easily sated, seemed to deepen. The demons tasted like ash upon his tongue, and no matter how many millions he consumed, he was unable to ease the gnawing in his stomach. He looked back at the blooming paradise he'd left behind, wondering.

Millennia passed and the emptiness inside of him grew. It was driving him to madness and, in desperation, he returned to the world. He fell to his knees before his siblings and begged. He had fought for them, he said, and had protected them from the demons. Now, he was in pain and to fix himself, all he needed was a taste. A simple taste of all they had created would sate him for all eternity, and he could return to the war beyond the stars.

But the gods knew that the locust's hunger would never diminish. Sek had been corrupted by the demons he had consumed, and so, they turned him away lest he devour them all.

Betrayed, Sek turned to the evil that he had once fought. They knew his strength and, unlike the family he had known, welcomed him. He lay with the mightiest of the infernal matriarchs, and from his seed, she birthed an uncountable swarm.

So was born the locust. Each was made in Sek's image, and each bore an echo of their father's boundless hunger.

I saw this legend and more painted on the walls of the tomb's antechamber.

The large room was surprisingly bright, with light spilling in from the entrance behind me and from long slits cut into the cliff face. I could see much of the chamber from where I stood a half-dozen paces within, including a statue in the center and the three entrances at the far end that led deeper into the maze.

"You can come in," I told Eshi, keeping my voice low. "Stay five paces behind me, and be quiet while we move. There aren't usually any traps in the antechamber, but if you hear a click or feel the stone shift beneath your feet, dive backward."

She made no sound of acknowledgment, I was pleased to note. We made our way toward the sculpture in the center of the room. Our footsteps were loud in the empty space, and I kept my attention on anything that might come shambling out of the three dark archways.

"Watch the doors," I murmured when we reached the center. "Touch me if you see anything."

The statue, predictably, was of the stork-headed Tel'aman. The god of knowledge and wisdom was depicted in a flowing vizier's robe and holding a clay tablet. At the god's feet was another tablet, its surface turned toward the outside.

"The wise fly on the wings of the stork," I murmured, *"to nest, immortal in wisdom's source."*

"Should you really be this chatty here?" Eshi said, her voice low.

I started, not having realized that I'd spoken out loud. I glanced over, seeing that her frame was tense beneath her pack. Her ears were high and alert, her eyes flicking over every bit of this room.

"As long as we don't get too close to those doorways, we're probably fine," I answered, turning back to my examination. "If there were any guardians nearby, they'd have come by now. Do you see those skulls set right above those doorways?"

"Yes," she said after a few moments. "Although, why are they only over two of them?"

"The third one was broken," I said, leaning over to see if anything was written on the tablet Tel'aman held. It was blank. "That's the tunnel we're going to go down."

Eventually, just as I was deciding that there wasn't anything else to gain from staring at this statue, Eshi let out a little huff of annoyance and asked, "And are you going to tell me why?"

"Why we're going down that tunnel?" I asked, lowering my pack to the floor. "Those skulls are alarm constructs. I'm not sure how the magic works, but they start screaming if anything larger than a rat gets too close. Divers would have broken that third one, and I bet that we'll be able to follow a trail of tripped traps all the way to the sarcophagus."

"Or they picked the wrong tunnel and we're following those idiots to our deaths."

"Kashir seemed pretty certain that this place was ransacked. I think he sent divers through here at some point, and they would have done what we're about to do." I straightened with my sling in my hand. "Do you think that you could hit those skulls from here?"

She glanced over at me for a moment before considering the distance between us and the nearest arch.

"Probably not on the first stone," she admitted.

I flashed her a smile and tossed her the pouch of alchemical powder I'd tied to my belt. "You get a glowstone ready, then."

"You can hit it?" She set her pack down, her voice skeptical, "From here?"

Instead of answering, I turned away and fished within my pouch of stones. I drew out one of the smooth, vaguely oblong-shaped rocks and rolled it in my palm while I considered the distant skull.

It really was rather far.

But I was damned good with the sling. I could, and often had, made shots like this with a furious guardian bearing down on me. I didn't let myself think too much, simply setting the stone within the sling's central cradle and whirling it three times through the air before letting fly.

The stone hissed, cutting forward in a tight arch until it hit the skull dead-on. The ancient bone shattered, and there was a loud retort as my stone cracked against the wall behind it. I had the second stone loaded in an instant, sending it tearing toward the final skull while the first was still ricocheting off the wall.

But in the moment before that second stone met the skull, I saw bright, purple flames flicker to life within its eyes.

"Fuck!" I swore, my heart pounding. "Gods of fucking death! What the—"

"What?!" Eshi had been crouched by her pack but now leaped to her feet. "Do we run?"

I let myself swear for a few moments longer, trying to stop the sudden tingle of my limbs from worsening into tremors. Eventually, I let out a shaky breath and turned to where Eshi stood stiffly enough that I thought she might crack.

"We're fine," I said. "Although, we almost weren't."

Eshi's ears lay flat against her skull and her cheeks were flushed with tension. "What happened?"

"Were you watching?"

"I looked up after you broke the first one. Wasn't the point of this to be quiet?"

"Yeah." I ran a hand through my now sweat-dampened hair. "It was always going to be loud. I wanted to break them close together so that there's only one loud crack, instead of two."

"Why break them at all, then? We're not going down those tunnels anyway, right?"

"Calculated risk," I said, finding that explaining myself was actually helping calm my racing heart. "Most lamians don't bother putting any guardians by the entrance. It's too easy to lure them outside and lose them. The maze is a different story, and you never know what will happen down there, so, I'd rather break these skulls now than risk having to do it while we're escaping something."

"So what happened?" Eshi let out a long breath. "I'm guessing that the purple in the other one's eyes wasn't a good thing?"

"Yeah," I said, looking back to the shattered bits of skull. "That purple was the construct waking up."

The hyenaling, who'd started to relax, stiffened right up again.

"It shouldn't have been possible. Every tomb I've ever gone into has these same skulls and they're only ever able to see. It shouldn't have been able to pick up sound."

My heart was still racing and, despite the severity of the situation, I was fighting off a wild grin. This was magic I had never seen before. It was something new, something different, just like the image of Marduss I'd found.

Gods of death, I couldn't wait to see what else was buried here.

"So if you'd been too slow with the sling ..." Eshi began.

"Or missed."

"Or missed." She glared up at me. "Or if you'd gotten me to fucking do it, then, what? It would have started screaming?"

I nodded. "And this tomb would probably be flooding with undead now."

Eshi stared at me in silence for several long moments. "Why did I ever think that you were good at this?"

I chuckled, feeling the last of my tension drain away. "It's not too late to go back outside."

To my surprise, Eshi's lip quirked upward. She stared at me for one long moment and something shifted within the depths of her amber eyes. "Yes, it is. Do we need to do anything else before moving on?"

I shook my head, and we were hefting our packs back up after another few minutes. We headed towards the entrance above which the skull had long since been broken. It was a wide, empty arch, and the darkness beyond was absolute.

The murals surrounding this door were of the war in the heavens. I saw Sek at the head of a legion of demons, marching towards our world. The other gods rose to meet them, leaving their paradise behind to fight, kill, die and be born again in the titanic struggle against the Locust God and his demons.

Then came the Devastation.

Sek's uncountable children slipped through the battling deities. Hunger entered the world for the first time and swarms of locusts landed amongst the lush, ever-blooming paradise that the gods had created. They began to devour, consuming everything they touched and turning vast swathes of green into empty deserts. The land was being consumed, and yet, the gods could not turn away from their battle, lest they be overwhelmed. In desperation, Eanna, the Mother of Life, gave birth to new children, ones that would steward the realm while the gods were away.

The lamians were born in the image of their father, the serpent-headed Djed. Each of them was born with a fragment of his dominion over death and, using this power, the lamians were able to fight off the locusts. They decimated the insects, saving the world from annihilation. Though, Sek's children could never be wiped out for good, and every few years, the swarm would once more take to the skies and consume all in its path.

To this day, hunger and gluttony were the worst sins for a lamian to indulge in. Hunger, the priests said, was the domain of the locust. It is what ruined the paradise that the gods had created. With the locust's arrival, beasts suddenly hungered for the flesh of others. There was a hunger for power, a hunger for wealth, and things that shined. Neighbor hungered for the possessions of his neighbors, and lust grew from a different sort of flesh-hunger.

Hunger, they said, was the root of all evil.

I thought of that as I turned away from those final murals. The lamians might believe their priests, but I never had. I'd been hungry my entire life and, as of now, all it had done was drive me to reach for something beyond the bounds of my village.

I strode into the darkness of the tomb. The lamians might fear their hunger, but I would show them what mine could do.

Glowstone, as a name, was fairly misleading. It wasn't so much a stone as a handful of different powders that, when mixed with water, hardened into a sticky lump of material that emitted a faint, blueish glow. It was cheap, easy to find, and lasted several hours. Though the light it emitted was faint, it was more than sufficient for the pitch-blackness of the tomb.

For a historian who was chronically short of funds, they were a blessing.

I held the glowing mass up to the nearest wall, revealing more details of the shape that had been carved into the stone. It was an ankh, a vaguely tear-shaped loop set atop a T. It was the ancient symbol of necromancy, representing the union of life and death. It was made up of the cross of Eanna topped by the hooded, serpent head of Djed.

It was the dozenth such section of wall that we'd come across since first leaving the antechamber. It stood out from the blank stone making up the rest of the tunnel. And though it was perfectly reasonable that this symbol would be found all over the tomb of a lamian necromancer-king, I wasn't convinced that this wasn't some sort of trap.

Though, as of yet, I hadn't figured out what it was supposed to do.

After a few more minutes of fruitless examination, I settled back on my heels and frowned. It looked as safe as the others we had passed, but tomb divers thrived on paranoia, and I couldn't quite bring myself to dismiss these out of hand.

Finally, I gave up and turned back to where Eshi stood a few paces away. The hyenaling's back was straight beneath her pack. Her cheeks, hair, and the exposed flesh of her stomach were streaked with dust and grime. Her ears were stiff and alert, though I saw fatigue creeping in to dull the brightness of her eyes.

I could feel the same exhaustion scratching behind my eyes and my limbs creaked with tension. Tomb diving was slow, nerve-wracking work. The cold and silent darkness were heavy, sapping at us and draining us of warmth and energy. The sun wouldn't set on the outside world for several more hours, but it had already been a long day.

This wasn't, however, a good place to rest.

'Ready?' I asked Eshi with a tilt of my head.

She nodded, reaching up to sweep a few sweat-matted strands of hair from her face.

I turned to lead us deeper into the dark, moving at a pace that would make a tortoise sneer in contempt. I marked every trap and intersection with lines of chalk to make sure I could retrace my steps. My glowstone rested against my chest, kept in place by a loop of string. My every sense and Eshi's more considerable ones, straining for any sign of the dangers lurking beyond our small circle of light.

Guardians, toxic air, traps... a lamian tomb was a place of death.

We'd passed blade traps, collapsible ceiling stones, rigged walls, and jaws of metal. There'd been jutting spikes, metallic tripwire, and a hundred variations of pits and crevices. We'd come across the remains of guardians as well, unmoving heaps of bone and desiccated flesh. These had also come in nightmarish variations; from armored, crocodile-headed behemoths to stalking, blade-handed assassins made from the bones of children.

There were more pedestrian obstacles as well; the darkness and silence, uneven floors to catch a foot, dead ends, and weirdly shaped stairs.

I was also happy to find no signs of any dangerous wildlife. Some of the newer tombs I'd raided kept small chambers open to the elements, allowing some vegetation to grow. Then, they'd release populations of rodents within their halls, along with several species of venomous snakes, lizards, and scorpions to feed on them. These artificial ecosystems could survive for centuries, ensuring that ambushing death lurked in every crack of stone.

Lamians were, unfortunately, rather creative as a species.

I stopped suddenly, as my eye caught something on the floor. Behind me, Eshi froze as well. I felt her stiffen, though she didn't otherwise react.

Good, she was getting used to this.

I set my pack down and crouched, bringing my glowstone closer to the patch of ground that had caught my eye. I could see it more clearly now, the shadowed edges of a square set within the rough stone of the floor. It was clay, a tile that was just a bit larger than my foot and likely thinner than the width of one finger.

I settled down onto my knees, getting more comfortable. I motioned Eshi over, keeping my gaze on the empty tunnel ahead while the hyenaling set her pack down and knelt beside me. She shifted close, resting a hand on my shoulder as she leaned in to breathe a few words directly into my ear.

"A trap?"

Her warm breath swirled over my skin, leaving a layer of rising gooseflesh in its wake. Strands of her hair tickled my neck, and I had to repress a shiver as my nose was filled with the wild, sun-scorched scent of her sweat. I swallowed as she leaned away, and the twinkle in her eyes told me that she'd noticed.

I pushed all of that aside as I leaned toward her. Eshi ducked her head, letting me whisper directly into one of her spotted ears.

"See that tile?"

Her ears flicked as my breath tickled her fur, and I grinned to see a shiver crawl down her back. She glared at me for a few heartbeats before turning to examine the floor before us. She nodded after barely a moment.

"Watch," I mouthed, raising a clenched fist above the tile.

I broke the clay with one swift punch, my knuckles throbbing as the shattered pieces of tile tumbled into the pit they'd been obscuring. The sound echoed around us, and neither Eshi nor I moved as we kept an eye out for anything that might have been attracted to the sound.

Nothing came. After a few moments, I got the hyenaling's attention with a touch to her arm. Together, we leaned over the now-exposed trap, my glowstone showing us the entirety of the knee-deep pit.

Inside was one of the nastier sort of spike traps. A single lance of iron thrust up from the center. It was long and sturdy enough to completely impale a plunging foot. There were four other spikes within, their tips pointing diagonally down towards the center from where they'd been set near the rim of the pit. They were designed to let the foot pass through, but would then rip savagely at the leg if the victim tried to jerk their limb free of that first spike.

Eshi made a small sound of disgust. We stepped carefully over it when we were once again ready to move on. We were making good time, despite everything. My earlier logic had proven to be sound, and my day had consisted of keeping us within the worn footprints of long-passed divers. I navigated a trail of tripped traps and broken constructs, using them to guide me through the twisting tunnels and splitting junctions of the maze.

That didn't mean that we were safe. In the following hours, I found a dozen more hidden spike traps. I took the time to break the obscuring tile over each one. Finally, when fatigue had started to blur my vision and we'd had to cross an honest to the gods chasm, we started to get close.

Paint started to appear on the walls; more depictions of the Gods and scenes of mythology. These, however, were more focused on the underworld. They showed a soul's journey from their tomb, up the river of souls in the boat of Mish, goddess of the sun. The soul then appeared before her husband Osirin, their life and deeds weighed on the scales of the falcon-headed Judge. Those found unworthy were torn apart by Antu, the jackal, while those of sufficient greatness were permitted entry through a door guarded by Sobak and Ninshubur, the twin, crocodile-headed protectors of the underworld's final domain.

Djed ruled from there, and he welcomed all who arrived before him into a paradise.

This last scene was painted right before a large arch of stone. Its pillars were intricately carved and sculpted into the forms of Djed and Eanna. There was an ankh, chiseled in the center of the arch that spanned between them. The emptiness beyond called to me, but I took my time in examining this final threshold.

Then, once I'd decided it was safe, I led Eshi into the sarcophagus chamber of Nabonassara the Third.

Chapter Twelve

THE SARCOPHAGUS CHAMBER WAS, in fact, a suite of five connected rooms. Each one was large, beautifully decorated, and utterly useless.

I scrubbed at my face with my hand, letting out a long breath. Gods of fucking death, I was tired. As best as I could make out, Eshi and I had been in this tomb for close to two days now. We'd eaten little, rested less, and I'd just spent who knew how many hours going over every inch of these chambers.

I shook my head clear and headed back into the main chamber.

"You don't look too happy," Eshi said, her figure emerging from the darkness as I approached with our single light source. "Didn't find anything?"

She was sitting on the steps leading up to the sarcophagus's rectangular dais. Eshi wore the strain of the past few days in the drawn lines of her grime-streaked face. She looked as exhausted as I felt, her bright eyes set within deep, dark rings. Her body was stiff, kept rigid by the silence, the darkness, the constant tension, and the sheer alien unfamiliarity of this place.

I climbed the wide stairs towards her, my eyes flicking to the sarcophagus rising from the center of the dais.

It was a fairly typical example of a lamian coffin, large enough to fit a coiling tail and made of solid stone. The sides were painted with scenes from Nabonassara III's life, and the slab of stone that served as a lid had been carved into her image. The same lid was pushed open now, nudged aside by the divers who had removed the mummified lamian corpse and plundered what artifacts she'd had with her. There was a smooth, unadorned obelisk that rose behind the head of the box, and my first few hours here had been dedicated to the fruitless examination of them both.

"Oh, there's a lot." I flopped down beside the hyenaling. I gestured to the painted walls around us, all of them depicting the life and deeds of Nabonassara III. "All of this stuff is fascinating. Like, look over there. The pharona apparently had to deal with an incursion of centaurs during her reign, but the first one that I'd ever heard of was when Temuja Khan led his horde through the Eastern Mountains and ended the Khamosse Dynasty several centuries later."

I didn't bother to keep my voice particularly low. Once cleared, the burial chambers were as safe a place as could be found within a lamian tomb.

"There was also some sort of elven slave revolt," I continued. "One that looked pretty serious. I saw a picture of the city of Basri and its olive groves in flames."

I went on to describe what I had found in each room. The two treasure rooms, as expected, had been empty. Only the long, stone tables remained, watched over by several large sculptures of the sinuously curved Nabonassara III. The third chamber I'd examined had been a library, though my initial elation had twisted into heartbreak as I'd discovered that all the clay tablets it had once contained had been smashed and scattered around the feet of a statue of the stork-headed Tel'aman.

"Was that what that sobbing sound was?" Eshi said, a smile tugging at her lips.

"Who knows what sort of stories and knowledge had been written there!? We might have lost something important just because a few idiot divers didn't see the value in them."

"Hmm." Eshi shifted so her knee rested against mine. "That is sad, but finish telling me about that revolt. Were my people involved?"

"I think so," I said, thinking back to what I'd seen of the murals. "I didn't see anything about it, but it was pretty normal for the houses to send their dog-soldiers in to try and solve things before getting the undead involved."

"Don't call us that." Eshi scowled, her ears stiffening.

"What?"

"'Dog-soldiers,'" she said. "I hate that name. Hyenas don't look anything like dogs, and we as people certainly don't."

"Right," I said. "Sorry."

She nodded and motioned for me to continue. I carried on telling her about what I'd learned, fitting everything into the historical tapestry and connecting what threads I could. I still wasn't convinced that Eshi actually found any of this interesting, but slowly, as the words continued to flow out of me, I saw the worried lines of her face start to smooth. The unconscious stiffness of her frame bled away enough that she leaned her elbows back on the step above us and stretched out her legs. Then, she closed her eyes and let out a long breath.

I trailed off after a few moments, not wanting to disturb her.

"Don't stop," she murmured, her eyes remaining shut. "Please."

I nodded and kept speaking, holding the silence of the tomb at bay for as long as I could. I told her about the last room, the armory, and the tales of war I'd seen painted in bright colors. Its walls showed a chariot-borne lamian pharona at the head of an army of the dead with her snake-headed scepter pointed towards a mass of savage-looking centaurs.

This chamber was by far the biggest, and other than the painted scenes of battle, it contained the remains of a hundred and more canopic jars.

They'd been made of clay and would have held the magic-saturated organs that had been responsible for powering all of the tomb's most powerful guardians. Something like the alarm skulls were too simple to need them, but those crocodile-headed monsters, as well as the creeping, assassin constructs, would have been tied to this chamber.

The undead were hard to put down, and that was four times as true for the ones that the lamians actually spent real time preparing. In battle, the best way to stop them was to shatter their skulls. This would take away their senses of sight and hearing, as well as destroying an important part of their magical framework. Headless corpses weren't much of a threat to anyone, blindly flailing about until they were torn apart or the magic completely leaked from them.

The lamians, of course, knew this and did all they could to eliminate this weakness.

The jackal-headed constructs of House Malash, or these crocodile-headed ones, would be nigh unstoppable in battle. Shackled in magic-amplifying gold, their skulls would have been heavily reinforced. Even the flesh that remained, other than being for plain intimidation, added an extra layer of protection.

To put them down, it was better to go for their canopic jars. There were five for each guardian, one for each of the construct's most important organs: the brain, lungs, liver, stomach, and guts. The undead were intrinsically bound to their jars, the vessels preserving the organs within and keeping them saturated with the magic needed to power the construct. So protected from the decay and passage of time, a guardian could, theoretically, exist forever.

Though the canopic jars inarguably made the undead stronger, they were also their greatest weakness. A guardian couldn't travel more than a league from their jars. Destroying them severed the construct from the corresponding organ, crippling their effectiveness and weakening the magic that powered them. Without a brain, it couldn't follow orders or experience the world around it. Without lungs, it would be slow and weak. Its guts made it physically tough, and though I had no idea about the liver and stomach, I was sure they were just as important.

When I eventually fell silent, I realized that I felt better than I had since coming down here. Our meager light seemed brighter, and the air had lost some of its stifling weight. It was good to speak again, and I was relaxed enough to lean back against my own elbows and mirror Eshi's pose.

"All that," the hyenaling said, after a while. "And nothing about where the first Nabo is."

"Nabo?" I said, glancing over to her.

Eshi cracked open an eye. "Nabonasarana is too long to keep saying."

"Nabonassara," I corrected.

"Whatever." She pushed herself upright, lifting her arms into a long stretch. "What's the plan, then?"

"We'll have to go back into the maze." I blew out a breath. "Do we have enough water for a few more days?"

"We do." She looked down at me. "Do you really think that we'll find anything else in there?"

"I don't know. But this is the only lead I've got, and I'm not ready to give up on this tomb."

"We," the hyenaling said, her eyes narrowing. "It's the only lead *we've* got. Don't think that you're cutting me out of this, Naroh."

I smiled, though fell short of actually laughing. This was a place of silence, and the tomb had a way of stifling such expressions of obvious delight.

Yet, that didn't mean that I didn't feel a momentary surge of energy. I moved without thinking, shifting along the step until Eshi and I were as close as when we shared the seat behind Asu's head. Then, I wove my fingers behind my skull and lay back down atop the steps, the side of my hip and leg pressed into hers.

"I wouldn't dream of it." I grinned into her still-narrowed gaze. "Oh, I'm sorry, should I move back? Is this uncomfortable?"

"Hmm, a little," she answered with a glimmer of light appearing to dance within her amber eyes. Her tail swept the stone behind her as she reached for my closest arm. She pulled it out from behind my head and stretched out along the step. Then, she lay with the back of her head on it, using my arm as a pillow as she shifted so that every part of her side pressed against mine. "There," she sighed. "Now, I'm comfortable."

My whole body was stiff with surprise, my heart beating faster in my chest. Eshi was right here, her hair tickling my skin and smelling of sun, sweat, and dust. She was so intimately close, her body so warm and so softly feminine. It felt... incredible. And yet, a part of me demanded I move away. I couldn't do this. I had to focus on the path ahead. This woman would hold me back, distract me, and get me killed. She was a thief, a manipulator who had stolen her way onto the trail that should have been mine alone to follow.

But as I lay there, breathing her scent and feeling the press of her body, that voice within me faded into nothingness. Eshi was my partner. She had followed me into this dead place, and she was warm, so much more so than the grave cold of the surrounding air.

"You're right," I said, my body relaxed even as I tightened my arm around her. "This is better."

And it was. Despite the stone being dusty and the edge of the step digging painfully into my back, it was better. Holding her like this felt better than I could have possibly imagined.

"Mmm." The hyenaling let out a pleased sound and I felt some little bit of tension leave her as she wiggled to somehow burrow herself even deeper into my side. "We do this together, Naroh. Don't forget."

I chuckled and tilted my head to press it into hers. Her hair still smelled like the sun and the fur of her ears was so soft. I closed my eyes, letting out an easy breath. It was so nice, I thought, my mind drifting off, to not be surrounded by nothing but the dark.

I settled back on my heels, carefully extracting my fingers from the teeth of the bladed trap I'd managed to disarm. My breath misted in the dark, grave-cold air of the tomb, and I let myself fall backward onto my ass and out of my weary crouch.

Behind me, I heard the rustle of cloth. Eshi's hand fell on my shoulder a moment later, and I felt her chest press into my back as she leaned in to whisper in my ear.

"You need to rest."

She was kneeling directly behind me, and I relaxed back into her. She stiffened to support my weight and the hand that had been on my shoulder sliding down across my chest. Her chin was just over my other shoulder, her hair tickling my neck.

"I know," I murmured, tilting my head to press my cheek against hers. "Soon."

Eshi let out a displeased huff and her arm tightened around my chest. She hugged me to her, running her other palm up and down the length of one of my own arms.

Immediately, I felt some of the tension within me loosen and I wondered briefly at the easy intimacy we now shared. We'd slept on two separate occasions since first arriving at the sarcophagus chamber. It had become our base; a place to rest before venturing out into the trap-filled darkness of the maze. In that time, we'd grown a lot closer. We sat to eat with legs and hips pressed together and curled up around each other for what hours we took of sleep.

I closed my eyes, sinking into her warmth and scent.

Would this have been possible up in the light of day? Perhaps, though I imagined that it would have taken longer. Right now, being close to her like this felt like the most natural thing in the world. Eshi was with me and she was so warm and strong, fierce and heart-poundingly beautiful. She had followed me into this place of silence, darkness, and death, and the simple heat of her touch did so much to ease the knot of tension within me.

"You didn't sleep much before we left," Eshi murmured. I felt the shape of her words in the press of her cheek. "Let's go back."

She was right, sleep was getting harder for me to come by. I was too keyed up, despite being both mentally and physically exhausted. We'd found nothing in these twisting tunnels, and the longer I searched, the harder it was to keep that doubting voice to the back of my mind.

There's nothing here, it whispered. This is where your road ends.

I let out a breath and opened my eyes, pushing the thought away as best I could. I blinked in the faint light of our glowstone, the seventh one we'd needed to make, and forced myself to examine the tunnel before us.

It, like everything else in the forsaken place, was dark and devoid of anything of use. We'd found only traps in these forsaken tunnels, as well as more of these large slabs of stone that had been carved with the necromancer's ankh. I glared at the one I could see a few paces ahead, at the edge of our little circle of light. The damned things were still a mystery, and I let my eyes slide off it a few moments later. A stone archway loomed past it, almost completely out of sight.

"Not yet." I planted my hands down and started to shift forward. "Let's go a bit further."

The hyenaling growled softly into my ear, and her other arm snaked across my chest. Her grip tightened, keeping me from standing. "That's stupid."

"Eshi," I said, letting out a breath. "We don't have too much water left. We have to find something soon, or we'll leave with nothing."

She shifted against me but remained sullenly silent. Her grip did not loosen either. That brought a faint smile to my lips, and I reached up with one hand to squeeze one of her forearms. I pressed my cheek tight against hers for a moment and murmured, "We'll just go see what's past that arch, alright? Then, we'll head back."

She pushed back against my cheek for a few heartbeats more before letting out a breath and loosening her arms. "Fine. But I'll kill you if you die and leave me alone in here."

"Deal," I chuckled, finally pushing myself to my feet.

A dozen slow paces later and we'd gotten close enough to the archway for it to loom clearly in the glowstone's meager light. I took a few minutes to examine it from afar, forcing my tired mind into focus. But there was nothing, no concealed pits, loose ceiling blocks, or bladed traps. It was nothing but cold, blank stone, identical to the hundreds we'd passed through already.

I nudged Eshi with my hip, signaling the all-clear. I took the first step, and then, I tripped.

Whether by exhaustion, an eagerness to be done, a particularly shoddily constructed bit of floor, or some combination of the three, my foot caught on something. I stumbled forward, passing through the open archway to land on all fours on the ground beyond.

I was unharmed, but looking back in response to the sound of Eshi's sharp intake of breath, my eyes caught a flash of purple. There was a skull there, grinning down at me from a niche set in the center of the archway. My heart lurched, my wide-eyed gaze fixing on the necromantic fire that blazed within both of its eyes.

I opened my mouth, but before I could make a sound, it screamed.

Chapter Thirteen

The skull's scream was a high, constant shriek that stabbed through my head like a spear. The sound careened off the walls around us, racing deeper into the maze. It didn't fade or lessen, powered by something other than the breath in one's lungs.

"Naroh!" Eshi shouted over the screaming skull, her eyes wide and wild. "What the fuck is going on?!"

"Skull!" I roared back, scrambling to my feet.

The hyenaling rushed over, reaching me as I started to unwind my sling from around my forearm. I had a stone loaded a few moments after it was free, whipping it through the air in two tight circles before releasing it. The stone smashed through the screaming skull, shattering it and cutting off the sound.

Eshi and I stood stiff and still, my heart racing and my ears ringing with the high screams' leftover echoes. The sound was fading but it didn't disappear. It must have awoken the alarm skulls set in other parts of the tomb. Gods, the magic here was weird. Luckily, with all the canopic jars within the central armory already having been destroyed, nothing seemed to be happening.

"I think we're okay," I said after a few moments. I let out a ragged breath, my hands shaking with the energy surging through me. "There might be a secondary armory with more canopic jars tucked away somewhere, but whatever guardians are left will be distracted by the rest of this noise. We should get back, though."

"Stupid!" Eshi's glare hit me like a hammer. "I said it was fucking stupid to stay, right?"

I winced, turning to meet her furious gaze. "Yeah..."

"Yeah?" Eshi bared her canines, her ears stiff and angry. She took a half step towards me and stabbed a finger into my chest. "You tumble into a trap, nearly stop my fucking heart and all you can say is *yeah*?"

"Sorry?" I held my hands up as the hyenaling's amber eyes flashed. "I'm sorry! We should have gone back!"

"And?"

Eshi's pale, sweat-matted mane fell around the razor-sharp lines of her face. The shadows of my glowstone gave a predatory gleam to her exposed teeth and the dirt-streaked muscles beyond her open robe were taut.

She was every inch the hyenaling warrior-huntress; feral and fierce, savage and strong.

"And... I'm an idiot?"

Her spotted ears twitched. She blinked, her eyes crinkled and her snarl relaxed into a smile. "Well, I was waiting for a 'you were right, Eshi,' but that works too."

My heart, which had just started to slow, sped up once again. I saw warmth bloom beneath her cheeks to set her amber eyes alight and something in that wide, teasing smile pulled at me. Sparks rose through me, swirling together into something so much more.

Eshi was with me and she was here, beating the darkness back with her smile. She was beautiful. Gods of death, even here, she was so, so...

"Beautiful."

"What?" Eshi said, her ears going stiff. "What did you say?"

I hadn't meant to actually speak. The word had just slipped out, and yet, I felt no rising roar of embarrassed heat. Filled as I was with the manic buzzing of my limbs, I felt nothing but the urge to move forward. I was burning with an altogether different sort of fire, an energy that pushed me to charge down this path.

"You're beautiful," I said, my breath hot in my chest. "Eshi, I—"

"Stop!" She shoved me, and I stumbled back. "Shut up!"

"Wha—"

"Shut up!" She stalked after me, her eyes blazing. "You can't fucking say that!"

"I can't say—?" My heart thundered, my blood roaring in my ears. "Why not?"

"Because," she almost screamed. Her body was stiff and she gestured wildly with her hands. "Look at me, Naroh! I haven't washed since we came into this fucking hole! My hair is disgusting, I smell like a pig and I'm covered in days worth of dirt!"

"I don't care about any of that!"

"Liar," she hissed.

"I'm not lying!" My fists were clenched tight. We were less than a half-pace apart, the roar of my blood not letting me back away or remain silent. "I like your laugh and I think you're beautiful! Why is any of that so hard to believe?"

"Because it's too early!" Her breath was coming faster and her ears folded back against her skull. "I haven't done enough! I haven't helped, and you don't see me as a part of—"

She clicked her teeth shut, cutting herself off. Scarlet blazed beneath her dirt-smudged cheeks and she looked away.

"Eshi," I started.

"It's not the right time." Her eyes were hidden behind hanging locks of hair. "We're in a fucking tomb, Naroh."

"So?"

Her head whipped up. I saw the snarl twist her features and her palms slammed into my chest. But I'd been ready, and in that split second before she shoved me away, I leaned forward.

And I kissed her.

Eshi's entire body stiffened. Her lips, soft and cool, were slack with shock. I pulled back after barely a heartbeat, having surprised even myself with the gesture. Lightning arced through me, the whole of me alight with that fleeting, all too brief taste of her.

"Sorry! Eshi, I—"

"You bastard." Her voice was soft and her palms slid down my chest. I saw the world open in her amber eyes and her breath, heated by the same fire that burned within me, escaped through parted lips. "This wasn't the right time."

"I know." I swallowed, struggling to force the words past the emotions searing my throat. "Eshi, I know that we're in a tomb, but—"

The hyenaling threw her arms around my neck and kissed me. It was fierce and passionate, and I lifted my arms to wrap around her narrow waist. I pulled her body tight against me, the press of her lips fanning the flames in me into a veritable inferno. We opened ourselves to each other, and Eshi let out a little mewl of sound when my tongue first slid against hers.

And that, unfortunately, was when the tunnel around us was filled with the loud crack of breaking stone.

I broke the kiss, jerking my head up in time to see the ankh carved into a section of stone burst into purple flame. Eshi reacted almost as quickly, spinning away from me so that, together, we watched that burning slab tip forward and crash to the tunnel floor. A torrent of sand spilled out into the dark corridor; a dozen desiccated corpses tumbling out with it. Several other crashes echoed throughout the tomb, and I had a brief moment to wonder how many hundreds of bodies had just been released into the tomb.

Then, purple fire burst into life in the eyes of each corpse, and heads turned toward us.

"Naroh," Eshi said, not looking away from the dead rising just beyond the arch of stone. "I thought you said all the guardians are gone."

"They are," I answered. "This is just the extra."

It was generally known that there were two forms of undead; those whose organs had been stored in canopic jars, and those whose organs had not.

Those constructs whose organs had been properly stored, like those jackal-headed monsters in Ikkad, were powerful. They were incredibly hard to kill and were even capable of something approaching thought.

Those whose organs remained, however, were not.

They were little more than puppets, filled with and pulled along by strings of magic. They were slow, stupid, inefficient, and were only useful for the handful of weeks it took for their organs to rot away within them. Even the corpse-drudges that worked the street and sewer cleaning gangs had at least had their brains and lungs properly stored.

They were impossible to use long-term, and were thus incredibly rare to see nowadays.

Their only real use, in fact, had been in times of war. In the chaotic centuries of the empire's infancy, the lamians had had to fight off many rival nations. Legions of hyenaling dog-soldiers would march into battle, killing and dying and carpeting the field with corpses. Necrophants would follow on their chariots, raising all who'd fallen to send shambling back in the lines of the enemy.

Yet, even with this strategy, the empire had come to the brink of being worn down. The battles had been endless, and lamian necromancer-lords of the past had needed to find some way to make their war-dead last until the next campaign.

These sand-dried, desiccated corpses were their solution.

"The extra? That doesn't—" Eshi spun back to face me. Her ears and tail were straight and stiff. Fear coiled within her, though she stayed clenched tightly around it. "What do we do?"

I could feel my heart slamming against my chest, sending waves of fire coursing through me. My fear was evaporating, boiled away by the heat of Eshi's kiss and an inferno of reckless energy. This was it, I thought, glancing back up towards the rising corpses. My face split into a too-wide grin, and my limbs started to shake.

This was it!

"Naroh! Stop fucking grinning and tell me what to do!"

"What do we do?" I turned my grin towards her. "This is it, Eshi!"

I laughed at the flash of anger in her eyes, the sound shrill and uneven. This was it! This was tomb diving! The guardians always found you, no matter how much you slithered and sneaked.

"Naroh! What do we fucking do!"

I bit down on my bubbling laughter, leaned forward, and gripped both of her arms. I squeezed hard without really meaning to, bringing my too-wide grin to within a handsbreadth of her face.

"This is it, Eshi! We run. We run, and maybe we die or maybe we don't."

Just out of sight, I felt, more than saw, the first of the undead gain its feet. I didn't look away from the hyenaling's eyes, ignoring the slow, silent death shambling towards us.

"I'm going through this and back to the center of the maze," I told her. "Are you running with me?"

And then, because that same mad, beautiful fire burned within her, Eshi bared her teeth. She grinned her scavenger's grin and let out a high, yipping cackle. Together, we turned and charged through the arch and toward the mass of living corpses.

We reached them within heartbeats.

I bowled over the first one, hardly slowing as my shoulder made contact with the walking, stick-thin corpse. They were dangerous only in high numbers; we reached them before most of the heaving mass had yet to even gain their wobbly feet. We crashed into the rest of them, stumbling over sand and bodies, tearing past grasping fingers, and flailing limbs. We were through in moments, and Eshi's cackle rebounded off the walls around us as we raced off into the darkness.

The run through the maze was a frenzied blur of purple fire, ragged breaths, and pounding footsteps. The glowstone against my chest bounced and jerked, making the shadows twist and dance.

And the dead were everywhere.

Corpses spilled out of every ankh-covered alcove, dozens of them pushing themselves out of the sand. We went around those groups we could, luring packs of them away with stones sent clattering down random corridors. I shattered skulls with my sling, thinning groups before we hammered into them. And once in their midst, Eshi never failed to jam a knife through one or two heads.

Then, we would be running once again.

By necessity, we stayed in the tunnels that we knew. We followed a trail of chalk marks and tripped traps on our back to the center; vaulting over pits and spike traps, diving through dark intersections, and wading through mounds of desert sand.

Throughout it all, Eshi was at my side. She was my long-legged shadow, her hair and open robe streaming back with the ragged breaths we left in our wake. We ran as we had through the rooftops of Ikkad, keeping each other going. Our bodies reacted to each other without the need for thought or speech, hauling each other up when we tripped or stumbled. I was there to yank her back from traps she didn't see, and when I got tangled up in a particularly thick mass of corpses, she cut me free with her knife.

Finally, when the air seemed to burn my lungs and my body was slick with blood and sweat, we burst into the central chambers. It was empty, luckily, save for the shadowy shapes of the obelisk and sarcophagus. There was a mass of undead a bare few corners away, and I didn't pause as I ran toward the center.

I noticed that one of our packs was leaning against the stairs, and only now did I realize that we'd left another sitting in the tunnel from which we'd started our flight. Most of our food and water was here, thankfully, though I'd lost a lot of rope and expensive tools.

"Get the pack!" I told Eshi, dashing up the dais steps.

My manic energy was nearly spent, and the fire within me was getting low. Still, enough of it burned within me that I was able to reach the sarcophagus within moments. The stone coffin was empty and, more importantly, the lid hadn't been pushed to the floor.

We couldn't have asked for a better hiding place.

I found the energy to grin as Eshi joined me with the pack atop the dais. The hyenaling looked as spent as I was, her ears drooping and sweat soaking her hair and flesh. Her eyes were still bright, however, and she understood my look within an instant.

"You're serious?" She flicked her eyes to the box's black interior. "Will we even be able to breathe in there?"

"Lamians always drill little holes into the sides of their coffins," I said. "So that their souls can escape. Ladies first."

Eshi didn't hesitate after that. She jammed the pack down at one end and slipped in over the side. I scrambled in after her, ripping the glowstone from my neck and hurling it out through the entrance arch.

Darkness swallowed us and I lay on my back within the empty sarcophagus, wedging myself between the hyenaling and the stone side. I reached up, feeling until I grasped the edge of the lid.

"On three," I said, as Eshi's hands found a place beside mine. "Two, three!"

We heaved, stone ground against stone and my muscles creaked. With our combined strength, we were able to slide the lid back into place above us, entombing ourselves in cold, dark stone.

Though the interior had been made to fit a lamian queen and her coiling tail, it was a little tight for both Eshi and me. We were, however, well used to this tangled sort of proximity by now. In those first few moments, we silently shifted and wiggled around each other to get as comfortable as we could. I ended up on my back while Eshi was on her side between my arm and torso. She rested her cheek onto my chest, slinging both an arm and a leg over me.

Then, we were still.

We waited for the dead to come, staying silent in the dark, our hearts pounding and chests heaving.

The mad, burning energy within me guttered and died. Suddenly, all the aches, pains, and fears that it had kept at bay came roaring back. I started to shake, suddenly cold, my exhausted chest laboring to rise and fall beneath the weight of Eshi's head.

She stiffened atop me, one fuzzy ear brushing against my chin as it twitched.

"They're here," she breathed.

I didn't answer, straining my senses. Soon, even my ears could pick up the shuffling steps of the desiccated war-dead. I heard the scuff of feet on stone, and the sliding crunch of sand and grit. My mind conjured up images of a shambling horde, a veritable flood of purple-eyed corpses pouring in to swirl around our stone prison.

My breath quickened. I was used to running from the dead or even fighting them with my sling. Though I'd hidden from guardians before, never had it been from so many. I screwed my eyes shut, reminding myself that these weren't true guardians. We were safe here. They were too stupid to pry open this coffin or even think to look into it.

But, blind to anything but my own overworked mind, I felt my panic rise.

Something scraped against the stone right outside, and my entire body locked itself into terrified rigidity. There came another hiss of flesh against stone, and it was all that I could do not to let out a whimper.

I could feel myself slipping away, my breath refusing to slow. So, I did the only thing I could and reached for something to hold on to.

I wrapped my arms around Eshi, squeezing her tightly to my chest. I anchored myself to her, pulling her body a little higher along mine so that I could press my face between her ears and into the top of her head.

Her entire body shook with suppressed emotions. She sank into my arms, digging her fingers into my flesh, snaking her leg between mine, and clinging to me as desperately as I clung to her.

Eshi was here.

I breathed her in, squeezing her tighter, lashing my mind to her. Her hair was soaked and slimy with dust and sweat. She smelled of sour exertion and movement, of femininity and life. The scent was powerful, but it was hers. And there, deep amongst the roots of her hair, I swore that I could smell the touch of the sun and the warmth of her laughter.

She was here, I told myself again, my heart starting to slow. Whatever happened, Eshi was here.

I wasn't alone.

Chapter Fourteen

Somehow, despite the dead periodically scratching at the sarcophagus, I managed to drift off into something resembling sleep. I awoke to Eshi shifting atop of me, feeling a lot better once I'd worked through the momentary flare of panic I'd felt waking up surrounded by cold stone and darkness.

"I think they're gone," the hyenaling murmured. "I haven't heard anything in a while."

She stretched and wiggled cramped limbs, her legs sliding over mine as she rolled more of her weight on top of me. I let out a soft groan, feeling the stiffness in my back and stretching out as best I could. The coffin was apparently quite deep because Eshi was able to prop her forearms on my chest and lift her head. My arms, I also realized, were still loosely wrapped around her.

And they fucking hurt.

"Don't," the hyenaling said, as I let my arms slip from around her. "Hug me."

"Can't," I gasped, clenching my fingers against the fire now chewing its way up my forearms. My damned circulation had been cut. "Hurts."

"Too bad," Eshi said. "You owe me for filling the tomb with undead. And for kissing me out of nowhere."

I winced. "Right, I'm sorry about—"

Eshi's palm slipped over my mouth, cutting me off. I felt the tickle of her hair as she leaned closer, and the warm swirl of her breath as her voice ghosted from the darkness above me.

"Just so that we're clear, if you're next words are 'I didn't mean to kiss you, it was a mistake,' I'm going to bite you."

I swore that I could almost see the gleam of her scavenger's fangs in the darkness and I smiled beneath her palm.

"No," I murmured, once she'd removed her hand. "I wasn't going to say that. But this really isn't the time, or place, to be talking."

"Any close enough to hear would have come over by now," Eshi countered. "And they're not as quiet as you think, I'll hear any getting close." She slid her body down mine a little, and I sensed her drop her head down to rest her chin atop her crossed forearms. "What were you going to say, then?"

"Well," I said. "I am sorry about the alarm. I also probably shouldn't have kissed you there."

The truth was that I hadn't been planning on doing it at all. What I'd said about her had been true, of course, I did find her incredibly beautiful.

But finding Marduss's tomb was hard enough without any other sort of complications. She was my partner in this, and I'd been hesitant to ever even act on that attraction.

Until, of course, I had.

Gods of fucking death, I'd kissed her in the middle of a tomb? What was wrong with me? I'd gotten carried away, swept away by crazy emotions and the roar of the skull alarm that had still been pounding through my veins. I'd kissed her.

Gods, why'd I kiss her in a fucking *tomb*!?

I didn't so much hear Eshi's low growl, as feel it rumble through my chest. "You regret it, then?"

"No," I answered, not even needing to think. "But I wish that I'd done it somewhere else."

"Hmm." Eshi relaxed, and then she pushed herself up a bit so that she could arch her back into a long stretch. The motion had the effect of grinding her body against mine, and I was suddenly reminded just how much she curved. "Your timing was terrible."

She settled back atop me, the open flaps of her robe falling on either side of my body. The skin of her stomach was warm through the thin linen of my tunic. I could feel the soft squish of her chest as well, and her waist ...

I lifted my arms, keeping them extended to slide my palms along the side of her muscled thighs.

"That's better," she breathed. "I like it when you touch me."

My heart beat faster at the throaty edge in her voice. I felt a stir between my legs as she shifted slightly and ground her navel along mine.

"Yeah." I cleared my throat softly, deciding that I needed a distraction. "I'm surprised that you'd even want to kiss me. Didn't I ruin your life?"

"I ruined my own life long before I met you," she said and I could hear her grimace.

"Your exile?"

She stiffened, and I cursed myself silently. Clan was life to a hyenaling, and for a moment, I worried that I'd pushed her too far. But I wanted to know everything about this woman and hard conversations, I'd always thought, were better had in the dark.

Finally, she let out a breath and sank back into me. "You knew?"

"I guessed," I admitted. "But I was pretty certain."

"Because I look like one?" Her voice was bitter. "That's it, right? I look like a dirty fucking exile who's all alone and hated by her family?"

"You look beautiful," I told her. "And I love it when you laugh."

Her fingers dug into my chest, and when she didn't respond, I raised my still-aching arms up to wrap her in a hug.

"Naroh," she said, her voice thick. "My clan threw me away, my sister... I'm all alone. How could you ever trust someone whose own family didn't want them?"

"I'm an exile too." Without thinking, I reached up and wove the fingers of one hand through the hair at the back of her head. I pulled her down to the crook of my neck and pressed my cheek into the top of her head. "And I've been alone for a long time. But since meeting you, I don't think that I want to be anymore."

Those words came from deep within me. They came out heavily, weighed down by the truth they bore.

"I'm really happy that you're here with me. You're keeping up, and I—I really hope that you keep diving with me."

"Really?" She asked, her voice smaller than I'd ever heard it. "You want me to stay?"

"We're both alone." I slid my hand down her back as she raised her head. "But maybe you can start your own clan someday. And until then... Maybe we can be alone, together?"

Eshi's palm slid along my cheek, and the next thing I knew, her lips were pressed against mine. The kiss was soft and salty with the taste of tears that I hadn't known she'd shed. I tried to pull away and ask her what was wrong, but she wouldn't let me. She made a small sound of protest and pressed herself harder against me.

And it was this kiss, long and slow, that made my entire being burn.

"Together," she eventually murmured, lying back on my chest. "I like that a lot."

We were silent for quite a while after that, filling the air of the sarcophagus with our breaths. My attention was focused inward, and Eshi's, I suspected, was pointed there as well.

The intensity of the emotions I was feeling surprised me. I hadn't even known Eshi for a month, and somehow, the fiercely beautiful hyenaling woman was in the process of radically changing my life.

The same fire burned within us, and she was quickly becoming so much more than just a partner. Her strength was incredible. She was smart and fierce, and shone like the sun even in so dark a place. She'd been right when she said that some battles were too big to fight on my own, and I felt, deep within my soul, that she was the one to fight them with me.

My throat tightened. I squeezed my arms around her, ignoring the painful stiffness of my limbs and the spot of wetness on my chest beneath her cheek.

I trusted her, I realized. I already trusted her with everything. Eshi had wormed her way into my heart as easily as she had wiggled into a place on the bench behind Asu's head.

And now that she was there, I didn't think I ever wanted her to leave.

Time passed, and eventually, Eshi stirred. She let out a long breath and shook herself out as best she could in the tight space before raising her head. "What do we do now? We can't stay in here forever."

"You could kiss me again?" I suggested, sliding my palms down the curving length of her body. "That seems like a good first step."

"Oh?" I could hear the smirk in her voice. "And how will that help?"

"I think better after kisses."

"Well," she said, her voice low and breathy. "In that case..."

She shifted back into place above me, pressing every curve and divot of herself into me as she slid her body along the length of mine. I let my hands rest on the swell of her hips, gripping her tightly as her nose brushed mine. I smelled sun and sweat and dust as her hair fell around me like a curtain.

Our lips touched, the kiss slow and deep. We each took the time to explore each other. Her tongue was teasing, darting forward to caress mine in quick, smoldering flicks of spiced heat that sent explosions of sparks showering through me. I pushed my entire body up against her, wrapping her tongue in mine and tasting all of her while I slid my hands down to her curving butt cheeks.

Eshi had a fantastic ass, firm and plump, shockingly soft where the rest of her was lean and hard. I squeezed, drawing a pleased sound from the hyenaling's throat. She wove the fingers of one hand into my hair, grinding herself harder against me and rolling her hips to push down on the hardness swelling between my legs.

I groaned softly, and her lips, still pressed against mine, curled into a smile.

"Better?" Eshi panted, pulling back. Her warm breath swirled over my face. "Or do you need another one?"

My breathing was as ragged as hers and my head spun with the fiery taste of her. It felt as if I'd downed an entire body of warm, spiced wine.

"I think," I eventually grated. "That another kiss like that would set me alight."

"Hmm." Eshi's cheek brushed mine as she brought her lips to my ear. "We'd better save it, then."

Gooseflesh erupted all over me. My fingers dug into the flesh of her ass, causing her to chuckle low in her throat. Her tail began to move in languid sweeps and she planted a slow kiss on my cheek after which she settled back onto my chest with a happy sigh. "Who knew being trapped in a coffin could be so much fun?"

That brought my focus back on the situation at hand, though it was still several minutes before the fire in my blood cooled enough that I could start thinking again. When I did once again start to consider our plight, the reality of our situation settled atop me like a shroud.

"We have to leave," I said, at last. The words were like shards of glass through my throat. "I hate to leave with nothing, but with the dead flooding the tomb, we don't have much of a choice."

Eshi was silent for a bit, sliding off me to lie on her side between my arm and torso. Her head remained on my chest, however, and one arm was slung across me, letting her fingers run absentmindedly up and down my arm.

"Where else can we go for clues?"

I let out a breath, lifting my head and thumping it back against the stone. "Ow. I don't know. Nabonassara I was Necrophant of Ikkad before he became pharon."

Eshi's ear brushed my chin as it twitched. "Just say 'Nabo,' it's so much easier."

I cracked a smile. "Never."

She sighed, still running her fingers up and down the bare flesh of my arm. It felt good, and though I'd been lying on cold stone for hours, her body had been keeping me warm.

"I thought all pharons were buried in the Valley of Kings, way to the south. Couldn't Nabo's tomb be there, somewhere?"

"We're not in the valley now," I pointed out. "That tradition only started about fifteen hundred years later, with the pharons of the Neferu

Dynasty. Even then, there aren't as many tombs in there as a lot of people think."

"But he could still be buried somewhere else?"

"It's possible," I admitted, lifting my arm to rub at my eyes. "But I don't think so. Everything I'd been able to find so far tells me that the Nabonassarans were pretty attached to the area. They built the most storklings here, and given that numbers three and four are buried up here, it seems very likely that Nabonassara I had his tomb built in the province as well."

"Isn't the Northern Province the biggest?"

"Yeah... Are you regretting your choice to come with me, yet?"

"No," she said, pausing the run of her fingers for a moment to squeeze my arm. "I'm in this for as long as it takes."

I'd been expecting a similar answer, but still, the lack of hesitation and matter-of-factness of her tone took me by surprise. I hugged her to me with the arm at her back, trying to swallow past the sudden lump in my throat.

"So," Eshi said, somehow wiggling closer to me. "We get out of this box, somehow get through the hordes of undead, and escape the tomb. We climb back up the cliff, get on Asu's back, and then what?"

"We go back to what I was doing, I guess. We go through villages and talk to people, we do jobs for small-time sifters who know the local region."

"We just wander around?"

"Basically," I sighed. "These tombs are so old that there really isn't any other way to do it. They aren't grand or well-known, so we kind of just have to hope that we stumble on something." I settled back, getting as comfortable as I could. "Anyway, we'll wait a few more hours to let the war-dead scatter through the tunnels a bit more before heading out. It's going to be a crawl to get out of here."

I expected the conversation to be over after that, but Eshi surprised me by asking another question. "Did you look in here when we first arrived?"

"Like when we were examining the chamber?" At her affirmative grunt, I continued. "I just checked to see if the body was in here. Why?"

I felt Eshi's cheek shift as she chewed the inside of it.

"This is probably nothing," she warned. "But when you dozed off earlier, I felt around with my hand, and—" She grabbed my hand, lifting it to the lid above us. She slid my palm along the cool stone, to the spot directly above my face. "Could this be a clue?"

Beneath my fingers, I felt the lines of what I thought were letters carved into the stone. Though, they were like nothing I had ever seen before.

"It could be, Eshi," I said, my heart beating faster. "It could be."

Chapter Fifteen

We crept around a corner, into a tunnel that was long and straight. I could see the glow of daylight at the end, and my shoulders sagged in relief. Finally, after an uncountable number of sleepless, stress-filled hours, we'd reached the exit.

Beside me, Eshi's pace quickened, but I reached out to grab her.

"Wait," I hissed, pulling us both to a stop. "Not yet."

"Naroh," she said, drawing my name out into something very near to a whine. "There aren't any undead or traps ahead. I want to get out."

"I know." I let go of her arm and used that hand to rub at my eyes, trying to dislodge and blink away some of the grit. "Gods of death, I know. But there's one last rule to tomb diving."

Eshi closed her eyes for a moment, her ears and head drooping. By the fading light of our final glowstone, I could see the same desperate exhaustion lining her face.

The journey back had been brutal. Corpses infested the tunnels, and the route to the outside world had been too long and too winding to risk the mad dash that had brought us back to the sarcophagus chamber. Any noise we made could draw the dead to us like flies and so we'd had to move at a slow, grinding crawl. We'd made detours and squeezed into out-of-the-way corners, alert for the undead silently shambling through the dark.

I shifted my weight towards Eshi, brushing my arm against hers. "We can rest here for a bit."

My whole being felt raw, my nerves stretched to the point of snapping from the unending tension. That was nothing, however, compared to how drained the hyenaling must be. She had been the key, more than I, in our escape. Her sharpened senses had been invaluable, and she'd spent every hour straining them to the absolute limit in order to pick up on movement in the dark and the scuffing step of the dead.

"No," she said, opening her eyes. She straightened. "I want to get out of here. What's this last rule?"

I shook my head. Gods, this woman was a wonder.

Her lip curled into a frown. "You're not going to tell me?"

I huffed out something that was just a bit too tired to be called a laugh. "Give me a second, I'm not as tough as you are."

Eshi snorted, watching me as I blinked my eyes rapidly and slapped my palms against my cheeks a few times.

"Alright. The last rule with tomb diving is that you never know who's waiting just outside to hit you over the head and take whatever treasure you managed to grab."

"We didn't grab any treasure," she pointed out.

"Yeah..." I started, trailing off for a moment before my tired mind finally latched onto an answer. "But we might have."

Her amber eyes shone in silent mirth, her tail swishing through the air in a handful of slow sweeps.

"But we might have," she conceded. "And I guess that it is easier to wait outside for some other idiot to go through all this than do it yourself."

"Or for a pair of idiots."

She cracked a small smile, and I smiled back, suddenly feeling a great deal better.

"Anyway," I continued. "Ambushers have to wait pretty close to the door, and if we move slowly and let our eyes properly adjust, we should be able to see them first."

In the end, the only thing waiting for us out in the open air of the canyon was a lone, dried-out corpse. It had stumbled out of the tomb and was shambling around the edge of the flowing Gibris. I shattered his skull from the doorway with a well-slung stone, and together, Eshi and I hurried down the coiling steps. It was late in the afternoon and the sun was hidden behind the rim of the canyon. We strode along the hissing river towards a patch of sunlight. We only had one pack, the other one abandoned, along with most of my diving gear, in a faraway tunnel. I let it fall to the ground before following Eshi as she stepped out of the cliff's shadow and into the light of the sun.

Spring had rolled over into summer in the days that we'd been beneath the earth, and the sun was hot. It hammered down onto my shoulders, but I didn't care. I closed my eyes, relishing the burning heat and the way the Gibris's burbling kept the silence from my ears. I soaked it all in, breathing in the dusty air, and finally felt the tomb's chill leech from my bones.

When I finally opened my eyes, I looked towards Eshi.

She was standing nearby with her eyes closed, having swept her grime-matted locks of speckled hair back from her face. Her robe was a puddle of cloth around her feet. The golden, dirt and sweat-streaked skin of her naked shoulders and stomach seemed to smolder in the light of the late afternoon sun. A small smile curled her lips as she tilted her face up to the light. Her tail slowly swept through the air behind her and her chest rose and fell beneath a loop of cloth made filthy by days spent below ground.

"Happy to be out of there?" I asked.

"Mmm," she agreed. Then, she lifted her arms in a long, luxurious stretch and I watched her muscles ripple beneath her skin. "You have no idea."

When she opened her eyes to meet mine, I saw something within them shift. There was a question in the fold of her ears, an uncertainty in the shape of her smile. Eshi looked unsure, as if what had taken place between us in the dark wouldn't survive a return to the light.

I, however, was well used to emerging from a tomb with something wonderful and new.

Eshi watched as I crossed the space between us, tilting her head back ever so slightly to hold my gaze as I came to a stop directly before her.

I smiled and reached for her. "How do you feel?"

Her belt was loose and her pants were riding low around her waist. And so, when my palms slid in just above her hips, it was onto warm flesh that they settled. The physical contact seemed to ease something within her and she took the final half step needed to press herself into me.

"Better," she murmured, snaking her arms around my neck. "Much better."

I shifted my grip along the tightness of her waist and stomach. "You're so warm."

"Hmm, the sun loves me."

"I can see why," I said, blinking at the sudden surge of emotion making my eyes prickle. "Even in the dark, you shone so bright."

Her eyes were two pools of liquid honey and the lines of her face were soft beneath her warm, freckled flesh. I pulled her to me and felt her arms tighten around me as our lips met in a long, sun-drenched kiss. I lost myself for a time, my mind drifting in a haze of Eshi's touch, taste, and the wild, powerfully feminine scent of her sweat.

"We need to wash," the hyenaling said when we eventually broke our kiss. Her ears flicked in amusement. "But at least you taste a bit better than you smell."

I grinned. "You're the one with her arms around my neck. Imagine how much I can smell, right now."

"Oh, so my smell does bother you?" She flashed me a wicked grin and shifted her body to grind her navel against my swelling hardness. A delighted flush bloomed high up her cheeks and made her amber eyes sparkle. "Are you sure?"

"Well," I adjusted my grip on her waist, keeping the curves of her body tight against me. "I never said that it bothered me."

Eshi laughed and I pressed another kiss onto her smiling lips. We stayed like that for several more moments. Although I wanted nothing more than to spend the rest of the day wrapped around Eshi, the sun was getting low and we still had quite a bit to do.

"Let's check on the rope," I said, reluctantly stepping away. "I'll make sure the pack is strapped and then we can wash up in the river before heading back up to Asu."

"I can't wait to get out of this." Eshi hooked a finger into her filthy chest wrap. "This thing is disgusting."

I also couldn't wait to see her get out of that, though I didn't say it aloud. I did, however, get the feeling that she noticed me surreptitiously adjusting myself as we walked the handful of paces back to the pack. She trailed her hand along my shoulders as I squatted down before it, then she continued on toward where we'd left the rope.

Before checking on the pack, however, I was hit with the overwhelming urge to do something else. I hesitated a moment, noticed that Eshi still had a little way to go, and reached into an inner pocket of my tunic. My fingers emerged clutching a folded-up piece of parchment, and I could finally examine the words the hyenaling had discovered in the light of day.

A line of script, carefully copied with a stick of charcoal, was what stared back at me. It had been the only thing carved into the sarcophagus's interior and was set directly above where the dead Pharona's head would have lain. And though I'd already examined it a dozen times by the light of a glowstone, it looked even more alien in the light of day.

The script flowed and twisted, whorled, and curled back on itself. I couldn't even be sure that this was even writing; there were no spaces to differentiate between words, and every letter was connected to the last. It put me in the mind of a swirling wind, or a sea of rolling dunes, and the whole of it seemed designed to draw my eye along its looping path.

It was like nothing I had ever seen and the sheer mystery of it set my heart racing. Was this some clue as I so desperately wished it could be? Or was it a prayer to some unknown god? Maybe it was some lost poetic masterpiece or the secret to whatever strange magic had suffused the tomb. Or, perhaps it even was—

"Naroh!" Eshi called. "Come here!"

I looked up to find her standing a few dozen paces away, just on the other side of the tomb's entrance. She was holding something, though it wasn't until I'd stuffed the parchment away and gotten closer that I realized what it was.

"Someone cut it," she said, showing me the severed end of our rope. The rest of it was at her feet in a lumpy pile. "We're stuck down here."

"Fuck," I said, not having the energy to do anything more than tilt my head up and glare up at the faraway ledge. "Fuck."

"This has to be that fucking elf's doing." Eshi let the bit of rope fall back to the rocky shore. "That slimy bastard is the only one who knew we were here."

"Kashir?" I said, sweeping a hand through my hair. "I don't know."

"He's Broken Mountain." The hyenaling's glare found me next. "And he hates us."

"Yeah, but—"

"We've been over this, Naroh! He's Broken Mountain and we're not. He thought about it some more and sent a gang of elves to cut our throats and rob us."

"Why didn't they just wait outside the entrance, then? Just cutting the rope doesn't make any sense."

"That doesn't fucking matter," she snarled. "They're coming after us, Naroh and if you can't see it, then you're an idiot."

"Whoa," I said, holding up my pants. "Don't get mad at me, Eshi. I'm just trying to figure this out."

"I'm not mad at you." She clenched her fists and her ears were stiff and upright. "I'm tired, hungry, dirty, and that fucking elf just cost me a chance at a change of clothes!"

"Yeah, I was really looking forward to another one of your stews." I blew out a breath, turning up to stare into the sky. We had a few hours before dark. "Well, with the dead stumbling out we can't spend the night so close to the tomb. We have to move."

Eshi let out a low growl, her eyes bright in their exhausted rings. She stomped forward and shoved her body into me. "Hug me," she demanded, "Like before."

The hyenaling was tight with anger and exhausted tension, her breath rapid. I stepped behind her and wrapped her in my arms, then I pushed my chin over her shoulder to press my cheek against hers. Immediately, her breathing slowed. This was how we'd whispered to each other in the grinding crawl to escape the tomb, and the contact had comforted us both in that endless darkness.

"The trail down here is supposed to be somewhere upriver," I murmured. "We'll head towards there for an hour or two and find somewhere safe to sleep."

Eshi pushed herself against me and folded her arms up to grip one of my forearms. Her cheek was warm against mine and her tail was a lump sandwiched between our bodies. "We'll go together?"

I frowned and squeezed her tighter. "Of course."

"Okay," Eshi said, letting out a long breath. What remained of her tension flowed out of her, her ears losing their stiffness as the rest of her body melted into mine. "Okay. I'm sure that Kashir's team will be waiting for us at that path, but you're right, we need to rest. We'll figure something else out in the morning."

"That's it," I said, pressing a kiss onto her cheek. "We have a plan."

I made to unwrap her and step away, but Eshi's grip tightened on my forearm, keeping me in place.

"Are you okay?" I asked, settling back into place.

"Can you..." She trailed off, ducking her head. Her cheek, still pressed against mine, blazed hotly. "Do you... can you kiss my neck?"

The embarrassed uncertainty in her voice and the sudden stiffness of her body told me that this was something important, even if I didn't understand why. Instead of arguing, however, I just bent my head and planted a gentle kiss on the crook of her neck.

A shudder ran through Eshi's body and her breath hitched. She dug her fingers into my forearms for a moment before she relaxed, and her tail started to wiggle against me. I loosened my grip on her and Eshi spun in the circle of my arms. She quickly brushed her lips against my neck before stepping away.

I arched my eyebrow but the hyenaling wouldn't meet my gaze. Her ears were folded back and her freckled cheeks were burning brightly. Her tail, however, didn't stop wagging.

We headed out a few minutes later, walking along the rocky ground between the canyon wall and the flowing Gibris. Our pace was slow, and we encountered a couple more war-dead in the first hour of our journey.

In the light of the sun, their purple-eyed forms were simultaneously more hideous and less threatening. They were so thin, their bodies little more than bones wrapped in papery flesh. Their movements were awkward and jerky, their hair falling in stringy clumps.

I brought each of them down with my sling, and we moved on.

The shadows had grown deep within the canyon depths when, beside me, Eshi suddenly froze. I stopped with her, following her gaze and the forward perk of her ears to the bend in the canyon ahead.

"I hear something," she said, after a handful of heartbeats. "It sounds like... singing?"

"Singing?" I asked, softly. "Are you sure?"

She nodded, not taking her eyes from the Gibris's bend. I saw her ears twitch, searching for every scrap of sound that made it past the river's burble. "A woman... I think."

"Just one?"

The hyenaling waited nearly a full minute before nodding again. I sighed, digging my thumb and forefinger into my eyes. Gods, there was always something.

Eshi touched my arm. "What do you want to do?"

I shook myself, forced my back straight, and held my arm out to her. "Should we go say hi?"

She gave me a tired smile and looped her arm in mine. We set out over the rocks and as we neared the bend in the canyon, I too started to hear the unseen singer.

The woman's song was wordless. It wrapped around us, flowing like the wind through moon-drenched dunes. It was beautiful, yet filled with such a yawning depth of emptiness that my chest ached to hear it. In my mind, I saw a hearth without a flame, a dream broken by time, and an empty sheet of parchment crumpled by a poet who had lost his muse.

I blinked away tears I hadn't felt come while, beside me, Eshi's pace slowed. We took the final few steps in a sort of hypnotized haze, enveloped in the notes of a song neither of us had the words to describe.

When we rounded the bend, we stopped to stare at the scene before us.

The singer was an elf, a young woman whose skin was the color of the desert beneath a morning sun. We saw her in profile, her face and song turned towards the river. She wore a sturdy-looking robe of gray cloth with a strip of bright red cloth cinched just above the swell of her hips. A scarf of the same color covered her hair, and in her hand, she held a long stave.

And surrounding her, was a crowd of at least two-dozen war-dead.

My heart lurched in my chest, and I felt Eshi's grip tighten on my arms. I was about to shout a warning when my exhaustion and music-fogged mind registered something important. The dead weren't attacking. They were gathered around her, swaying on their feet as if... listening to her sing.

I blinked. She was a—

"Spellsinger," Eshi hissed. "Naroh, the elf's a magic user!"

The art of singing magic into being was a uniquely elven gift. It was a power that was much more subtle than lamian necromancy, having more to do with the practical elements of nature and illusions than anything else. As far as I understood it, the spellsinger was not the actual source of the magic. Rather, their song was meant to speak to the spirits of the land; to the djinn, efreet, and nyads, and entreat their aid.

As with glowstones, the name, I'd always thought, was somewhat misleading.

Now that I was actually looking for it, I noticed an odd sort of shimmer dancing over the middle of the river. It was towards this that everyone faced. The glow twisted and swirled, swayed and waltzed, with every note of the elf's song.

"We have to go," the hyenaling said. "Kashir probably sent her to find us."

"I'm not sure," I said, resisting her insistent tug on my arm. "I've met one or two spellsingers before and they always show up in weird places. She's probably here to try and talk with the Gibris."

"The river?"

I shrugged. "It's supposed to be one of the greater spirits."

"All that," Eshi yanked hard enough on my arm to draw me back, "Means dangerous. Let's go."

Then, before either of us could turn away, we saw the undead start to move. A dead hyenaling took a jerking step toward the river. Its burning eyes were turned upward, lost in the whirling dance of whatever spirit the elven woman sang to. It didn't even seem to notice the moment it stepped into the water, continuing to wade forward, its focus never shifting.

Within moments, the fast-moving current had torn it from its feet and swept it away.

Over the next few minutes, Eshi and I watched every other walking corpse step into the water and be pulled away. The Gibris was one of the empire's great rivers, and in this canyon, the waters crashed through rocks, careened into walls, and tumbled off high ledges. The war-dead would be smashed to pieces long before the river slowed into the wide, life-giving channel it was around the Ashuran heartland.

When the last corpse disappeared, the elf fell silent. She bowed her head towards the bright shimmer and then cocked her head to the side. She turned to face us in the next moment, her face splitting into a wide smile as her eyes took us in.

"Hi, there!" Her voice was high and melodic and she waved at us with one hand. "You're Naroh the tomb diver, right? My Uncle Kashir has told me so much about you!"

Beside me, Eshi drew her knives.

Chapter Sixteen

THE SPELLSINGER'S NAME, IT turned out, was Amna.

That was something that we only learned some time into our encounter with her. She might have mentioned it before, but I was busy trying to keep Eshi from sticking a knife into her belly, so I couldn't be sure.

Whatever enmity Kashir had for us would only worsen if we stabbed his niece.

Except, it turned out, that the two elves were more distantly related than what we'd been led to believe.

"He's not actually my uncle," Amna said, once I'd gotten Eshi somewhat calmed down. "He's my mother's cousin, but we've always just called him uncle. And I know he's a bit stiff, but why would he want to rob you?!"

The elf was only a handful of paces from us now, one end of her stave planted in the rocky ground. Night was falling in the canyon, and though it was getting dark, there was still enough light that I could get a proper look at the strange elf.

She was of a height with Eshi, her body full where the hyenaling's was lean. The robe she wore, though obviously utilitarian, fit her well. It hugged her tightly, accentuating her curving chest and the wide swell of her hips. Her crimson headscarf was long and loose. It covered her like a hood, the cloth hiding her pointed ears and pooling around her shoulders and neck. A few curls of black hair emerged to tumble around a face whose sun-darkened skin glowed with the day's final heat.

And her eyes, dark as the richest ebony, were made wide by a mix of bafflement and incredulity.

"Because he's a bastard," Eshi growled. Her ears were stiff and though I'd managed to get her to sheathe one knife, she held the other blade low and ready. "And you're Broken Mountain just like he is. You cut our rope and now that we've actually found something you—"

She clicked her teeth shut, red flaring beneath her cheeks. I winced at Amna's loud, delighted gasp.

"You found something in the Nabonassaran tomb!?" The elf's smile was bright with sudden excitement. "What was it? Uncle Kashir was sure that it had been picked clean!"

Eshi gave me an apologetic stare but I didn't have the energy to muster any sort of anger toward her. She was beyond exhausted, and expecting any sort of subtlety from her was unfair.

With that in mind, I looped my arm around hers, holding her before she could do anything rash.

"We didn't find anything." I might not want this elf dead, but I certainly wasn't going to share our clue with someone I'd just met. "Just some old history."

"But that's the best part!" Amna's smile split into a wide grin. "Was there anything about the Basri Revolt?"

"The Basri Revolt..." I blinked at her. "Wait, are you talking about that elven slave revolt? How did you know about that?"

"How could I not?" The elf said. "The lamians slaughtered thousands of my people that summer, but it's what kicked off the next three centuries of resistance leading up to the Dyers Revolution."

"And then to the abolishment of slavery," I said. "Sure. But how did you even know about that? I've never seen it written anywhere before."

"So there is something about it there!" The elf crowed. "Uncle Kashir will be so excited! What did you learn? Ishran's account from that time is so spotty."

I gaped at her. Ishran was an elven terrorist, or hero, active during the reign of Nictossis I, the pharon who had succeeded Nabonassara IV. He was widely considered to have been the elf who kicked off the first, and bloodiest, century of the elven uprisings. His life and deeds were the stuff of legend, and the Broken Mountain had long ago enshrined him as a saint of their order. It had been he, they said, who had once again taught the lamians to fear the symbol of the notched triangle.

"You read an account of Ishran's life!" I nearly shouted. Eshi hissed as I tightened my grip on her. "Where!? I didn't even know that any existed!"

This had been a chaotic era of the empire's history, and not a lot of contemporary sources had survived. There were a ton of stories about the elf, but I'd never actually been able to find anything that was truly verifiable.

"My uncle has one," Amna said. "It was written by Ishran's wife's cousin. He was a child in Basri when the lamians burned it down. I wish there was more written on it, but the account mostly focuses on the years after the assassination of Sargon's grand vizier."

"Kashir has one?" I felt my shoulders slump and turned pleading eyes back to Eshi. "You still have some of that silverware, right? Maybe if we give it back he'll let me read it."

"That was you?!" Amna said. "Emran was tearing through the house looking for that."

This time, I was the one to shift uncomfortably beneath Eshi's glare. After a moment, the elf's smile faded. Her eyes seemed to take us in for the first time, noting the bloodshot depth of our gazes, our haggard, filthy appearance, and the way Eshi and I seemed to be holding each other up.

"Look," she said. "Whatever you think, I'm not here to attack you, or rob you, or anything like that. The truth is, I want to dive the tomb myself. I was excited to see you because I thought you could help."

Eshi snorted. "We're not going back in there, especially now that Naroh let all those corpses out."

"You let those out, too?" Amna said. "My uncle spoke as if you were a great diver, but I suppose even the experienced can make mistakes."

"His reputation is very exaggerated." Eshi let out a breath and finally sheathed her second knife. She rested her palm on my tangled forearm.

"He tripped over his own feet, and suddenly the dead were pouring from the walls."

"I should have left you down there," I grumbled, trying to pull my arm from around hers. Her grip instantly tightened and something like a growl rumbled from her. The hyenaling narrowed her eyes, daring me to keep trying to free myself. "Anyway, Eshi's forgetting about the weird magic or the fact that I then saved her ungrateful life."

"Weird magic? What did you—" Amna interrupted herself with a quick shake of her head. "No, sorry, you're both obviously exhausted. I'm not asking you to go back into the tomb with me, just to answer a few questions. I'm camped on a sandbar not far away, and I'll make you a hot supper and give you a safe place to sleep in exchange."

The hyenaling and I exchanged a glance. A warm meal sounded heavenly, and I could see that Eshi's natural wariness was also crumbling beneath the hollow weight of her stomach.

"Are you a good cook?" I asked the elf.

Amna lifted her hand to tuck a few loose strands of hair back behind her scarf. Then, I saw a sparkle come into the dark depths of her eyes, and she gave me the sort of smile that might have stopped my heart.

"You'll have to come with me to find out."

She was, it turned out, an excellent cook.

Barely an hour after Eshi and I had collapsed into the sandy ground of her camp, the elf had gathered an armful of driftwood, brought a small fire to life, and had a pot of water boiling. Ingredients started flying in not long after, and soon, the air was filled with the scent of the bubbling soup. We were digging into our meal not long after that. I don't remember exactly what it was we ate, but it was hot, filling, and delicious. I sat up a bit straighter once I'd finished, feeling a warm tingle of energy curling through me.

The meal seemed to have the opposite effect on Eshi, however. She lay her head on my shoulder almost before she finished, leaning heavily against me and struggling to keep her eyes open.

"Go to sleep," I told her, taking a moment to press my cheek to the top of her head. "I'll talk with Amna."

The elf had pushed herself to her feet as soon as we'd finished eating, taking the dirty pot and bowls beyond the firelight and to the edge of the water. She was scrubbing each with a handful of sand, the sound of her humming reaching me over the burbling hiss of the Gibris.

"I don't want to sleep alone," Eshi murmured, her voice thick with exhaustion. "What if you're gone when I wake up?"

"I'll be here," I said, softly. I lifted an arm to wrap it around her shoulders. "Go to sleep."

"Too risky." She snuggled closer to me with a sigh. "You might leave."

"Here," I said, ignoring her mewl of protest as I untangled myself from her. "Give me a second."

I'd put my usual robe on over my diver's tunic before we'd started our journey away from the tomb. I slid it out of it as Eshi watched and spread it out on the sand behind her.

"There," I said, settling back beside her and giving her a quick grin. "If you sleep on that, I'll have to wake you up before I leave."

Eshi's eyes were little more than thin, heavy-lidded slits. Yet, I still saw a light shift within them as her lips curled up into a tired smile.

"Okay." She lay back, stretching out over my open robe. "You'll sleep beside me?"

"I promise."

"Good." She curled up on her side and closed her eyes. Her fingers dug into my robe, pulling a section of it to her chest a moment later. She let out a long breath, her voice coming out as little more than a murmur. "Smells good."

Then, before the next breath escaped her, she was asleep.

I smiled down at her for a time, watching the fire's warm shadows flicker and dance over her sleeping form. Then, I leaned back against my palms and stared up into the open sky. Night had well and truly fallen, and I could see bright points of light twinkling far above us. The stars were beautiful tonight, as they always were after days spent below the earth.

"I'm going to make tea," Amna said, returning to set her pot back over the fire. "Would you like some?"

"Please."

The elf gave me a small smile and settled down on the opposite side of the fire. She pulled over her large leather pack, rooting through it with practiced ease. That wordless hum started to flow from her once again, filling the space around us with the gentle depth of her voice.

Amna was only the third elven spellsinger I had ever met. The talent was rare, I'd been told, especially amongst the elves who spent their lives in the hubbub of the larger cities. The two I'd previously met had been very different, but they'd each had this sort of... ethereal quality. It was as if they were turned towards a world that was only half there.

I could see that same quality in Amna, wrapped as she was in the fire's gentle glow and the notes of her song. Her eyes were warm, dark pools. Her lips were full and her small smile was made brighter by the red scarf tumbling around the smooth, burnished flesh of her face.

She shone, beautiful in a way I didn't have the words for.

"That song," I said, accepting the small cup of tea she handed me. It was hot and smelled powerfully sweet. "Is it the same song you were singing to the dead?"

"No," she said, settling back onto the sand with her own cup. "This song is the one my grandfather used to hum when we traveled. It's just a silly little thing."

"And the other one isn't?"

"It is not." She tilted her head to stare out into the darkness beyond me. "That is a song about the deepest sort of loss. I don't like to sing it."

"But the spirits do?" I asked, bringing the cup of tea to my lips.

Her lips curled into a sad smile and her dark eyes refocused on me after a long heartbeat. "There is only one spirit who likes it when I sing that song, despite the pain it causes him."

"That shimmer we saw over the river? The one that all the war-dead were staring at. That was it?"

"Him," Amna corrected. "Ko is a *djinn*. He is a spirit of the deep desert, one of light, air, and fire." She paused for a moment to take a sip of her tea, following it with a long breath. "But yes, that was him you saw."

"Djinn are tricksters, right?" I said. "Illusionists and... mirage-makers?"

"They are, although, I don't think 'mirage-maker' is a term."

"But is that what he did? Did he bewitch the undead? Did your song give him the power to trick them into destroying themselves?"

The elf arched one dark eyebrow. "Weren't you supposed to be answering *my* questions?"

I blinked, then gave her a sheepish smile. "Yeah, sorry. You're the first spellsinger I've met who's interested in talking. I'm curious."

"Oh, don't worry." She reached up to tuck a loose curl of hair behind her scarf. "I like curiosity. But how about this; I'll answer your questions once you're done telling me about the tomb."

"Or we could do one for one?" I suggested. "I answer one of your questions and then you answer one of mine."

Amna's lips quirked upward. "That wasn't the deal."

"I'm curious," I said, with a deliberate shrug. "And you're fascinating."

The elf's smile widened. "Well, alright, but we'll do five to one."

"As in I get the five?"

Amna didn't even bother to answer, simply raising her cup back to her smiling lips to take another sip of tea.

"Fine," I said, settling myself a bit more comfortably. "What do you want to know? I'm guessing that Kashir told you quite a bit before sending you out here."

"Well," she said, drawing out the word. "Not exactly."

I frowned. "What do you mean?"

She shifted, looking a bit uncomfortable. "My uncle doesn't know that I'm out here. Well, he probably does by now, but I left without telling anyone."

"But you knew my name. You knew who I was, what I was doing here and you're here to dive a tomb."

"Well," Amna said again, giving me a sheepish smile of her own. "That's a bit of a story."

I raised my eyebrow, staring at her until she shifted and let out another sigh. "Fine. But this counts towards your first three questions."

I smirked, and Amna took a last sip of tea before continuing.

"I'm from a family of caravaners, though we don't trade much in the summer. My sister and I like to spend the season with Uncle Kashir in Ikkad, while the rest of my family prefers to be outside the city. We got to his house not long after you and Eshi left, and the whole place was in an uproar. What I heard made me... curious."

Light danced within her eyes, and I smiled at her use of the word.

"You seem to know your history," I said. "I'm guessing you learned that from him?"

She nodded. "My uncle knows more about elven history than anyone I'd ever met. He would travel with us at times when I was younger, and at night, around the fire, he would tell us the most amazing stories about our history. I used to sit beside him for hours as we traveled and fill his ears with questions."

"That's nice," I said. "Nobody in my town knew anything beyond the basics. I had to climb in through the vizier's library window on nights when he was out drinking."

"Wow. You were certainly determined."

"No," I corrected. "I was curious."

The elf laughed, the sound flowing out of her bubbly and bright. I grinned back at her and took a moment to flick my eyes down to where Eshi slept. She hadn't so much as stirred.

"Curiosity really does motivate you," she said, dark eyes shining with mirth. "Is that why you became a tomb diver?"

"The vizier only had four different books," I said. "Diving was a much better way to learn."

"What were the books?"

"They were all from Chronicler Jimbe."

"Oh," Amna winced. "My sympathies."

"Yeah..."

"Well," the elf continued. "Lucky for me, my uncle has a much better library. I'd torn through his entire collection before my twelfth summer.

I started on the artifacts after that, and the days his diving teams returned started to feel like birthdays."

I cocked my head to the side. "You know Kashir is a sifter?"

"Of course." Amna gave me a wry smile. "Do I look that inexperienced?"

"You don't look like any other diver I've met."

"This will be my first dive," she admitted. "What gave it away?"

"Your excitement," I said. Then, I nodded to her pack, "And you don't have enough rope."

She followed my gaze. "Really? I have four coils of it."

"For this tomb, you'll be fine with that, but if you're going to keep doing this, you'll need to start bringing three times that." I hesitated a moment, flexing my fingers as I briefly wondered if there was a more diplomatic way of saying this. Then, I gave up and just plowed ahead. "Why do you want to do this? If you know Kashir is a sifter, you must know how dangerous diving is. Most of us don't survive our first tomb."

"I know," she said, letting out a breath. "But when I saw that artifact that you brought my uncle, I knew that I couldn't wait. Marduss in a headscarf... I have to know what it means."

I nodded, swallowing whatever objections I had. I could see it in her dark eyes, the flicker of a flame that matched my own. Trying to dissuade her would be a waste of breath.

"Yeah," I said, instead. "Me too."

We looked across the fire at one another for several long moments. She smiled and I could see the light of understanding in the depths of her eyes. Amna was like very few people I had ever met and, despite the circumstances of our meeting, I found that I was starting to like her quite a bit.

"Did you cut our rope?"

She blinked. "Your rope? Ah, Eshi said something about that, didn't she?"

"Yeah. We climbed down to the tomb from the top of the cliff, and we left the rope there to climb back out when we were done. But when we got out today..."

"…the rope was gone," Amna finished. "And now you're headed for the path."

"Someone cut it at the top," I confirmed, keeping my gaze on her. "Eshi thinks Kashir regrets telling us about this tomb and sent a team after us."

Amna frowned, though she had no trouble holding my stare. "Why does she think that?"

"Because we're not elves." I ran a hand through my hair and leaned back. "Something like this… this connection between Marduss and the elves; I know your uncle and I know that this is the sort of discovery he'd want for himself."

"You might be right," she admitted after a few moments. "But my uncle isn't the sort to send people to, what, kill and steal from you? He's not that sort of elf."

"He's Broken Mountain."

Amna's shifted, her expression growing uncomfortable. "He… believes in a lot of the same ideas they do. But he also believes that the Broken Mountain should return to what it was before Ramesh the Great wiped them out. My uncle's not a criminal, well, not a violent one, at least."

"And do you? Believe in the same ideas, I mean?"

"I believe that my people have a right to know the truth about their history," Amna said. "But as for everything else… I can see why a lot of elves are angry, but I'm not."

"So you didn't cut our rope? And you're not Broken Mountain?"

"No," she answered, "to both those questions."

And I believed her. Whether it was because of her beauty, the way she spoke, or the kinship I had felt starting to grow between us, I decided that in this, at least, I could trust her.

"Well," I said, finally taking another sip of tea. "I'm still curious about how you knew my name and how to get here."

"I listened to him talk about you with someone from outside his office door," she said. "Then, I snuck in to look at the artifact in the middle of the night."

I laughed. "For the richest sifter in the northern half of the empire, your uncle has terrible security."

"Lucky for both of us." Amna grinned, and much of the tension left her face. "Now, by my count, you owe me about twenty questions."

"Fair enough," I agreed, then drained my cup. "What do you want to know?"

Amna and I spoke until the fire was no more than a pile of glowing embers between us. By then, I could barely keep my eyes open, and the answers I gave her were growing increasingly nonsensical.

We decided to bid each other goodnight, and I let myself flop back onto my open robe. While sleeping on sand without a bedroll was not the most comfortable thing, it sure as hell beat lying on naked stone.

I tucked myself in beside Eshi and was asleep in only a few moments.

I woke up on my side, stiff and sore, groaning at the light seeping in through my eyelids. Our camp was set in a shadowy part of the canyon, almost right against the rocky wall. But even this indirect sunlight was a lot for eyes that had gotten used to waking up in the pitch darkness.

I shifted, stretched, and felt a sudden prickle crawling beneath the skin of my face. I slid an arm up to scratch and rub at my still-closed eyes, but stopped when I found them both wrapped around a warm body.

It stirred and I heard a sleepy little exhalation. I blinked my eyes open to find Eshi snuggled up against me, her back pressed against my chest and much of my face buried in a cloud of her bright, speckled hair. I don't remember hugging her last night, but she'd somehow wormed her way into the circle of my arms. She'd evidently woken long enough to slip out of her robe to drape it over the two of us, and the flesh of her bare shoulders and back was warm and a bit sticky in the rising heat of the early morning.

It was, I decided, a fantastic way to wake up.

I stretched, finding her legs thoroughly tangled around my own. Flexing my arms, I pulled her closer, squeezing her tightly to me and breathing deeply of the wild, sun-drenched scent of her body.

Eshi let out a pleased little hum, her tail twitching. She stretched long and slow, the entire length of her body shifting along mine. That was when I noticed that it wasn't only my back muscles that were stiff. Eshi's rear was folded into my waist, my morning hardness pushing against the pillow-soft curve of her ass.

What drowsiness I had was quickly lost beneath the rising beat of my heart. I tried to shift back before she noticed, but Eshi wasn't having it.

"Where are you going?" She murmured, pushing her hips back against me. "You promised to... ah." That last word was a breath swirling through parted lips.

"Sorry." Heat seared my cheeks. I loosened my grip on her to shift my erection away. "It's morning, and I—"

Instead of pulling away, the hyenaling moved with me. She slid her ass in, arching her back to slot herself into place over my crotch.

"Sorry?" She purred, her voice low and breathy. "Why are you sorry?"

My heart was pounding in my chest, my throat going dry. "I... I don't know."

"Hmm." Eshi wiggled in the tight circle of my arms, rubbing her ass up and down my stiffened manhood. "This feels a bit painful."

I groaned, pushing my hips into her. My manhood was a bar of iron between my legs, hard and locked upright. Even separated by both my pants and hers, I could feel so much of the tender firmness of Eshi's ass.

"Am I making you uncomfortable?" I could hear the smile curling her lips. "Should I go?"

She adjusted herself just so, enough that my bulging hardness slipped between her ass cheeks. I had one arm wrapped around her stomach and the other supported her neck. She laughed low in her throat, folding one arm back to weave her fingers into my hair. Her other hand gripped one of my forearms. I felt her nails dig into my flesh and her stomach ripple as her hips started to roll.

"Stay," I grated.

My blood coursed through me, filling my ears. I pushed my hips into hers, moving with the rhythm of her warm, leanly curved body.

"Hmm." Eshi's grip tightened in my hair. I barely felt the tickle of her hair as I pressed my forehead tight against her skull, my spinning with the sour, feminine reek of her sun-dried sweat. "You sure?"

"Gods, Eshi," I groaned, my aching cock squished between her two firm mounds of soft flesh. "Yes"

The hyenaling's breath came faster as she ground herself harder against me. She pushed my forearm up the sweat-slickened length of her stomach and freed my hand from where it gripped the underside of her flank. Her palm slipped over mine, guiding my hand up to the bound swell of her chest.

Her breath hitched as I dug my fingers into the cloth of her wrap. I squeezed, marveling at the sinful softness of her flesh. Eshi pressed down on my hand and a moan slipped from her lips as I massaged one breast.

Then, there was a loud clatter of stones, and the hyenaling and I both froze. Our paralysis lasted only a heartbeat, and we were both sitting up even as we heard another grinding shift of rock.

"Ah," Amna said, looking up from where she'd been approaching from the river. "You're both awake!"

The elf's smile was sunny, the morning light making the red of her headscarf bright and vivid. If she noticed our flushed faces and rapid breathing, she did not comment.

"I was just about to get going," she continued, moving to crouch by her pack. "I'm happy I didn't have to decide whether to wake you up or not."

"Yeah," I said. "I—uh, yeah."

I coughed, shifting my legs, happy that Eshi's robe was still covering my waist. I swept my hand through my hair, trying to calm my racing heart.

Beside me, there wasn't a shred of embarrassment on the hyenaling's face. Instead, Eshi's cheeks seemed to be flushed more with anger than anything else. She pushed herself to her feet, her amber eyes glaring frustrated daggers at the elf.

"I'm going to bathe," she said, digging through our pack and coming out with a single bar of soap. "Try not to die, elf."

With that, she ripped her robe off my waist and stomped towards the river.

"It was nice to meet you!" Amna called after her, turning back to me when the hyenaling didn't answer. "I don't think that she likes me very much."

"I wouldn't worry about it," I said. "She tried to stick a knife in me the first time we met."

"Now that is a story I wish that I had time to hear."

I laughed and pushed myself to my feet. I was still tired, though the hours of undisturbed sleep and the... *wake-up*, had done wonders. I felt great, and I took the time to shake my own robe free of sand before slinging it over my shoulders.

"I forgot to ask you last night," I said, moving to join Amna by her pack. "Will your *djinn* follow you underground? There are still a lot of war-dead in there."

"Ko's not a pet," she chided, straightening from her crouch. "It is his choice whether or not he answers my call."

"Sorry, sorry," I said, holding out my hands. "I'm just worried."

"Worried? We're strangers, Naroh."

I shrugged. "Sure, but you're not the usual sort of diver I meet. It would be a shame if your career ended before you discovered something."

"Well, you shouldn't worry," Amna said, bending at the waist and reaching for her pack. And because the blood hadn't entirely left my crotch, my eyes darted to the slice of her cleavage to stare into the shadowy crevice between her two large breasts. "If there's an obelisk in the sarcophagus chamber, as you say, there will be a few spirits around to help me."

I tore my gaze from her chest as she lifted the pack to her shoulders, and flushed at the knowing sparkle in her eyes.

"Good," I said, clearing my throat. "I—wait, obelisks?"

Obelisks could be found throughout the empire. The pyramid-topped pillars of stone were used for everything from marking the center of villages, decorating the entrances of crypts and palaces, and guiding wanderers through the desert. They were everywhere, and though the lamians had been building them for millennia, not many knew that the tradition was actually elven.

I'd been told that it had arisen in the ages before the elves had found their Ashur. Back when they had lived on the backs of carrier beetles in the vast, featureless ocean of sand that was the Great Desert. They'd been nomads and had erected obelisks at important gathering points such as natural shelters, oases, and hunting grounds.

And though they were but stone, there were stories, legends, and whispers that they might actually be more.

"Do obelisks actually draw spirits?"

"Oh yes," Amna said, shifting beneath her pack's heavy straps. "But drawing them to a place, and keeping them there are two very different things."

"I… don't know what that means." I had about a thousand more questions buzzing through my head, but I could see that she was anxious to get going. "Do you remember the traps I told you about last night?"

"Yes, yes," she smiled. "I'll be fine."

I liked Amna, and our conversation the night before had been more than pleasant. The elf was fascinating; beautiful, mysterious, wickedly smart, and with a knowledge of history that very few possessed. I had meant it when I said that I would be sad if something happened to her, and though I'd told her a lot about the Nabonassaran tomb, I hadn't said anything about the strange words carved inside the lid.

She was my competition, after all.

"You know," she said, pushing that stray curl of dark hair back beneath her scarf. "After everything I've heard about you; you're nothing like I expected."

I smiled wryly. "I hope that's a good thing."

"It is." She bit her lip and hesitated a moment before darting in to plant a kiss on my cheek. "Thank you for all your help. Maybe we'll meet outside another tomb, someday."

"Yeah," I said, resisting the urge to rub at the warmth the touch of her lips had left behind. "If this one doesn't satisfy your curiosity, that is."

"I'm curious about a lot of things." Light danced in Amna's eyes, and a splash of red bloomed high on her cheeks. "And I'm a hard woman to satisfy."

"Well," I said, my throat suddenly dry. "I'm sure that we'll see each other again, one day."

"I hope so," she said. "Goodbye, Naroh. Stay curious."

With that and a last little wave, Amna turned and stepped out into the sun and towards the entrance of the tomb. She left a faint cloud of floral sweetness in her wake. I watched her until she disappeared around a bend in the canyon, a part of me feeling inexplicably empty now that this stranger was gone.

I suddenly hoped that she'd find those words beneath the lid and that she would step onto the path to Marduss's tomb. Perhaps she'd discover something that Eshi and I had missed and would already be there when we figured out our next clue.

I would like that, I decided, if only to see her again.

Chapter Seventeen

Breakfast this morning was more of our dried provisions.

I stared rather dejectedly at the strip of dried meat in my hands before popping it in my mouth. I chewed on the tough, flavorless hunk, thinking about all the extra supplies we'd left outside the canyon. Asu should be there by now, and as soon as we got back, I would ask Eshi to make that stew again.

The hyenaling still hadn't returned from bathing by the time I finished a second piece of meat. We only had one bar of soap, so I lay back in the sand with my head on our pack to await my turn. I stared up into the endless blue of the morning sky, not feeling particularly rushed. Amna had said that the path up the cliff was only a handful of miles upriver and that she hadn't seen signs of anyone else when she'd come down it the day before.

We'd have no problem making it there today, so, I relaxed and let my thoughts wander.

This clue, an unknown, weirdly looping script, hadn't been what I'd been hoping to find in the depths of the Nabonassaran tomb. I had no idea what it could mean and only the vaguest notion of who in the empire might even recognize it. Deciphering it would likely take months of work, if it was possible at all, and I had no guarantees that whatever it said would even be helpful. This might all be a huge waste of time.

And yet, I thought, grinning to myself, it might not be.

Then, I heard the rocky clatter of approaching footsteps. I sat up to see Eshi step into the shade of our little sandbar. She was clean; her flesh scrubbed free of dust and sweat. It glowed a healthy pink, and the shining beads of moisture that remained accentuated the slopes and ripples of her body. Her speckled hair was dark and damp and water dripped from the thick mane to soak her robe. She carried her belt slung over one shoulder, causing her pants to ride low on her waist. The thin linen clung wetly to the shape of her thighs, letting me see her muscles flex and ripple.

It looked like Eshi hadn't taken the time to dry herself. Neither, it seemed, had she remembered to bind her breasts.

I blinked as, through her open robe, her chest wrap was nowhere to be seen. Her breasts, so much rounder and fuller than I had imagined, quivered delightfully with every one of her swaying steps. The skin was paler than the sun-drenched gold of the rest of her, and though both edges of her robe kept her nipples hidden, I could still see so much of their naked shape.

"The elf's gone, then?" she asked, stopping not far from me. "I guess that you couldn't talk her out of diving the tomb last night?"

"I—uh, yeah. No."

The hyenaling flicked her ears and arched an eyebrow. "Which is it?"

"No," I said, clearing my throat. "It's no. She's gone."

Eshi made a little noise in her throat and turned her head to look in the direction Amna had gone. "You know, I looked through her stuff while you were all asleep."

"She's not Broken Mountain, Eshi," I said, getting to my feet. "She wasn't hunting us."

"I think you're right." The hyenaling was still staring down the canyon. "She looks like she can handle herself. Hopefully, she doesn't die in there."

"Yeah, I liked her too... Eshi?"

"Mmm?" She looked back at me and cocked her head to the side. Her expression was one of innocent curiosity, though I could see her tail swishing through the air behind her. "What's wrong, Naroh?"

"You—uh, you didn't put your chest wrap on."

"Of course I didn't." Her face twisted into a grimace. "You saw how disgusting it was, right? I washed it and left it in the sun."

My heart drummed against my ribcage. "That makes sense."

"I think so too." She glanced down at herself and a small shift of her hips was enough to pull her robe open a hairsbreadth wider. "Besides, I'm so much more comfortable like this."

Red heat bloomed beneath the pale flesh of her chest as my eyes followed hers down the near-naked length of her body. The pounding of my blood was making it difficult to think and it was like ten thousand sparks were cascading through me, making my chest and limbs tingle.

"Yeah," I said. "But your pants... They're a little dirty too, aren't they?"

Eshi's face, when I glanced back at it, was splashed by a scarlet flush. Her eyes were sharp, alight with a smoldering heat, while her lips curled into a languid smile.

"Oh?" She slipped two of her fingers into the top of her pants and pulled at the fabric. "Should I also leave these somewhere, then?"

"Well..." I stepped up to her, sliding my palms along the warm, wet flesh of her waist. "You want to be clean, right?"

"Mmm," she purred, running her palms up my forearms. "That's a good point."

Eshi leaned into me as I pulled her hips into mine. She smelled fresh, like water on a sun-warmed rock. Her chest pressed against mine and I felt the brush of her nose a heartbeat before her lips found my own. The kiss was long and slow and when we parted, my head was spinning with the spiced heat of her tongue.

"I'll think about it." Her grip on my arms tightened and her breath, warm with the heat staining her breasts, swirled over my lips. "While you go and wash."

Then, before I could react, she gave me a little nip on the chin and spun out of my grip.

I blinked. My hands hung in the air, frozen in the place Eshi's hips had been. My mind spun and stuttered and the hyenaling's smile widened into a wicked grin. I blinked again and she burst into a stream of high, cackling laughter.

"That wasn't nice," I grumbled, letting my arms fall. "You could have just given me the soap."

"Poor, Naroh," Eshi teased, her freckled cheeks red and happy. "Forced to kiss a beautiful hyenaling."

I twisted my features into a scowl, drawing out a fresh peal of high-pitched laughter. My expression was difficult to maintain, however, and it wasn't long before the smile I was fighting broke through.

I really did love it when she laughed.

"The kiss was pretty nice." I grabbed the bar of soap she held out to me. My manhood pulsed between my legs, pushing painfully against my loincloth. "Can I get another one?"

"Not until you're clean," Eshi said, giving me a little push towards the Gibris. "Hurry up, and I'll keep thinking about this pants idea you had."

Her smile sent another wave of heat through me, and I practically ran to the edge of the water. I didn't bother moving out of sight of our camp as she had, though I kept my back to her as I leaped out of my clothing and into the river.

The cold water did absolutely nothing to cool the fire raging through me. Things between Eshi and I felt like they were coming to a head, and I soaked and scrubbed and washed myself as quickly as I could. I didn't know exactly what would happen next, but I did know I needed to finish here if I wanted to find out.

And I *really* wanted to find out.

"Don't forget your back."

Eshi sounded much closer than she should be.

I swept my dripping hair back and peeked over my shoulder, confirming that she'd indeed come to the river's edge. Her robe was tied shut now, though a wave of tingling energy rippled through as I saw that her legs and feet were bare beneath the hem.

"I—" I coughed, my whole body growing hot. "I can't reach it."

"You can't?" Out here, in the light of the morning sun, Eshi's speckled hair seemed to almost burn. Her blonde tumbling locks shone with dampness and flickered with many-layered depth. It was a fire to match the one I saw alive in the amber depths of her eyes. "I guess that I'd better come and help, then."

Eshi pulled open her robe, letting it slip from her shoulders to puddle over the rocks at her feet. She took her first step into the water, predatory in the grace with which she prowled forward. I turned to face her and whatever clever words I might have spoken evaporated beneath the sun-wrapped glory of her nakedness.

The hyenaling was all sharp muscle, the feral leanness of her body underpinned by a shocking softness. Her breasts were dollops of creamy flesh topped by bright, cherry nipples. They quivered with the sway of her sun-drenched hips and the muscles of her naked thighs played beneath smooth, golden skin. And there, nestled at the center of her, was a seam of soft, pale flesh topped by a pale tangle of lush pubic hair.

I stumbled over to meet her, my movements jerky where hers were smooth. We stopped a bare pace from each other, the entirety of me filled with the wonder of her.

"Well?" The challenge in Eshi's voice was made less by the shiver of uncertainty in her amber gaze. "You got anything to say?"

"You're perfect," I croaked, hoping that the truth of my words shone behind my eyes. "Gods of death, Eshi, you're so fucking perfect."

Her lips parted and her eyes melted into warm pools of gold. My hands found the circle of her hips and her arms slipped around my neck as I pulled her into me. Her body molded itself to mine, her breasts soft against my bare chest.

"Say that again," she murmured, her eyes liquid. Loose strands of her hair tickled my neck and shoulders. "Tell me that you mean it."

"You're amazing." Emotion made my voice thick. Gods, she shone so brightly; a light beside me to ease the darkness of even the blackest tomb. "You're the most amazing woman that I've ever met."

She kissed me, and I tasted the sun in the warm press of her lips.

Eshi leaned her chest back from me when we parted, her arms still looped around my neck. She gave me a teasing smile. "Wasn't I supposed to help you wash your back?"

"Hmm," I said, sliding my palms down the length of her hips. "I don't really feel like washing anymore."

"I can see that." A mischievous sort of pleasure flickered over her face as she flexed her stomach to roll her hips. Suddenly, I became aware of my swollen hardness. It stabbed upward, spear-straight, and pressed between our flesh. "And feel it."

"That's your fault," I said, unashamed.

I leaned in to press a kiss onto her smile, sliding my palms behind her to dig my fingers into the fleshy firmness of her ass to pull her into me. She giggled into my mouth, the fur of her tail brushing over my hands. Her arms tightened around my neck, squeezing me as I ground her hips against me.

"Is it?" Eshi's cheeks were flushed and the heat flared in her eyes. "Well, maybe I should help with that instead?"

Even as she spoke, Eshi unwound her hands from around my neck and folded her legs beneath her. She slid out of my grip and trailed her fingers along the slopes and ridges of my chest and stomach as she sank to her knees in the shallow water.

I watched her settle herself on the smooth pebbles of the river's bottom, my heart rate spiking. My naked cock speared through the air a handsbreadth from her face, twitching as Eshi's hands traced the muscles of my thighs.

"Naroh," Eshi said, her lips parted to release swirls of heated breath. Her amber eyes were fixed on my engorged manhood, her stiff, cherry-red nipples quivering with the rhythm of her chest. "Do you want me to help you?"

"Yes," I groaned. My hips twitched as she trailed the tip of one finger along the scalding length of my cock. "Gods, Eshi."

"Good," she said from low in her throat. Her finger slipped along the bottom of my shaft, the whole of it spasming as she ran the back of her nail up along the underside of it. "I like helping you."

"Eshi," I panted, fire pulsing through me. "What are you...?"

I trailed off, unable to finish as the hyenaling wrapped her palm around my cock. Her flesh was warm and she started to stroke me, slowly working her wrist up and down my swollen length.

"You're so hard." She purred, the flush of her cheeks growing deeper. Her ears folded back as she breathed in the scent of my masculinity. "Isn't it painful?"

"Gods, no," I said, reaching down to run my fingers through her damp hair. "This feels incredible."

Eshi leaned into my touch, stroking me from base to tip. She lifted her gaze to mine, her amber eyes bright through the few strands of wet hair that clung to her face. "Do you like it when I touch you?"

I nodded, mesmerized by the sight of her naked, heaving breasts and the gentle part of her lips. Her flesh was golden and smooth, her body reddened by the sun and the heat of the fire rising within her.

Her fingers flexed around my cock, stroking me faster. "Say it."

"Eshi," I groaned, tightening my grip on her hair.

"Say it, Naroh." Her eyes never left mine and I felt the fur of one ear brush my hand as it shifted. "Please."

"I love it when you touch me," I told her. "And I loved waking up with you in my arms."

"Mmm, I liked that too." She smiled and her ears relaxed atop her head. Then, her eyes slipped from mine to drift down the length of my body. "You kept your promise."

The hand caressing me slowed, then stopped after one long, final stroke. Her fingers stayed wrapped around my base and the flesh of my manhood now rolled back to expose its swollen head. She shifted in the water of the river, leaning closer.

"You stayed with me," she murmured, her warm lips a bare finger-breadth from the tip of my cock. "That deserves a reward."

I frowned, but before I could speak, her tongue flicked out to kiss my head. She licked me and my whole body stiffened, my thoughts obliterated by the warm, languid flex of her tongue. Then, almost before I had time to recover, she bobbed her head forward and pulled my cock into the silken dampness of her mouth.

I let out something between a gasp and a groan, my whole body tense. I held onto her hair as she took more of me in with every rhythmic bob of her skull. The urge to shove myself into the back of her throat was nearly overwhelming, but I resisted, my breath growing ragged as Eshi's tongue writhed and danced around my cock.

Then, she took all of me.

She slapped her hands onto my thighs, anchoring herself to me as she ground her nose into the curling hair of my navel. A shudder ripped through me and my fist tightened in her hair as her throat flexed and clenched around my swollen head. She held herself there, digging her fingers into my thighs. A moan thrummed through her, her jaw working, the heat of her tongue molding itself to my cock.

"Eshi." I folded at the waist, nearly overwhelmed by the sensation. "Fuck."

She came off my cock with a ragged gasp, her ears shifting. Ropes of bright saliva spilled out down her chin to splash over her chest, coating her tits in shining moisture. My member gleamed with liquid spit, her fingers slipping over its length as she took it in her hand.

"I like this," she panted, pumping her wrist up and down the slick length of my cock. "I like the way you taste."

Then, she peeled my foreskin back and pulled me back into the silken heat of her mouth.

"Gods of fucking death," I groaned, making small, rolling thrusts of my hips. "Eshi."

Her head bobbed with me and her hands went back to my thighs as she swallowed the length of my cock. I still held onto her hair and I reached down towards her breasts with my other hand. My fingers flexed as I ran my palm over her warm, spit-covered chest, tugging and squeezing the soft, pillowy flesh. Her ears twitched and another moan thrummed through her as I found one of her stiff, pink nipples. I massaged it between my fingers, thrusting my member into the liquid heat of her mouth.

Eshi, wonder that she was, took me with ease, her tongue slurping and throat flexing.

Her ears twitched again, and, suddenly inspired, I loosened my grip on her speckled hair to touch one. I took the furred flesh between my fingers and rubbed it.

Her reaction was immediate.

A shiver rippled through her as she moaned low and deep. Her eyes rolled back beneath fluttering lids, and she came off my cock with a mewling gasp. I continued to massage her ear and her tongue lolled, letting another flood of saliva spill over her lust-reddened tits. One hand slipped from my thigh, while the other hung onto my aching hardness.

Her obvious pleasure delighted me, and I worked my fingers over the whole of her ear. I caressed it carefully, adjusting to every moan and gasp I drew from her. Eventually, I pushed the tip of my cock back between her parted lips, groaning as she latched on and eagerly sucked on it. The sensation was incredible, but the fire in me was burning hotter and hotter.

I wanted more.

Pulling my cock from her mouth, I bent and heaved her to her feet. Eshi leaned against me, almost boneless. Her flesh was flushed a deep red, and her pleasure-glazed eyes fluttered open behind a screen of her speckled hair. I slid my hands down to grip her hips, her skin cold from the river water.

"How was that?" I asked, giving her a lopsided grin. "I didn't know your ears were so sensitive."

"Hmm," she shivered and her lips curled into an expression of languid pleasure. "You were so gentle with them. It felt really good, Naroh, and even better because I could finally taste you."

"Finally?"

"Yes," she purred, looping her arms around my neck. She pressed her naked body to mine, her breath hot and sour from the heat of my cock. "Finally."

Eshi reeked of lust and dripping sex and the scent fanned the fire within so that it flared into an inferno of all-consuming need. I crushed her to me and her arms tightened around my neck. My mouth was hungry for hers and her lips met mine with eager, bruising strength. Her mouth was as hot as her breath. She moaned into me, the spicy heat of her tongue wrapping around mine.

When our lips parted, I pushed her hips back just far enough that I could slide one of my hands between us. Eshi let one of her arms slip down my chest, shifting to create a bit more space. She opened her legs, her breathing edged with the hint of a desperate whine.

Great gouts of heat billowed through me, the raw need in her making all of me burn.

I slid my fingers between her legs and curled them through the cold, river-soaked tangle of her pubic hair until I reached the super-heated flesh of her pussy. Eshi gasped, one hand clutching at my chest while the other gripped the hair behind my skull. I explored her, my fingers slipping along the outside of her lush, steaming seam of flesh. She was so hot, and so wet, her folds slick with her own shining moisture.

"Naroh," she moaned, her body writhing and shivering. "I want—"

I slipped a finger inside her, my flesh prickling as her words vanished into a throaty moan. She shifted her head, bared her teeth, and bit down on the meat of my shoulder. I growled, working my finger inside her as her canines dug into my flesh. She didn't break the skin, but there was still pain. My heart hammered against my chest and I curled a second finger into her hot, silken depths.

The hyenaling mewled into my shoulder. She shuddered as I stroked the soft, inner ridges of her center, dropping her hips, and flexing her stomach to grind her pussy hard against my hand.

Gods, she was so hot and wet, so strong, and so *ready*.

With my free hand I lifted one of her legs, hooking my forearm beneath her knee and opening her wide. Her jaws tightened as I pushed my fingers deep into her, pulled them partly out, and thrust them back into her eager pussy.

"Fuck!" Eshi gasped, releasing my shoulder with her teeth. "Fuck, Naroh."

Her leg buckled and more of her weight sagged into me. The muscles of my thighs and shoulders bunched as hers turned watery with the rhythmic pumping of my fingers. Then, her grip tightened in my hair and her other hand slid between us to find my cock. She gripped its molten length and started to stroke.

"I want you, Naroh," she panted, finding the strength to lift her hips off of my fingers. She pulled my manhood to the silken folds of her center, stroking it, a fog of lust heating her face and dulling the amber of her eyes. "I want to feel you inside me."

I groaned as my tip brushed against her soft, wet flesh. I adjusted my grip on her, positioning myself, all of me yearning to thrust all the way into her.

"Put it in," she begged. Locks of her wet hair were stuck to her face and shoulders, her spit-bright tits quivering as she pumped her hand up and down my cock. "Put it in me."

"Yeah, Naroh," another voice said. It was gruff, masculine, and strangely accented. "Jam it in there."

I wrenched my head to the side, spotting a trio of rough-looking men watching us from the shore. The three of them were human, their faces dirty and beards tangled. They looked like bandits. One held a bow, and the others had their hands resting on the hilts of the knives belted to their waists.

The big man who'd spoken grinned evilly, sliding a long knife from its sheath. "Give the little slut a good pump, and then the rest of us will take a turn."

My gaze flicked back to Eshi and time slowed to a crawl. I met her eyes, a cold wash of shock and fear snuffing out the fire within me.

We were naked, vulnerable, and had nowhere to run. I didn't know what to do, but I swore, in that eternal moment between heartbeats, that I would die before I let these men do anything to her.

Then, because we were so close, I saw the amber of her eyes brighten. The haze of lust disappeared, and time sped up.

Eshi's leg slipped from my grasp, and she screamed.

The hyenaling launched herself forward, howling her rage and furious frustration. Her ears were stiff and her fingers curled into claws. Sudden, overwhelming violence was her answer, and water fountained beneath her bare feet as she tore toward the three men.

The bandits, especially the one with the bow, might have ended her assault before it even began. Shock, however, kept them frozen in place.

Their weapons remained lowered as Eshi closed in, their wide-eyed stares focused on the roaring blur of nakedness and fury.

She threw herself at the nearest of them, hands reaching and canines bared. This happened to be the man who'd spoken, the broad-shouldered man who'd already drawn his blade. He reacted at the last moment, hand spasming to bring his knife flashing forward. Eshi crashed into him an instant later, and I didn't see if he'd managed to cut her before the two of them tumbled to the rocky ground. They rolled around together in a screaming pile of limbs and flashing metal.

The bandit without the bow was the next to react.

He was only about two paces from where Eshi and the big man were wrestling for control of the knife. He ripped his own dagger from his belt, face twisting into a wordless yell. That knocked me from my own paralysis, and my body was moving before my mind was able to latch onto anything resembling thought.

The riverbed below my feet was made up of pebbles and water-smoothed stones. Bending low, I reached for a rock that my eyes told me was properly shaped. I straightened with a smooth, vaguely oblong stone nestled in the palm of my hand, my body immediately flowing forward to hurl it at the second knife-wielding bandit.

I wasn't as good at throwing rocks by hand as I was with my sling, but still, this was something that I'd practiced a lot as a kid. My skill hadn't deserted me, and the stone cracked into the bandit's chest just as he was lunging forward. He screamed and crumpled sideways into the ground.

I turned away, my arm hot with the whip-crack force of my throw. There was something on the edge of my hearing, barely audible over the rasp of my breath and the roaring of my blood. It was a constant, high-pitched whine; a sound that I quickly dismissed as irrelevant.

Eshi and the broad man had stopped rolling. Bright blood poured down her forearms and coated her naked stomach and chest, but she was atop the man, straddling him, her knee pinning his knife hand to the ground. The bandit clawed at her with his other hand, punching and screaming and bucking to try and throw her off. Eshi would not be dislodged, however, and was digging the fingers of one hand into his throat while the other came up holding a heavy, fist-sized rock.

Movement tugged at the corner of my eye and my focus skipped to where the bowman was shifting to face me. He'd evidently decided that, with his companion there, shooting at Eshi was too much of a risk.

This left me as his most convenient target.

I swept my hand back in the water for another stone, finding one as the man was hauling back on his bowstring. I had time to note the flash of his snarling teeth, shockingly bright against his dirty face, before he sent his arrow slicing towards me.

My body flowed through my throw, even as my mind flinched from the expected pain. Yet, it never came. The arrow hissed past my ear. The archer, whether from luck, nerves, or the flash of sunlight on the milky pallor of my thighs and still-hanging genitals, missed me completely.

The stone I sent whipping towards him, however, did not.

He went down clutching at his stomach, and in the next moment, I was running towards where the first bandit I'd hit with a stone was even now struggling to his feet. I didn't know if Eshi saw him. Her focus was on the man beneath her, and her teeth were bared in a snarl as she brought the rock in her hand crunching down onto his skull. I ignored the pain of running barefoot through the rocky river, desperate to reach the now-standing bandit before he could plunge his knife into her.

But I needn't have worried.

Not only did Eshi have the naturally superior strength and speed of all hyenalings, but she was also more warrior than the rest of us combined. I hadn't even reached the shore when she let the bloody rock clatter beside the still form of the bandit beneath her. She scooped up his knife in the next motion, getting her feet beneath her and throwing herself at the other man a moment after that.

Her knife was cutting into his stomach and chest even as I stumbled to a halt, the bandit's own panicked thrusts slicing along her arms and sides.

Instead of getting in her way, I bent and hurled another stone at the still-recovering archer, and then a third. I kept him hurting and off-balance, screaming and panicking in the time it took for Eshi to finish her opponent off. She streaked towards the archer next, her bloody knife held low and ready. She stabbed it into him without hesitation, killing her third man in as many minutes.

It was over.

But then, in those following few beats of stillness, the sound that had never truly faded from my hearing crystallized.

It was laughter, the high, gleeful cackle of the scavenger.

Eshi whipped her head around, her gaze and stiffened ears swiveling towards the source of the sound. I followed a heartbeat later, turning towards the patch of sand that had been our camp. There was a hyenaling there, a man, his frame hunched around a stream of unending laughter.

Eshi sprinted towards him, blood dripping from her naked blade and body. She moved fast, reaching the man several paces ahead of me, though I started a bare moment after her. I expected to arrive in time to see her cut this fourth bandit's throat, but instead, she'd stopped a handful of paces from him.

"I told them!" The hyenaling cackled, his wide grin and bright eyes turned towards us. "I told them!"

Fresh laughter burst from him as I slowed to a halt beside Eshi.

The man was fairly young, his features sharp and cheeks free of any sort of hair. He didn't look much older than Eshi and I, likely just into his third decade of life. He wore a long, worn robe the color of sand and dust. It was in the elven style that was so popular amongst those of us who roamed the furnace-hot Ashuran territory. A dirty strip of cloth was looped around his head in a ragged imitation of an elven headscarf. His spotted ears, one missing the top where it appeared to have been sliced away with a knife, poked through the mass of stained fabric.

"I told them!" he cackled. "I told them, and now they're dead!"

I had absolutely no idea what to make of this man, and one glance at the mix of revulsion, wariness, and fear on Eshi's face did not help.

"They're all dead," the hyenaling said, his laughter fading even as his grin stretched wider. "I told them a sex-hungry matriarch was no prey, but they were hungry too."

"Eshi," I started. "Why— ?"

"We can't kill him," she said, cutting me off. She kept her eyes locked on the giggling hyenaling, her chest heaving and body clenched tight enough that I was sure she was about to vibrate. "He's a priest of the Laughing God."

I sucked in a breath.

"I told them," the mad priest said, an echo of ancient malevolence tugging at the edges of his too-wide grin. "And look at how their little jaws choked on so big bite!"

Chapter Eighteen

WHILE THE LAMIANS WORSHIPPED an entire pantheon and the elves looked to nature's spirits for guidance, the hyenalings recognized only the Laughing God.

He was eternal, a deity without a name. The Laughing God was a lord of scavengers, a god of tricks and carrion grinning atop a mountain of bones. He'd been there to feed on the first creature to ever die and would be there when the last one fell. And on the day when the rivers were salt and the land itself was nothing but sand-choked death, He would be there to gnaw on the bones of the world itself.

Yet, that day was long into the future and the Laughing God was endlessly patient.

He remained atop his mountain, grinning down at the mortal lives below him. He laughed at their struggles, their love, greed, and jealousy. He laughed at their victories and defeats, their carefully laid plans, and their black-hearted betrayals. He laughed because all that lived must one day die, and no matter how mortals fought and schemed, no matter their deeds or how high they rose, their bones would one day crack between his teeth.

All this drifted through my mind as I peered up from beneath my hood to the vultures circling high in the endless blue sky. It had been little more than an hour since we'd killed those bandits, and already the scavengers were gathering. I shook my head and squatted down beside the corpse I'd been next to.

This was the archer. His body had been torn by Eshi's knife and his face was still twisted in the agony of his death. He'd died hard, but I felt no remorse.

Life was hard on the empire's periphery, and they'd have done much worse to us.

I searched the man's pockets, coming away with a bare handful of coins. He didn't have anything else worth taking, and I added those coins to the ones I'd taken from his companions. I wasn't sure that I believed in the Laughing God, but if he did exist, I thought that he would approve of me taking from the dead.

Finally, I pushed myself to my feet, gritting my teeth as I put pressure on the bandaged cuts beneath my soles. They throbbed in my boots, wedged tightly in the worn leather. The river's rocky bottom had torn them up, and I moved slowly back to the sand bar on which we'd camped.

Eshi was there, her chest wrapped in bandages and her robe folded in the sand beneath her. She was seated across from the hyenaling priest with the remains of last night's fire between them. I saw her shift as I approached, my throat tightening at the pain graying her face.

"How are you feeling?" I lowered myself beside her, sitting close enough for our legs to touch. My palm found her thigh. "Do you need anything?"

Her torso and arms were a mass of bandages. Despite her ferocity and skill, Eshi had been naked when she'd thrown herself at the bandits. There was a deep gash across her chest from where the first bandit had cut her from collar to breast before she'd taken him to the ground. The second man's knife had also given her several more cuts along her ribs and forearms before she'd killed him.

And her feet... if the rocks had torn the soles of my feet, they'd shredded hers.

"No," she said, resting her hand atop mine. "I'm fine."

"Are you sure?"

I looked down from the wan smile she gave me, already seeing spots of red soaking through her ointment-smeared bandages. The lump in my throat swelled, and my fingers tightened on her thigh.

"I'm fine, Naroh," she said. "I'll be ready to get moving soon."

I blinked, but before I could address the idiocy of *that* statement, the priest seated across from us spoke.

"She grins at the pain. Like every good child of the Laughing God must."

Eshi's ears stiffened and she bared her teeth. "Be silent, priest."

The hyenaling, who'd introduced himself as Kur, let out a stream of laughter. I winced as the high-pitched cackle scraped across my mind.

"Put your fangs away, matriarch. There are none here for you to bite."

"What are you doing here?" She leaned forward. The two of them had been silent while I'd been gone, but my arrival seemed to have given Eshi a flash of energy. "Why would a hyenaling priest be with a group of human bandits? There aren't any clans for you to curse this far north."

Kur's ears twitched above his dirty headwrap, his eyes bright. "I'm ministering to a hyenaling now, am I not?"

"Answer the fucking question," Eshi growled.

Without the unsettling laugh and his too-wide grin, the priest might be mistaken for any other traveling hyenaling. He wore no symbol of his faith, nor did he carry a book with any of his god's teachings.

In truth, I don't think that any of those things even existed. For only the idiotic, desperate, or hopelessly insane would ever risk drawing the Laughing God's eye with worship or prayer.

"Perhaps I'm here searching for the same thing you are?"

Eshi snorted.

"Oh?" Kur's face split into one of those too-wide grins. "You think that you're the only one making a circle, matriarch?"

I had no idea what that could possibly mean. Eshi, however, flushed deeply. Her hand squeezed mine for a moment while the priest let out another yipping stream of laughter. Her eyes flicked to me before dropping to the sand.

That, of course, only confused me more.

But, with a measure of self-control that surprised even me, I managed to swallow the tide of questions rising through me and turn back to Kur.

I'd met a lot of hyenalings in the decade since fleeing the village of my birth, though never one of their priests. And while most hyenalings were reluctant to even speak the name of the Laughing God, I'd heard a thousand cautionary tales about his chosen clerics.

As far as I could tell, they performed little in the way of religious ceremony. No one prayed to the Laughing God. There were no places of worship, no sculptures or icons, no teachings or sacred commandments passed down through wild-eyed prophets. Most hyenalings wanted as little to do with their deity as possible. They were like toys to him, one man had told me, and the Laughing God broke most of what he played with.

In fact, his priests seemed to exist to do nothing but meddle.

The Carrion Lord did not create. He was a force of chaos, a being that represented the eventual desolation of the world. The order of his priests was small and untethered from society. They roamed alone through the world, wandering between the clans and lighting fires in the lives of all they touched.

What those flames left behind was always different, though it was hardly ever better.

After a priest's arrival, a powerful matriarch might suddenly die, leaving the clan to fracture around the squabbling of her too-young heirs. Prey might vanish from a rural clan's territory, or a city hyenaling might insult a passing lamian and bring a noble house's anger down upon the familial compound.

No hyenaling clan was ever happy to see one of their priests, though killing or driving them away would be worse than whatever change they brought. There was no surer way to draw the Laughing God's eye than getting rid of his chaos bringers.

Yet, for all that, Kur had saved Eshi's life.

"Thank you," I said, speaking as the priest's laughter finally faded. "For the bandages and medicine. We owe you."

Eshi hissed, digging her nails into the back of my hand. Kur turned his grin to me. "The Laughing God will have his due, human, never worry."

I nodded. Kur had been the one who'd supplied most of the bandages and the entirety of the infection-fighting salve that was even now covering Eshi's wounds. With how much of our supplies we'd lost in the tomb, that very well might have saved her life.

This deity could have whatever he wanted, as far as I was concerned.

"Your choice of center is uncommon, matriarch," the priest said. He flicked his ears, returning his attention to the injured hyenaling. "But he seems fitting."

Eshi stiffened, her cheeks blazing even brighter than before.

"Why do you keep calling her that?" I asked, wincing at the strength of Eshi's grip. "I thought you had to lead a clan to be a matriarch."

"Indeed, but all circles must start small."

I frowned in confusion, but Eshi released my hand and spoke before I could. "We're leaving, Naroh."

That drew another high-pitched cackle from the priest. She ignored him, gritting her teeth against the pain in her body as she reached across for her boots.

"Eshi," I said. "What are—"

"We have to go!"

She was still barefoot, her feet too swollen and bandaged to get into her boots. She growled, sweat beading her forehead as she slid them out from where they'd been folded beneath herself. Fresh spots of blood soaked through her bandages.

"Eshi, stop!" I grabbed at one of her ankles. She was trying to push a foot into one of her boots. "What are you doing?"

"Leaving," she panted, flicking too-bright eyes towards me. "Let go of me."

I didn't. "Eshi—"

"We have to go, Naroh!" She kicked her leg free, speaking through a gasp of pain. "Priests can't be trusted! There's probably a whole other gang of bandits coming this way and he's just trying to keep us here."

"That doesn't make any sense," I said. "Why patch us up, then?"

"You don't understand!"

No, I didn't, but I didn't think that Eshi did either. She was already one of the most stubborn people I knew and, right now, her face was bright with anger, and embarrassment, and twisted in pain. Arguing with her now wouldn't do me any good.

"Alright," I said, shifting onto my knees and reaching for the boot she held. "But at least let me help."

"I'm fine," she growled, pulling it away. "I don't need help."

I settled back on my knees and glared at her. She didn't meet my gaze, going back to trying to fit her too-injured foot into one boot.

"She's worried," Kur said. I could hear his grin even if I didn't turn to him. "Who would want a warrior too weak to fight?"

"Shut up!" Eshi almost screamed. "Shut the fuck up and leave!"

"Oh, don't be like that, little matriarch. Don't you want to know if I'm the one who cut your rope?"

She froze, and I turned incredulous eyes back to the grinning hyenaling. His own eyes were bright and merry.

"Two little mice, diving in the dark. They sneak and they scurry, they steal and they hurry. Laughing, they away from the serpents, too clever and unmarked."

"How do you know about the rope?" I demanded, ignoring the prickle that those unsettling words had provoked. "Did you do something to Asu?"

It was probably ridiculous of me to worry about what a single person, or even four if he'd been with the now-dead bandits, could do to the massive war-scorpion.

Yet, he was a priest of the Laughing God.

"Asu?" Kur cocked his head, ears twitching. Then, his expression shifted into a more natural smile. "Ah, the scorpion? Don't squeak and worry, little mouse. I'm sure that the creature is fine."

"But you saw him," I insisted, "And our rope. Did you watch us climb down? Were you and those bandits here to try and rob us?"

"I've seen many things," Kur said. "And I know some more. Neither I, nor those small-jawed fools you killed, cut your rope. But we met those who did."

"Who?"

"Friends of yours," the priest said, grinning once more. "From the big city."

"Kashir," Eshi spat. "I knew that fucking elf sent people after us. We have to go, Naroh."

"Go where?" Kur said. "You have no rope, and your friends are so eager to see you. They're camped at the bottom of the path, their teeth hungry for the bones of two little mice."

"Then, we'll go downriver," Eshi said through gritted teeth, her mangled foot halfway into her boot. "The canyon ends eventually."

"No," I said, my thoughts still spinning. "None of this makes sense, and you can't walk! We can't just—"

With a loud, gut-wrenching cry, Eshi shoved her foot all the way. A shudder wracked her frame, and her wounded chest heaved as she settled back.

"I'm... *fine.*"

"Gods of fucking death, Eshi!" I shouted. "Can you just stop one fucking second so we can think?!"

"No, we can't." She snarled, baring her teeth at me. "Kashir's men are coming for us, Naroh! We can't just sit here!"

"We don't even know if Kur's telling the truth," I said, not backing down from her stare. "And we don't have the food or the energy to just wander off without a plan. You're hurt, and we need to think through our options."

"I'm fine," she growled for what had to be the hundredth time. And then, as if just to spite me, she reached for her second boot. "Besides, priests never lie."

I snorted. "Come on."

"I'm serious. Priests never lie. They twist and hide the truth, but they will never tell a lie."

"That's..." I didn't even know what that was. "So, we can trust him?"

"No." She glared at me, the effect diminished by the pain tightening her eyes. "Didn't you hear what I just said?"

"Why lie?" Kur grinned. "We all end up broken between the Laughing God's teeth. And now, if you're done talking, I have a suggestion."

"We don't want to fucking hear it," Eshi said.

I let out a long breath and ran a hand through my hair. I suddenly felt so tired. This day had started off so well, and now... I sighed again, resisting the urge to reach for one of the pockets inside my robe. I'd already checked if the scrap of parchment that contained our only clue was still in its place, but the way everything was going, part of me thought it would simply vanish.

"What's your idea?" I said.

"I know another path to the top," Kur said. "A secret one, not far away. I'll take you there."

"You'll help us?" I asked. "Why?"

"Why?" The mad priest grinned, and I saw another echo of that ancient malevolence. "For a laugh, of course."

Eshi and I argued for several long minutes about whether or not we should follow Kur. She was fervently against it, but in the end, with no other real way out of the canyon, we had no choice.

"There'll be a price," she had argued. "There's always a price."

I'd asked her what she'd meant, but Eshi had simply shaken her head.

We'd been walking for a pair of hours now, shuffling through the almost physical weight of the afternoon's heat. The priest was in the lead, his furred ears perked and alert. He walked quickly over the sun-scorched rock, moving in a strange, skipping gait; slowed by neither the afternoon heat nor the weight of his pack.

My pack, though emptier than ever, dug uncomfortably into my shoulders. I shifted it over my sweat-soaked back, huddling deeper into my robe. Gods, it was hot. The burnt air clawed at my throat, and I kept my head bowed beneath my hood, ignoring the pain in my feet and focusing on the simple act of putting one foot in front of the other.

Beside me, Eshi tripped.

I reached out for her, catching her before she fell. She was a shambling mess, her movements jerky and uncoordinated. Blood soaked through what bandages I could see, and she didn't so much walk as stumble forward.

Eshi steadied herself and beneath her hood, her eyes were dull with pain.

"Hold onto me," I told her. "At least for a bit."

She tilted her head towards me, and for a moment, a spark of fire flashed within her eyes. "I'm fine."

"Eshi—" I started, but she was already stumbling after Kur.

I gritted my teeth and followed. For several long moments, sheer frustration kept me from feeling my own discomfort.

I didn't know what was going through her damned skull. Eshi loved physical contact, and during the last few days, the difficulty had been in getting her to actually *stop* clinging to me. Yet, now that she was hurt and could use the support, she didn't want to be anywhere near me. This damned hyenaling had more spiteful stubbornness packed into her frame than any four other people. We'd had this same 'conversation' nearly a dozen times since leaving and trying to speak to her now would just further drain whatever willpower was keeping her moving.

I was still quietly seething when, ahead of us, Kur stopped before a section of cliff. There was a sliver of shade at its base, and Eshi and I gratefully stumbled into it to join the priest.

"Is this it?" I asked, sweeping my eyes over a sandstone wall that looked as sheer as all the others. "I don't see a path."

"I told you it was a secret, yes?" Kur said, giving me a grin. "Seen secrets don't stay secret for long."

"So, this is it?" I pressed.

"Stop your squeaking, little mouse." The priest never lost his grin. "Your friends are close, so we must sneak and scurry."

I stiffened, my eyes darting to look upriver. We'd been heading up towards where the bandits, and Kashir's men, were supposedly camped.

"You said that this path wasn't close to the other."

The priest cackled, though he did so quietly. "Everything is far to the mouse."

"Gods of fuck—" I bit off the rest of my retort.

I looked back to Eshi, ready to clamp my hand over her snarl of rage. But it looked like she hadn't even heard. She swayed in place, bludgeoned by the sun and lost in a fog of pain and exhaustion.

Gods-damned hyenalings; not one of them was normal.

I let out a long breath and took a few moments to set my pack down, stretch, and drink from one of our skins. The cool water helped wash the dust from my throat, and I pressed a full skin into Eshi's hands before lifting my pack back to my shoulders.

"Show us the way, and we'll follow you up."

Kur gave me one last grin before flicking his ears and turning back to the cliff face. He started to shimmy up a narrow ledge to where it met an outcropping of rock. A scramble later and he'd slipped over it, getting his feet under him and starting up what looked like a hair-thin ledge.

This, I thought, feeling every one of my aches and cuts, wasn't going to be easy.

I turned away in time to see Eshi start forward, though it only took three steps before she tripped and fell to her knees. She let out a low gasp, the sound turning into a low groan as she tried to push herself up.

I hurried over and pulled her to her feet. She held onto me as she steadied herself, only this time, when she went to step away, I held onto her bicep.

I was done playing whatever game this was.

She tugged on her arm, trying to get free. Weakened as she was, I had no trouble keeping my grip. She glared at me, and this time, I glared right back.

"I'm fine," she growled. "Let go."

I leaned in towards her, meeting her too-bright eyes without blinking. "Make me."

Eshi bared her teeth and once again tried to pull herself free. I held on through several more attempts, growing more frustrated by the moment.

"Gods of fucking death, Eshi," I hissed. "We don't have time for this!"

"Let go!"

"What is wrong with you!?"

"Let me go!"

Her cheeks were red, blazing with the same fevered heat in her eyes. She wasn't thinking, had latched onto the idea of getting there on her own, and wouldn't, or couldn't, let it go.

I held onto her, helpless, as her movements became frantic. Her too-bright eyes rolled around wildly, unable to settle on anything. I didn't know what to do. Kur was getting further ahead and the other bandits were likely on their way here. We had to go, but Eshi would kill herself if she tried to do this alone.

What the hell could I do? How could I make her understand? Desperation, fear, panic, and a thousand other emotions swirled through me. I had to snap her out of this, but I didn't know what to do.

Out of time, and out of ideas, I did the only thing I could think of; I wrapped my arms around her. I pulled her into a hug, squeezing her to my chest. Eshi stiffened, momentarily frozen, and I took the opportunity to slide one hand up to the back of her hooded head and tuck her face into the crook of my neck.

She shifted against me, her fingers digging into my robe. I thought for a second that she would try to push me away, but instead, she bit me. Her teeth dug into the flesh of my neck, hard enough that I was sure a few of her teeth had punctured my skin. The pain was sharp and immediate, though I didn't let her go.

"Please, Eshi," I whispered, my voice hoarse. "Please."

The world around me faded until all I could feel was the woman in my arms. At that moment, she was everything to me, and the pain of her bite was nothing compared to the fear I felt at the thought of losing her. I told her of it, holding onto her as I repeated her name and spoke of the emotions roiling through my depths.

I don't know how long we stood like that, and I don't know what I said. The words left no impression on my mind, their weight and depth too much for me to comprehend. I kept speaking, and eventually, the force of Eshi's bite eased. Her entire frame started to shake, and I almost fell back as she let herself sag into me.

"Naroh?" She murmured.

"I'm here. I'm right here."

She shifted her arms to hug me, and slowly, the world around me started to bleed back into my awareness. I lifted my eyes up the cliff and blinked as I saw Kur staring down at us. He wasn't yet very far, and as soon as my gaze settled on him, he bared his teeth into a grin.

"Scurry and hurry, little mice, before the snakes slither over."

I shook my head, and then, after making sure that my grip on Eshi was secure, I started up the path.

It was a trail that even a goat would balk at, and most of the ascent was a blur. Guided by Kur's mostly nonsensical words, I half-pushed and half-carried Eshi up the series of narrow, snaking ledges. We scrambled over boulders and I lashed her to me with rope so we could get over short walls and through tight chutes of rock.

By the time we reached the top, it was nearly dark. I was lost in my own fog of pain, torn flesh, and screaming muscles. Eshi and I leaned heavily against each other, and it was all we could do to stumble after Kur as he led us along the cliff, away from the trail and the bandits that weren't camped too far.

Night fell before we could make it to Asu.

Kur finally stopped when it was nearly too dark to see, setting his pack down in a sheltered little copse of rock and brush. I barely managed to slip my own pack off before Eshi collapsed into my arms. She was asleep almost before I set her on the ground.

I lasted only the time it took to lay down and curl up next to her on my side. I wrapped her in my arms and fell asleep.

Chapter Nineteen

Eshi was still curled up against me when I was eventually woken by the brightness of the day. I felt the weight of her head on my arm, the tangle of her legs with mine, and the tickle of her breath swirling over me. I was lying on my side and when I blinked open my eyes, I found Eshi's face a bare handsbreadth from my own.

She looked so peaceful, her freckled features made soft by sleep and the absence of pain. Something warm buzzed deep in my chest. Her blonde, speckled hair was a cloud around her, and I felt the urge to reach out and brush her hair away.

Then, I made the mistake of trying to move.

I'd meant to roll onto my back, but my entire body seized up. I groaned as pain throbbed through me and every single one of my muscles locked into agonized stiffness. I felt like a chewed-up chunk of dried meat, every part of me raw and pummeled by yesterday's brutal climb.

My pained spasms must have woken Eshi, because it wasn't long before she started to stir. I let out one last groan as her eyes fluttered open, cold sweat erupting all over me when I finally regained control of my limbs.

"Naroh?" She murmured, blinking slowly. "What..."

I smiled, relieved to see that yesterday's fevered brightness had disappeared from her amber gaze. "Good morning. How do you feel?"

"Mmm," she said, her breath hitching as she pushed herself closer to me. "Hurts."

With a bit more wiggling, she pressed her forehead into my chest. I grunted as fire exploded through my arm, blood roaring back into my extremities now that Eshi was no longer sleeping on it.

"Yeah," I said, at last, pressing my lips to the top of her head. "Yesterday was a long day."

She let out a pleased little hum, and I hugged her tightly. For a while, neither of us spoke. I concentrated on holding her close and on breathing in the sweat, dust, and sun of her hair. In time, I felt the stiffness in her body ease, and her breathing became smoother.

When Eshi spoke again, her voice was noticeably stronger. "Are we with Asu?"

"Not yet. I'm not sure where we are, actually. We stopped here when it was getting too dark to see."

"I think I remember that?"

I chuckled, loosened my grip on her, and, together, we helped each other sit up. That was when I noticed that we were in the shade, sheltered from the late morning sun by an outcropping of stone. I turned my head to examine the rest of our surroundings, but Eshi's gasp wrenched my attention back to her.

"What?" I said, looking her robed body up and down. "Are you ok? Does it hurt?"

"Someone bit you!"

"I—what?"

"Your neck, Naroh!" Eshi said, her amber eyes were fixed on the base of my neck. "Why is there a huge bite mark there!?"

I blinked and brought my hand up to touch the spot that suddenly throbbed with pain. The flesh was incredibly tender, and I did not doubt that the color of the bruise was particularly vivid. I could even feel spots of dried blood.

"Eshi—"

"Who did that?!" She snarled, her bared teeth bright through her flushed features. "Who's the bitch you let bite you?"

"Bitch? Eshi, what are you talking about!?"

"Who was it!"

"You!" I said, utterly lost. "You bit me!"

She stiffened, her ears sticking straight up from the mess of her hair. Scarlet deepened the flush of her cheeks and her amber eyes stared into mine. Something flickered there, just beneath the chaotic swirl of her emotions; a fire, brighter and more wondrous than anything I'd ever seen.

Then, she blinked and looked away. "I did?"

"Yeah," I said, my voice strangely thick. "Don't you remember?"

"You..." Her ears folded back and the red heat staining her cheeks crept down to color her neck and chest. "You let me bite your neck?"

"Well, I didn't..." I trailed off, swallowing the rest of that joking response. Her reaction, so much more powerful than I ever would have expected, threw me off. "Yeah, at the base of the cliff. You were pretty out of it, so I hugged you. That's when you bit my neck."

She wouldn't meet my gaze, and her lack of response worried me enough that I reached out to her. She flinched when I placed my hand on her thigh, but she slapped her own hand over it to keep me from sliding it away.

"Are you okay?"

Her fingers squeezed mine, and her voice, when she spoke, was small. "Do you regret it?"

"Letting you bite me?"

She nodded quickly, jerking her head up and down. I didn't answer right away; this question was obviously important to her, and I gave it all the consideration it deserved.

"No," I said. "I mean, I wish you hadn't done it so hard, but I was really worried about you. This seemed to help."

"Naroh," her eyes darted up to mine and then away. Her cheeks were, somehow, burning even hotter than before. "You're human, so maybe you don't know this, but biting, for a hyenaling, is... it's a sign of... affection, usually."

"Ah," I teased. "So, you like me."

Her hand shifted on mine, her gaze still low. "This is important."

"Sorry. I'm sorry."

She nodded again and let out a shuddering breath. "A bite is like a kiss for us, but not just between mates. Mothers nip their children, close siblings might bite each other and so would friends, cousins, clanmates... it's something we all do."

"Okay. So, the neck is...?"

"Different," Eshi finished. Her fingers squeezed mine, most of her face hidden by a curtain of her falling hair. "Teeth to the neck is... special. It's baring one's throat and caring and trust and... it's more. Actually leaving a mark for everyone to see is... even more than more."

"Oh," I said, then swallowed. Heat rose to stain my own cheeks, a wave of tingling energy buzzing through to my extremities. "So, outside the tomb when you asked me to kiss your neck?"

"That was..." She shifted uncomfortably. "A kiss on the neck is close to a bite. But not the same."

"Then, do you regret it? Biting me, I mean"

She stiffened, but responded with a barely audible, "No."

"Then," I swallowed again, my throat almost painfully dry. "Do you ... do you want to do it again?"

Her eyes flew up to mine, and for a moment, I saw nothing but the naked glory of that fire burning within her. It was so bright, shining more beautifully than anything I'd seen.

"You want me to?"

"Yeah," I said, flashing her a quick grin. A fire to match hers burned within me, and all my pain and discomfort were lost beneath a shower of tingling sparks. "Hopefully Kur won't mind waiting... huh."

I don't know why my mind had chosen that moment to turn to the hyenaling priest. But once it had, I finally swept my gaze around the rest of our campsite.

It was empty.

"He's gone," I said, turning back to Eshi. "Did you hear him leave?"

The hyenaling stared at me with narrowed eyes, anger changing the flush of her face. She let out a low growl and pushed herself away from me.

"You're such an idiot, Naroh."

Once I'd gotten to my feet and taken a proper look around, I noticed that our campsite wasn't, in fact, totally empty.

There was no sign of Kur, nor did I have any idea when he'd actually left. But the Laughing God's priest had left a pile of fresh bandages on the ground not far away, along with a couple of jars of salve for our wounds.

That salve... worried me. Not because I thought it was poisonous or somehow harming us, just the opposite, in fact. That morning, when I unwrapped the first of Eshi's feet to help change her dirty bandages; the wounds, of course, looked bad. And yet, at the same time, they didn't. Fever should have been raging through her and her foot, at the very least, should have been swollen and hot to the touch.

But it wasn't, and instead, the bottom of her foot seemed to be healing.

Her wounds were thickly scabbed and new, silvery flesh was already appearing at the corners. They still hurt her, but it was as if Eshi had been resting for three days instead of spending hours walking on her wounded feet. The cuts on her chest and forearms looked even better.

I didn't know how that was possible, but Eshi's scowl told me that she wasn't surprised. And so, I swallowed whatever doubts I had, smeared some more of the stuff over her wounds, and bound them in fresh cloth.

The rest of the morning went a bit smoother. Eshi was eager to leave, worried that the priest had gone back to fetch Kashir's men. That didn't make much sense to me, especially after all he'd done for us. But I was also ready to get back to Asu and finally move on from this damned tomb.

We started to work our way along the edge of the canyon, away from the trail we'd come up. Neither of us knew exactly where we were, so we went looking for the place we'd first gone over the edge. I was surprised when we came upon it less than an hour later, the severed section of our rope left looped around a tree marking the spot as clearly as any obelisk.

Less than an hour after that, we were approaching our first camp.

"Asu!" I cried out, a grin splitting my face as I caught sight of the great, white insect. "Where's my Asu-boy?!"

The war-scorpion, who'd been waiting with an ambusher's stillness in the shadow of a great rock, sprang into motion. He let out a loud chitter, flowing towards us in a tidal wave of churning legs and pale chitin.

Beside me, Eshi tensed, but I reached for her before she could step away. "Naroh—"

"Stay here," I interrupted. "It's past the time you two became friends."

The hyenaling had been a bit peeved with me since this morning and had regained enough of her stubbornness that she'd made this short journey without hanging onto my arm. I worried that she'd try and argue with me now, but when I stepped behind her and pulled her into a hug, I was pleased to feel the lump of her tail as she relaxed against me. I kept my arms higher around her than I normally would, conscious of the wound on her chest, and by the time Asu was halfway to us, Eshi had dipped her chin and pressed a gentle bite into one of my forearms.

The great scorpion slowed when he noticed that the hyenaling wasn't moving away. I kept him coming with a steady stream of encouragement until we were in the circle of his great pincers. He settled back into stillness, his large eyes on us. His mouth pincers were tucked away, and both he and Eshi looked stiff and uncomfortable.

"Good boy, Asu. Did you have a good hunt, my big boy? You look so full and strong. Give me your hand."

That last was directed at the hyenaling, her ears straight and head tilted to stare up at the looming war-scorpion.

"Are you sure?"

"Oh yes," I said, gripping her forearm. "Asu loves getting scratches. Isn't that right, my big boy? We're going to show Eshi how to do it, okay?"

I pushed on the hyenaling's arm and, after a moment's hesitation, she let me lift it.

"She's going to be with us for a long time," I said, guiding Eshi's hand up beneath his head. "It's important that she knows how to do this for you, isn't that right, Asu-boy?"

Eshi's other hand came up to grip my forearm. I ignored it, along with the shift of her tail and the way she leaned more of herself back against me. I focused on the great scorpion before us, speaking continuously, making sure that Eshi's fingers found the right groove.

Then, I lowered my hand and let the hyenaling scratch him alone.

Nothing happened for several long moments. I was at the point of bringing my own arm back up when Asu's whole body twitched.

"Don't stop," I hissed when Eshi froze. "It's working."

She obeyed, her ears stiff and grip tight on my forearm. Asu twitched again and then his whole body relaxed. His tree-length tail curled in and he lowered his pincers. He also let his mouth pincers hang loose in what I, at least, took to be an expression of contentment.

"Good boy! What a handsome boy you are, Asu," I cooed, lifting my arm to give him my own scritches. "Isn't he just the best, most handsome boy?"

"Yeah..." Eshi said, staring up into the scorpion's many-segmented mouth. She swallowed. "He's... yeah."

"We'll do this a few more times in the next few days, but he should be a lot more tolerant of you now."

"Right..."

It was several more minutes before we headed back to the actual campsite. I was happy to see that what supplies we'd left there remained untouched. We got started loading everything back onto Asu.

Then, we found the body.

"It's an elf," Eshi said, squatting down. "He's only been dead a day or two."

The corpse was on the edge of our camp, lying broken and blood-soaked in the dirt. His headwrap and pointed ears marked him as an elf, and the armor he wore over his robe and the curved sword at his waist painted him as some sort of warrior.

"Yeah," I said, letting out a breath. "This was Asu. You can see where his pincers crushed him before tearing him up."

Eshi's ears flicked in acknowledgment. She reached down and pulled the sword from the dead warrior's belt, examining the curved blade for a few moments before raising her eyes back to me.

"This sword is well made, Naroh and no backwoods bandit could have afforded armor like this. Only a house guard or..."

"...or a rich sifter could have paid for this," I finished for her. "When I spoke with Amna, she was sure that her uncle wouldn't ever do something like this."

"He's Broken Mountain," Eshi said, pushing herself to her feet. "And you don't get as rich as he is without spilling a little blood."

I let out a breath. "I guess so. Anyway, I hope that this wasn't one of Amna's cousins or something."

Eshi shrugged. "I just can't figure out why he'd been stupid enough to get close to a war-scorpion. Asu isn't exactly hard to miss."

"I have no idea." I nodded to the blade she still held. "You gonna keep that?"

"It's a good sword and I should be able to sell it for quite a bit. The armor's also worth taking, even if Asu broke a lot of it."

"Yeah, we'll get it off of him before we leave." I swept a hand through my hair and chewed on my lip for a few moments. "With the Broken Mountain after us like this, finding someone to ask about the words we found is going to be *a lot* more complicated."

"Because all the good sifters are Broken Mountain?"

"Exactly." I reached into my robe for the slip of parchment. "I know a human woman in Niveh who might be able to help. But she..."

I trailed off, frowning as my hand found only an empty pocket where the clue had been. I checked a few more pockets, my heart beating faster as I repeatedly came up empty-handed.

Finally, I lifted my wide eyes to Eshi. "It's gone."

She stiffened. "What's gone?"

"The parchment. The fucking parchment with the words on it is gone!"

"What? How is it gone?"

"I don't fucking know!" My heart was pounding in my chest and sweat prickled my skin. "I don't have it anymore! Did you take it?"

"When would I have fucking taken it?" Eshi answered. "I've been half-dead since yesterday! Naroh, this is—"

"I know," I interrupted, my fists clenched. I let out a quick breath, trying to bring my racing thoughts to bear. "I know. Fuck! Okay. I checked my robe after we killed those bandits and it was still there. You don't have it, and the only other person we've seen is..."

"The priest," Eshi snarled, her tail lashing the air behind her. "That fucker! I told you we should have just left him, Naroh!"

"You'd have died if we'd stayed in there," I snapped back. "And he couldn't have been the one to steal it."

"Open your fucking eyes, Naroh!"

"I'm telling you that we couldn't have *physically* taken it. He never came near us during the hike."

"While we slept, then."

But I was shaking my head before she'd even finished speaking. "I kept it in my breast pocket, and you spent the night pressed against my chest. There's no way he could have gotten to it without waking us up. It must have... fallen out somewhere?"

It was Eshi's turn to shake her head. "Priests have power, Naroh. He took it, and I bet he's been giggling about it all morning."

"Power? You mean magic? I didn't think hyenalings could use magic."

"We can't," she confirmed. "We're as magicless as humans. But the priests have this... ability. They're chaos bringers."

Despite everything, I felt my curiosity roused. I kept my eyes on her, waiting.

"It's like... I don't know." Eshi let out a long breath. "Wherever they go, it's like they know just what to do to bring the most chaos. No matter how impossible it seems, they're always there to fuck everything up. If a matriarch has an important secret, they'll ferret it out. If a clan gathered their wealth for something, a priest will get to it without the dozens of warriors on guard noticing a thing. And if two outcasts catch a single fucking break after days of fucking misery, they'll just laugh while they tear it all apart."

Eshi's anger drained away while she spoke, her body sagging into resignation. "We're fucked, Naroh."

I... had so many more questions.

I'd never heard anyone talk about the Laughing God's priests like that before. Historically, hyenaling clerics had been a nuisance for more than just the clans. One of the more well-known ones had been Tiamen Firedancer, so named because she'd once set a necropolis-palace in Uruq ablaze. She was seen vaulting and spinning through the burning building, laughing and dancing as an entire lamian noble house died around her.

Some sort of innate magic would explain how she'd skipped away from the devastation. And how she had avoided capture in the decades-long hunt that had come after.

This was all so *fascinating*, and I think that curiosity is what kept my own energy from dimming. I had just learned something new, and, although the path to Marduss's tomb may have just gotten a little longer, I was beyond excited to see what else I would come across.

"Alright," I said, clapping my hands together. "If Kur has the clue, then we either need to go find him, or go back into the tomb."

"We're fucked, Naroh," Eshi repeated, crossing her arms over herself. "We'll never find him, and I don't know if I can go back into that tomb."

"Are you giving up?"

Her eyes flashed. "Did I fucking say that?"

"Then, what's the problem?"

"The problem?" She growled, ears going stiff. "The problem is that I'm fucking exhausted and my body is torn to shit!"

"Torn to shit? You're not the one with a huge bite mark on their neck!"

Her whole body went rigid, heat searing the entirety of her face. I laughed, stepped forward, and pulled her into a hug. After a few moments, she let out a breath and relaxed.

"How do you have so much energy?" She mumbled into my chest.

"Because I haven't given up either," I said, breathing in the sunny scent of her hair. "It's taken me more than ten years to get this far; going a little longer doesn't bother me."

Eshi shifted in my arms, tucking herself in more comfortably. She was silent for a few moments before she said, "What if I can't keep up?"

"That's crazy." I pressed my lips to the top of her head. "You were right about what you said back in Ikkad—this is too big for me to do on my own. I need you with me, partner."

I felt her nod and her fingers tightened their grip on my chest. "Okay."

Despite everything that Eshi had told me, I hadn't given up on finding Kur. The grinning priest was out there somewhere, and thanks to Asu, he'd have a much harder time actually outrunning us.

With that in mind, we were heading back to the spot we'd slept. We'd look for some sort of trail, and if that failed, we'd see about finding that camp of bandits in the event that he'd returned.

Once again, thanks to Asu, a group of Kashir's mercenaries didn't worry me.

I spent the short trip trying to remember everything I could about the strange writing. The shape of the letters, the exact way they looped and curled. I wanted to see if I could retrace them from memory, but I wasn't confident. With everything that had happened in the last few days, I hadn't had the time to properly examine them.

"Stop here," Eshi said, when we reached the section of cliff we'd first rappelled down. "I was too tired before, but I want to see if I can find anything about who cut our rope."

I nodded, tapping on Asu's head and slowing him down. We both jumped off the great scorpion, and Eshi moved to peer at the ground around where our rope had been lying.

I watched her search for tracks, keeping out of her way. Now that we were moving, and had some semblance of a plan, the hyenaling had regained a lot of her energy.

Eshi was a survivor and much too stubborn to ever really quit.

After a few minutes, I got bored of watching her look at dirt and moved to the edge of the cliff. The canyon was open below me, illuminated by the same summer sun that beat down on my hooded head.

From where I stood, I couldn't see the actual tomb, but I thought I could feel it, like a snarl of malevolent darkness beneath my feet.

My eyes were instead drawn to the Gibris, that ribbon of water winding its way toward civilization. I stared into that rippling current, and even from all the way up here, the sun sparkled and shone within those life-giving waters.

Inexplicably, I found myself thinking of Amna. An image of the beautiful elf drifted through my mind. I saw her smile, saw her reach up to tuck away that one curl that kept escaping her red headscarf. I remembered the way her skin had glowed in the firelight.

As I stared into the dancing light of the river, I wondered if she was still in the tomb. Then, my vision of her changed. Instead of being as I'd seen her that first night, I now saw her surrounded by darkness. I saw her moving through a tunnel, a glowstone held high in her hand. Her head was turned towards the markings on the wall ahead, and she didn't see the open, spiked hole that her foot fell into. She screamed as the trap tore her open.

I blinked, hearing something behind me. Then, the vision changed again.

Amna was still in the darkness, though she was singing now. Her voice was cracked, made reedy by overuse. She held another glowstone out before her, and by its meager light, I could see that her face was drawn, her skin and headwrap soaked with sweat. She was limping, moving slowly, notes of pain woven into her song.

Behind her, held back by her voice and keeping pace with her in the darkness, were dozens and dozens of burning, purple eyes.

I blinked again. Amna was hurt. She was trapped there. I had to go. I had to help her. I had—

"Hey!" Eshi said, bumping her shoulder into mine. "Were you ignoring me?"

"What?" I said, blinking rapidly. "No, I was... I was just looking at the river."

"The river?" Eshi said, settling in beside me. "I couldn't find any useful tracks. We can keep going... "

She trailed off, and after a few moments, I glanced over to find her staring out into the canyon.

"Eshi?" I asked, calling her name again when she didn't respond. "Eshi!"

The hyenaling started, her ears shifting beneath her hood. "What? Sorry, I was just looking at... Amna?"

I blinked. "You saw her too?"

"In the water," Eshi murmured, her eyes still forward. "She was hurt."

And then, suddenly, I understood. A surge of energy buzzed through me and I hauled back on Eshi, getting us away from the edge of the cliff.

"Naroh!" She squawked. "What—"

"Ko," I said. "Get away from the edge."

"Ko? Who?"

"Amna's djinn, the one we saw luring those war-dead into the river. I think it was trying to hypnotize us."

We were a dozen paces back from the edge, far enough away, I hoped, that we wouldn't be mesmerized into throwing ourselves off of it.

"The visions?" Eshi said, rubbing at her eyes. "That was her magic?"

"Yeah. I got the same ones."

I risked a glance back towards the top of the canyon. Now that I was looking for it, I could see a strange shimmer in the air above the open emptiness. No more visions entered my head; instead, the djinn seemed to just be waiting there.

"Do you think what we saw was true?" I asked.

"I was thinking the same thing," Eshi admitted. She looped one arm around mine. "She's part of Kashir's family, but I..."

"...know what it's like to be in the dark."

"Yeah."

I chewed my lip for several moments, feeling Eshi's grip shift. "I think I should go down there."

"Naroh..."

"I know," I said, letting out a breath. "But we can't just leave her. You saw all those undead trailing behind her."

"We don't know if what we saw was true," she said, but I could hear the uncertainty in her voice. "That thing could just be trying to kill us."

"Then why is it just waiting there?"

Eshi just shook her head.

"I think," I continued after a brief moment of hesitation, "That Amna sent him to find us. She'll die without help."

"I don't like this."

"I know, but could you really just leave someone to die down there? Someone who welcomed us into her camp and fed us?"

The hyenaling's fingers tightened around my arm and she tilted her head to glare at me. "If you're asking me to choose between her life or ours, my answer is yes."

"It's not going to come to that. Look, we have another long coil of rope, and this time, I'll loop it around Asu so that nobody can fuck with it."

"So, we go down, and then what? Do you want to go back into the tomb after all?"

"No, I don't want to go in. I have a feeling that she's on her way out, in any case." I wanted to help Amna, but if I went back into that corpse-flooded tomb on my own then neither of us would make it back out. And speaking of which... I let out a breath, bracing myself. "I'm going down there alone."

Eshi stiffened. "No."

"Eshi—"

"No!" She interrupted, turning to face me properly. "You're not going alone, Naroh! I'm not going to let you leave me so that you can go and die down there. I'm coming with you!"

"You can't," I said, holding her gaze. "You're injured, Eshi, and I can't carry both you and Amna up this rope."

Her amber eyes flashed. She bared her teeth, but I didn't stop speaking.

"I need you to help me from up here. You'll be able to keep watch from the edge of the canyon, and I'll teach you a few commands for Asu in case anything happens. He'll have the rope tied around him, and if you're here, you can get him to help pull us up."

Eshi's expression was a blend of helplessness and anger. After a few moments, she let out something between a growl and a whine. "Fine."

I smiled, untangled my arm from her grip, and pulled her into my chest. Amna was in danger, and we didn't have a lot of time, but this was important. After a handful of heartbeats, Eshi exhaled and relaxed into me.

"Naroh?"

"Hmm?"

"Come back to me." She leaned back, far enough that I could see the intensity of the emotion swirling within her amber eyes. "I need you to come back."

Then, she kissed me, long and deep. The softness of her lips and the warm spice of her tongue scattered my thoughts. Before I could do much more than start to gather them, she brushed her teeth against my neck and spun away.

Chapter Twenty

THIRTY MINUTES AFTER MAKING our decision, I was once again peering over the cliff's edge.

Ko, Amna's spirit companion, had disappeared at some point during our preparations, and so, my vision was unclouded as I watched the coil of rope I'd thrown tumble through the open air until it reached the ground.

"Looks like everything is set," I said, turning back to Eshi. "Make sure that Asu doesn't run off."

The big scorpion loomed over her, a dozen paces from the canyon's edge. I'd looped the rope around one of his arms, tying it just below the flare of his pincer so it wouldn't slip off. Asu wouldn't let anyone but Eshi come near enough to touch it, yet the tradeoff was that the rope would shift with each movement he made.

And with me dangling from it, even just a twitch, if it came at the wrong time, might be enough to knock me loose.

"He'll stay put," the hyenaling answered.

She was clutching the guiding stick in one hand, and she'd practiced giving Asu a few commands while I'd been getting the rope ready. I could see the worry in the fold of her ears, but I trusted her to have everything well in hand.

Besides, scorpions were ambush predators. The smaller breeds hunted by tucking themselves into some dark hole and remaining frozen until the moment that something scurried by. That instinct was still very present in the colossal war-scorpions, and Asu could remain immobile for most of a day if he had to.

"Thanks," I said, lowering myself to the ground. "Keep us safe, partner."

She nodded, and I saw some of the tension ease from the lines of her face. She advanced as I swung my legs over the cliff, squatting before me as I wrapped myself around the rope. Pain from her injured feet tightened her eyes, but she didn't move as she watched me slip into the empty air.

For a moment, I let myself hang there. The rope creaked, and my tired muscles were already making themselves known. Yet, all that was easy to ignore, lost beneath the tingle of energy washing through me.

I grinned up into Eshi's amber eyes and started down.

Her face stayed with me as I worked my way towards the distant ground. The prickle in my limbs became a buzz in my chest. My smile stayed in place, the feeling warming me more than the summer sun.

I was falling for her, and the thought that she might somehow feel the same delighted me in a way that I wouldn't have thought possible. I'd known a few women in the past, with few being the operative word. And though I'd cared for each of them in turn, none had made me feel anything like Eshi did.

She was amazing; a warrior-huntress, fierce and strong. She was dependable, smart, sun-kissed, and bright. Her fierce beauty made all of me ache, and just the shape of her smile, or the sound of her laughter, was enough to send sparks shooting through me.

But more than anything, Eshi just *fit*.

The ease with which we existed together was nothing short of a wonder. To touch and be touched by her had already become as natural as breathing. Her passion burned as hotly as my own, and no matter where this path took us, I knew that she would have no trouble staying beside me.

That companionship was something I'd never thought I'd been missing, but now that I had it, I couldn't imagine going without it ever again. She was everything I'd never known I'd been searching for.

And gods of fucking death, the way she used her *mouth*.

My crotch stirred as I thought back to our time in the river. I pictured the glory of her lean, sun-drenched nakedness, and felt my heart pound as I once again saw her get onto her knees before me. The heat of touch, the warmth of her lips, and the wetness of her tongue… gods, with the memory of that playing through my mind, even the bite mark on my neck felt almost good.

That, of course, led me to wonder exactly how good she was with the rest of her body. And, before I knew it, my feet were touching down onto the rocky riverbank.

I blew out a breath, untangled myself, and shook out my aching limbs. My palms ached from gripping the rough hemp, and I used the pain as a way to clear my head. The tomb's extravagantly carved entrance was just before me, and I had to focus.

There were, as of yet, no signs of either Amna or the djinn.

I could wait out here, but the sun was hot and that really didn't sit well with me. My eyes trailed up the coiling staircase to settle on the rectangle of darkness cut out of the rock. I'd get closer, I decided, maybe poke my head into the antechamber to see if I could hear her sing.

A fresh tingle of energy washed through my limbs, and beneath the stone-gazes of the twin, sinuously curved forms of Nabonassara III, I took a few moments to unwind my sling from around my forearm. Other than that, I had a pouch each of glowstone and ammunition, as well as a pair of waterskins slung across my chest.

I set a smooth, fist-sized stone into my sling's cradle and started towards the stairs.

No war-dead jumped out at me on my way up to the entrance, and after a few minutes spent crouched on the threshold, I decided that none were waiting for me just inside either. I slipped inside, staying right by the door while my eyes adjusted, ready to flee at a moment's notice.

But there was nothing.

The antechamber was much as I remembered it, mostly empty and illuminated by the sunlight pouring in through slits carved into the cliff face. I could see the lamian gods painted on the walls around me, and the statue of Tel'aman in the center. I tucked myself into a shadowy corner to wait, finding a place where I could keep all three entrances to the maze in my field of vision.

A few minutes later, I started to hear Amna's song.

Her voice was high and cracked, the notes hoarse and pained. She sounded worse than in my vision, and I figured that she must have been singing for hours to keep the dead at bay. I slipped from my darkened corner, reaching the stork-headed statue just as the elf stumbled into the chamber.

Amna looked haggard, her face gray and deeply lined. Dust and sweat streaked her skin, and the cloth of her robe was torn and filthy. She limped into the antechamber, leaning heavily on her wooden staff, her back bent beneath the weight of her pack. Her left foot was a swollen lump of bloody bandages, and I saw more red staining her hands and forearms.

The tomb had gouged pieces from her, doing all it could to keep her within its depths.

I'd started to move towards her as soon as she'd emerged. But she turned away, her exhaustion dulled eyes sweeping over me without settling on my form. She faced the tunnel from which she'd come, a broken song still pouring through her cracked lips.

I slowed when I was most of the way to her, seeing the glowing eyes of the dead that were shambling in her wake. I saw dozens of them, their withered faces slack and hypnotized. They rippled to a stop when the notes of Amna's song changed, their purple eyes following her as she took a staggering step back toward them.

She laid a hand on the stone arch of the entrance and then fell silent. My stomach lurched as I saw another ripple through the dead. Immediately, they started to come out of their stupor, sharpened gazes falling onto the elf.

But then, after one, and then two wheezing, splintered breaths, Amna began to sing once more.

This song was just a single note, low and deep. It came from the depths of her stomach, thrumming through the air around her. She held it, the note growing louder and deeper with every passing heartbeat.

The sound washed over the dead infesting the tunnel, though it did nothing to stop the first of them from starting towards her. I set my sling whirling beside me, launching a stone and shattering the skull of the nearest corpse. It crumpled to the ground, thrashing and tripping those behind it.

They were just starting to get through, their clawed hands reaching for Amna, when I heard stone crack. The rock of the arch beneath her hand shattered, and she fell back into the antechamber. The clatter of her staff hitting the floor was lost as the tunnel began to rumble and shake.

Then, with a groan of tortured stone, the ceiling collapsed over the mass of desiccated dead, entombing them once and for all.

It took several long minutes for the echo of that grinding thunder to fade. I didn't even think to worry about the stability of the chamber around us, instead spending that time gaping at the elf.

After a while, she started to slowly push herself to her feet, and I was able to shake myself into motion once again.

"Amna," I called out, starting towards her. "Are you ok?"

She whirled towards me, her eyes going wide. "Naroh?"

"Yeah. Although, it doesn't look—"

"Naroh!" She cried out, letting her pack fall to the floor. "You came!"

She threw herself into the space between us and I had to lunge forward and catch her as her injured foot failed to hold her weight. We went down in a tangle of limbs, and I ended up on my back beneath her.

"You came," she said, her voice thin and cracked. She shifted atop me, burrowing herself into my chest. "You actually came.

"Yeah," I said, hesitating for only a moment before wrapping her in my arms. "Yeah, Amna, I'm here."

"You're here. I'm so happy you're—"

Then, her voice broke. Her frame shook, and whatever else she might have said was lost beneath a storm of sudden tears.

"You did it." I shifted my arms around her and squeezed her tight. "It's over. You made it out."

Amna's breathing was short and gasping, her tears coming in great, full-bodied sobs. I held her through the entirety of those long minutes, neither shifting from beneath her nor offering any more words of comfort. She wasn't some weeping damsel in the arms of her valiant rescuer.

Amna had, in point of fact, been more than capable of rescuing her own damned self.

She had pushed herself to the absolute limit. I don't know how long it had been since she'd impaled her foot on that trap, but since then, she wouldn't have stopped pushing herself. She'd have continued through the darkness and death of the maze, her entire being clenched tightly around her fear and pain.

But right now, the danger was past. She had survived, and the tension that had let her so push herself had slipped from her grip. It rushed out of her now, released in this very literal flood.

Sometime later, when the shaking of her shoulders had started to ease, I shifted my arms around her. I ran my palm up and down the small of her back to remind her that, even though we were still strangers, she wasn't alone.

Eventually, when she had fallen silent, empty of all she had to give, Amna let out a long breath.

"I'm sorry," she murmured, forcing the words out past a torn throat. "I don't know what just happened."

"Don't worry." I breathed in her scent, blood, dirt, and sour sweat blended with a floral sweetness. "I've cried like that more than once in the past years."

"I doubt it." She shifted her head and I became aware of the puddle of tears and snot that had soaked through the cloth of my robe. Her tone became disgusted. "Fuck me, I made a mess here."

I laughed softly, releasing her to lace my hands behind my head. "That's alright, this robe has seen a lot worse."

"You're kind, Naroh," she said, raising her head off my chest. I suddenly became aware of the press of her body, feeling the softness of her curves, the squish of her large breasts, and the length of her legs. Her dark eyes were rimmed in red and set in exhausted pits, and yet, I could still see something of her strength. There was a burning core within her, wrapped in an iron will and hidden beneath a layer of lush femininity.

"Thank you so much for coming. When I sent Ko out to find you I wasn't sure..."

I gave her a small smile. "Being kind is easy when I don't have to do anything. Gods of fucking death, Amna, that thing with the tunnel was insane."

She flashed me a quick grin. "It was, wasn't it? Although, I think that Marduss managed a lot more at the walls of Uruq."

Her body was a blanket of softness atop me and the wash of her scent quickened my pulse. And yet, for all that, it was that smile, pained and yet full of genuine excitement, that reached furthest into me.

She'd been beautiful when we'd first met, but now ... was there anything more wondrous than a woman with the strength to walk alone through the darkness and emerge smiling on the other side?

Amna shifted again, and, as if she could see something of my thoughts, a flush bloomed beneath her cheeks. She pushed herself off of me, but in my mind, I still saw that smile. And even though it soon faded, my entire being thrummed with the change it had wrought.

"Sorry," she said. "I'm—"

She bit down on the rest of her words, letting out a long groan of pain.

"Your foot," I said, pushing myself upright. "How bad is it?"

She managed to shift herself until she was seated, the agony of the effort coating her skin in a fresh layer of sweat. Wordlessly, I handed her one of my two, thankfully unbroken, waterskins. She nodded her thanks and took a long draught.

"Pretty bad," she eventually panted. "I know you told me to watch out for those spike traps, but I..."

"But you got distracted," I finished with a grimace. "Ko showed us what happened."

"Us?" Amna said, reaching up to push back on her headscarf. "Ah, of course, the hyenaling."

"Eshi," I answered with a nod. "And yeah, she saw what happened too. She's waiting for us back on top of the canyon walls."

"I'm surprised that she was alright with you coming after me."

"Eshi's been down here as well," I told her. "She wouldn't leave anyone to die down here in the dark."

She nodded, then gasped as she once again shifted her bandaged foot.

"Come on," I said, pushing myself to my feet. "I'll get your pack and help you up. There are fresh bandages up with Eshi, and a salve that's been doing wonders to fix our own feet."

"What happened to your feet?"

"That's a long story," I said, hefting her pack.

"Does it have something to do with the bite mark on your neck?"

"Sort of? That was Eshi."

"Hmm, you two really have gotten close," she murmured. Then, she cleared her throat. "And the rest of the story?"

"Let's get going," I answered, returning to where she sat. "I'll tell you later."

Amna shook her head. "Tell me now."

I grinned, reaching a hand down towards her. "Curious?"

She reached for my hand, something shining in her dark eyes. "Always."

Amna paused for a moment as we stepped out into the sunlight. She closed her eyes, tilted her head up towards the endless blue sky, and let out a long, shuddering breath.

"Feels good to be back outside, doesn't it?"

The elf opened her eyes and gave me another heart-stopping smile. "More than I ever thought possible. I wasn't even in there that long, but it felt like an eternity."

I grunted in agreement. "It doesn't take long for the cold to get into your bones."

Amna shuddered. We'd spent several more minutes in the tomb's antechamber, waiting for her eyes to adjust to the light of the bright, midday sun. In that time, I'd filled her in on what Eshi and I had gone through in the thirty or so hours since we'd last seen each other.

Though, of course, I'd left out a few of the more personal details.

We hadn't, unfortunately, gotten to talk about her time within the maze. I desperately wanted to hear about it and had come up with a few more theories about some of the scenes I'd seen painted in the sarcophagus chamber that I would *love* to get her thoughts on.

The subject was a little difficult to broach, however. With how things had ended for her, it was probably best to give her the chance to rest first.

I could be patient... at least for a few more minutes.

"Are you ready to go?" I drew my hood back over my head.

Amna took a moment to adjust her own headscarf before nodding. As I'd done to get her this far, I took some of her weight by looping an arm around her waist. She slung her arm over my shoulders after a moment's hesitation, a slow flush creeping over her features.

"Spirits, I must stink worse than a herd of camels."

I chuckled, guiding her faltering steps over to the stairs. "Don't even worry about it. Eshi and I smelled absolutely feral when we got out of there. Some of our clothing wasn't even salvageable."

"Oh, I remember," Amna said, a twinkle in her dark eyes. "Believe me."

I winced. "Right, I guess we did meet you before washing. Sorry about that."

"You're here now, Naroh. I'd say that more than makes up for it."

"So, we're even then?"

"Hmm, maybe not. You did *really* stink."

I chuckled and we fell into an easy silence. Her staff thumped rhythmically on stone as I helped her navigate the steps to the beach.

"You two must have been in there for quite a while," she said, at last.

"Almost a week. Although, to be fair, a lot of that time was spent hiding from the war-dead."

"A week? Really?"

"I think so, although time is hard to keep track of down there."

Amna shook her head, a few of her dark curls spilling out from beneath her scarf. "Even so, I couldn't even manage two days without being carried out. I'm really not much of a diver."

"If anyone ever tells you that, just sing them into a river. Or drop a tunnel on their head."

She snorted. "I have a particularly generous rock spirit to thank for that last one, and Ko is only ever dangerous to those who don't realize he's there. It might sound stupid, but I expected to be a lot better at this."

"You survived, Amna," I told her, helping her off the last step. "That's more than what most first-time divers accomplish."

The elf tightened her grip on me before letting out a long breath. "Yeah, you're right. I just wish that I had more to show for losing a few of my toes."

My stomach twisted and my eyes darted down to look at her bloody foot. "The trap?"

She grunted. "I keep telling myself that I was lucky. With the way I fell into it, the spike tore through a few of my smaller toes instead of impaling my foot. I don't know if I'd have been able to walk, otherwise."

"You... are speaking very blandly about this."

"I also haven't slept since the night we met," she answered. "It's possible that I'll feel worse about this when reality starts to settle in. Is that how we're getting up the cliff?"

Amna's tone had become something between disbelief and horror. We'd finally gotten over to the rope, and she paused for a moment to stare at it. "Naroh... I don't think I can climb this."

"Me neither," I said. "That's why we're gonna let Eshi and Asu do all the work."

"Asu?"

"You'll see," I said and then grinned at her annoyed frown. "Come on."

"I really don't like unanswered questions." She huffed but moved with me towards the rope.

It was the work of only a few minutes to get her pack tied down. I got her to sit atop it next, and I looked up towards the top of the cliff as soon as she was secure. I'd spotted Eshi looking down on us almost as soon as we'd reached the riverbank and I waved up at her now, letting her know that we were ready.

I had time to wrap my arms and legs around the coiled hemp before we lurched up into the air. Amna let out a surprised squawk and clutched at the rope, the ground getting farther away with every passing moment.

"Are you going to tell me who this Asu is, now? He must be really strong."

"He is," I said, grinning down at her from where I hung not far above. We were ascending smoothly, Eshi doing a fantastic job of keeping the war-scorpion's movements steady. "But first, you have to tell me how far into the tomb you got."

"Ah, so you are curious." Amna's eyes shone, and she risked letting go with one hand to tuck a curl back beneath her scarf. "I was starting to think that you'd never ask."

"It's been killing me," I admitted. "Did you make it to the sarcophagus?"

"I did. I didn't learn anything new about the Basri Revolt, but when I got into the armory and— "

"—you saw the centaur incursion? Did you notice the—"

"Yes!" Amna's voice was high and excited. "House Hidalu was there! Those centaurs must have been the first of their cavalry legion. Did you ever read Vizier Sopdat's account of the war against Temuja Khan's horde?"

"*Hoof met hoof, though bone proved stronger than flesh.*" I quoted, speaking faster as I understood what she was implying. "It was a reference to this!"

Amna laughed. "It has to be, right? That line has been bugging me since I was twelve years old."

We spoke excitedly for several more minutes before the rope jerked to a stop. I looked up, startled to find that the edge of the cliff was just a handful of paces above me.

"Looks like we're here," I said. "Give me a second and I'll get you up."

I started up the rope and Eshi's bare head popped out above me when I'd almost reached the top. She reached down with a bandaged arm to help me the rest of the way up.

"Thanks," I grunted, scrambling to my feet. The war-scorpion was stopped dozens of paces away, the entire length of the rope stretched out between us. "Can you bring Asu back? I'll pull Amna up."

The hyenaling's eyes flashed, and before I knew it, she'd gripped my robe and yanked me into a hard, ferocious kiss. My head felt light when we parted; my breath was ragged and my lips bruised.

"Don't ever leave me like that again," she growled, her cheeks flushed. "Especially if you're going to break your promise and do something stupid."

"What? I didn't do anything!"

"The rumbling," she snarled. Her ears were folded back and her tail lashed the air behind her. "I thought you'd pulled the whole fucking tomb down on yourself!"

I frowned. "How would I even have done that?"

"Same way you made thousands of guardians appear out of nowhere!"

"That was... never mind. The rumbling was actually Amna. Do you remember the guardians we saw shambling after her? I went into the antechamber in time to see her collapse a tunnel on top of them."

The hyenaling blinked.

"It was amazing," I continued. "Although, if I tell you about it now, she might get impatient and sing this whole section of cliff down into the canyon."

"I heard that!" The elf called up from where she still hung in the air below us. "And that's not something I can do!"

I grinned as Eshi's face twisted into a scowl. Her ears shifted. "Now, I'm definitely not leaving you alone with her."

Together, it was the work of barely a minute to pull Amna and her pack up onto solid ground. Eshi's glare was suspicious as we helped her to her feet, and I noticed that the hyenaling kept her hand not far from the hilt of her knife.

"Thank you," Amna said. This last bit of effort seemed to have drained away the last of her energy. She held onto my arm for balance, and I could tell that it was taking a lot of her willpower to not simply let herself sag against me. "Both of you, thank you so much. I—I don't know how I would have made it out here on my own. I owe you both my life."

"You do," Eshi said before I could speak. Her scowl had lost none of its force. "How are you going to pay us back?"

"Eshi—"

"No," Amna said, cutting me off. Her grip tightened on my arm and then relaxed as she let out a long breath. "She's right, Naroh, you've already done so much for me. I'm a merchant's daughter and I pay what I owe." She met the hyenaling's gaze without flinching. "What do you want? I'm warning you now that I don't have much."

The hyenaling stared at her for a few moments before she nodded. With a glare in my direction that screamed 'Keep your fucking mouth shut,' Eshi slipped over to Amna's other side.

"Put your arms around our shoulders," she ordered. "We'll get you over to Asu before anything."

"Asu?" Amna asked, looking around for the first time. Her eyes widened when she spotted the colossal war-scorpion waiting in the distance. "Oh."

"That's our Asu-boy," I said, looping my arm back around her waist. Eshi did the same thing on the other side, and soon, we were traveling with Amna hopping between us. "Isn't he handsome?"

"I..." The elf started. "I don't know how to answer that. Is that really a *war-scorpion*?"

"Naroh told me a bit about what you spoke about the night we all met," Eshi said, ignoring Amna's reaction. "You saw the artifact he found?"

"I—yeah." She shook herself, pulling her attention away from Asu's handsome shape. "I snuck into my uncle's office to see it when everyone was asleep. Marduss in a headwrap ... I came out here to find what that means."

"And did you find anything about that in the tomb?"

"Maybe," the elf said, her tone suddenly wary. "But something like that is valuable."

"And you owe us your life."

Amna let out a breath.

"Wait," I cut in. "You actually found something?"

"It wasn't much," she admitted. "I found an inscription on the inside of the sarcophagus."

I sucked in a breath. "Did you copy it?"

"Better," she said, giving me a tired smile. "I know what it says."

Chapter Twenty-One

NEST AND FLOW THE wise ones from wings of stork, immortal in wisdom's source.

Those words tumbled through my head, filling my thoughts. I gripped them, twisted, turned, and pulled them apart. I dissected every letter and tore the sentence apart in my hunt for meaning.

Yet, no matter what I did, I just couldn't make sense of this.

Well, that wasn't really true. I understood the phrase; they were a variation of House Nabonassara's motto, subtly different but broadly similar. Why they had been changed for only this specific instance, I had no idea. That was one of several questions nagging at me, though I wasn't sure if the answer would be particularly helpful.

No, the real mystery, the one that delighted and frustrated me both, was that the words had been written in elvish.

I shook my head and blinked myself back into some sort of awareness.

It felt like I'd been kicked by a camel and while I'd been busy staring at nothing, Eshi and Aman had gone on with what work needed doing. They were on the ground in the shadow of Asu's bulk. The hyenaling had spread some of Kur's salve over Amna's ruined foot and was now wrapping it in cloth.

I stared at it for several long moments before my eyes drifted upward. The smooth skin of Amna's features was drawn tight, made gray by exhaustion and the constant agony of her foot. Her eyes, however, were still alert, and she spoke quietly with Eshi while the other woman worked.

I couldn't see Amna's pointed ears beneath her dirty headscarf, but... elvish.

Everyone knew that the elves had once had a language of their own. Before Marduss pulled down the walls of Uruq, the elves had built an entire civilization between the banks of the Nazlun and Gibris. They'd had trade and writing, music and culture; they'd built vast monuments whose surfaces had been decorated with scenes from their myths and legends.

And while some of that survived to this day, their language and writing had not.

The lamians had outlawed it as soon as they'd clapped manacles around the wrists of the first elf. They'd ripped families apart, forcing elven children to learn their language while setting the adults to work chipping away the words carved into their temples and obelisks.

Those ancient pharons and their necrophants had decreed that the elven language was to be purged, and generations of slaves had had the flesh stripped from their backs for speaking the tongue of their fathers.

Things became less brutal after emancipation, though by then, the elven language had been largely wiped away. As far as I knew, the lamians had never repealed the law, and in the centuries that followed, several accounts had been written of vicious crackdowns on any who had tried to bring back the dead language.

So why, by every fucking god of death, had a lamian pharona from that time had elvish words carved in her sarcophagus?

"Naroh!"

I started, finding Eshi standing directly before me. She'd set aside her robe now that we were in the shade, exposing her bandaged chest and arms to the air.

"What?"

She frowned. Behind her, I could see Amna leaning forward to peer at me.

"You've been staring at us for the last few minutes," the hyenaling said with a flick of her ears. "What's wrong?"

"What? Oh—nothing." I flushed. "I was just thinking."

Her frown became suspicious. "About what?"

"Everything," I said, letting out an explosive breath. I pushed my hood back to sweep a hand through my hair. "Amna just completely shattered my world."

"Sorry about that!" The elf called.

"Elvish... I still can't believe that you can—" I shook my head, swallowing the rest of my words. I'd said that enough in the past hour. Kashir had taught her the language, she'd told us; though, she wasn't sure from where he'd learned it. She suspected that he'd taught himself, which, I conceded, might be possible given enough time and resources.

One of which, I knew, Kashir certainly had in abundance.

"Anyway, I'm fine. And you," I met Eshi's gaze, "shouldn't be on your feet."

She set her jaw, but I spoke again before she could. "Yes, yes, you're also fine. I'm going to go sit down, though."

With that, I stepped past her and lowered myself to the ground not far from Amna. I leaned back against one of Asu's legs. Once I'd made myself comfortable, I held out a hand to where the hyenaling was still glaring down at me.

"Sit with me?"

Eshi's face softened. After a moment, her lips curled into a small smile and she limped forward to take my hand. She lowered herself between my legs with her back to me. I wrapped her in my arms and pulled her into my chest.

"You may have had a point," Eshi murmured, settling herself more comfortably. "This is better than standing."

"Mhm," I said, shifting so that her head was tucked beneath my chin. The fur of her ears was soft against my cheeks and strands of her speckled, sun-warmed hair tickled my face. "I'm full of good ideas."

The hyenaling laughed, relaxing against me with a contented sigh.

"How about we rest here for a few hours?" I glanced at Amna. "We can all leave on Asu afterward."

The elf was silent for a moment, an expression that I couldn't decipher shaping the tired lines of her face. Then, she shook herself and smiled. "Rest sounds good, although, I don't think I could sleep right now."

I smiled back, drawing an appreciative murmur from Eshi when I shifted my grip on her. "You're so tired that you're not tired at all?"

The elf chuckled. "I guess so."

She adjusted herself and that laughter became a groan of pain as she jostled her wounded foot.

"Gods, if Kashir didn't hate us before, he definitely will once he sees you like this."

"Well," Amna said, letting out a ragged breath and leaning back against one of Asu's legs. "Lucky for you, I don't plan on going back anytime soon."

I blinked. "Where will you go, then?"

"I left Ikkad to discover why Marduss appeared wearing an elven headscarf." She reached up to tuck away a loose curl of hair and relaxed with another long sigh. "I haven't found that yet."

"You're not done?" I asked, incredulous. "Even after what happened in the tomb?"

"I'm curious, Naroh." She gave me a tired smile, though I saw something glimmer in her dark eyes. "I told you that I'm a hard woman to satisfy."

Eshi cackled, shifting within the circle of my arms. The hyenaling said something, but her words washed over me. The smile on the elf's face, so similar to the one I'd seen in the tomb, reached deep into me and answered a question that I hadn't yet thought to even ask myself.

Abruptly, I made a decision.

"Amna?"

The elf had been responding to Eshi, but something in my tone caused her to stop and turn to me with a quizzical expression. "Yes?"

"Eshi and I are hunting Marduss's tomb. I want you to come with us."

The elf's eyes widened, and in my arms, Eshi stiffened.

"Naroh!" The hyenaling exclaimed. "What the fuck are you doing?"

"We need help, Eshi." She squirmed in my arms, and I let her go before she decided to bite me. "It's what we talked about this morning."

Eshi pushed herself off my chest, her ears stiff and angry. She turned to look at me, sitting back on my outstretched legs with her knees straddling my waist.

"This morning," she growled, red blooming beneath her freckled cheeks, "you told me that you needed me with you."

"Exactly," I said, looking into her bright, amber eyes. "Because this is too big for me to do on my own. And now, I think that it's too big for even the two of us. Amna is exactly who we need."

"She's Kashir's niece," Eshi snarled. "Did you forget that he's been trying to fucking kill us?"

"But *she* hasn't! Think about it, Eshi. Amna speaks elvish. I don't know why the elves seem to be so tied into this, but she knows more about their history than anyone except Kashir. If we keep finding more connections to the elves, which is looking pretty fucking likely, I'm going to need help."

"You'll figure it out. We don't need her."

I shook my head. "I'm out of my depth. Maybe I could eventually piece some things together, but that could take years. She can also do magic, Eshi! Real magic that can be useful. You remember how she dealt with those undead by the river, and then there was the tomb and even what she did with Asu!"

That had been something that neither of us had expected.

The great war-scorpion had flowed towards us while Eshi and I had been helping Amna walk. He'd stopped when he caught sight of a stranger, stiffening into that dangerous, predatory stillness. I'd pulled us to a stop as well, readying myself for several minutes of keeping Asu steady while Eshi got the elf up onto his back.

Yet, it had been the elves who had first tamed the great insects of the desert and Amna had not been afraid. She'd slipped from our grip and, before I could say anything, she had started to sing.

The song had been high and rich with those otherworldly tones that signaled the use of her magic. It had been beautiful, despite many of the notes emerging frayed from her already abused throat.

Asu had, apparently, thought so as well.

He'd remained still for more than a minute, letting Amna's song wash over him. Then, abruptly, he'd relaxed. He'd flowed towards us once again, quickly wrapping us in the circle of his great arms. Still singing, the elf had reached up to touch his face. And one happy chitter later, Asu settled onto his stomach, as comfortable around Amna as if he'd known her all his life.

When she'd fallen silent, the elf had smiled into Eshi and my gaping astonishment. "A creature's spirit isn't so different from those of the land. It's good that Asu is so friendly, otherwise, I might have been singing here for hours."

I blinked as Eshi growled something. I reached for her waist but she shoved my hands away.

"I don't care," she said. "She's not coming."

"Eshi—"

"No, Naroh!" She snarled. "No. I'm not fucking doing this."

"That's not how this works. You don't get to just say no and have that be it."

"You mean like you did when you invited her without talking with me?"

"That's... okay, fine. You're right. I'm sorry, I should have spoken to you about it. But my point still stands!"

Eshi's eyes burned. Her hair was a wild mane around her face, and when she bared her teeth, I saw the sharpened points of her canines.

"I don't care, Naroh. We don't need her."

"Gods of fucking death, Eshi." Frustration roiled through me and my fists were tight balls. "You're not making any sense!"

"Hey," Amna said, cutting into that beat of silence. "Sorry, but I'd like to say—"

"No!" Eshi snarled, whipping her head towards the elf. "Shut up! You're not fucking coming. This isn't happening!"

She made to push herself to her feet, but I clamped my hands around her waist. The eyes she turned to me were murderous.

"Wait, Eshi, I'm sorry. Can you just..." I let out a shuddering breath. "Please."

Her tail cut through the air behind her. She shifted over my legs but didn't make any more effort to move away.

I relaxed my grip on her waist, doing my best to swallow my anger. There was something here that I wasn't seeing.

"Listen, Eshi," I began, holding her gaze. "I should have talked to you before saying anything, and it was really shitty of me that I didn't. I wasn't treating you like a partner, and I'm really sorry."

The hyenaling didn't react, her feelings locked behind an expressionless mask. I kept talking, speaking the words that rose from within me.

"I—I've been alone for a long time. This," I said, shifting my palms over her hips. "This is all very new to me, and I'm sorry. I'll do better, Eshi, I promise that I will. I want you to stay as my partner. I want that more than anything and I—I'll do better."

More words were pushing to get out, but they stayed stuck in a throat that was suddenly blocked. A distant part of me was embarrassed to bare myself like this in front of another person, but it was easy to ignore. I only had eyes for Eshi, and whatever answer she might have.

Finally, after what felt like an eternity, her shoulders loosened a degree and she nodded.

"Thank you." Then, I let out a breath, aware that my next words would likely shred whatever moment of understanding we'd found. "But Eshi, about Amna, can you tell me why you don't want her along?"

Her eyes flashed. "I already told you. She's Kashir's niece, and I don't trust her."

"Eshi, please."

She bared her teeth, but I didn't look away. After a moment, she made an effort to rein back her anger. She let out a long breath, fresh scarlet blooming beneath her freckled cheeks.

"I had to *beg* to get you to take me with you." Her voice was thick and her eyes had lost their fire. "Even after days together, I had to beg and plead and argue before you'd agree to let me join you. And then, this elf comes along and you just offer her a place?" She blinked rapidly, her eyes liquid. "It's not fair."

"You're right," I said, forcing the words past the lump in my throat. "You're right, it's not fair and I'm so sorry. But you're the one who got through to me and it's only because of you that I even realized how lonely and unprepared I was. You saved my life, Eshi, even before those bandits found us."

Moving slowly and giving her all the time in the world to pull away, I reached up to brush her hair aside. Her breathing quickened as I brought my face to the curve of her neck.

"I can't be without you," I murmured, her pulse fluttering beneath her golden flesh.

And then, I gently bit down on her neck.

Eshi let out a gasping breath, and I felt a shudder run through her. Her skin was warm and tasted of sweat and dust. I released her neck as she sagged back into me, my arms rising to fold her into a hug.

"You're an idiot," she whispered, her breath tickling my ear. "You're such an amazing, stupid, wonderful idiot."

"Yeah," I said, my voice hoarse. "I'm sorry, Eshi."

She shifted against me, nuzzling her face into the unmarked side of my neck and wrapping her arms around me. She bit down gently, and my face split into a smile of pure joy. I closed my eyes and held her, feeling the beat of her heart through the press of her chest and breathing in the sunny scent of her hair.

After several long minutes, Eshi stirred. She shifted within the circle of my arms, gingerly stretching out her wounded feet and turning so that she was once again lying with her back against my chest.

"I'm sorry, Amna," she said, settling herself against me. "I promise that I'm not normally this crazy. It's been a really long few days and Naroh's just..." She let out a breath and shook her head. "Anyway, again, I'm sorry."

The elf nodded slowly, watching us with eyes that shone with an almost wistful sort of glimmer. "You don't need to apologize."

"I do," Eshi said, meeting her gaze. "I haven't been nice to you, but the truth is that I do like you. I think you're strong and smart and your magic is amazing. We really could use your help looking for this."

"That's nice of you to say." Amna smiled and reached up to tuck that stray curl back beneath her headscarf. "And, well, for my part, I've been thinking about asking to join you since the night we met. Naroh coming back into the tomb for me sealed the deal." She looked down at herself and grimaced. "Although, I was hoping to rest and wash myself off a bit before bringing it up."

"Naroh's timing is terrible," Eshi agreed. "You know, the first time that he told me I was beautiful was after four days in the tomb?"

"Naroh!" Amna exclaimed, her expression scandalized. "That's horrible!"

"Right!?" Eshi shifted to better face the elf, lying with her side against my chest. "I was so mad. Then, he kissed me!"

The weight of the elf's glare made me wince. I ran a hand through my hair, fully ready to fight and justify my actions when something that Amna had said finally sank in.

"Wait, you were already going to bring up coming with us? Did Kashir tell you that we were hunting Marduss's tomb?"

"No. Like I said, he didn't want me to know about any of this." She hesitated a moment before giving us an embarrassed smile. "I suppose that it's time to come clean. I'd actually seen you once before we met by the river. My sister and I walked past you in Ikkad on the way to my uncle's house. You were arguing in the street and, well, you shouted rather loudly about searching for the grand necrophant's tomb."

A flush crawled up my face, growing hotter as Eshi pushed herself into a seated position to stare pointedly at me. Amna wasn't done speaking, however.

"I thought you were just some crazy people, at first. But then I got to the house and I heard about what had happened and saw the artifact you'd found, and, well... the *mystery* just swept me away. I left to come after you the very next morning."

"How did you get here so fast?" The hyenaling asked. "We left Ikkad in a hurry and didn't stop anywhere for too long."

Red once again bloomed beneath Amna's cheeks. She cleared her throat. "I, um—may have stolen one of my uncle's horses."

I raised an eyebrow at that. Unlike camels, horses weren't that common in the empire. As far as I understood it, very few breeds of the creatures did well in the dry, desert climate. Those that did exist, however, were fast.

And ruinously expensive.

Eshi's face split into her wide, scavenger's grin. "Oh, I like her, Naroh."

I shook my head, though I couldn't keep the smile off of my own face. I spent the next few moments considering Amna.

"This path won't be easy." I flicked my eyes down to her wounded foot. "There'll be more traps and tombs and fighting."

The elf met my gaze. "Marduss is responsible for the enslavement of my people and the annihilation of much of our history. I've got a thousand questions, and it seems like his tomb will be a good place to find some answers. A little pain doesn't scare me."

I nodded, and the fire within me flared to see itself in the eyes of yet another. Then, my lips quirked into a smile. "You're curious."

Amna flashed me a quick grin. "Just so."

"Alright, then, you have my approval to join us. Eshi?"

The hyenaling didn't hesitate to nod. "Mine too. I want you to come with us."

"Thank you." Amna's smile was brighter than the sun. "I promise that I won't slow you down. Well, not for long, anyway."

"Perfect." The hyenaling made a humming sound as she lay back against me. "We'll need to figure out where we're going to go, and what to do next. But I think that that can wait until we find a better place to camp tonight. Hopefully, beside a stream."

"I can find one," the elf said. "Water spirits are loud."

"Really?" Eshi said, her ears perking up. "What else can you find?"

I leaned my head back against Asu's leg, listening to the two women talk. This tomb hadn't provided us with any real answers, and our path forward was as long and difficult as it had ever been. Despite that, I felt lighter and better than I had in a long time.

It wasn't just Asu and me anymore, and with Eshi and Amna walking beside me, I felt like I could do anything.

"One last thing," Eshi said, drawing my attention back outward. She gave me a mock glare. "We have to agree not to talk about this out loud anymore. We got lucky with you, Amna, but Naroh's big mouth has gotten us in enough trouble already. We don't need anyone else knowing and making things more complicated than—"

"Squeak, squeak, little mice," a voice interrupted. "Peer out from your safety and shelter!"

Asu stiffened, rising up from his belly. Eshi pushed herself back upright, turning with me towards the voice we both recognized and hadn't wished to hear ever again.

Kur stood a few dozen paces behind Asu's tail, his face split into that too-wide grin. Above his ragged headwrap, he folded his notched ears back in a gesture of mock concern.

"But take care, little mice, for here come snakes that hiss and slither."

There was a squad of warriors behind the grinning priest; hyenalings, elves, and even one human woman. They were armored in the same way that the elven corpse at our old campsite had been, and a dizzying variety of weapons hung from their belts or were otherwise clutched in their hands.

One of them stepped forward, a hyenaling man that I'd last seen in the company of a purple-eyed, jackal-headed construct.

"Naroh," the House Malash guard said. "Come out and talk."

Eshi swore and the three of us scrambled to our feet as quickly as we could. Asu moved with us, spinning to face the warriors he'd somehow failed to notice approach. He raised his pincers only to fall into a lethal sort of stillness a bare moment later.

The three of us tucked ourselves against his side, my beating heart sending sparks of tingling energy rolling through me. Our two groups considered each other for several long moments and I spent that time trying to wrap my mind around this newest wrinkle.

Malash guards, brought to us by a priest of the Laughing God.

Gods of fucking death, nothing was making any sense. I let out a breath, too tired to try and reason my way through it.

"I guess we blamed Kashir for nothing. It looks like these guys were the ones who cut our rope."

"He still could have been the one to tip them off," Eshi said, rather unconvincingly.

She was on her feet beside me, her hands on the hilts of her knives. Her body was stiff with pain, though she still looked ready to throw herself at them.

"Maybe, but Asu's pretty easy to track."

"Do you know that smiling hyenaling?" Amna murmured. "And those soldiers... house guards? Why have they come all the way out here to find you?"

The elf was directly behind me, leaning onto her staff for balance.

"Kur is a priest of the Laughing God," I answered, keeping my eyes on the crowd of warriors. Though many shifted on their feet, they mostly seemed content to watch us mutter amongst ourselves. "He helped us get out of the canyon. I don't know why the guards are here, but their leader is Issia Malash's personal guardsman. They tried to arrest us in Ikkad."

"House Malash? Sand and fucking spirits," Amna swore. "What have I gotten myself into?"

Eshi was the first one to call something out. "Kur, you thieving bastard, what are you doing here?"

"Thief?" The priest's eyes shone with mirth. "I haven't stolen a thing from your circle, little matriarch."

Eshi bared her teeth. "Twist the truth all you like, priest. You stole from us and we want it back."

Kur hummed in thought and reached into a fold of his robe. He pulled out a familiar slip of parchment and held it up for us to see. "Do you mean this? I didn't steal these funny little words."

"I sure as hell didn't give it to you," I said.

"Ah, but you are free from the canyon, you are on your feet and your wounds heal faster than fever or infection can take hold." The priest grinned, his gaze returning to Eshi. "And look, matriarch, look how your circle has already grown. What you call thievery, I call payment. The Laughing God's blessing does not come freely."

"Blessing?" Eshi said, her body stiff enough that I thought she might shatter. "What!?"

Kur tucked the slip of parchment away, his too-wide grin erupting into a high, grating cackle.

"Enough of this," the hyenaling guard said, shouldering the priest aside. He was armored like the rest and as broad-shouldered as I remembered. A khopesh hung at his hip, but he kept his hands well away from it. "Naroh, I'm here on my mistress's orders. Come away from the war-scorpion so that we can talk."

I shook my head. "We can keep talking like this."

The hyenaling scowled. "You're not in any danger from us."

I didn't bother to answer, keeping my eyes on the warrior while I waited.

"Fine, I guess that I can respect a bit of caution. Like I said, I'm here on Lady Malash's orders. She wishes to speak with you back in Ikkad."

Eshi stirred enough to snort, and I had to say that I agreed with the sentiment. We'd suspected as much back in the city, but to me, this was proof that my shouting in the street had reached even Issia Malash's ears.

Either she wanted Marduss's tomb for herself, or wanted it to remain hidden. In both cases, I'd end up dead.

"Alright," I said. "Next time we stop in Ikkad, I'll be sure to come speak to your mistress."

"You will obey, mongrels," one of the guards, a human woman, growled. She stepped forward and pointed a spear in our direction. "Your betters have—"

The hyenaling leader reached up and cuffed her on the side of the head hard enough to send her stumbling. She recovered faster than I would have believed possible, dangerously graceful even in the armor she wore. She straightened to glare bloody murder at the man.

"Are you done?" He said, meeting her gaze impassively. "I told you, that's not how we're going to do this."

"We were ordered to bring them in, Captain," she hissed. "We should just take them."

"Get back in line."

A few tense moments later, the woman lowered her gaze. She slunk back into her place, and the hyenaling captain didn't again look away.

"Sorry about that," he told us. "My name is Sarach. How about we start over, eh?"

I gave him a cautious nod, curious, despite myself.

"Like I said, Lady Issia Malash is very interested in you. I don't know why, but I swear that you'll be safe with her."

"Safe?" I said. "You already tried to trap us in the canyon and we found one of your men dead at our camp. Even if you hadn't already chased us through Ikkad, none of that paints you as very trustworthy."

Sarach grimaced. "I know, but I have a job to do. I tried to get to you before you could get back to the war-scorpion. Obviously, that failed."

"With a priest," Eshi said.

"Believe me, I wouldn't have relied on his kind if I'd had any other choice. The bastard already ruined a perfectly good ambush." The priest cackled, but Sarach ignored him. "Listen, I'm a soldier, so I'll tell it to you straight. House Malash is powerful, my mistress could make your lives very difficult if you refuse her."

"She's already made our lives difficult," I said. "We're doing fine."

"My mistress is also rich and generous to those who follow her commands. I don't know what you're doing out here, but I bet that a bit of her gold would help you out."

He had no idea how right he was about that.

"Anything to get these little mice into your jaws," Kur grinned. "Three fat squeakers for your snake to swallow."

"Be quiet," Sarach growled, not looking away from me. "Think carefully, Naroh. It would be a mistake to refuse the lamians."

I tilted my head to the side. "Ladies?"

"Fuck no," Eshi growled. "We're dead if we go back to Ikkad."

"Returning now does seem a little unwise," Amna agreed.

"You could go back," I told her, shifting to face the elf more fully. "If you split from us now, you could go back to your family. You haven't done anything to them, yet."

"I'm in this, Naroh," Amna said. "Till the end."

I grinned and warmth buzzed through my chest as I turned back to face the hyenaling captain. "Sorry, captain, we're going to have to refuse."

"You're making a mistake." Sarach shifted almost imperceptibly forward, one hand finally finding the hilt of his khopesh. "There are enough of us here to kill you if we attacked."

"Sure," I said, keeping my eyes on his. "But then Asu would make sure you all died with us."

We stared at each other for several heartbeats longer before the captain finally relaxed. He waved his warriors, speaking even as he turned away.

"Alright, then. I hope that you'll remember this next time we see each other."

With that, the warriors moved away. I watched them leave, wondering if I should just set Asu on them now and save me whatever trouble they might bring me in the future. Instead, I just looked away. I didn't have the stomach to murder a dozen or more people for something they might never even do.

"There's no room for you here, priest," Eshi said. "Asu will kill you if you come too close."

I blinked, realizing that Kur hadn't left with the others.

"Don't worry about me," he said. "I think I'll follow the captain for a while. It's been a while since I've seen Ikkad."

"Leave, then," Eshi said.

Kur cackled, flicked his notched ears, and turned away. "The Laughing God is watching, little mice. Make sure you keep him entertained."

Chapter Twenty-Two

We ended up spending the night not far from where Kur and the Malash guards had left us. The three of us were exhausted, worn thin by the stress of the past few days. We'd stayed on Asu's back just long enough for Eshi to spot a suitable camping spot.

We were all asleep long before the sun went down.

I woke with the following dawn, feeling better than I had in days. It was dark enough that I could still see Tel'aman's Flight twinkling in the sky to the north, though most of the other constellations had already disappeared.

Eshi lay with her head on my chest, and her sleepy murmurs of protest drew a smile from me as I untangled myself from her and pushed myself up. She was sitting up and rubbing at bleary eyes by the time I returned from checking on Asu. Amna woke up not long after and the two women hobbled off to relieve themselves while I prepared our breakfast of dried rations and water. After a quick meal, we turned our attention to our bandage-wrapped injuries.

"You know," Amna said. She was seated on the ground beside me, staring at the jar of Kur's salve. "I was too out of it yesterday to notice, but there's something odd about this stuff. I can feel a sort of... resonance. It's unlike anything I've ever felt before."

"It's definitely magic." I straightened from where I'd re-bandaged the first of my ointment-smeared feet. The three of us were in the shade of Asu's bulk, sheltered from the heat of the rising summer sun. "You look way too good for someone who had a few of her toes ripped off. And it's the same for Eshi and me."

The elf nodded, and my stomach twisted as she lifted the naked ruin of her foot up for a better look.

Unwrapped and cleaned of dirt and dried blood, it was a lot easier to see exactly what sort of damage the trap had done. The wound was messy, her flesh ragged and torn. The two smallest toes on her right foot were missing entirely, as was about half of her third toe. They'd been torn away by the trap's central spike, and the downward-facing lances along the pit's edge had ripped three long, bloody rents.

Although her injuries looked bad, the skin seemed to already be closing. There was no swelling, her skin wasn't hot, and it did not smell or look to be going bad. The wound was a healthy-looking red. Instead of just a day, it looked like her foot had already been healing for close to two weeks.

Though judging from the way she moved, it was still incredibly painful.

"When I was younger," the elf said, staring at her foot. "A man in our caravan had impaled his hand on something. He did his best to keep it clean, but it went bad after a few days, and it had to be cut off. I thought the same thing would happen to me, but I don't even think I'll have a limp when this is healed." She set her foot back down and scooped a finger into the viscous ointment. "This is powerful magic."

There's a price for it," Eshi said. "I think that I'd have almost rather lost a limb."

The hyenaling was sitting on my other side, near enough for our legs to touch. She was scowling down at her unwrapped forearm, the cuts already well on their way to closing.

"You're still going to use it, right?" I said, frowning at her. "It's already saved all of our lives."

I expected her to turn her glower on me and argue. Instead, she just folded her ears back for a moment and let out a long breath.

"Yes, Naroh, I'll use it. Spitting in the face of this gift will just make things worse."

I didn't really have an answer to that, so I just nodded and turned back to where Amna was still examining the salve. "You need to use it too. Even if the magic makes you nervous."

The elf smiled. She leaned forward to look past me, a lock of her dark hair tumbling out from beneath her red headscarf.

"He's a bit of a worrier," she told Eshi. "Isn't he?"

The hyenaling made a sound of assent, and her bitter expression softened. She let her hand fall to my thigh. "He is. You should see him fret when I go through his junk."

"Junk!" I exclaimed, turning to the wide smile that had appeared on Eshi's face. "A shard from a Nictossis era canopic jar isn't junk."

Amna let out a gasp and slapped a hand down to grip my other thigh. "What! Where did you find something like that?"

I grinned. "I pulled it out of the tomb of Nictossis II a couple of years ago. It's got this beautiful pattern baked into the clay, I think that they had something to do with —"

"Great," Eshi interrupted with a groan. "Now there's two of you."

A flush crept over Amna's face, but I just laughed. We fell silent after that. I leaned back against Asu, letting my thoughts drift while, on either side of me, my two companions tended to their injuries.

"Nest and flow the wise ones from wings of stork, immortal in wisdom's source."

"You still think that's important?" Eshi asked.

I blinked, not having realized that I'd spoken the words out loud. "I think so? Those words feel like a modified version of the House Nabonassara motto, and my gut tells me there's a reason the pharona had them written like that."

"Weirdly, you mean?" Eshi finished pulling her boots on over her second freshly wrapped foot and leaned back against my side. "It doesn't even sound like a real sentence."

"That's my fault." Amna's knee brushed against mine as she shifted. "Elvish grammar and syntax are very different, and some of our connector words don't have a direct translation."

I chewed on my lip for a few moments, slinging my arm around Eshi's shoulder to let the hyenaling settle more comfortably against me. "How sure are you of the translation?"

"As sure as I can be. My uncle might be able to do a better job, but..." Amna let out a long breath and shook her head. "The lamians worked very hard to purge our language."

"But you speak elvish," Eshi said. "The snakes obviously failed to kill it."

"They didn't kill it," Amna confirmed, her voice bitter. "But they did break it."

The hyenaling flicked her ears in confusion. Amna didn't respond right away, taking a few moments to adjust her headscarf while she gathered her thoughts.

"My people were slaves," the elf eventually continued. "Everyone knows that, but I don't think that anyone alive today can actually understand what that means. An elf's body literally did not belong to them. Can you imagine that? Can you imagine not having any say in what happens to you? The lamians could bend and break us in any way they wanted. Our men were sent to work and die in the mines and fields, while our women were forced to serve and please and birth new generations of slaves. A slave's life was short and filled with horror and pain."

"Fucking snakes," Eshi muttered.

Amna nodded. Her eyes flicked to mine for a moment, and I saw her make a visible effort to change tack. She was choosing to omit the fact that many hyenalings and humans had been just as intrinsically tied to, and profited from, the slavery of the elves.

"In any case," the elf continued. "Our language was outlawed. I'm sure a lot of us resisted at first, but the lamians were ruthless. Submitting to their rules was the best way for a slave to lessen the misery of their existence. Speaking elvish brought pain, so we stopped using it. There were only a few who clung to it, and they did their best to pass on what they could before they were caught and killed. The language became fragmented, and the only reason that a few of us know some of it today is because hundreds of elves throughout the centuries dedicated their entire lives to collecting and piecing together those fragments."

"And those fragments might have mutated," I said. "Words change their meaning over time, even without something like the purges."

"Exactly, and almost nothing of our writing exists to corroborate what we do know. We have no real way of telling how closely our elvish matches the one spoken by our ancestors."

Eshi blew out a breath. "So, we have nothing. The writing on the sarcophagus could be anything."

"In theory," Amna answered with a shrug. "But, contextually, it makes sense for those words to be the Nabonassaran House motto."

"Nest and flow the wise ones from wings of stork," I repeated, *"immortal in wisdom's source.* This is literally how you would say their motto in elvish?"

"As far as any of us can tell."

Eshi wiggled herself against me so that my arm draped over the front of her chest and my palm rested on the warm flesh of her naked stomach. I was careful of the still-healing slash that cut across her upper torso, which meant that my forearm rested directly over one of her breasts.

A result that I was not at all annoyed with.

"Alright," the hyenaling said with a pleased little hum. "What was the original motto again, Naroh?"

"The wise fly on the wings of the stork, to nest, immortal in wisdom's source," I said. "This is what was carved into the medallion I've found and on that statue in the tomb's antechamber."

"They're close," the hyenaling remarked.

"They are," I agreed. "But *flow the wise ones from wings of stork...* are you sure it's not 'fly' like in the original?"

Amna nodded and used one finger to trace two symbols into the dirt in front of us. "I don't know how much of it you remember, but this," she pointed to one of the whorling and curling symbols, "is how you write 'fly.' This other one is 'flow,' and that's what was carved into the lid."

"Flow," Eshi mused. "I've seen storks fly, and I don't think I'd ever describe that as flowing."

"I don't think any birds flow," I said.

"Unless they're on a river?" Amna said. Then, she leaned back against one of Asu's legs and rubbed at her eyes. "No, never mind, that's stupid. This is what it translates to, but I have no idea what it means."

"Maybe it's some sort of weird riddle?" Eshi said, tugging on my arm with both hands so that I hugged her tighter. "Is that common to find in tombs?"

"Sometimes." With some difficulty, I pulled my focus away from the soft squish of the hyenaling's breasts. "But they're often just related to the tomb itself. Lamians never seal their corpses away—it's why there were holes in the sarcophagus we hid in and why there wasn't just a big slab of stone over the main entrance."

"Why is that?" Amna asked. "I wondered about that when I first went in."

"You don't know either," Eshi asked. "Really?"

The elf shrugged, self-consciously. "I've always been more focused on my own people's history. Until a couple of weeks ago, I never cared enough about diving to study lamian burial traditions. Although I wish I had... this sort of information feels crucial now."

"Not as crucial as learning a supposedly extinct and highly illegal language turned out to be," I said, giving her a wry smile.

Amna's lip quirked upward, then she made a rolling sort of 'go on' gesture with one hand.

"It's not much of a secret," I said. "Lamians believe that for their soul to ascend to the afterlife, it first has to leave the body behind and make its way to the outside world. But their tombs are built to be these large, deadly mazes, that most of them don't know as well as they should. A lot of lamian pharons and necrophants worry that their souls will lose themselves in that same maze and never be able to reach the gods. Their solution is to leave little clues to help their souls navigate the tomb. Sometimes there will even be treasure hidden in faraway chambers, and a clue might point to that."

"Spirits can't move through rock?" Eshi said.

"Souls," Amna corrected. "Sentient beings like us have souls."

"What's the difference?"

"Spirits are more natural?" The elf shook her head, and a curl of her dark hair slipped from beneath her headscarf. "Sorry, it's not quite that. Souls are natural too, but they're different."

"Fascinating," Eshi drawled.

"I still have a thousand questions," I agreed.

"I'm getting there," Amna flushed, giving me a light smack with the back of her hand. "It's complicated. There's... alright, I'll just skip all the theory—"

"What?" I interrupted. "I want the theory!"

"I'll tell you later, then."

"But I'm curious!"

"Hush!" Amna said, giving me another light smack. "I need to think!"

I grinned, and against my side, Eshi let out a high cackle. Amna let out an annoyed huff, but I could see her fighting off a smile.

"Alright," the elf said after a few moments. "Practically speaking, the important difference comes when we are talking about magic. Have you ever wondered why lamian necromancy doesn't work on animals?"

I nodded, and Eshi flicked her ears in assent.

"Well, that's because creatures like Asu have a spirit. And compared to souls, spirits are ... simpler is the wrong word, but they're—"

"Different?" I said.

"More natural?" Eshi added.

"Yes." Amna stuck her tongue out at me and silenced the chuckling hyenaling with a pinch to the arm. "Spirits are different and more intrinsically woven into the natural world. They're a part of it in a way that we could never be, and operate on instinct and impulse rather than thought. Asu can't help wanting to mate at certain times of the year, just like water spirits will always babble."

"So," Eshi said, rubbing at her arm. "Your magic works on all animals?"

Amna nodded. "All spirits and animals can hear my call, though whether or not they choose to answer, or how they will respond, depends on the individual."

"When we first met you," I said, speaking slowly while I chewed on my thoughts. "By the river, when you were singing, I... felt something. It was like I was in a daze."

"That was mostly because of Ko," Amna said, with a small smile. "He's powerful, especially when you don't know he's there."

"But in the tomb, you were singing to the undead. You had them hypnotized, but Ko wasn't with you."

The elf inclined her head. "You're right, and that leads to my next point. Souls, like we all have, are complicated. Only sentient beings, like us, have them, and the main theory is that they're a sort of... evolved spirit. Parts of them are the same, and that's why my magic has some small effect on you, though you can easily shake it off."

"But those zombies were too stupid to?" Eshi asked.

"Exactly. My magic doesn't affect the soul— only necromancy can do that." Amna reached up to tuck away a loose curl of hair. "A lamian could probably explain this better, but how I understand it, a body that housed a soul isn't like the remains of a fox or scorpion. Our soul affects our flesh and bones somehow, marking them. Something of that stays with our remains once the soul leaves, and that's what the death magic latches on to. Without it, the magic just can't find purchase."

It was interesting, fascinating, really. I had dozens of other questions bouncing around my head, but managed to reel myself in after some effort.

"I would love to hear more about this later," I said. "But we got a little sidetracked. *Nest and flow the wise ones from wings of stork, immortal in wisdom's source.* My gut tells me that this is the key to finding the tomb of Nabonassara I. We just have to figure out how."

"You're the tomb diver," Eshi said. "You should be good at this."

I chuckled. "I'd have been able to actually pay you back if I was any good at this."

"Mmm." The hyenaling pressed a gentle bite onto my bicep. "That's true."

"Anyway," I continued. "Between the two versions that we know, 'wisdom's source' is what stays consistent."

"It also sounds like it could be a location," Amna said, her eyes going distant. "Like... the Nabonassarans were the ones who built a lot of those old libraries. Could that be it? As slaves, my people were excluded from them, but everyone else went there to learn how to read, right?"

We all spent a few moments mulling that over.

"Well," Eshi said, after a moment's hesitation. "If it is talking about Nabo's tomb, 'nest' is close to 'rest,' as in, 'resting place.' Maybe he's buried under one of those libraries?"

"I don't—" I started, only to be cut off by an excited clap of Amna's hands.

"Oh! We should go to the capital!"

"Uruq?" I asked, "Why?"

"That's where the last great storkling library is!"

"Right," I nodded. "There was supposed to be one in every major city, but they were all destroyed or fell apart and were built over. You think Nabonassara I is buried there?"

"Just say Nabo," Eshi muttered.

"Maybe," Amna said. "It's a bit of a long shot, but there's also someone in the capital who might be able to help us with the translation. He's an elf named Lushran, and my uncle used to write to him all the time about elvish history. I know for a fact that he speaks elvish, and next to my Uncle Kashir, he's the most knowledgeable elf I know."

"Mmm," Eshi mused. "I've never been to the capital before."

"It's worth a try," I added after a few moments. "And I can't think of anything else right now. Uruq is a long way south, so we'll have time to come up with better ideas as we go."

"Let's go, then!" Amna said, carefully pushing herself to her feet. She looked down at herself, nose wrinkling in disgust. "We're stopping at a stream tonight. I am *not* going another night without bathing."

I blinked as the otherworldly notes of Amna's song faded. The world came creeping back from the edges of my awareness, my focus returning as I stirred within the depths of my robe.

Gods of fucking death, that woman could *sing*.

"There's a river not too far away," the elf said, letting out a breath. "Over to the east."

She was seated in the dirt with her back to us, sheltered from the summer by her long, layered robe. She looked out over the dry, empty wilderness from the crest of a small hill, the red of her headscarf bright in the light of the late afternoon sun.

"East?" Eshi squinted in that direction, her arm hooked around mine. "Are you sure?"

Amna turned to smile at us, embarrassed. "It's around here, though it might be more south than east. Water spirits are friendly, but it's hard to get anything but gossip out of them. They're not too great with directions either."

We were on the crest of a small hill, one of several that Amna had pointed to throughout the day. Certain landmarks, she'd said—specially shaped hills, rock formations, and copses of trees—were places where nature's spirits tended to gather. She'd had us stop at a few throughout the day, taking a few minutes to learn what she could about the land around us from the spirits that answered her song.

"Looks like there might be a ripple in the land over there," the hyenaling pointed. "I don't see any greenery, but there isn't anywhere else the stream could be."

"I guess that's where we'll first look," I said. It was getting to be late in the day, though there were still a few hours left of daylight. "Shall we?"

Both women nodded, and Amna gingerly pushed herself to her feet. We climbed back onto Asu's back, the colossal scorpion waiting still and uncomplaining. Eshi squeezed in beside me on the too-small driver's bench while the elf settled into place on the platform behind us.

"Let's go." Amna tugged the neckline of her still-filthy robe away from her ample chest. "I'm going to faint if I have to sit in my stink for too much longer."

I laughed while Eshi's ears shifted amusedly beneath her hood. She draped one leg over mine and shifted to tangle herself more comfortably around me.

"You should try sitting next to Naroh. He didn't even really wash before we left the Gibris.

"That," I said, getting Asu moving with a few taps of my guiding stick, "was totally your fault."

"My fault?" Her amber eyes were bright beneath her hood. "You're the one who told me that the rest of my clothes were too dirty."

I coughed, feeling heat bloom beneath my cheeks. "Well, you can still sit somewhere else if I smell too bad."

"I'll survive." She slid her leg along the top of my thigh and adjusted her grip on my arm. "Although, I can move if you're not comfortable."

My heart beat faster at the embers I saw smoldering within her gaze. I shifted myself closer to her. "I'll survive."

Eshi laughed, her tail wiggling. She pulled my hood back for a moment to press something between a kiss and a playful nip against my cheek before settling back against me.

Behind us, Amna let out a sigh. "You two are so good together."

Eshi's tail moved faster, and I smiled at the sudden warmth that buzzed within me. She was right, I thought, shifting my arm to better wrap it around the hyenaling at my side; we were good together.

"I'm liking you more and more, Amna." Eshi glanced back to where the elf sat. "I'm sorry again for how I first treated you."

"Oh, don't worry. I'm just happy that we're becoming friends."

"Me too," Eshi said.

I guided Asu around a scattering of boulders, keeping an eye on the ripple of land that Eshi had pointed out. The flesh between my shoulders prickled, and I glanced back to find Amna's eyes on us. I was puzzled by the expression I saw on the beautiful elf's face.

Eshi, evidently having noticed it as well, spoke before I did. "Are you alright?"

"What? Oh, yeah, sorry." She blinked and shook herself. Heat flushed her cheeks. "I didn't mean to just stare at you like that."

"What were you thinking about?" The hyenaling asked.

Amna's flush deepened, and she reached up to adjust her headscarf. "It was nothing."

Eshi shifted against me, twisting her neck back. "Tell us."

"No. It was just a stupid thought."

"Come on," I said, giving her a quirked smile. "We're curious."

She laughed, though her flush didn't fade away. "Don't worry, it's nothing serious. It was just a silly thought, and I don't want to say something that will make things uncomfortable now that we're all starting to get along."

"Well," I said, after exchanging a glance with Eshi. "Now you have to say it."

The hyenaling made an affirmative sound and detached herself from me. She shifted until she was kneeling on the seat beside me to fully face the elf.

"We're waiting," Eshi said, and I could hear the smile in her voice without having to see it.

"I don't—" Amna started, but then cut herself off with a quick breath. "Fine. I'm just a little ... jealous of you, Eshi."

"Really?" she answered. "Why?"

"You two." I felt Amna shift. "You're both so close and cute, and Naroh is so handsome and interesting and kind that I just... I just want something like that. That's all I was thinking."

"Hmm," Eshi said, laying a hand on my shoulder. "He is."

"But I'm not going to try anything," Amna hurriedly assured her. "We're still almost strangers and I'm not even sure about me or what I feel or—sorry, I'm not making sense. It was just a random thought, Eshi, and I promise that I won't ever try and get between you two."

I felt strangely hot and my head was a swirl of thoughts and emotions unfamiliar enough that I struggled to get a handle on them. I didn't know what to say. There was no doubt that I was attracted to Amna. She was fascinating and her beauty, knowledge, the confidence with which she spoke, her magic, and the sound of her voice when she sang were all intensely appealing.

Eshi, however, had wiggled her way into my heart. She made me feel better than I could have possibly imagined, and I was surprised at just how ill the thought of being without her made me. There was no chance that I was ever going to give up what was developing between us, and I was opening my mouth to say just that when Eshi spoke.

"Well, the smell of him now might change your mind. Come sit with us." She nudged me with her hip. "Naroh, budge over."

"What?" I blinked, pushing my hood back to glance up at her. "You want her to come sit with us?"

She flicked her eyes to mine for a moment, and I saw a strange sort of light in her gaze. "That's what I said. Come on, Amna."

"What?" The elf echoed me, and I shifted my eyes to find her staring at the hyenaling with an expression of disbelief. "Didn't you hear what I said?"

Eshi flicked her ears, amused. "I don't have Naroh's hearing problem."

"Then, I don't understand."

My own confusion pressed against my teeth, desperate to be voiced. I didn't know where Eshi was going with this, but some instinct told me that it was best to keep quiet.

"Come sit with us," the hyenaling repeated. "On the bench."

"Why?"

Eshi lowered her hood, exposing her features and letting the sun soak her speckled hair. She leaned her elbows on the platform, still kneeling on the bench beside me. Asu's steady, flowing gait made balance easy for the graceful hyenaling.

"Marduss's tomb isn't going to be easy to find, so you're going to be with us for a while, right? I think that it's better that we're close."

"But—" Amna's eyes flicked to me. Our gazes met, and both of us flushed and looked away. "Eshi, I—I don't—"

"You don't want to?" The hyenaling shrugged. "It's okay if you don't. But if you're curious...?"

She let the question hang in the air. The elf gaped at her for another few moments before closing her eyes and letting out a long breath. Then, she straightened and uncrossed her legs, seeming to have come to a decision when she looked at us again.

"Make some space."

Eshi bared her canines in a wide grin. "Shift over, Naroh."

"I'm already half off the bench." My heart was beating inexplicably faster as Amna slipped both of her legs beside Eshi. "I can't move anymore."

The hyenaling considered me for a moment, then her tail started to wag. She was slipping into my lap in the next instant, shifting so that her side was against my chest. She looped an arm around my neck, holding on as she settled atop me.

"There," she said, her breath and hair tickling my cheek. "Now there's room."

I chuckled, shifting my legs and wrapping my outside arm around her back to keep her from falling. "Creative."

She made a pleased sound, molding her lithe body to mine. Her scent, an intoxicating blend of spice and sun-warmed sweat, washed over me. It, along with the supple firmness of her ass and the soft squish of one breast, helped ignite my blood. Heat bloomed beneath my flesh, and I felt my crotch stir.

"Thank you." Light danced in Eshi's amber eyes, and she did a slow roll of her hips to slide her ass over my growing hardness. "Are you a little uncomfortable?"

"Mmm," I answered, leaning forward for a kiss. "Not at all."

Delight flushed her cheeks as she laughed. She smiled into our kiss and cupped my cheek with her free hand. Sparks exploded through my mind. Her palm shifted over my cheek and my entire body buzzed with the taste, scent, and feel of her.

I gazed into her when our lips parted, her smile softening into something warm. Words, powerful and laden with feeling, bubbled up from deep within me. Racing through my stomach and chest, they burned their way up my throat until they were on the verge of flying free.

But then, Amna slid down on the bench beside us, and Eshi had to pull in her legs. We both turned away from each other, and the words slipped away.

"Wow," the elf said, wedging her side against me. Her cheeks were as bright as her headscarf, and a dark curl of hair tumbled free. "There really isn't much room here."

"You have to get close," Eshi said, folding one leg between Amna's. "Wrap yourself around Naroh's arm, there."

"I still need to steer," I reminded them, waving Asu's guiding stick.

"You'll be fine," the hyenaling answered with a flick of her ears. "Come on, Amna, you look like you're about to fall off."

After another moment's hesitation, the elf looped her arm around mine and slipped closer. She pushed one leg beneath my own and shifted to slide her shoulder behind mine. Her chest pressed against my arm, my limb almost swallowed by breasts that were so big, round, and soft. She was... fuller than the hyenaling, her body softer and more obviously curved. There was an allure to that softness, and the scent of her sweat was a strong, feminine blend of sour heat and floral sweetness.

I swallowed. The feel of them both so close to me, the warmth of their flesh, the curve of their bodies, and the way their scents swirled together within me was... intoxicating.

"Comfortable?" Eshi asked.

"Mmm," Amna answered, before shifting her body just so and letting out a long breath. "Yeah, this is nice."

"And the warmth," the hyenaling said, leaning the side of her head against mine. "Do you feel it?"

The elf gave the two of us a soft smile. "I think so."

Eshi smiled back, and the two shared a look I couldn't decipher. I briefly wondered if this bench made for one could continue to hold the weight of three, before settling back into the soft tangle of feminine bodies.

Amna made a small sound in her throat, glancing at me with dark, dancing eyes. "I see what you mean about the smell." She shifted so that her breasts pressed more comfortably into my arm and flank. "Although, it's not at all unpleasant."

Eshi hummed her agreement and did another wicked little roll of her hips.

I spent the next several minutes lost in a warm haze of the two women's touch and scent. My blood was hot, and my crotch was a bulging, painful lump beneath the soft flesh of Eshi's ass.

It wasn't long, however, before we came upon the ripple of land and the narrow ribbon of water that cut through the dusty wilderness along its bottom. The stream was overgrown, sheltered from the sun by a snarl of gnarled brush and woody vegetation. We traveled downriver until we found a rocky section of the riverbank with less plant life.

We carefully slid off Asu onto still-healing feet, and the two women focused on pulling down the supplies we needed while I tended to the great scorpion.

"You did so good today, Asu-boy," I cooed, scratching beneath his chin. "Having the three of us behind your head wasn't too much for you? What a strong, handsome boy you are."

The war-scorpion chittered happily, flexing his pincers and settling what parts of him he could within the narrow strip of flowing water. I eyed the saddle for a moment, making sure that I hadn't loosened the supporting straps too far.

I spent a few more minutes lavishing attention on the big bug before turning away and heading over to where the two women were digging through our packs.

"—have to see how much money we have before we get too much further south," Eshi was saying. "We'll be passing through villages again soon, and we'll need to pay for more supplies."

Amna grimaced. "I have a little left over, but I sold my uncle's horse at a huge loss to pay for my own supplies. Let's spend tomorrow morning going through everything we have."

Eshi nodded. "An inventory is a good idea."

The hyenaling pulled a bundle of clean-looking cloth from the depths of her pack and stood. She had already taken off her robe, as was her habit when the sun sank low enough for the heat to be bearable. Her golden flesh glowed an amber to match her eyes in the evening's deepening light, and her pants were belted low enough that I could see much of the muscled V of her naked stomach.

"I've been slowly going through Naroh's stuff on our way up here, but he's got so much junk, and he's about as organized as a sackful of kittens."

"I have a system," I said, joining the women. "I know exactly where everything is."

"Really?" Eshi said, raising both ears and eyebrows. "What about the stone bowl?"

I... had forgotten I had an old bowl, but I'd be damned if I admitted to that now. "I know exactly where everything is, minus that."

Eshi's canines flashed in a scavenger's grin, and, seated on a rock not far away, Amna laughed.

"Well," the elf said, reaching up to pull at her headscarf. "That will be tomorrow's job. I'm not doing anything but bathing and washing my clothes tonight. My hair is a disaster under here."

The hyenaling limped over to me and looped her arm around mine. "We'll go and wash as well. Naroh, at least, could really use it."

"We're going together?"

"Obviously." She pressed her chest against my arm, her tail swishing behind her in languid sweeps. "Someone has to make sure you get properly clean."

Chapter Twenty-Three

Eshi and I picked our way downriver, arm in arm, looking for another clear stretch of water. We walked through a rising chorus of bird and insect songs, past scuttling lizards and coiled serpents. Mice scurried over the rocky ground, their twitching noses alert for any foxes stalking in their wake. The sun was low against the western horizon and, past the worst of the day's heat, the world was coming alive around us.

"You know," I said, once we were a few minutes from camp. "I'm not going to be able to focus on bathing if you come with me."

"Hmm." The hyenaling squeezed my bicep with one hand, holding soap and a bundle of clean cloth in the other. "As unfocused as last time?"

"Worse." My cock, which had never fully softened, swelled back into prominence. "Having you on my lap was pure torture."

"Was it?" Heat bloomed beneath the freckled flesh of her cheeks and my heart beat faster as I saw the smolder return to brighten her amber eyes. "You know, I thought I felt something."

"So did I." I pulled Eshi to a stop beside a relatively clear section of stream. "What do you think about this? It looks private."

The heat in the hyenaling's eyes flared. "Take off your robe."

She let her arm slip from mine, turned, and took a few steps away.

"I don't think that's very fair," I said, admiring the sway of her hips and the curve of her ass. "I only have my loincloth underneath and you're still wearing all of that."

Eshi dropped her bundle down on a nearby rock and watched as I pulled the robe from my shoulders. Her eyes traced the naked contours of my chest and thighs.

"Mmm, you're right." Her voice emerged as a low, breathy purr. "That isn't fair."

She hooked her thumbs into the top of her pants and, with a delighted flush and wicked little smile, Eshi spun so that her back was to me. She bent forward, arched her spine, and, in one smooth motion, pulled down her pants.

Heat flared through me as I watched the cloth slip over her tail and down the curve of her ass. Her waist wrap was coiled tightly around the flare of her hips, looping between her legs to hug her center. The pale linen was striking against the golden smoothness of her exposed flesh. It left most of her bare, and Gods of fucking death, I loved the way her ass devoured the single, narrow strip of cloth between her cheeks.

Eshi bent lower, pulling her pants down to her ankles. She flexed her thighs, her muscles shifting and playing as she stepped out of them. A groan rolled through me as the motion made her ass quiver, and through the rippling screen of her soft, golden flesh, I saw hints of the curving, snuggly wrapped shape of her sex.

"There we go." She straightened and peered back at me over one shoulder, letting her pants dangle from the tips of her fingers. Her amber eyes shone through the tumbling waves of her blonde, speckled hair. The pants fell to the ground with an audible thump. "Now, we're even."

"Uh, not quite," I coughed, my flesh hot. "I don't have anything over my chest."

"Ah." She turned to face me and ran her fingers over the bound swell of her breasts. "You're right. Should I take it off?"

"It's only fair." I swallowed, finding it hard to speak through my dry throat. "And to bathe, you'll need to take it off anyway."

"Well," she dug one end of the winding cloth free, her eyes hot. "In that case."

With a slow pull, she unraveled her chest wrap. The knife slash she'd taken across her torso was still bandaged and it stayed in place while the rest of the cloth fell away and freed the soft, rounded flesh of her naked breasts.

They were as I remembered—shockingly pale and plump compared to the rest of her sun-kissed leanness. Her nipples were mouth-wateringly stiff and bright as cherries, the delicate flesh already prickling in the cooling air.

"You know." She stretched long and cat-like beneath my gaze. "This does feel better, actually."

Heat roared within me as I drank in the sight of her near-naked body. I stalked towards her, my heart pounding with a wild and sudden hunger.

"Gods of fucking death." I slid my hands over the warm, nearly naked flesh of her hips. "You're perfect, Eshi."

"Mmm." She bit down on the corner of her lip and rested both palms against my chest. "I love seeing my mark on you."

The bruise on my neck throbbed and I chuckled low in my throat. "Do you want to leave another?"

Her ears twitched and crimson bloomed beneath her freckled cheeks. "You don't know what you're saying."

"I think that I do," I murmured, folding her in my arms.

I kissed her, slow and deep, marveling at the spiced warmth of her tongue and the softness of her lips. She leaned into the kiss and a little mewl of sound escaped her throat. Her body melted into mine, the naked flesh of her breasts and legs achingly smooth.

Static buzzed through me as our lips parted. Her nose brushed against my cheek on her way down to nuzzling the unbruised side of my neck. My skin prickled beneath the heat of her breath and a groan rumbled through me as I felt the gentle press of her teeth and the warm caress of her tongue.

"Fuck," I said when she pulled away. "Eshi—"

Her touch, her scent, her beauty, and her very being were making the fire within me flare and rage. Great clouds of heat billowed within me, the flames rising ever higher and reaching for her through the silken contact of our naked flesh.

Gods, I *burned* for her.

"Let's get into the river." Her arms snaked around my neck, her near-naked hips shifting as she ran a smooth leg against mine. "We have to wash first."

"First?" I asked, shifting my grip to hook my thumbs into the top of her loincloth. "What happens after?"

"After," she breathed, her eyes bright and burning, "I reward you for staying with me."

I frowned, her comment like a bucket of water on the fire coursing through my blood. She'd already turned away, however, holding onto my neck with one arm as she reached down to pull off the first of her boots.

"What are you doing?" I shifted my grip to steady her. "Eshi, your feet."

"I'm fine," she said, though couldn't hide the pained grimace as she pulled her bandaged foot free. She placed it gingerly on the rocky ground. "See?"

"You need to keep your wounds clean." I moved to take more of her weight. "Here, let me help you get to the water."

"I'm fine, Naroh," she said, folding her other leg up to reach her boot. "Take yours off, and the waistwrap. I promise that I'm worth it."

There was so much wrong with that last statement that I didn't even know where to begin. I stood blinking for a few moments before my mind finally latched onto something.

"Worth it? Eshi, what are you even talking about?"

The hyenaling had gotten her other boot off and threw it aside without meeting my gaze. She reached for my waist, tugging at the cloth that covered my crotch.

"That I'm worth staying with."

I stiffened, those words breaking something within me. Eshi noticed. She folded her ears back atop her head and hunched her shoulders as if cringing from a blow she knew would come.

"Eshi," I said. "Stop."

She shook her head in denial, looking anywhere but at my face. The fire between us had cooled, but still, she tried to re-ignite it. She pulled harder at my loincloth, her movements made clumsy by haste and rising emotion.

I grabbed her wrists. "Stop it. You need to put your boots back on."

"I'm fine, Naroh. Come on, let's have sex." Her breathing was coming faster, and she tugged her arms against my grip. "Please, let's just have sex. I know that I've been crazy and useless and just slowing you down, but don't leave. Please, Naroh, if we have sex, you'll see."

"Leave? Eshi, I—" My voice broke. Where was this all coming from? And why was she still on her fucking feet? "Let me help you."

"I'm f—"

Something very much like anger tore through me. I moved without thinking, scooping her into my arms and turning that damned platitude into a startled squawk.

"Naroh!" Eshi squirmed against my chest. "What—"

"Be quiet."

I swept my gaze over the darkening landscape, spotting a large, flat section of rock not too far away. I stomped towards it, easily ignoring the pain in my feet from the hyenaling's added weight.

"Put me down! Naroh, I'm—"

"Eshi," I interrupted, stopping to glare down at her. "If you tell me that you're fine one more fucking time, I swear to all the fucking gods of death that I'm going to muzzle you."

She stilled, finally meeting my eyes. A thousand emotions swirled within the amber depths of her gaze—fear, shame, anger, helplessness, confusion, desperation... it covered the glorious fire of her passion like a pall of smoke, smothering her ferocious strength and will.

My anger flared hotter.

"You are the most frustrating woman that I've ever met." I started back towards the flat section of rock. "Gods and fucking demons, Eshi, sometimes, you make me want to scream and rip my fucking hair out."

She shifted in my arms, but I squeezed her harder against me.

"For someone so smart, confident, and all-around fucking amazing, you say some of the dumbest fucking things I've ever heard. Seriously, what in the hell was all that fucking garbage? You'll *reward* me? You'll show me that you're worth keeping around? Are you fucking serious?"

"It's true," she mumbled, her cheek hot against my chest.

"It's a steaming pile of fucking scorpion shit. Gods, you make me so fucking mad. And why won't you ever let me help you? That's the worst thing. You were acting totally crazy in the canyon, Eshi, and you almost fucking died because of it."

She didn't answer, staying stiff and still in my arms. We reached the flat section of rock a few moments later. I inhaled deeply, and let out a long breath. What was left of my anger drained away, leaving behind a strange dullness.

I set her down on the stone. "Don't move."

I turned away, returning a few moments later with my robe in one hand and her boots in the other. She was still seated where I'd left her, facing the river and hugging her knees to her chest.

Her ears twitched, but she otherwise didn't react to my approach.

"Here," I said, wrapping my robe around her shoulders. "We're going to talk."

She didn't meet my gaze as I knelt in front of her. I reached for one of her bandaged feet with a boot in the other hand. I felt her tense, but the weight of my glare kept her silent.

I was done humoring whatever this nonsense was.

"You fought those bandits at the river." I slid the first of her boots on as gently as I could. Eshi watched me with a sullen expression, her face flushed beneath a falling curtain of hair. "You saved my life."

I moved more slowly with her other boot, taking a moment to examine her bandaged foot before sliding it on. Spots of blood dotted the pale cloth.

"You got hurt fighting for me. You could have died." I settled back on my knees and emotion made my voice thick. "Why won't you ever let me help you, Eshi?"

She closed her eyes, folding her knees back to her chest and wrapping my robe more tightly around herself. I waited, silently watching her, my chest aching at how tightly clenched her frame was.

Eventually, she let out a ragged breath and opened her eyes.

"Do you remember back in Ikkad when I told you I could help you?" She continued at my nod. "I said that I would take care of the present, I would fight, hunt, trade, and do whatever else so that you could focus on the past. You've got this impossible task to do—finding Marduss's fucking tomb. I'm supposed to help you, but I haven't."

She dropped her gaze, grimacing at the sight of her boots. "I promised to keep up, but all I did was get hurt and slow you down."

"Eshi," I reached out and laid my hand on one of her feet. "You saved my life. Even before the fight at the river. I'd still be trying to make it out of the tomb if it wasn't for you."

She shook her head. "That's not what I mean."

"Then, what?"

"Who would want a warrior too weak to fight?"

"Wait," I said, recognizing those words. "Is all this because of what Kur said?"

"It's the truth," she said, still not quite meeting my gaze. "I knew it before he said it."

"Eshi..." I was stunned, and for a moment, I didn't know what to say. "That doesn't make any sense. You're not weak because you need time to heal!"

She shook her head again, more vigorously this time. "I haven't done enough."

"You saved my life!"

"You don't understand."

Her eyes flicked to mine and I flinched, completely unprepared for what I saw there—fear, and a yawning pit of despair that was as deep and black and gnawing as it had been the morning Asu had killed her camel.

Gods, she was terrified, and somehow, it was because of me.

I rose to my feet and circled behind her. She didn't move as I lowered myself to the stone. The rock was rough and gritty beneath my mostly bare legs, but the discomfort was easy to ignore. I scooted forward, stretching my legs out on either side of her to wrap her in my arms.

Even through the cloth of my robe, I could feel the warmth of her as I pulled her to my chest. It relieved me, though she remained stiff, silent, and still. Her hair smelled of dust and sweat and sunshine, and I leaned into her body to rest my chin on her shoulder and press my cheek to hers.

"Tell me, Eshi," I murmured. "Please."

She pushed her cheek hard against mine for several moments. Then, she sagged against me, and I adjusted my grip on her, hugging her tight.

"Three years ago, my father and I were hunting. A priestess of the Laughing God found us one night. She followed us back to the clan a few days after that, and not long after, people started getting sick. It wasn't anything our healers knew how to treat. People started to die—my mother, father, cousins, and siblings. I got sick too, and for a while, I thought that I would die as well."

She relaxed into me as she spoke, and I could feel her jaw move against my cheek.

"When the sickness burned itself out, Tannah, my eldest half-sister, became matriarch. She was my mother's favorite and blamed me for causing all of that death. Everyone else agreed, and I was exiled the very next day."

"How was that your fault?"

She let out another breath. "Because I brought the priestess, Naroh. She might not have visited the clan if it wasn't for me."

I still wasn't sure I agreed that the two were related, but I let it go.

"Anyway," she continued. "That was all a long time ago. I spent the next few years wandering around, scraping and saving, and finding work where I could."

"That must have been hard."

"Yeah." Her hands came up to grip my forearm. "It was hard, but I could always go out and hunt if I got too hungry. It was just..."

"...You missed your family," I finished.

I hugged her tighter. I felt like understanding was right there, just out of reach.

"I was alone." Her voice cracked and she dug her nails into my forearm. "I was all alone, for years. I tried to join other clans, but everyone could see I was an exile. Nobody wanted me. Nobody wanted a girl whose own family threw her away."

"Eshi," I murmured, pushing my cheek hard against hers. She'd stiffened up again, her body clenched over a knot of old, old pain. "I'm so sorry."

"And then I met you. We spoke and you were interesting and you made me laugh. I had this... feeling about you, and it didn't go away even after Asu killed my camel and smashed all of my figs. We spent more time together and it grew more powerful, and I thought that maybe—Maybe I wouldn't be alone anymore."

Loneliness, Eshi had lived with it for years. It had been a constant weight on her back, no doubt momentarily kept at bay by companions that were as easy to lose as they had been to gain. But that wasn't enough. It wasn't family or clan. There was no security in it, no true companionship, warmth, or acceptance.

The isolation had been destroying her. She needed somewhere to belong; a place to call her own surrounded by people that were hers.

Gods, I hated that it had taken me so long to see.

"Eshi," I said. "I'm never going to leave you."

Someone to belong to— it was something that I hadn't known I was missing until this hyenaling had come howling into my life. She had taught me the wonder of it by pushing her way into a place beside me. She was beautiful in her strength, confidence, and ferocity, and in the tomb, surrounded by nothing but death, she'd pushed the darkness back with the warmth of her touch, laughter, and smile.

"But you might!" She broke through the circle of my arms as she pushed herself away with my robe still wrapped around her. Her hands pushed down on my legs as she spun to face me, her features tight and eyes bright with unshed tears. "There's nothing tying us together, Naroh! We're not clan or family. And sure, we've kissed, but that's it! We aren't even lovers. I wanted to do that now but..." She closed her eyes for a moment, tears spilling down her cheeks. "We're just partners, and you'll replace me if I don't do enough."

Me, Asu, and maybe even Amna—we were her chance to belong. I had no idea why she had first chosen me, but at some point, using the impossible goal we shared, Eshi had started to build a place for herself. What had Kur called it? A circle or a center? A clan? I didn't remember, but it wasn't important. What mattered is that, to Eshi, it was as precious as it was still fragile.

If I broke it, she would be left with nothing. If I decided that I didn't need her help, she would once again be left alone and abandoned and forced to start again.

And that terrified her more than anything.

That final piece of her clicked into place and finally, it felt like I could see the whole, shining wonder of her. Gods of fucking death, I'd never seen anything so beautiful.

Then, I burst into laughter.

Eshi's body went rigid, her eyes flew open and rage burned across her features. "Are you fucking laughing at me?"

"No!" I gasped, reaching for her hands. "I'm not!"

I laughed again. I couldn't help it. This fear of hers was so crazy and I felt so happy and so light. Eshi was the fire at my side, the warmth in the icy blackness. This woman—this beautiful, wonderful, fierce, *amazing* woman—was the most important thing in my life.

"Naroh..." Her voice broke.

Rage turned to hurt, and Eshi's face was twisting into an agonized grimace. That killed the laughter in me, though, I couldn't keep the smile from tugging at my lips.

"No, no, no," I said, squeezing her hands. "I'm sorry. I'm not laughing at you, Eshi, I promise. It's just that you don't understand. You're worried for nothing. We're already tied together too tightly to ever be pulled apart."

Her ears were stiff, her expression guarded and tight. "What do you mean?"

My mind was clear; certainty blazed within me, brighter than it ever had before. I let the heat of that wondrous feeling burn behind my eyes, and my smile grew as her expression softened into a more hopeful sort of confusion.

"You marked my neck, Eshi," I told her. "And you let me bite yours."

"Say what you mean."

I laughed, and the words that I'd first become aware of in the sarcophagus, the ones that I'd meant to say just a few hours ago, came as easily as breathing.

"I love you, Eshi."

Her lips parted to let out a little hitch of sound. I saw the world in her amber eyes, a joyful future lit by a fire more wondrous than anything I'd ever seen before.

"Again," she murmured. "Say it again."

"I love you. I need you beside me."

A shiver ran through her and fresh tears spilled from her still shining eyes. "Again."

"I love you." My voice had grown hoarse and I felt wetness flowing down my own cheeks. "You're my life, Eshi, and I never want to be without you again."

The hyenaling leaped from my robe, launching herself at me with a low mewl of sound. She crashed into my chest and knocked me onto my back. The rock and grit tore at my skin but Eshi's nakedness was so soft and warm atop me. She buried her face into my neck and I wrapped my arms around her as she sank her teeth into my flesh.

I laughed at the sharp pain of her canines, squeezing her tightly against me. Her entire frame shook, and I blinked away what was left of my tears as I listened to the hitch of her uneven breath.

"Careful," I said, wincing as her jaws tightened. "Your fangs are sharp."

"Sorry!" She gasped, releasing me at once. "I'm sorry."

"It's alright."

Eshi shifted atop me, her naked chest and legs sliding smoothly against mine. She raised her head and bit down on her lip, her expression suddenly unsure.

I gave her a lopsided grin as her eyes found mine through the falling strands of her speckled hair. "Does the mark look as good as the first one?"

She flushed, propping her elbows on my chest to touch her fingers to the fresh bite mark. "I bit you too hard. I'm sorry."

"Don't worry," I said, running my palm down the warm curve of her back. "You have years to make it up to me."

She shivered, sliding her own hand up to cup my cheek. "You meant what you said? You're not going to leave me?"

"Never," I said, seeing the heat of my love reflected in her amber eyes. "You're the light of my life. I need you beside me."

"I love you, Naroh." She brushed her nose against mine. Her hair tickled my shoulders, and her warm breath swirled over me. "I love you so, so much."

Then, her lips were on mine, and she filled me with the spiced, liquid taste of her tongue. I could feel her heart beating through the squish of her breasts. We sank deeper into each other, our kiss stretching into eternity, her body molding itself to mine. I let my hands roam her lean, silken curves, a small sound of pleasure escaping from between her soft lips.

Those lips were still on mine when she started to roll her hips. I suddenly became aware of the bulge between my legs. I slid my hands down to squeeze the flesh of her ass, groaning into her mouth as she ground her cloth-wrapped sex against my crotch.

"Naroh," she panted, breaking our kiss. Her breath was hot and her flesh was burning as she pressed her forehead to mine. "My Naroh."

I wove the fingers of one hand through her sun-soaked hair, pressing hard against her. My voice was ragged, made hoarse by the taste of her love. "My Eshi. You'll never be alone again."

Then, I pulled her into another deep, endless kiss.

She pushed herself off of me once we parted, rearing up to settle her ass back on my thighs. Her hands rested atop my stomach and her knees straddled my hips. The naked flesh of her chest and stomach was stained red. Heated air slipped through her soft, parted lips, her breasts shivering with every one of her heaving breaths.

I slipped one hand behind my head, unable to look away from her. Gods, she was radiant; her hair was ablaze, her flesh glowing gold in the light of the setting sun.

"You're perfect," I said, forcing the words through the lump forming in my throat. "Gods, Eshi, I'm so lucky that you're here."

She smiled down at me, her features melting into an expression of such softness that it made my chest ache. I had to blink back another flood of tears. Gods, nobody had ever looked at me like that before.

It felt good. It felt better than I could have possibly imagined.

"My Naroh," she breathed. "How did I ever find you?"

"By sitting with the weirdest-looking guy at the caravansary?"

She laughed, shifting her hips over my still-bulging manhood. Fire flickered within her eyes and her hands drifted down the ridges of my stomach to pull at the cloth wrapped around my waist.

"Eshi," I murmured, my heart beating faster. "You're still hurt."

"I know," she said, fingers working at my wrap. "I'll rest after, but I need this, Naroh."

I groaned as my cock sprang free. It twitched in the evening air, upright and eager. Something between a moan and a purr slipped from her and I saw the flash of her canines as she bit down on her bottom lip.

"I want to feel your love for me." She blinked hooded eyes, and her voice was a breathy thrum. She wrapped her palm around my cock, working her wrist in long, languid strokes. "I need to feel it."

"Eshi," I dug my fingers into one of her naked thighs. "Gods..."

"I need you, Naroh." With a flex of her thighs, she scooted her hips forward to press her still-wrapped sex to the swollen length of my cock. "I need to feel you inside me."

Even had I still wanted to, there was no way that I could have ever refused her after that.

I pushed myself upright and pulled Eshi into a kiss. My tongue slithered into her, caressing the silken dampness of her tongue. She moaned, arching her chest into mine, and released my swollen manhood to wrap both arms around my neck.

I slipped one arm around her waist, feeling the stiffened base of her tail. I hugged her to me, folded my legs beneath me, and, with a heave, I pushed myself to my feet.

"Naroh!" Eshi squawked as I lifted her into the air. "What are you doing?"

"One sec," I answered, carefully setting her down on her feet. "We're doing this properly?"

"Properly?"

I felt Eshi's eyes on me as I turned to pick up my discarded robe, her ears perking as I spread the garment out over a flat patch of ground. I turned back to her when I was done, conscious of my naked cock spearing into the air between us.

"Come here."

"Hmm," Eshi said, stepping onto it and lowering herself to her knees before me as she had beside the Gibris. "Like this?"

"Oh, no," I said, nodding to the rest of the garment. "Lie down."

A fresh layer of heat bloomed beneath her flesh and her eyes got a shade brighter. She obeyed, stretching herself out on her back.

"You've pushed yourself hard enough, my Eshi." I took a moment to admire the delicious, near-naked curves of the hyenaling spread out before me. I got down on my hands and knees atop her, my palms on either side of her shoulders and my knees between her legs. My face was just above hers, her eyes gazing up at me from a nest of her speckled hair. "Now, it's my turn."

I folded my arms to settle my weight onto my elbows and kissed her, slow and deep. Eshi responded eagerly, coiling the spiced warmth of her tongue around mine. She arched her back to press herself into me as I pushed my forearms beneath her back to smother her body with my own. I felt her run her palms along my ribs and slide the warm, sinfully smooth flesh of her legs against mine.

I pushed my face into the crook of her neck once I broke the kiss and the fire within me flared as she gasped into my ear. Her fingers dug into my back and her pulse shivered as I ran my tongue over the soft flesh of her neck.

"Naroh," she gasped, high and breathy, pushing harder into me. "Naroh."

I kissed the curve of her neck, working my lips over her golden skin and sucking on gentle mouthfuls. Her breath was warm and wet against my ear, her body soft and deliciously curved. I shifted one hand beneath her head, pushing my fingers through the thick tangles of her hair until they brushed against one of her ears.

She moaned as I rubbed it between my fingers, clawing at my back and shifting her hips to grind her still-wrapped navel against the length of my cock.

"Mark me," she panted. "Show the whole world I'm yours."

I bit down on her neck and her body went rigid. My fingers kept working the furred flesh of her ear, my jaws flexing and squeezing. She seemed to almost vibrate beneath me, stiff enough that I thought she might shatter.

Finally, she sagged back, a long, low moan slipping through her parted lips. I released her neck, shifting my arms to once again prop myself above her.

"You know," I smiled, brushing my fingers over the reddened indent of my teeth. "This does look really good on you."

"Now, everyone will see." Her face was flushed and her amber eyes shone. She slid a hand over the twin bite marks on my neck. "I love you, my Naroh. I'm yours."

"You're my life, Eshi." I leaned down to the softness of her lips. "I'm yours."

I pushed myself off of my elbows after another long, slow kiss. I kissed the flesh beneath her chin, going lower, skipping over her bandages to trail my lips and tongue down the length of her body.

Her skin tasted of sun, dust, and the salt of her sweat. She gasped, arching her chest as I flicked my tongue over one nipple. Her stomach flexed and rippled as my kisses trailed lower. I pushed myself up when my lips reached the cloth around her waist.

"Stay still," I said, settling on my knees between her legs. I dug my fingers into her waist wrap. "I'm not done kissing you."

"Mmm, really?" Eshi's eyes were hot, her reddened chest shivering with every ragged breath. She lifted her hips as I worked to unravel her wrap. "We haven't bathed yet."

"I don't care."

Within moments, I had pulled the rest of the cloth away to reveal the naked glory of her sex. Gods, it was perfect. Her folds, lush and pink, were already soaked with moisture and her soft curls of pale pubic hair were damp with ready wetness.

Eagerness flooded my mouth as I scooted back to settle on my stomach between her legs. Down here, her scent was rich and full, wild and nearly overpowering. It was sweat and sour femininity, heat, and liquid sex. I breathed her in, feeling my head spin and my blood roar.

Using my tongue, I pressed a wet kiss against the pale flesh of her navel. Her pubic hair was soft against my chin, the blonde curls steaming with a jungle's heat. Eshi's breath caught, her legs sliding against my shoulders. I felt the muscles of her stomach flex beneath my lips and tongue.

She pushed herself onto her elbows, but I continued to focus on kissing her. I trailed my lips and tongue over her navel and along her soft, inner thighs, careful not to touch the gleaming heat of her pussy. Her scent was intoxicating, and I was desperate to taste her and to quench myself in her liquid femininity.

But I wanted to prolong the moment. I kept my tongue gliding along her inner thighs, enjoying Eshi's every twitch and shiver.

"Naroh." Eshi was propped up and watching me, her heated breath swirling over her naked tits and down the rippling length of her stomach. "We didn't wash. Are you sure?"

"Don't you move," I told her, looping my arms beneath her thighs to hold her in place. "I finally get to taste you."

Light danced in her eyes. "Finally?"

I grinned, happy she'd remembered this from the edge of the Gibris. "Finally."

"Mmm," she said, shifting her hips to lift her ready slit closer to me. "Then, stop teasing me."

Instead of obeying, I tilted my face and pressed a gentle bite along one of her inner thighs.

Eshi gasped as my teeth sank into her flesh. She pushed herself up onto one hand, taking a fistful of my hair with the other. Her thigh flexed and she ground my face into her leg.

"Oh, you bastard." She laughed from low in her throat, the sound thrumming with pleasure. "A bite like that is... mmm."

I released her thigh with my own chuckle, shifting so that I was lying down more comfortably. My cock throbbed, trapped between my stomach and the bottom edge of my robe. I pushed back on her hips with my arms.

"Lie back down, love. Relax."

"My Naroh," she said, releasing her grip on my hair to brush her fingers against my cheek. "I'll do anything you want if you keep calling me that."

"Well, right now I want to taste you. Hurry up."

She laughed, making her breasts bounce and quiver. She stretched out onto her back once more, stretching her legs further apart to spread her wet and ready pussy. I closed my eyes as a fresh wave of scent washed over me. The sight of her pink, moisture-drenched folds followed me into the darkness as I breathed in the wild, sour swirl of her femininity.

Then, burying my nose in the soft curls of her pubic hair, I dove in. The taste of her exploded through me as I ran my tongue along her seam in a long, languid stroke. Eshi moaned, pushing her hips into me. I adjusted my grip on her, working my lips and tongue through her every ridge and fold. Her sweat was salty and sour, sharpening the spiced, liquid heat of her arousal. My tongue found the little nub tucked in just below her tangle of pubic hair. I kissed it until she squeezed my head between her thighs. I loved and caressed it until she tensed, shivered, and screamed.

"Don't stop," she panted, a shiver wracking her body. "Please, don't stop."

I glanced up from between her silken thighs, drinking in the sight of her stretched-out nakedness and loving the way her breath made her lust-reddened tits shake and quiver.

"Naroh," she breathed as I brought one hand down to tease her steaming lushness. She moaned as I slipped two fingers past her moisture-laden folds, and I felt her hand snake down to grab a fistful of my hair. "Oh, fuck."

Eshi's insides were warm and tight, flexing around my curling digits as ground her pussy against my hand. She pulled on my hair to bury my face into her eager slit, rolling her hips while I licked and fingered her, coating my lips and chin in her liquid arousal.

After another tense, mewling shiver, she loosened her grip on my hair. I finally lifted my head from between her thighs, pushing myself up to my knees as Eshi slid her legs along my waist.

"Inside me, Naroh." The woman I loved spread her legs wide, panting as she opened herself to me. Desire glazed her amber eyes, and her ears were floppy over the tangled mess of her speckled hair. "I need to feel you inside me."

The fire within me, banked while I was focused on her, roared to life once again. My heart was a hammer in my chest, her scent fanning the heat coursing through my blood. I lay a hand on one of her warm thighs, positioning my cock before her wet and ready pussy with the other.

I stared into her eyes, letting her see how much I wanted her. I let her see how I wanted to love her, to taste and worship and hold her in my arms while she bucked and writhed with pleasure.

"I love you, Eshi."

The hyenaling pushed herself onto her elbows, her lips curling into a smile. "Then, show me."

I thrust forward and slid into her with slow, wondrous ease.

Eshi moaned, low and breathy, stretching out onto her back as her body pulled me into its liquid depths. I groaned with her, digging my fingers into her thigh. She took all of me, and for a moment, I was overwhelmed by the wet, flexing warmth completely enveloping me.

"Naroh." She shifted her hips, stirring my cock within her. "I feel you. Fuck, Naroh, I feel you filling me."

"Gods." Still on my knees, I gripped both of her hips to pull her harder into me and grind her moisture-matted pubic hair against mine. "You feel so fucking good."

I thrust my hips, moving slowly, sliding myself most of the way out of her before spearing back into her silken depths. Propped on her elbows, Eshi watched me enter her. Her freckled cheeks blazed, and she twisted her fingers into the robe spread out beneath her, holding on as I thrust into her again and again.

I kept my movements slow and deep, at first, taking my time and not letting myself lose control. I concentrated on the feel of her, on the shape of her, on the liquid flex of her pussy, and the soft, silken pressure of her body's inner ridges.

Eshi's flesh burned, her breath coming in measured gasps. Her stomach rippled, her breasts bouncing and her hips rolling as she moved with me. Then, she lay back with a long moan. I breathed in her scent, the air filled with the soft, wet clap of our meeting flesh. Pleasure swirled over her features and sweat made her body shine.

Eshi was glorious in her nakedness, beautiful in her abandon.

When I shifted to crawl overtop her, the hyenaling moved with me. She looped her arms around my neck as I planted my hands on either side of her. Her tongue slipped into me as I kissed her, and I felt the smooth flesh of her legs as she wrapped them around my waist. My cock thrust into her as our tongues danced around each other, her taste and scent and the slide of her sweat-soaked flesh making the heat within me rage.

I rocked my hips, groaning into her mouth as I lost my grip on my slow, deliberate rhythm. Eshi broke our kiss with a throaty gasp as my cock speared into her. She rolled with me, staring into my eyes and sliding her palms down my muscled arms as I thrust into her harder and faster.

"Say it again."

I settled onto my elbows, pushing my forehead into hers. "I love you."

Her nose brushed against mine, my hips still thrusting. I breathed in her every mewl and gasp, the air sweeter than any field of flowers.

"Again."

"I love you."

"You love me," she said, her chest and forehead slick against my own. "You're mine."

"I'm yours."

Her pussy was so warm and wet, taking the whole of me with delicious ease. She moaned as I pushed harder into her, sliding her hands over my side and along the muscles of my ribs and stomach.

"You'll never leave me."

"My Eshi." I lifted my forehead from hers, pausing for a beat to stare into her. "We're a clan of two."

She yanked me down to her, burying her face in the crook of my neck. I felt the sharp pain of her teeth as I wrapped her in my arms. She mewled into me as I hammered my cock back into her. I moved faster, feeling her suck and nibble at my neck, losing myself in her silken, liquid heat.

Eventually, the fire within me flared and I bit down on her shoulder. Her legs slipped from around my waist as I drove my hips into hers harder and faster. My cock skipped over her inner ridges, spearing her depths as Eshi bucked beneath me. She released my neck, gasping and moaning in my ear. Her pussy, so hot and so wet, wrapped and flexed, and loved every inch of my molten shaft.

"Naroh," she panted, arching her body. "Naroh!"

The heat kept building within me, an inferno that flared and swirled and raged. I was getting close, but so was she. Our movements were growing stiff, our limbs tensing into rigidity.

"Eshi," I grunted, dripping sweat onto her body. "I'm close."

"Inside me. Finish inside."

"What !? Eshi—"

"Inside!" Her legs once again encircled my waist, trapping me. "I need," she gasped. "I need to feel you."

"Fuck," I growled. "Eshi, I can't—"

"You love me. Show me. Show me you're mine."

I bit down on her shoulder, our bodies slapping wetly together as I pounded into her. Eshi threw back her head and howled, clutching at me as an orgasm ripped through her. My mind was the inferno's mindless roar and I couldn't hold back anymore. I thrust past a fresh spray of her liquid arousal, burying myself deep within her before my own orgasm exploded out of me.

I squeezed her to me as my body jerked and shivered. My cock twitched inside her, spurting and spraying and coating her depths with my seed. I collapsed atop her a moment later, feeling her thrum with satisfaction.

"My Naroh, my love," she purred, planting a soft kiss against my neck. "Thank you."

I rolled off her, groaning at the kitten-like weakness of my limbs. "Remember this moment when your belly swells up."

Eshi laughed and draped herself over my chest as soon as I'd settled onto my back. She folded a bare leg over mine, letting out a breath as she tucked her head beneath my chin. "I can't get pregnant. Not yet, anyway."

I frowned, trailing my fingers up and down the arch of her back. "Why not?"

She shivered and somehow managed to burrow even closer to me. The amused flick of her ears tickled my jaw. "We're not the same species, Naroh."

"I'm sure that I've seen mixed children before."

"Mmm," Eshi said. "They do exist, but human seed rarely ever takes within us. I think it's because of how weak you all are."

I chuckled, feeling the shape of her grin against my chest. "So, we can have as much sex as we want, and you'll never get pregnant?"

"That's not what I said, love," she tsked. She trailed her fingers along the curve of my bicep. "It'll happen eventually if you keep finishing inside me, but it will take a long time."

I didn't have an answer to that, so I just folded her in my arms and pressed a kiss into her sweat-darkened hair. Eshi returned my hug, squishing her breasts against me. We were silent for a while after that, holding each other and letting our bodies cool in the evening air. My mind drifted as I stared up into the stars emerging from the darkening sky, marveling at how drastically my life had changed in the past few weeks.

I searched within myself for any sort of doubt, anxiety, or regret, but I came up empty.

"A clan of two," Eshi said, pulling me from within myself. "I liked it when you said that."

"Hmm," I said, shifting my grip on her. "Should I start calling you matriarch?"

She lifted her head to meet my gaze, folding scarred forearms across my chest to hold herself up. I'd meant the comment as a joke, but Eshi appeared to be seriously considering it.

"No," she eventually said. "I like the way you say my name. And besides, you're the center of this circle."

"Circle? That's what Kur kept saying."

Eshi grimaced, shifting atop me. "I don't want to talk about that dog."

"I know," I lifted my head to plant a quick kiss on her cheek. "Sorry. I do want to know what it means, though."

The hyenaling made a small sound of pleasure, flicking her ears in a mollified gesture. "The circle is the heart. It's—oh, I'm so sorry, Naroh." She brushed her fingers over my neck, the flesh weirdly tender now that my blood had cooled. "I bit you way too hard."

I winced as she applied a bit more pressure. "You definitely marked your territory."

"Fuck," Eshi swore, her tail lashing the air behind her. She tilted my chin to the side, crimson blooming beneath her cheeks. "Look at what I did to you! I'm a grown woman, not some love-drunk pup!"

"I mean, I bit you pretty hard as well."

"You're bleeding!" Eshi exclaimed, completely ignoring my comment. "Naroh, look what I did! What in the hell was I thinking?!"

"It's fine."

"It's not! I promise that I won't bite you like this again."

"What!?" I let my outrage color my voice. "Don't you dare!"

Pain had never been something that turned me on, and I don't think that that had changed. Rather, I loved the way she gave herself to her passion. There was nothing sexier than causing a woman to lose control, and that more than made up for the pain of her teeth.

"I'm still going to mark you," she muttered, the color of her cheeks deepening. She bent to brush her lips against my chin. "I like to use my mouth."

I grinned, folding my arms behind my head. "I also like it when you use your mouth."

She shook her head, but I could see her fighting a smile. She settled her chin onto her forearms a few moments later, her expression turning considerate.

"Do you really love me, Naroh?"

I groaned theatrically. "Are you going to ask me this every day?"

"Probably."

Her tone wiped the smile from my face. I met her eyes and reached up to brush away a few locks of her speckled hair.

"Well, you'll hear this every day, then. You're the light of my life, Eshi. I love you and I never want to be without you again."

Her ears folded back and she tilted her face to kiss my hand. "Thank you."

"Mmm," I said, shifting beneath her. "And I loved you first, so, you know it's not going to change."

She glared at me. "That's not true."

"I bet that it is."

Eshi raised her head. "It's not. I felt it at the storkling."

"You tried to kill me at the storkling!"

"That doesn't matter," she growled. "And besides, this was before that."

"I feel like that should matter."

I chuckled as the hyenaling bared her teeth. She settled back atop me with a huff, sliding her shoulder into the crook of my armpit and tucking her head back beneath my chin.

"I was first, Naroh. Don't forget."

"Alright," I said, sliding my palms along her naked flank. "You were first."

"Good." She let out a breath, the air tickling my chest. "Ugh, we really need to wash."

"Yeah..." I trailed off, the stars of Tel'aman's Flight blazing in the sky above. A thought popped into my mind. "At the storkling... from wings of stork ... "

"Hmm?"

"Flow the wise ones from wings of stork," I murmured. *"Wisdom's source...* and you were first."

"Naroh?" Eshi raised her head. "What's going on?"

Her words washed over me, lost beneath the rising thunder of my heart. Was that it? Could it really be that simple? I let myself sit with that idea for a few moments, turning it over in my head, and concentrating on it. Gods of fucking death, it would be a gamble. A wild roll of the dice based on a few random, gossamer-thin connections.

But it felt good. It felt *really* good.

Blinking back into focus, I found Eshi staring at me with a mixture of worry and annoyance.

"Eshi," I told her. "You are the most brilliant, amazing, and wonderful woman that I've ever met!"

Her eyes narrowed in suspicion, her tone wary. "Why?"

"Because you did it!" I laughed, grinning into her frown of confusion. "We have to get back to camp!"

"Slow down," Eshi said, hauling back on my arm. "My feet hurt."

"Right, sorry." I bounced up and down on my toes as the hyenaling steadied herself. "Do you think we're still far from camp?"

"We've been walking for less than two minutes."

"I know, I know." I stared longingly out into the darkness before shaking my head clear. Eshi was still wounded, and I couldn't hare off now that she'd actually started taking her injuries seriously. "You're right, sorry. Let's go."

"We're almost there," Eshi said, releasing her hold on my arm. "Relax."

That, of course, was impossible.

It had been more than an hour since my revelation, and I was practically vibrating with suppressed energy. Lightning arced through me, a storm of doubt, certainty, epiphany, and excitement. The path before me seemed wider and more open than ever before. I knew where to find the tomb of Nabonassara I.

I knew where to find this fucking tomb!

"Naroh!" The tips of Eshi's fingers snagged my robe, pulling me to a stop for a second in as many seconds. "Will you wait!"

"I'll carry you," I told the hyenaling. "Get on my back and I'll run."

Night had fallen some time ago, though the moon was bright enough that I could see the annoyance on Eshi's face.

"Just tell me about this idea you have, Naroh. Talking about it will calm you down."

I shook my head. "Amna needs to be there when we talk about it. I'm really not sure about this and I need both of your opinions."

No matter how much I'd insisted, Eshi had flat-out refused to leave our section of the stream before we'd washed. It had taken what felt like an eternity. She'd been, to my eyes at least, absolutely unhurried, having taken the time to scrub her hair clean before slipping into the fresh loincloth and chest wrap that she'd brought.

She'd carried a clean change of linen for me as well, a fact that I'd be a lot more grateful for if I wasn't currently on the verge of literally dying of impatience.

"Then stop trying to run off. We'll be there in a few minutes."

"Eshi," I whined. "Come on."

The hyenaling sighed. "Fine, but first let me finish with this."

Since we'd started picking our way back towards Amna and Asu, Eshi had been busy doing something with her hair. I could see a braid taking shape along one side of her skull, and though I hadn't yet seen her so much as tie her hair back, the hyenaling's fingers wove her speckled tresses with an expert's speed and precision.

After what felt like an eon, Eshi tied off the final section. She'd made one thick braid that ran along the side of her head, weaving together the locks of hair that normally tumbled over the side of her neck and shoulder.

"What do you think?" She asked, tilting her head. "Do you like it?"

"Eshi," I coughed, my nervous impatience suddenly forgotten. "Wow."

I slid my eyes along the now-exposed flesh of her neck, collar, and shoulder, noting the spotted pattern of little dark bruises that were now prominently displayed. They were the marks I'd left with my lips and teeth and were evidence, more than anything, of the sex we'd just had.

"Well?"

"I don't—" I blinked, feeling heat rush to both my crotch and cheeks. "Aren't you worried about what people will think?"

Eshi snorted, taking a slow step forward to loop her arm around mine. "I don't care what a bunch of prissy humans or elves think. Braids like this are a hyenaling tradition. I want everyone we meet to know that we belong to each other, that we're together, and that we're clan."

"Alright," I said, the back of my neck still flaming. "Sure, if that's what you want."

She stopped me from turning away with a tug on my arm. "You still haven't told me if you like it."

"Eshi," I said, sliding my hands along her hips and staring into her eyes. "This is one of the sexiest things I've ever seen. Seeing you like this makes me want to mark you a hundred more times."

"Mmm," the hyenaling purred, snaking her arms around my neck. Her tail swished languidly behind her. "Good."

We kissed, long and deep.

"But not right now," I said, once we parted. I crouched onto the ground with my back to her. "Climb on, we've gotta run."

"You're so frustrating," Eshi growled but wrapped her arms back around my neck and latched on. "You owe me for this."

I didn't answer, already charging back upstream.

Not long after, the glow of a small fire came into view. I slowed as Asu's silent bulk came into view, jogging the final few paces to where the elf was seated beside the flickering flames.

"Amna!" I called out. "The tomb! There's something... uh, wow."

I trailed off, once again losing my train of thought. Amna's many-layered robe hung on a nearby line, washed and drying by the fire. She was now wearing a thin linen dress, the material clinging to the swell of her hips and every delicious curve of her ample chest. I could see more of her skin than ever before, the dark, smooth flesh of her neck and bare shoulders glowing softly in the firelight.

She wasn't wearing her headscarf either, and despite the obvious beauty of her face and curving body, it was this first glimpse of her uncovered head that took my breath away.

The elves, more than any other people, had a history with the land around us. Before settling into what would become Ashura's heartland, the elves had been nomadic. They'd lived their lives amongst the dunes of the Great Desert, wandering in familial bands between its life-giving wadis and oases.

Much of that tradition had survived the intervening millennia of agriculturalism and slavery. Many elves still lived as wandering caravan masters, and the clothes that they had first designed to protect themselves from the savage desert sun were what many of us still wore.

"Amna," Eshi gasped, sliding off my back. "Your hair!"

The elf tilted her head towards us, her cheeks coloring as she gave us a small smile. Her hair was jet black and shone with obsidian depth. It was long and straight, a river of liquid midnight, cascading past knife-shaped ears down to her waist.

"There you are." She was running a comb through it in long, smooth strokes. "I was starting to get worried."

"Your hair!" The hyenaling repeated.

"Do you like it?" The elf's eyes flicked to mine before watching Eshi limp closer. "I'm happy that I could finally get it clean."

"It's beautiful, Amna," I said. "Really, I've never seen anything like it."

Her flush deepened, though she didn't meet my gaze. For a moment, I swear that her smile curled wider.

"It's really amazing." Eshi's tone held the same amount of reverence as I felt. "How'd you get it to shine like that?"

"Argan oil. I use it every time I clean it, and it works miracles. Do you want to use some?"

"You have extra?"

"I have two jars of it." Amna's dark eyes sparkled. "I wasn't sure how long I'd be gone for."

"Smart. Do you need help brushing it?"

"Would you? I'll be here for another hour otherwise."

It wasn't long before the hyenaling had dug a brush out of Amna's pack and positioned herself behind the elf.

"It's so strong too," Eshi said, separating one shining lock. "And how do you have no split ends?"

"The oil helps with all of that, but I also rinse it with fenugreek-infused water every few days."

To this day, the headscarf is a distinctly elven garment. It had evolved from the need to protect their heads from the desert sun, and while the rest of us were content to just wear a hood, the elves had held on to their headwraps.

I'd been told that it had held a religious significance once, that some of the great spirits they'd once worshipped had demanded they hide their hair from all but their closest family. That commandment, whether real or not, had evolved into tradition through the lamian purges and centuries of slavery. Some of the more conservatively minded elves, like Kashir, still held onto that belief, though that wasn't common.

Nowadays, most elves wrap their heads simply to protect their hair.

Whether man or woman, child or elder, an elf's hair was a great source of pride. Most I'd met went to extraordinary lengths to care for it, going far beyond simply protecting it from the sun, wind, and sand. They bought tinctures and oils, creams, and perfumes. They hunted for rare ingredients, and entire mercantile dynasties had risen from those who could supply them.

"—difficult with Naroh." I blinked at the sound of my name, listening to Eshi speak as she continued brushing Amna's hair. "He's impossible. You don't know how hard it was to get him to stay and wash."

"Well, at least you're clean," Amna's eyes flicked back to mine for an instant. "I also like what you did with your hair, Eshi."

"Thank you." The hyenaling's eyes found mine, a flicker of heat curling within them. "Some things, Naroh is very good at."

"I'm sure." There was something odd about the elf's tone but she was speaking again a moment later. "Anyway, why did you guys come back running?"

"The tomb!" I said, my face splitting into a wide grin. *"Nest and flow the wise-ones from wings of stork, immortal in wisdom's source.* I figured it out. I know where Nabonassara I is buried."

Chapter Twenty-Four

I LOOKED DOWN AT the Storkling River for what was likely the millionth time. Barely a pace wide, this narrow ribbon of water we'd spent the past two weeks following was little more than a stream. The cold, clear water burbled as it wound south through the tight, mountain valley. It cut its way through the dry earth, cascaded over rocks, and hissed past scraggy bushes and stunted trees.

Gods of death, it was such a small thing to gamble everything on.

"It's getting late," Eshi said, shifting against me. "We should stop soon."

Blinking, I untangled my arm from around the hyenaling to push my hood back and rub at my eyes. Despite the hour, it was already starting to get dark. We were deep within the wild Northern Mountains range. Snow-capped peaks loomed high on either side of us, blocking the sun's light.

I tapped Asu on the side of the head, guiding the great scorpion around a large boulder. We were following the Storkling River north through a narrow valley, our pace having dramatically increased once we'd stumbled upon it the day before. The ground here was flat, and I was reluctant to stop after so many days spent picking our way through the sheer, rocky mountain slopes.

"There's a curve in the valley up ahead," I said. "Let's at least see what's on the other side."

"And what if the valley curves again after that?" Eshi asked, her voice teasing. She was with me on the too-small bench behind Asu's head.

Her hood was down and the cool, mountain air tugged at her locks of speckled hair. "Or if we see another weirdly shaped tree?"

I flushed. "That tree kind of looked like a stork, it could have been important."

"Good thing you spent two hours looking it over," Eshi said, her amber eyes dancing. "But I guess you had to be sure that it was just a tree."

I chuckled, shaking my head. She tangled herself more thoroughly around me as I draped my free arm back around her shoulder. I took comfort in the warmth of her presence, in her scent, and in the firmness of her body. My eyes, however, stayed fixed on the not-so-distant horizon.

"We'll find it," Eshi said, gently. Her head was against my shoulder, her ears and hair tickling my face. "It doesn't have to be today."

I smiled, pressing my cheek against her head. "You can read my thoughts, now?"

"We're clan," she said, squeezing my thigh with one hand. "Your body can't keep a secret from me, love. Now, stop worrying, we'll find it eventually."

"But we don't have time for 'eventually.' Winter comes early in these mountains, and we haven't seen anything but rocks and dirt." I shifted, Asu's eight legs drumming steadily against the earth beneath us. "With the supplies and new diving gear we had to buy, we've got no money. If I'm wrong about this, then we'll be left with nothing."

"You're not wrong," Eshi said, firmly. "I felt it as soon as we came into this valley. We're going to find this tomb, Naroh."

"She's right," Amna said. The elf was seated on the saddle behind us, her long, lustrous hair hidden beneath her red scarf. I felt her lean forward, her hand coming to rest on my shoulder. "Your logic is sound, Naroh. This tomb is out here somewhere."

I shook my head, let out a breath, and tried to settle my nerves.

They were right—the first Nabonassara was buried somewhere out here. He had to be. We'd discussed it every day and night for nearly a month and had come to the same conclusion time and time again.

Wisdom's source, that's what we were looking for. Whatever it was, my gut told me that Nabonassara I's tomb would be there.

And it was the Storkling River that would lead us to it.

Nest and flow the wise ones from wings of stork, immortal in wisdom's source.

'I was first,' Eshi had told me on the night we'd first made love. 'I'd felt it at the storkling.' Those words had put a simple thought into my head, one that had quickly grown and bloomed into a full-fledged idea.

Eshi had been first; could the river have been first, as well?

What if the Storkling River hadn't been named after the storkling libraries? What if the libraries had been named after the river? Nabonassara I and his descendants had venerated Tel'aman above all other Gods, and if this river was already tied to the stork-headed god, it followed that they would have seen it as sacred.

Nest and flow the wise ones from wings of stork, immortal in wisdom's source.

Wisdom flows like water down from the source within these mountains. Wise ones gathered at the libraries, making them into nests of knowledge along the banks of the river. From there, it spread throughout the empire.

Even in my own mind, that felt thin. But my theory was reinforced, I thought, by the very stars themselves.

Tel'aman's Flight, the constellation that looked like outstretched wings. It was a star formation that hung in the north of the sky, directly over the Northern Mountain range. The source of the Storkling River was here, in a place that was, in a sense, wrapped in Tel'aman's great, astral wings.

"Gods of fucking death," I groaned. "I wish we had some actual proof about any of these conclusions. Now that I'm thinking about it all again, it all just seems like I made up a bunch of random nonsense!"

Eshi pushed off of me, giving me an annoyed look. "You're making yourself crazy, Naroh. Stop worrying."

"I'm not." I flicked my eyes down to the river for a moment. "All of this relies on the fact that Nabonassara I was particularly devoted to Tel'aman, and there isn't any proof of that."

The hyenaling snorted. "You mean other than all of the bird statues they put everywhere?"

"Or the stork in their heraldry?" Amna added.

I glared at both of them.

"This is a leap of faith, Naroh," the elf said, smiling sweetly. "And we're with you on it. Now, move over, I want to sit with you when we go around this bend in the valley."

Eshi quickly slid into my lap, shifting to sit on my outer thigh. The arm I used to steer Asu was around her waist and she folded her feet onto me while Amna squeezed in beside us. By now, the three of us were well used to sharing the bench behind Asu's head. It wasn't comfortable, and I'd actually suggested building a bigger one when we'd first set out together a few weeks ago. Both women had flatly refused, however, and part of me was glad they had.

I'd grown to really enjoy having them so close.

"You're not going to fall, Amna?" Eshi asked, wrapping an arm around my shoulder and extending her legs onto the elf's lap.

"One sec." Amna threaded her limbs around me, snaking one leg between mine and hugging my arm to her ample chest. "There, that's better."

"Much better," Eshi agreed, grinning at the other woman. Her tail slowly swished through the air. "I like it when the three of us are together."

"Mmm," Amna agreed, tucking a lock of hair beneath her scarf. "Me too."

We fell silent as Asu came around the bend. I held my breath, searching the valley ahead of us. But there was nothing, only more dirt, rock, and sheer mountain slopes. The stream continued, disappearing around another bend in the distance.

"At least the ground is still flat," I sighed, trying to ignore the frustration spiking through me. "Let's camp here."

"No," Eshi said, tightening her grip on my shoulder. "Keep going."

"We should stop. I'm getting hungry."

"One more bend," the hyenaling insisted. "Let's just see."

I opened my mouth to refuse but decided it was pointless. I shrugged and tapped Asu forward.

"It's here, Naroh," Amna said from my other side. "We'll find it."

"Okay."

"I'm serious!"

"Alright."

"He needs kisses," Eshi cut in. Her head was just above mine and she leaned down to press her warm lips against my cheek. "Give him one like this. It's the best way to cheer him up."

Her smile was sly and her amber eyes were bright when I quirked an eyebrow towards her.

In more ways than one, the woman I loved was a mystery to me. There was a bond between the beautiful elf and me, a mutual attraction that Eshi seemed determined to help nurture. The hyenaling was as loving as ever and our own connection had only grown deeper over the past weeks. But ever since our first night together, Eshi had gotten more... pushy when it came to Amna.

I had no idea what to make of it.

And what was, perhaps, even more worrying, was how happily the elf had started going along with it.

"Is it?" Amna asked, her cheeks flushed and dark eyes twinkling. "I didn't know that."

Then, I felt the squish of her large breasts as she leaned forward and pressed a soft kiss against my cheek. I shivered, sparks of tingling energy rushing through me. Her lips were warm and full and the floral scent of her hair and body washed over me.

Eshi let out a pleased little sound. She shifted in my lap so that she could press a kiss onto my other cheek.

My entire body buzzed, and I felt so warm squashed between the lips and bodies of these two beautiful women. Laughter bubbled within me, fanned by the tickle of their loose hair and the force with which they were pushed against me.

"Okay, okay!" I laughed, my face scrunched between them. "Let go! I'm alright!"

"See?!" Eshi said, grinning as she pulled away. "Look how much better he feels."

"You're right," Amna said, her cheeks redder than her scarf. "That worked really well."

I shook my head, unable to wipe away my stupid grin. I relaxed back and, with the reckless energy still buzzing through me, pulled Eshi into the center of my lap and draped my other arm around Amna's shoulders.

"I like this," Eshi said, her voice low and pleased. "Isn't this nice, Amna?"

The elf had stiffened the moment my arm had gone around her as if she were suddenly worried or unsure. "I… is this really okay?"

I opened my mouth to speak, but Eshi silenced me with a grip on my chest.

"That's up to you," the hyenaling told her, leaning her head against mine. "Does it feel okay?"

My heart was beating faster, my body reacting to the feminine blend of their scent and the warmth of their proximity. I had no idea what I was supposed to do, so, I just held still. I kept my arm around Amna, though, ready to pull away the moment she objected.

"It does," the elf said, her cheeks crimson. "I know that we've been playing around a bit but you two are—"

"Do you like it?" Eshi interrupted. "Do you like being here with us?"

"I…" She looked at me, and I saw uncertainty swirling within her warm, earth-colored eyes. "I think so."

"Do you want to stay?" Eshi said.

Amna blinked, the uncertainty within her fading. She nodded.

"Say it."

"Yes," the elf said. "I want to stay."

"Do you want Naroh to keep his arm around you?"

Another pause, though much shorter this time. "I do."

"Do you like it?"

"Yes"

"Do you like him?"

The elf's cheeks blazed but she spoke without hesitation. "Yes."

"Do you want to kiss him?"

"Yes." Then, Amna's eyes went wide, and she let out a loud gasp. "Eshi!"

The hyenaling cackled and, after a moment, Amna was laughing too. The elf melted against me, her body soft and warm. I tightened my grip around her, hugging her close, unsure about anything other than the fact that it felt right.

Eshi settled back against me, teasing the elf with a few more grinning comments. Their voices washed over and something eased within me. It was as if my heart, which had already stretched to fit one, was starting to grow large enough for two.

Then, without any real guidance from me, Asu flowed around the bend in the valley. I stiffened and Eshi let out a loud whoop. Amna pushed herself off my chest, squeezing my thigh with one hand.

"Wisdom's source," she said, barely audible over the triumphant stream of Eshi's cackling laughter. "It's here."

Interlude II

ISSIA SAW IN SHADES of purple.

The magical latticework pulsed brightly in her vision, dulling the pale bone beneath it. Her fingers twitched and the gold banded around her arms and wrists was uncomfortably hot as she wove more strands of magic into the delicate construct.

Her head pounded, but her grip on the magic never faltered. She could feel the muscles in her back and shoulders begin to cramp, aching from the hours spent hunched over the jackal-headed skeleton.

Yet, Issia's focus was absolute.

She was reaching a critical part of her working, and would not squander more than a month of work on anything less than perfection.

"Now," she said, her voice made harsh by both lack of use and water.

Her many-armed servitor drudge moved at her command, locking a golden shackle around the guardian construct's wrist and stepping away.

The purple pulsed brighter within her vision, and Issia let out a sharp breath. Gold, above all other material in the world, was prized by necromancers. The metal amplified death magic and strengthened the strands pushed through it while simultaneously making them easier to control.

Pain lanced through her skull and her golden jewelry burned hotter as she pushed more of her magic through it and then into the latticework.

This was the most difficult part.

She had to weave the gold into her magical working, using it as a sort of secondary anchor. If she could do it properly, this shackle, as well as the one already clamped around the other wrist, would become part of the very fabric of the weave. The gold would amplify the framework as a whole, strengthening this construct and making it faster and more durable than any other of its kind.

Yet, it was a concept that was more easily spoken about than achieved.

What she was doing was many magnitudes of difficulty greater than simply pushing magic through the gleaming metal. Necromancy was power over death, after all, and the magic resisted working on anything that wasn't bone or cooling flesh.

It was only because of gold's perfect magical conductivity that binding magic to it was even possible. And to succeed, Issia had to be perfect.

When she had finished, Issia released her magic without hesitation. She watched the glowing threads sink into the skeleton, unable to help the spike of anxiety that came as she watched the purple framework pulse, shiver, and throb. But then it stabilized, and she sighed in relief.

The lattice had held. She had done it.

Then, all the pain that she had shut away came roaring through her. Issia staggered, as much as a legless being even could stagger, away from the bier. She felt raw, her limbs shook, her head pounded, and even the muscles of her stomach and underbelly were weak and watery.

A waiting pitcher of water waited for her at a table by her open balcony. She raised it to her lips with one, shaking hand. The liquid felt good sliding down her parched throat, even if the ice that had chilled it had long ago melted. She emptied it with a gasp and sagged back into her inky coils.

A soft breeze rippled the thin curtains of her balcony, and Issia closed her eyes, relishing the air swirling over her skin. Gods, she was tired. Her bed, large and sinfully soft, called to her from the floor below. She wanted nothing more than to collapse into it, or, failing that, to coil up on a patch of sun-warmed stone.

But Issia was due to meet her father.

"Tell me, darling," she asked her servitor. "What do you think the chances are that he even remembers our appointment?"

The drudge, of course, stayed silent.

Issia rubbed at her eyes for several moments before forcing them open. She lifted herself off her coils, picked up a second pitcher of water, and slithered through the curtains and into the daylight. Her breath came easier as the setting sun soaked her skin, and she felt a bit more like herself after gulping a bit more water.

Below her, the city was starting to come alive. The worst of the day's heat was behind them, and the citizens of Ikkad were returning to the streets. Market squares were filling with noise, the rich strolled along wide avenues and closer to the docks, and sailors stumbled from the taverns they'd taken shelter in towards the brothels set deeper within the city.

Issia let her gaze slide over the familiar sight, her eyes drifting north. She could see beyond the wall, and as she did every time she was out here, she scanned the road beyond for any sign of her returning guardsman.

She saw nothing, of course.

The road was much too far for her eyes to pick out any sort of detail. Still, frustration made Issia frown. It had been more than a month since Sarach had gone after the tomb divers, and she had long ago moved beyond simple impatience.

She was not used to waiting for what she wanted.

Eventually, she let out another breath and turned back towards her workshop. "I'm fairly certain you're right, darling. My father has likely forgotten, but we will go to him nonetheless." She wrinkled her nose as she noticed the sheen of sweat staining her skin and the soft white linen of her dress. "Right after I bathe."

Lamians, as a general rule, were creatures who loved the water. Most bathed daily, and Issia was no exception. She loved the feel of warm water on her skin and scales and could spend hours lounging in the baths below Ikkad's Grand Ziggurat.

Comprised of three large, ornately tiled pools of varying temperatures, those baths were a marvel of the city. The water was kept warm by some heat that rose from below the earth, and an army of attendants—masseurs, cleaners, maids, and porters—ghosted through clouds of steam.

No matter the time of day, members of Issia's extended family could be found lounging within. In addition, any noble visitor and their retinue were given access to the pools. Ikkad was the capital of the north, a city rich in minerals and livestock. Many arrived to petition House Malash, and lamians from every corner of the empire could reliably be found within its steam-shrouded rooms.

Such a concentration of nobility ensured that the baths became a hotbed of gossip and intrigue. Schemes were hatched beneath a masseuse's hands while lords of a more mercantile inclination might negotiate empire-spanning trade deals in the next pool. Marriages were negotiated and alliances were made and broken. Enemies watched and plotted, love could be found or torn to ribbons. Fortunes rose and fell, and everything from the pharon's mood, fashion, assassination, and the raising of corpses might be discussed.

Indeed, in Ikkad, as with most of the major cities, it was in the baths, more so than any formal courtly setting, that the true business of ruling took place.

All of which meant that Issia would rather die than appear there when she was actually dirty.

"The almond oil today, darling," she told her drudge when they reached her suite of rooms. She had her own bathing pool here. The water was piped up from the baths far below, though it was cold and unpleasant by the time it had made its way up to her. "And the argan for my hair."

Issia thought of those heated pools longingly as she slipped into the cool water. This simply could not compare and did nothing to improve her mood. She deserved a bit of luxury after spending weeks nearly shuttered up here.

Her thoughts unexpectedly turned to the great bathing chambers beneath the pharon's palace in Uruq. She'd only been there once, spending a whole summer there to attend her elder sister's wedding.

Samira had been her usual insufferable self, but the baths had been well worth the unpleasantness of her company.

"Come help me with my clothing," she said once she'd finished bathing. "I could use your opinion, dear."

Issia didn't have any servants to help her clean or dress. Her drudge took care of all of that. Silent and efficient, it was the only being in all the world that ever saw behind her perfect mask.

"What do you think?" she asked, slithering into her closet. "The pale silk, again?"

Issia liked white. To wear it was to be noticed and to stand out from the background. It invited admiration, for white was the color of perfection and purity, easily stained by anything less than flawlessness.

It also, coincidentally, paired beautifully with her golden skin, blonde hair, and black scales.

She considered the rows of white garments before turning away with a sigh. "You're right, I'll wear something a little more somber."

White reminded her father too much of his dead wife, her mother. And while Issia had long ago shed any attachment to the woman who had died birthing her, she was, above all else, a dutiful daughter.

It took most of an hour to get ready, and close to another to make her way down from her tower to the door of her father's laboratory. She passed soldiers and constructs standing at their post, one of her own jackal-headed guardians following in her wake. Issia only crossed paths with a few members of her family, though most of House Malash resided within the Great Ziggurat.

She exchanged what greetings politeness required, but the pain behind her eyes and the ache of her muscles kept her from lingering.

Necromancers tended to have their workshops set below the ground, surrounding themselves with layers of dark, cold stone. Sunlight was damaging to bones, not to mention the fact that a corpse's fleshy parts rotted away much faster in the heat.

Issia was an exception in this. She hated the cold, and could tolerate a bit of a smell. If she had to mitigate the sun's damage by working her magic faster, more efficiently, and within a smaller margin of error, then so be it. Properly raising a construct took months of work, and the thought of not seeing the sun in all that time sickened her to her very core.

Her father worked his magic in a dark cavern not far from the family crypts and sprawling catacombs. A legion and more corpses waited down there in the cold blackness, eternally patient, awaiting the day when they might be once more called to war.

"Issia?" He said, looking from the corpse he'd been hunched over. "What are you doing here, daughter?"

Ballasu Malash, head of House Malash, Necrophant of Ikkad, and one of the most powerful lamians in the Ashuran Empire, was a bit pudgy. He carried it mostly around his face, having a thick neck and soft, squishy cheeks. His shoulders were also broad, his bare arms were wide, and his skin was ridged with hundreds of old burn scars.

Issia kept her face carefully neutral, moving over the cold stone to her father's side. "We were due to speak today, father."

The two of them looked quite different standing side by side. House Malash tended to breed heavier, more muscled lamians, and her father was a perfect embodiment of this. He was thick, where Issia was curvy, squat where she was sinuous. She had inherited her mother's figure; though her coloration, from the warm brown of her eyes and the gold of her hair to the inky blackness of her scales, were her father's.

"I summoned you?"

"I received your note this morning," Issia confirmed.

Ballasu frowned, scratching at a fresh, angry-looking burn around one bicep. She repressed a shudder. Those burns came from the bands of gold that he, like her, wore around his arms and wrists. The metal warmed along with the amount of magic that was poured through it, getting hot enough to scald and burn with the more complex workings.

The pain could be excruciating, often shattering concentration and ruining the flow of magic. It was something that all necromancers had to deal with, and there were those like her father who embraced this agony, flaunting the scars of their power and showing the world their might and iron will.

Issia, and every other lamian that valued smooth skin, simply wrapped her gold in layers of protective cloth.

"Ah!" Ballasu snapped his fingers. "Yes, I remember. Word came from the capital in the night."

"From the pharon?"

"No, from your sister." Her father's face split into a grin that was not unlike a hyenaling's. "She's with child."

Issia blinked, surprise causing her perfect mask to momentarily slip. "Samira's pregnant?"

"After three years, I was starting to think that the old Harissanu didn't have it in him, but here we are." The Necrophant turned away with a flex of his black tail and slithered to a nearby table. He returned with a jackal's head cradled in his arms. "Samira will birth the Pharon's heir, and you'll one day take my place as Necrophant of Ikkad. Our family is ascendant, daughter."

"Indeed, father." The cold of the stone-bound room sank deeper into Issia's bones. She schooled her features back into neutrality, ignoring the twist of her stomach and letting nothing of her discomfort show.

"The Harissanus have been in power too long," Ballasu said, setting the head down. "Their blood is weak. Your sister will use this child to cement her control over her fool of a husband and consolidate power around herself. In the meantime, while news of her condition spreads, we must strengthen ourselves. House Malash must be ready to seize whatever opportunity comes."

"I'll redouble my efforts in the creation of constructs," she said. "The Imbayas of Basri and the Nar-Ssalims from Nippur will be the most problematic, and I can make sure that our legions eclipse theirs."

Her father shook his head, and Issia clamped down on her flare of anxiety. She knew what was coming. She might not be the political creature that Samira was, but she had grown up at court and was a long way from being any sort of fool.

"Our crypts are filled to bursting with constructs. We are stronger than we have ever been and your magic, I suspect, is already on par with my own. No, daughter, we must look to secure the future. It is past time that you marry and help ensure the continuation of our House.

These next few decades are of vital importance, and we might usher in a Pharonic Dynasty of our own if we play things right."

Issia hid the shake of her limbs with a bow and two, tightly clenched fists. "Your will, father."

The necrophant smiled, slithering closer to drop a hand on her shoulder. "I knew that I could count on you, Issia. You have made me nothing but proud during these past few years."

She smiled, making sure that it reached her eyes. The perfect daughter could do no less. "Of course, father. If there's nothing else, I will leave you to your work."

Ballasu waved a hand at her, having already turned away. "Think more about your prospects and we will speak of this soon. My instinct would be to try and enter into an alliance with the fleshsmiths of Sargon, but I would appreciate your input."

Issia bowed again and left her father's workshop. She moved through the Ziggurat; her mind was strangely calm, though her stomach roiled.

Duty, she reminded herself, was the most important thing.

Chapter Twenty-Five

Far from the empire's border, at the end of a long valley, nestled by cliffs and snow-capped peaks, we found a small lake. Rocks coated its bottom, and nothing grew along its edge. The little lake was fed from streams that tumbled down the surrounding mountains, and the water was as cold and clean as the alpine air.

Rising from the center of the lake's shallow water was an outcropping of rock. A statue of Tel'aman, carved from the granite bones of the mountains, had been placed there. The stork-headed god of wisdom was depicted with his head up-raised and his arms spread in imitation of the constellation that twinkled high above.

A library's worth of stone tablets were scattered about his feet, spilling into the knee-deep water. Words had been cut into each one of those tablets—ancient prayers, discoveries, and arcane-looking formulae of mathematics and the movements of stars.

The Storkling River flowed away from it, carrying these knowing-filled waters down into the empire. Earth and barren rock filled the rest of the valley, along with a scattering of low trees and prickly bushes.

Wisdom's source was a quiet place, empty, save for the lake and the wide doorway carved into the eastern cliff.

"Naroh," Eshi murmured, interrupting my thoughts. "You need to sleep."

I blinked gritty, fatigue-reddened eyes. I could see nothing in the pre-dawn night, the darkness made deeper by the cloth of the small tent the hyenaling and I shared.

"You're awake?" I asked, rolling onto my back.

The tent wasn't something I typically used on the warm, dry Ashuran nights. It was a lot colder in these mountains, however, and I was grateful to sleep out of the wind. There was also the added benefit of privacy, though the walls were far from being made of stone. Amna hadn't ever said anything, though the smile she sometimes gave me in the morning made me think that she heard more of what passed between Eshi and me than I was comfortable with.

"Mhm." The hyenaling shifted against my side, draping a leg over mine and resting her cheek against my bare chest. She was as naked as I was, her flesh smooth and warm. "How could I not be? You haven't stopped moving since we lay down."

"Sorry." I rubbed my eyes with one hand, trying to banish the vision of that wide doorway. "I can't sleep."

"You're still thinking about the tomb?"

"Yeah."

I'd rushed over to the entrance as soon as we'd entered the valley. Like the tomb of the third Nabonassara, this one had been dug directly into the rock. Unlike that one, however, the entrance was huge, bigger than any I'd ever seen, and large enough for even Asu to squeeze through without too much difficulty. The stone was also bare and undecorated, save for the image of a stork and crown carved into the gray granite.

This was it, the tomb of Nabonassara I.

Eshi lifted her head and I could see the shine of her eyes as she met my gaze. "You're not going to be able to relax, are you?"

"I don't think so."

"Hmm." Eshi's soft, naked breasts squished against me as she shifted atop me. She trailed her fingers down my flank, and I felt the smooth slide of her legs as she rolled her hips into place. "I can help with that."

"Yeah..." I said, knowing that her hyenaling eyes would catch my pained expression even in the darkness. "I don't think I'll be able to focus on that either. Sorry."

She let out a displeased huff but didn't press. Resting her cheek back against my chest, Eshi slid off me and tucked herself in the crook of my arm. She made herself comfortable, blanketing me in the soft warmth of her body.

We were silent for a time. I ran one hand down the curve of her back, drawing a small shiver from her when my fingers brushed against the base of her tail.

"We actually made it," I said, at last. "We actually found Nabonassara I's tomb."

"We did."

"What do you think that we'll find in there?"

"I don't know," Eshi said, her breath and hair tickling my skin. "But we're not going to make it far if we don't sleep a little. Remember what happened in the last tomb?"

I winced. "I'm not tired like that."

"Naroh..."

"I'm serious! There's just so much we still have to do." I propped my head up with my free hand. "We have to get all the gear and supplies organized, Asu's saddle needs to be dealt with, we should scout the valley a bit more and—"

"Those," Eshi interrupted, once again raising her head to stare at me, "are all things that we decided to do in the morning."

"Sure, but I don't want to take too long." I felt Eshi's glare in the stiffness of her body and the thickening of the air around us. "And what about all those tablets in the water? We didn't have time to look at them at all last night!"

"I care less about them than getting some sleep."

"You don't want to know what they say?"

"You should talk to Amna about that, love." Eshi wiggled atop me, nestling her head into the crook of my neck and pressing a kiss to my skin. "But, after we sleep."

"Amna," I said, still stroking her back. "I don't understand what you're doing with her, Eshi."

"Mmm?"

"She... feels something for me. I think."

"She feels something for you?" Eshi said, her voice amused. "Very specific."

"You know what I mean," I answered, a flush heating my face. "She's attracted to me."

"I should hope so." Eshi shifted against me, her ears brushing against my cheek. "That tells me that she has good taste."

"Well, shouldn't you put a stop to it?"

"Why would I do that?"

"Because... I don't..." I shook my head, frustrated. "Will you just tell me what you're doing?"

"You," she said, lifting her head for the third time, "are relentless."

"And you're trying to put another woman between us!"

"No," the word emerged from Eshi as a low growl. She lay a palm against my cheek, her body stiff. "You're mine, Naroh. We're clan, and nobody is going to ruin that."

Eshi's hair hung around me. I reached up to brush some of it aside, letting out a long breath. "Is this some hyenaling thing, then?"

"Do you love me, Naroh?" She said, her fingers flexing against my cheek. "Do you trust me?"

I nodded.

"Say it. I need to hear it."

"I love you, Eshi," I said, wrapping both my arms around her body. "And I trust you with everything."

"Good," she breathed, pressing a soft kiss onto my lips. "Then, trust me in this. Amna might not even be right, we still don't know that much about her."

"Right?" I asked as the hyenaling relaxed back atop me. "Right, for what?"

She gently bit my neck. "Go to sleep, love."

"I... don't think I can."

"You're lucky I love you this much," Eshi sighed, pushing herself up. "Come on, then. Let's go start getting ready."

We crawled out into the pre-dawn darkness a few minutes later and I was surprised to find that we weren't the only ones who couldn't sleep.

"Good morning!" Amna called. The elf was a shadow on the silvery edge of the lake, her form dark and indistinct. "I didn't expect to see you for quite a while."

"Blame Naroh," Eshi grumbled, burrowing into her robe. "Ack, it's so cold out here!"

"Why'd you let him drag you out here, then?" Amna teased. She turned to me as we approached, the moon's light just enough that I caught a hint of her smile. "Couldn't sleep?"

"Not at all," I said, matching her smile. "Were you trying to get a look at those tablets?"

"If only," the elf chuckled. She looked back out over the still water, her laughter fading. "No, there's something... odd about this place. The spirits aren't responding like they should."

"I thought that was normal," I said, stepping up beside her. "Spirits don't always answer you when you call, right?"

"Right," the elf confirmed, her breath misting the air. "But this is different. Even in the deep desert, where the spirits are few, I can feel a sort of echo of their presence. This valley feels empty, though. It's like there isn't a single one."

"Maybe it's because of him?" I said, gesturing to the statue of Tel'aman.

"The spirits are nature itself, Naroh. A minor lamian god wouldn't impede them." She shook her cloth-covered head. "A place like this should be thronging with them, or a great spirit might make this place their home. This is something else. I can't even feel Ko."

We all chewed on that for a few moments before Eshi pushed me with her hips.

"Well, let's just get this started. I want to get this done and get back to sleep. And you," she poked a finger into my chest, "won't be invited."

Hours later, I re-tightened the last of the saddle's straps and stepped out from underneath the great, war-scorpion in time to greet the rising sun.

"There we go, Asu-boy," I said, reaching up to scratch beneath his mouth. "We're all done. Are you feeling better now, my handsome boy?"

Asu gleamed in the weak light of dawn, his pale chitin bright and clean. I'd spent the better part of the last two hours scrubbing dirt from him, washing away the sand and grit from between each of his joints and beneath each saddle strap.

He chittered happily as I continued to scratch. He flexed his colossal pincers and let his pedipalps hang.

"You've been so good these past few weeks," I cooed. "My big, strong boy. You carried us so far. It's going to feel good to have a nice long rest, huh, especially with that big fat goat you caught filling up your belly."

"Naroh!" Eshi called. "We're ready to go!"

"You be good here, Asu-boy." I scratched more vigorously, smiling at the scorpion's dopey expression. "I know you don't like the cold much, but get as nice and comfy as you can. We'll be back soon, alright my boy? Be good."

I left the war-scorpion to settle himself into comfortable stillness. The tomb's entrance loomed ahead of me, and I hooked my pack off the ground and moved towards it. The straps dug into my shoulders through the light fabric of my diving tunic, but the weight was as familiar as the sling wrapped around my arm.

"What do you think about his diving tunic?" Eshi asked Amna, her amber eyes appreciative. "He looks good without that robe, doesn't he?"

The hyenaling was savagely beautiful in the light of morning, her grin hungry and her tail slowly swishing behind her. She was a warrior, a huntress whose golden flesh was marked by blade and claw. Her newest scar cut wickedly across the top of her linen-bound chest, though it, along with the wounds on all of our feet, had healed thanks to Kur's salve and the weeks spent immobile atop Asu's back.

She was waiting beside the darkened doorway, her own robe discarded. Her pants rode low on her hips, showing every rippling muscle of her naked stomach. Her shoulders were strong beneath the weight of her pack, one hand resting beside the knives belted around her waist. She'd braided her hair to reveal one side of her curving neck. The marks of our love-making spotted her skin, matching her pale, speckled locks.

"I like it," Amna said, speaking from low in her throat. She stood beside the hyenaling, one hand wrapped around her stave and her own pack ready at her feet. "Look at those arms..."

"I know," Eshi purred. "Now, imagine them wrapped around you."

The elf bit her lip, spots of color blooming high on her cheeks. Heat smoldered in the depths of her warm, brown eyes, and her dark skin shone richly in the dawn's glow. Her limbs were long and gracefully curved, her obsidian hair and pointed ears hidden away by a bright red headscarf. The rest of her body was swathed in a long, many-layered robe of dark blue cloth. The garment fit her perfectly, accentuating her ample curves while remaining loose and comfortable.

Amna was a vision of elven beauty, a spellsinger touched by the otherworldly grace of the spirits that served her. Her song would guide us through the darkness, her ferocious passion and intelligence a bulwark for my own.

"We have everything ready?" I asked, joining my companions. "Water, diving gear?"

"Yes," Eshi said, rolling her eyes. "We have everything. I packed us both an extra set of clothes too."

I frowned, flicking my eyes to where my pack lay in the dirt. "That's a waste of space."

"I'm not letting us get as disgusting as last time, Naroh."

"We've also got plenty of water," Amna said, hefting her leather pack. "And rope. Eshi and I went through everything carefully and split the gear between the three of us."

"So, we don't lose everything if you drop your pack and run," the hyenaling added.

"Perfect. Remember not to speak—"

"Naroh," Eshi interrupted, stepping forward and laying a palm on my chest. "My love and center of my circle, we've gone over this every day during the past weeks. We're ready."

I stared into her amber eyes for a long moment and then nodded. I shifted my gaze to the stone archway. The tomb's entrance yawned wide before me, the darkness within ancient and foreboding. Nabonassara

I had been a lamian of rare power, a necromancer mighty enough to ascend to the pharon's seat and forge his own dynasty.

What sort of knowledge might be hidden here? What sort of death had this ancient ruler woven into this place?

"Well, then." I felt my face stretch into a wide grin, waves of tingling energy rolling through me from the wild beating of my heart. "Shall we?"

Eshi bared her teeth into a scavenger's smile, her ears perked and ready. Amna nodded, her eyes were clear, unafraid about stepping back into the blackness that had already claimed a part of her.

I didn't know what awaited us in there. But gods of fucking death, I couldn't wait to find out.

Chapter Twenty-Six

NO GUARDIANS WERE LYING in wait within the tomb's antechamber, and neither were there any traps or shrieking skulls. In truth, there wasn't much of anything within the small, circular room. There were no murals, statues, or carved epitaphs. The floors were bare, and the stone walls were decorated with nothing but millennia-old tool marks.

The chamber was nearly empty, and that made me uneasy.

Lamians were creatures of extravagance, luxuriating in the wealth, power, and comfort that they spent their lives accumulating. Status in their society was a measure of what one might flaunt, and wealth, grandeur, large deeds, and gestures were the surest ways to rise and draw the favor of the gods. The lamian lords of today spent rivers of gold in the construction of their tombs, stuffing their burial chambers with riches in the hopes of improving their place within the afterlife.

And while it was true that the oldest burial sites—those from the turbulent centuries following the birth of the empire—tended to be smaller and less ornate, I'd never seen anything so plainly *gray* before.

I chewed on my lip, staring at a blank section of the wall. After a moment, I let go of my glowstone so that it dangled from the string around my neck. Even Het-Hassi, a pharona who'd lived two hundred years before Nabonassara I and had spent her reign putting down slave revolts, had put more effort into her resting place.

Turning away, I shook my head clear. Only one feature defined the antechamber, and it was there that I now headed.

In the center of the floor was an obelisk. It was made from a stone darker than the rock that surrounded us, and wasn't particularly large or imposing. It was simply there, its sides as plain as everything else in here.

Dust puffed upward with every one of my steps, and Amna, who'd been focused on the obelisk, glanced over at the sound of my approach. By the light filtering in through the wide entrance, I saw a smile flicker over her features. It was gone quickly, however, and her attention had returned to the marker by the time I reached her side.

"Can you feel anything?" I asked, keeping my voice low.

"I don't know." The elf's expression was troubled as she ran a palm down the wind and time-scarred stone. "There's the same emptiness as the valley outside but there's also an echo of... something."

"Something about the spirits?"

"Mmm," she confirmed, hesitating a moment before she continued. "That echo... it's a spiritual presence but *twisted* somehow. Something happened here. It's old and faint and I can feel... wrongness? Hatred? Grief? I don't know." She shook her head and let her hand fall away. "I've never felt anything like it before."

I turned away from the obelisk, once again chewing on my lip. On the far end of the chamber, directly opposite the wide entrance, was an equally large archway. It was the single passage leading deeper into the tomb, and I could just make out Eshi standing guard beside the dark portal.

There wasn't anything overtly menacing about this room, and yet...

"Come on," I said, at last. "Let's go see Eshi."

"I'm sorry, Naroh," Amna said, her staff tapping faintly against the stone floor. "I don't know if I'm going to be much help without any spirits to sing to."

"We're not out of here yet," I told her. "Besides, you're the only reason we even found this place."

The hyenaling turned to glare at our approach and let out a low hiss. "Will you two be quiet?"

I slid my palm along her bare lower back when I reached her. "I've told you before, love. It's better if the guardians find us here than in the maze. Have you heard anything?"

"Nothing," Eshi answered, leaning some of her weight against me. "I don't think anything is moving around out there, but I can't be sure."

"That's fine. We'll wait a few more minutes to be sure, and then, we'll go in."

Nothing attacked us in the first few steps beyond the undecorated archway. Neither was there anything in the few dozen steps after that. My unease grew the deeper we ventured through this large, empty tunnel.

There was nothing in here; no traps, guardians, or any sort of forking path. The single tunnel, long and straight, simply continued. Had this ancient pharon left his tomb undefended? That was impossible. We were in a remote part of the world, but the tomb wasn't otherwise hidden. Someone, in the time this was being built, would have known about this, and the fact that Nabonassara I might have left his tomb open for any of those people to stroll into was laughable.

And yet, there weren't even the crumpled remains of guardians or sprung traps that would have marked another diver's passage. There was nothing, only the endless darkness and the wide, blank passage that surrounded us.

We went around one corner, then another; and eventually, the tunnel opened up into a chamber.

I stopped at the threshold, the light from my glowstone reaching little more than a handful of paces into the large, open space. I squinted into the darkness as Eshi and Amna came to a stop behind me. After spending a few minutes ensuring that the entrance wasn't trapped, I motioned them over.

"Can you see anything in there?" I whispered into Eshi's ear.

A shiver ran through her as my breath tickled her fur. She flicked her ears and gripped my shoulder as she brought her lips to my ear. "Take the glowstones back. There's too much light."

"Be careful."

The hyenaling rolled her eyes, but I saw a little smile flit across her features before I turned away.

Other than the one shining over my chest, Amna had tied a glowstone to the end of her staff. It painted her features in its ghostly light, and I could clearly see her frown as she stared intently into the darkness.

The elf didn't react as I came near, starting with surprise when I laid a hand on her arm. She followed me when I inclined my head back down the tunnel, though her expression was still troubled when we stopped a dozen or so paces later.

I touched her arm again, frowning my concern. She pushed her headscarf back from one long, pointed ear as I leaned towards her.

"What's wrong?"

"That feeling," she said, her eyes far away. "It's stronger here."

"Are we in danger?"

Amna hesitated a moment before shaking her head. "No. Whatever it is, it's just a feeling."

She tried to smile her assurance, but the expression was thin. This was bothering the beautiful elf and, because I knew how comforting another's touch could be in a place like this, I slid my hand along her lower back to hug her waist.

Amna's smile immediately grew. Her fingers tightened around her staff, and she shifted closer to me. I hugged her to my side, feeling my own unease settle beneath the warmth of her presence. Her scent, floral and sweet, replaced the mustiness of the tomb, and when she lay her cheek against my shoulder, I kissed the cloth-wrapped top of her head.

"Ready?" I murmured.

"Hmm." She pressed herself closer to me and let out a long breath. Finally, I felt her start to relax. "Let's go."

I let my hand slip from around her waist to start towards Eshi. The elf, however, surprised me by wrapping her free arm around mine. She held onto me as we walked. Her palm, warm and soft against my forearm, slid down until it was nestled in my own. Our fingers were intertwined after a handful of steps and my throat had gone unexpectedly dry.

Eshi turned at the sound of our approach, both of her eyebrows going up at the sight of us. I expected Amna to release my hand, but her grip only tightened. Her cheeks were dark in the light of our glowstones and the look she gave the hyenaling was challenging.

Eshi smiled into the elf's stare, her expression wide and pleased. Her tail swished through the air behind her as she seemed to almost skip to my other side.

"Well done, love," she murmured into my ear. "Looks like she's making her choice."

"Is it safe to go in?"

"I didn't see anything," she answered. "Hold onto her for a bit. I'll follow behind."

Then, she pressed a quick kiss onto my cheek and spun away. I let out a huff of air, my exasperated expression softening into a smile when I caught Amna's suddenly uncertain gaze. I squeezed her hand and led us into the chamber.

The darkness grew deeper as we ventured from the shelter of the tunnel. A cold sea of silence wrapped around us, heavy enough to swallow the sound of our walking feet. Amna's hand was a spot of warmth against me, and the three of us moved slowly through the empty room. My eyes strained to see past the fraying edge of our glowstone's light, searching for anything that might leap out at us from the ancient darkness.

The room remained empty until, very suddenly, it wasn't.

Eshi was the first to react, her hiss of warning reaching me just as a monstrous shape materialized from the darkness ahead. Amna sucked in a loud breath, her fingers clenching. I dropped into a half crouch, my eyes wide and muscles tense. The hyenaling appeared beside me and for a few, heart-pounding moments, the three of us stared, frozen and ready to bolt.

But the monster before us didn't so much as twitch, and as my heart thundered and my muscles creaked, the darkness-blurred edges of the shape snapped into focus.

"It's a war-scorpion," I said, easing out of my stiffened crouch. "A dead one."

The corpse was huge, the dry, dust-covered husk as black as the surrounding darkness. It was stretched out atop the cold stone, its eight legs splayed outward and its great pincers motionless at the end of its long arms. I stepped towards it, raising my glowstone above my head. The tip of its stinger was just visible in the air above, the tail stiff and shriveled in death.

"Naroh," Eshi hissed, reaching out to grip my arm. "What are you doing?"

"Taking a look." Both women were holding onto me now, and it was getting difficult to move. "Do you ladies mind letting go?"

That, of course, only resulted in their grips getting tighter.

"Isn't this a guardian?" Eshi's teeth were bared and her ears were stiff. "What if it wakes up?"

"It can't be," I said with a shake of my head. "Necromancy—"

"Doesn't work on animals," the hyenaling interrupted. "Right."

"Thank the gods for that," I said, eyeing the dead war-scorpion. "This would make one hell of a guardian."

The elf's hand slipped from mine as she took a few steps away. The light of her glowstone revealed more of the dead husk as she drew near. Cracks split the chitin in several places, and though death had shriveled the great creature, I thought that it once would have been even bigger than Asu.

"Well," Eshi said, also loosening her grip on me. "What's it doing here if it's not a guardian?"

"This was probably Nabonassara I's war-scorpion. Lots of lamians have their favorite pets buried with them."

"Really? Why?"

I shrugged. From the corner of my eye, I saw Amna step over one of the scorpion's arms and into the circle of its pincers. "Same reason they fill their tombs up with gold; they think that it'll come with them."

That tradition had, at certain points in history, extended to a lamian's favored servants. Slaves, guards, handmaids, priests, and cooks; tens of thousands of men and women had been put to death throughout the millennia. Their mummified remains were placed within their master's tomb to serve them as they had in life.

Djassu V, a pharon from more than a thousand years ago, had even had an entire legion of his hyenaling dog-soldiers put down. Their corpses stood in silent, ordered ranks within his tomb, their servitude stretching into eternity.

"Fucking snakes," Eshi said, with a shake of her head. "Anyway, let's keep going."

I nodded, hefting my pack. "We'll go straight until we find a wall, then we'll follow it all the way around to be sure we don't miss any exits. Are you ready, Amna?"

The elf stood directly before the great scorpion's head. I don't think she'd heard me. Her eyes were intent upon the dead creature and her lips were moving in silent whispers.

"Amna," I said, a bit louder. "Are you okay?"

"That thing," she murmured, reaching her hand up. "I can almost feel..."

She trailed off, the words fading into a low, musical hum. Her fingers brushed against the side of the war-scorpion's head and, without warning, lines of purple light blazed to life beneath her hand and spider-webbed outward.

Amna stumbled back, letting out a loud gasp of pain. Her staff slipped from her hand as the weight of her pack pulled her to the ground. In front of her, purple fire raced through the great scorpion's corpse to settle within it. The light shone through the cracks in its armored shell, growing brighter with every panicked beat of my heart.

"Naroh!" Eshi cried out, her knives appearing in her hands. "What's happening?"

I didn't know, could only gape as embers of purple fire flared to life within the scorpion's dead eyes.

Then, impossibly, it began to move.

"Guardian!" I shouted, though everything within me screamed in disbelief. I pulled on Eshi's arm, yanking her back. "It's a fucking guardian! Run!"

The scorpion's legs twitched and scrabbled at the stone. Its pincers flexed and its body shifted and shivered. The purple fire burned brighter, bathing everything in necromantic light and letting me clearly see the struggling shape of Amna. Blood streamed from her nose and her face was twisted in pain. She was still on the ground, scrambling to get her feet beneath her.

"Amna!" I cried out, jerking the pack from my shoulders. "Get up!"

Reckless, tingling energy washed through me as I vaulted over the scorpion's rising arm and ran towards her.

Above us, the scorpion's head started to rise.

"Can you run?" I asked, drawing my knife when I reached her. My limbs were tingling and my heart was pounding. "Amna?!"

"My head," she said, her eyes dull with pain. Her hands fluttered weakly against my arms, blood dripping down her chin and onto her chest. "It hurts, Naroh. The scream..."

"We have to go," I said, sawing my knife into the leather straps of her pack. "Amna! Can you run?"

"Run?" She stirred, blinking rapidly. I saw her eyes sharpen, piercing through the fog of her pain. Then, she nodded, wiping at her bloody face with one sleeve. "Yes, I can run."

"Good." I jerked the elf to her feet, feeling the guardian's awareness sharpen. The purple shadows around us flickered and danced as the monster shifted and rose. "Let's go!"

I shoved Amna towards the gap between the scorpion's shifting pincers, sending her stumbling. I followed a step behind her, ready to catch her if she fell. The elf quickly found her balance, however, and a heartbeat later, we were racing out of the still-waking guardian's reach.

"Eshi!" I shouted. "Eshi?!"

"Here!" The hyenaling answered, a handful of paces ahead of us. Her ears were stiff above her braided mane of hair and the heavy pack was already gone from her naked shoulder. "Come on!"

"Get us to Asu!"

"Obviously!" She turned, leaping into a run. "This way!"

I charged after the keen-eyed hyenaling, sprinting towards the exit tunnel. I didn't look back, though the inferno of necromantic fire from the impossible guardian pushed the darkness back from the large chamber.

"What the fuck is this thing!?" Eshi shouted, pumping her arms. "How is it moving?"

"I don't know," Amna gasped, her scarf streaming behind her. "I felt something like a spirit, but when I called to it—"

She was interrupted by a loud roar.

Peeking over my shoulder, I saw that the massive, undead scorpion had fully regained its feet. A furnace of death magic burned within its center, growing brighter. Its mouth pincers churned through the air while its tail flexed and its legs stepped and skittered.

Then, with another roar and a flare of purple light, it started after us.

"Go!" I screamed, plunging into the tunnel on Amna's heels. I could feel the thing's hatred, something a construct shouldn't be able to feel. "Go, go, go!"

My glowstone bounced against my chest, making the shadows around us twist and jerk. The pounding of my feet on stone was a familiar rhythm, and as the seconds passed, I felt my breath become more even and my heartbeat slow. Running from guardians was something I knew, even if this one was unlike anything I'd ever seen before.

Purple light started to creep around the edge of my vision, and I risked another glance back as we careened around the first corner. The guardian had just entered the tunnel, its movements no longer stiff and awkward. It flowed through the wide passageway with pincers raised and head forward, an unstoppable wave of bone and burning magic.

Gods of fucking death, what was this thing?

The walls shook as a third roar chased around the second corner. The scorpion was gaining on us, but the entrance was straight ahead. I could see the light of the sun in the distance, a sliver of brilliance that sent fresh energy surging through me.

"Get to Asu," I shouted over the thunder of my heart and the guardian's charge. "We're almost there!"

We burst into the antechamber, Eshi streaking ahead of us towards the open air. Amna, for her part, was limping. She wasn't a natural runner and pain made her movements awkward and jerky. Sweat and blood soaked her face but, despite everything, she didn't slow down.

Gods, this woman was a wonder.

"Asu!" I roared, charging out into the open air of the valley. "Guard!"

The bright sunlight seared my eyes. I blinked rapidly, blinded by the sun's glare. Shapes flashed through my vision as the three of us stumbled and tripped over the rocky ground. I couldn't yet see Asu, but Eshi was still in the lead and I trusted her to find him.

We were only a dozen or so paces from the tomb's entrance when a roar of fury buffeted the air around us. Amna fell, but I was near enough to grab her arm and wrench her back to her feet. I saw a flash of white chitin ahead while, behind us, the guardian smashed through the antechamber's obelisk.

It would be out with us in the next few moments.

"Naroh!" Eshi screamed. "Amna, come on!"

I pulled the elf towards the hyenaling's voice, gritting my teeth as I tripped over another fucking rock.

"I'm fine," Amna gasped, her face tight and chin bloody. "I can run myself!"

I ignored her, taking some of her weight on my arm. My vision was finally clear enough to see. Eshi had stopped beside Asu, the two of them a bare few paces away. The great war-scorpion was a statue, his pincers raised and tail curled high. His entire body was coiled tight, an ambusher waiting in perfect stillness.

"Go!" I shouted to the hyenaling. "Don't fucking stop!"

I saw her bare her teeth, her body tensing to rush forward. Then, her eyes widened and I glanced back in time to see the Nabonassaran abomination crash through the entrance and out of the tomb.

The dead scorpion looked even more monstrous by the light of day. The thing was colossal, a creature that was even bigger than Asu. Great pincers flexed and a wicked stinger bobbed at the end of a skeletal tail. Its black chitin was shriveled and cracked, death magic burning through the jagged vents splitting its armored shell. The filth of millennia caked the entirety of its form and a hatred that was just as ancient burned within its undead eyes.

The guardian didn't slow for an instant upon emerging into the sunlight, its eight legs churning as it rolled towards us with the speed and unstoppable power of a landslide.

"Run," I screamed. "Run!"

With that, I wrenched Amna forward, twisted, and scooped her into my arms. The elf yelped in surprise as I caught her, throwing her arms around my neck as I squeezed her to my chest. Amna's weight pulled me forward, but I adjusted and lengthened my stride into an all-out sprint, rocks crunching and sliding beneath my boots.

The guardian tore down towards us, the entire valley trembling with the thunder of rage. It swung great pincers to blast through trees and slam boulders aside. The furnace of purple fire roared within its core and twin, burning eyes fixed on us.

"Asu!" I roared, charging past the great insect. Eshi was just ahead, having turned to run as soon as she was sure the elf and I wouldn't fall. "Kill, Asu! Kill!"

The great scorpion snapped into motion, lunging forward with an ambusher's speed. He lashed out with his tail and his stinger punched through brittle, black chitin. Where a hunting scorpion might back away and wait for its venom to take effect, Asu had been bred for war. The rest of his body slammed into the undead creature with the fury of a falling meteor, his pincers crushing and tearing.

The guardian crashed to the earth in a plume of rock and dirt. Chitin broke and magic flared. It roared, thrashing with tail and pincers as Asu, silent and unflinching, bore down on it. Great, white claws pinned the dead creature in place while Asu's tail whipped forward again and again, his stinger piercing armor with a sound like cracking rock.

"Can he actually do it?" Eshi said, slowing down now that we were beside the small lake and safely away. "Can your bug actually kill this thing?"

The hyenaling's ears were stiff and her chest rose and fell in deep, even breaths. Sweat slicked her naked flesh, staining her chest wrap and darkening her speckled hair.

"I don't know," I said, setting Amna down. The ground shook and the air reverberated with the rage of the warring titans. My stomach clenched as I watched Asu's pincers tear into the thing, his weight crushing it to the rock. "Without breaking the canopic jars, properly raised constructs are really hard to kill. They don't get tired, and they don't feel pain, and they never stop fighting. Asu's destroyed guardians before, but nothing like this thing."

"Listen to it," Eshi said, her tail snapping through the air behind her. "How does it roar like that? Undead are supposed to be silent."

It was true; the dead never made a sound. They had no lungs to take in air and no throats to shape it into a voice if they did. Even constructs like the jackal-headed guards of House Malash were incapable of anything but silence.

"This isn't an undead," Amna said. She'd wiped most of the blood from her face, her nose having finally stopped bleeding. Sweat soaked her robe and headscarf, and she stood with most of her weight off her injured foot. "At least, not really. I could feel it as soon as we entered the tomb."

"Then, why'd you go and touch it?" Eshi growled. "That thing almost killed us!"

The elf shook her head, letting out a long breath. "It didn't matter. That spirit became aware of us as soon as we entered its chamber."

"Spirit?" I cut in. "Are you saying there's a spirit in that thing?"

"It's what I started feeling in the antechamber," Amna confirmed, her expression troubled. "I don't know how it's possible, but that scorpion isn't just a mindless necromantic construct. There's a spirit bound within it, a powerful one."

As if in response, the guardian roared. Pincers and scrabbling legs tore through the rocky earth. Purple death magic flared through its cracked chitin as it continued to struggle against Asu's claws.

"Well, your magic works on spirits, right?" Eshi said. "Can't you sing to it?"

"I tried. I could feel it stirring when we first walked into the chamber. When I reached out to it, it *screamed* at me. Hatred, rage, pain..." Amna shuddered and reached up to touch her nose. "It's been bound like that for thousands of years, and it's not—"

She was interrupted by a loud, agonized chitter. Asu was backing away from the fallen guardian, his pincers blackened and his chitin smoking. The dead thing roared, great gouts of purple fire bursting through its cracked armor. Asu hissed, flexing his tail and pincers, but the heat was too much for him. He backed away as the guardian stood.

Then, with another flare of magic, the cracks in his chitin started to close.

"It's healing," I said, my stomach twisting. "It's using magic."

Chapter Twenty-Seven

THE GUARDIAN'S BODY SHOOK, his entire frame sheathed in an inferno of burning death magic. Chitin glowed hot as the dead thing's armored shell melted back into place, sealing holes, cracks, and fixing limbs that had been broken by rock and claw.

It roared, mouth pincers churning as magic repaired dead flesh.

"Magic?!" Eshi said, her body stiff and tail still. "How is this thing using magic?!"

"Spirits are beings of magic, but this..." Amna's stare was intent, her interest powerful enough to hold back whatever fear and pain she might be feeling. "This is necromancy. I can feel ripples of spirit magic, but something in the binding must be giving the spirit control over the necromantic weave."

"What the fuck does that mean?"

The elf shook her head. "It means that this guardian can use magic."

"Can it do anything else?" Eshi said through gritted teeth.

"I have no idea."

Asu circled the undead scorpion, his pincers spread wide and his tail curled high and ready. He was kept well back by the furnace heat searing the air around the guardian. The white scorpion's head and armored shell were scorched by fire and blue blood leaked from wounds and cracks.

"So, what the fuck can we do?" I felt Eshi's amber eyes land on me. "Naroh, can your bug still kill it?"

"I don't know." My heart beat faster, sending sparks of tingling fire rolling through me. "But I'm not letting him fight this alone."

"You have a plan?"

"It'll catch us if we run," I said, turning to face both women, "and Asu can't kill it. Amna, you said this thing is still mostly necromancy, right?"

"The spirit is bound within a lamian construct." The elf confirmed, though a frown creased her features. "Why? What are you thinking?"

"Guardians are nothing new and there's only been one surefire way to stop them."

"The jars," Eshi said.

"The canopic jars," I agreed, the flames within me flaring. "If we can find and break them, the guardian's body will fall apart. I don't know what will happen to the spirit after that but, well, one thing at a time, eh?"

"That 'one thing' is pretty big," Amna pointed out. "You really want to go back into the tomb?"

"We don't have a choice. Not unless your singing can stop its magic."

The elf's frown deepened, but it was Eshi who spoke next. "Didn't you say those jars are usually in the sarcophagus chamber?"

"They are," I answered. "They'll be in the tomb's center."

"And we have no idea where, or how deep it is?"

"We don't."

"Nor," Eshi continued, her ears perked and head cocked to the side. "Do we know anything about what sort of traps or other guardians might be waiting for us?"

"No." My limbs were practically vibrating and a grin, wide and reckless, split my features. "And we'll have to go fast. Really fast."

Another roar from the guardian shook the air around us. The undead scorpion was still sheathed in purple flames, and its burning eyes were locked on Asu. It lunged towards the white scorpion, reaching with its pincers and lashing out with its stinger. Asu scuttled to the side, staying out of the way and unable to attack with the heat pouring off the guardian's body.

"What do you say, my matriarch?" I asked, extending an arm out to Eshi. "Are you running with me?"

"We're clan." She stepped into me, her grin wide with the scavenger's savage hunger. "We run until we reach the end."

"To the end," I said, my heart beating in time with hers. "Side by side."

"Together." Her fingers twisted in my tunic and she pulled me down into a ferocious kiss.

I felt lighter than air when we broke apart, my entire being filled with the warmth of her love. Eshi was with me. She would always be with me.

"Amna," I said, turning towards the elf. Her eyes were on the warring scorpions, her expression intent. "We're going, you—"

The rest of my words were lost as Amna sucked in a breath and screamed. The sound, high and shrieking, tore at her throat. Amplified by the otherworldly hum of her magic, her voice was a lance of focused power. It speared into the dead scorpion and staggered it. Flames guttered, the purple fire flickering and fading as the guardian lost its hold on whatever magic it had been working.

The construct whirled on us, the spirit within howling its fury and fixing burning eyes on the spellsinger. But then, Asu was there. The war-scorpion's stinger slammed through newly healed chitin before he bowled into the guardian and crushed it to the ground.

"I'll stay here and fight with Asu," Amna said, turning to grin at our shocked expressions. "Although, I can't do that too often."

I laughed, feeling my heart swell at the wonder of the women beside me. One of my arms was still wrapped around Eshi and I reached for Amna with the other. I pulled her to me, and because my entire being buzzed and we might all die and she was so brilliant, so kind and so strong, I leaned down and kissed her.

Her lips were full, warm, and achingly soft. Her body stiffened with surprise. She didn't return my kiss but neither did she pull away. Nevertheless, I broke our kiss after only a few moments, my heart pounding with an entirely new sort of feeling.

"Stay away from that thing." My voice was rough, and I squeezed her waist. Amna's brown eyes were huge. Disbelief, joy, hope, doubt; heat bloomed beneath her cheeks, and I saw a dozen and more emotions flicker across her naked features. "Be careful."

Beside the elf, still in the circle of my arms, Eshi started to laugh. Her hyena's cackle rose high and loud around us and Amna's crimson flush deepened. She flicked her gaze to Eshi, then back to me before she turned and dashed towards the warring scorpions.

I gaped, staring at her retreating form. Gods of fucking death, what the hell had I just done?

"Naroh, you—" The hyenaling gasped, laughter still bubbling out of her. "Your timing!"

Guilt seared through me. "Eshi! I'm so sorry, you said it was okay, and I—"

She pressed a finger to my lips, her cheeks flushed and smile wide. "Not now, love. We have to go, but I am very happy with what you did."

She was right. We had to go.

I shoved everything to a corner of my mind as another roar from the guardian tore through the air as Eshi and I began to race over the rocky ground. We gave the scorpions a wide berth and, within moments, the tomb's entrance loomed large before us. I heard another high-pitched, otherworldly scream, but didn't look back as we burst into the rubble-strewn antechamber.

I crossed the remains of the shattered obelisk at a run with Eshi at my side. We plunged together through the darkness of the tunnel, our feet beating a steady rhythm on the stone floor. The hyenaling kept pace as I put on speed, her movements and breath working in time with my own.

The glowstone bouncing against my chest was our only source of light and the writhing shadows were a good representation of the lightning coursing through me. My whole body vibrated with energy and my awareness felt sharp and crystalline as we entered the guardian's chamber.

Despite our earlier light-heartedness, neither Eshi nor I were under any delusions about our odds of success. Amna and Asu were buying us time, exhausting themselves by fighting a battle they couldn't hope to win. We had to find the sarcophagus chamber before the guardian tore them apart, and we didn't have the luxury of slowly navigating whatever traps lay ahead.

Speed and bloody momentum were our only chance.

In the center of the dark room, Amna's glowstone-topped staff shone like a beacon. We sprinted towards it, and it was only when we were a handful of paces away that I noticed a dark hole in the floor where the guardian had laid.

It was a staircase leading downward.

My face split into a wide grin and beside me, Eshi let out a high, yipping cackle. We would likely die down here, our bodies broken by traps we didn't see coming. As we charged forward, I found myself unable to dredge up any sort of regret.

Because Eshi was with me.

I sucked in a breath, the musty air of the tomb suddenly sweeter than anything I had ever tasted. The hyenaling scooped up Amna's staff and I let out a loud whoop as, together, we plunged headlong into the dark.

The staircase was short; the dozen or so ancient stone steps were rough and choked with dust. No pit traps awaited us at the bottom, no blades reached for us from the darkness, and neither did the stairs collapse in our wake. Instead, our glowstones showed us that there was a single path ahead; a tunnel flanked by two stork-headed statues of the god Tel'aman.

It was a simple, straight corridor without any forks or bends. This passage was narrow, though still large enough for Eshi and me to run comfortably side by side. Sweat coated my back, and the air was hot in my lungs, but we didn't stop or slow. We flashed by statues tucked into nooks, and the bouncing light of our glowstones revealed the shapes of images and hieroglyphics carved into the walls.

I barely registered any of this, however. My attention was fixed forward, on the two pairs of burning, purple eyes that awaited us.

"Guardians!" I shouted.

Eshi laughed, filling the air with the scavenger's glee. As we ran closer, the forms ahead revealed themselves to be two, hulking constructs.

Fashioned in the image of Sobak and Ninshubur, the twin, crocodile-headed Gods who protected the doors to paradise, this particular form of undead was the purview of the Royal Guard. Independent from house or politics, this order of lamian warrior-necromancers could trace its history back to the founding of the empire. They were sworn to defend the capital, the ruling Pharonic Dynasty, and their tombs. The creation of this particular form of construct was their most closely guarded secret. They were larger, faster, and more powerful than any other form of undead.

The two that stepped towards us were typical examples of the great, crocodile-headed monstrosities. The scaled flesh of their bestial skulls was dry and colored a dull gray, and their feet were wide and clawed. Golden shackles gleamed around each wrist, and ragged scraps of cloth that had once been cloaks hung from their thick, skeletal bodies. Their fingers were clawed as well, and were wrapped around the hafts of millennia-old halberds.

They filled the hallway with their bulk and lowered their weapons towards us. Silent as death, their movements were smooth despite the weight of time on their shoulders.

"Go through them!" I roared, my muscles burning. "Don't stop!"

Eshi held Amna's staff low in her hand, her eyes eager and speckled hair streaming in her wake. The scavenger's laugh poured from between grinning lips, high and hungry. She put on a burst of speed when we were only a handful of paces from the gleaming points of the halberds, leaping ahead of me faster than I could react.

The royal guardians brought their long weapons to bear on her, thrusting forward with unnatural force and speed. The gleaming points dove towards Eshi's body, but she twisted at the last moment and lashed out with the staff. The weapon knocked one halberd aside, though the other ripped across her stomach.

Blood sprayed and still, she laughed, the sound an exhortation to her savage god.

The hyenaling was within the reach of their weapons and she crashed into them with a violent sound of impact. She tumbled to the floor, though the speed of her charge was enough to shove the heavy guardians off-balance. Their weapons were out of position, and I was there before they had time to recover, throwing myself into a slide over the floor.

I'd aimed for a gap between the wall and an unsteady leg, my speed carrying me through, though the rough stone tore at my pants and flesh. I gritted my teeth against the pain and scrambled to my feet. I was in a large chamber, my glowstone showing me glimpses of still statues and the shadowed shape of a large box atop a dais within the center.

The sarcophagus.

I hesitated.

Behind me, Eshi hadn't stopped moving. She was on all fours, tearing her fingers and knees on the stone floor as she lunged for a gap between the guardian's legs. The constructs kicked at her, stomping down as they turned. She avoided the worst of the heavy blows, though one swiped down with one hand and tore bloody rents into her back with its claws. Her cackle warped into a scream of pain but she managed to make it through and into the chamber.

Along with her flesh, the guardian's claws had torn through the back of Eshi's chest wrap. Ribbons of cloth fell away as the hyenaling regained her feet, the wrap coming away completely as she threw herself away from a thrusting halberd.

"Go!" She howled, somehow still clutching Amna's staff. "Go!"

Eshi's eyes were wild and her grin was feral through her falling locks of speckled hair. Blood and sweat coated the naked flesh of her chest, staining her bare breasts. She yipped and laughed as the constructs charged her, launching herself towards them with the staff held high.

In the turbulent centuries of the empire's infancy, before the crypts of the major lamian houses were stuffed overfull with ready constructs, it had been the hyenalings who had fought Ashura's enemies. Called dog-soldiers, as much for their appearance as their dogged loyalty, hyenalings were ferocious fighters. They were naturally stronger, faster, and more aggressive than any of the empire's races; and when Marduss had marched across the desert all those millennia ago, it had been the hyenalings who had broken the first elven armies.

Though the empire had long been at peace, I could see echoes of that bloody legacy in Eshi. She was a vision of savage glory, feral, strong, and beautiful; a warrior-matriarch who seemed to have stepped directly from the blood-soaked annals of history. Her movements were quick, sharp, and seemed almost instinctive. She twisted and ducked away from the guardian's thrusting halberds, dodging and spinning to avoid the slashing axe-heads. When she attacked, it was with hard, vicious strikes, and her cackling laughter accompanied the splintering sound of her wooden staff meeting bone.

Gods of fucking death, she was holding her own against two royal guardians armed with nothing but a stick and her naked tits.

I blinked and shook my head. Eshi, Amna, and Asu were fighting, spending their blood to buy me time. The rest of their lives would be measured in seconds if I didn't fucking move.

I dashed away, ignoring the sarcophagus-topped dais as I moved deeper into the room. The canopic jars would be within a sort of armory, and I ignored every decorative statue, carving, and artifact as I swept my gaze through the darkness.

At the far end of the chamber, I found two arches bored into the stone on opposite walls. Both led deeper into the tomb. Hieroglyphics were carved above each entrance; a string of birds and waves, an arm, a scepter, a boat, and dozens of others. I couldn't understand whatever phrase these symbols spelled out, and I might only have one chance to make the right choice.

And so, I guessed, diving through the arch that had a hieroglyphic chariot wheel carved into the stone.

The sound of metal ringing off stone followed me through the entrance and I heard Eshi howl. Sprinting through a short tunnel, I quickly came into a small chamber. My glowstone illuminated walls painted with scenes of war and the light gleamed off the remains of the war chariot that dominated the center of the space. Piles of weapons—axes, curved swords, and spears—lay scattered about the floor, their wooden racks having long since faded to dust.

There were no canopic jars, though another archway loomed out of the darkness on the other side of the room. Behind me, Eshi had fallen silent and my heart lurched at what that might entail. I clamped down on my emotions and charged ahead. Pain from my torn leg pulsed through me as I ran through this new entrance, my chest heaving, struggling to take in the thick, stale air.

The next chamber was larger and crammed full of corpses.

I didn't let myself stop, sprinting forward, though my breath caught and a scream wedged itself in my throat. Dozens of mummified bodies lay atop their biers, the stone blocks laid out in orderly rows throughout the large room. Bronze armor covered many of the corpses, and swords and daggers rested beside skeletal fingers.

The roaring of my blood and the pounding of my boots were all I heard as I raced towards the back of the room. Corpse-laden biers flashed past me, and I was ready to leap aside should necromantic fire burst within the desiccated eyes of a grinning skull. But the dead didn't stir, and the relief I felt was only eclipsed by the sight awaiting me along the far wall.

The canopic jars.

There were three rows of them, each line of five jars resting atop a separate stone shelf. A thick layer of dust covered the pottery, but even lit by only the weak light of my glowstone, I could tell that they were beautifully decorated. Lines of delicate symbols were carved into each one and the sealed lids had been sculpted into the animalistic heads of the god tasked with watching over the organ within.

I swept the first of them to the floor, the thousands-year-old artifact shattering with the crack of breaking clay. More of them followed and I kicked at the larger ones along the bottom with my boots. A tide of viscous liquid carrying slimy chunks of meat spilled from the broken vessels. I stomped and crushed, ground and jumped, gagging at the chemical stink of the embalming fluid that adhered itself to the back of my throat. The oversized organs of the scorpion were the worst, and my boots and legs were soon covered in chunks of bloody viscera.

When the last one broke, I was plunged into a world of silence.

A moment later, I was turning away, slipping and sliding through the mess at my feet. No sound met me as I sprinted back towards the sarcophagus chamber. That silence, heavy and all-encompassing, smothered me. It squeezed my chest, making it hard for my heart to beat and the breath to enter my lungs.

I burst into the central room, knowing I could have been faster and dreading to see what I might find here.

"I told you," Eshi rasped. She was atop the dais, the unmoving bones of the crocodile-headed royal guardians scattered around her. She was slumped against the stone sarcophagus, her breath ragged and her limbs trembling. Her pants were shredded and blood oozed from a dozen fresh cuts to stain the naked flesh of her breasts, stomach, and arms. But, for all that, her eyes were bright and her grin was fierce. "I told you that I could keep up."

Chapter Twenty-Eight

Something between a laugh and a sob escaped me as I rocketed towards the waiting hyenaling. Eshi stepped forward to meet me and fell into my outstretched arms. Relief washed through me as I wrapped her in a hug and squeezed her tight. She wiggled against me as I buried my face into her sweat and dirt-matted hair and breathed her in.

Immediately, her warmth eased the ache in my bones and her scent loosened the tightness of my chest.

Eshi was here. I hadn't lost her.

"Hurts," she mumbled, her face pressed into the crook of my neck.

"Fuck," I said, releasing her. "Right, sorry. You're injured."

I tried to step away but Eshi's fingers gripped my tunic, holding me in place. Her ears twitched and she glared up at me through tangled strands of speckled hair. "Don't let go, just don't hug me that hard."

"Alright, alright," I chuckled, wrapping my arms around her once again. "But I'm going to go back up the stairs in a minute. The bandages and the rest of Kur's salve should be in one of the packs we ditched upstairs."

"Not yet," Eshi said, and the breath from her contended sigh tickled my neck. "They didn't cut me too deeply and I'm enjoying this."

"We can hug again afterward."

Eshi growled.

"Fine," I said, pressing a kiss to the top of her head. "I'm just so... I can't believe you fought off two royal guards."

"Mmm, now do you see why you can't ever leave me?"

"There's no danger of that." I adjusted my grip on her, careful to avoid the wounds on her back. "Not ever."

"Why?"

"Because I love you, Eshi."

The hyenaling pressed herself harder against me, burying her face into the crook of my neck. "Say it again."

"I love you, Eshi. I never want to be without you again."

She shivered before gently biting down on the flesh of my neck. "You're my world, Naroh, my love, and my clan."

"I would have died a hundred times without you here..." I squeezed her more tightly for a moment. "I can't walk this path without you. I've never seen anything like what you just did."

"I wouldn't have lasted much longer," Eshi admitted. She let out one last sigh before finally releasing her grip on me and stepping back. "The bastards were fast."

"I guess I got to the jars at the perfect time." I shook my head, not wanting to think about what would have happened if I'd chosen the other chamber first. "Gods, I hope I wasn't too late for Amna and Asu."

"I'm sure they're fine. She's smart and the bug is tough." Eshi groaned as she shifted to sit at the top of the dais's steps. I stepped forward to help. Her body was stiff with pain and her muscles must have felt like water. "If I know the elf, she's running over even now to come and kiss you again."

The guilt, the shame, and everything else that I'd pushed away came roaring back. "Eshi, I'm so sorry I kissed her."

"Mmm?" Eshi asked, reaching for my hand. "What do you mean?"

"Amna," I said. "I just kissed her without talking to you!"

"It's fine, love." She tugged on my arm. "Sit down."

"I'm such an idiot." I resisted her pull, guilt and shame making my cheeks burn. "I just got overwhelmed and I kissed her and you were right there, and I—"

"Naroh!" Eshi interrupted, yanking on my arm. "Sit!" I did, and after glaring at me for a few moments, the hyenaling looped her arm through mine and leaned against me with a sigh. "Thank you. I told you that I was happy you kissed her, love."

"I know, but I—" I let out my own sigh and forced myself to relax. "I just wish I knew what your goal was in all this, love."

"Didn't I ask you to trust me in this?"

"I know, I know, but, well, maybe this is crazy after everything we've been through together but I just... I don't want to lose you, Eshi."

"My Naroh." The hyenaling kept a hold of me as she shifted to better face me. She was so warm; her skin, voice, and the light shimmering within her amber eyes. "You will never lose me. We're clan and I will be with you till the end."

I nodded, unable to speak past the lump in my throat. So, instead, I leaned forward and kissed her. She pressed herself against me with a low hum of pleasure. The taste of her lips and the soft, spiced caress of her tongue melted away the last of my doubt.

"This is my goal with Amna," Eshi said, once we had parted. "I like her. She's smart, knows magic and that body of hers is just..." She bit down on her bottom lip as another shiver ran through her. Heat bloomed beneath her cheeks and she darted forward to nip at my neck. "Right now, we're a clan of two, but what if we were three?"

"Well..." I trailed off, struggling to wrap my mind around what she had just said. "I don't know if she's going to want to stay with us now."

"She does."

"She literally fled when I kissed her."

"Your timing was terrible," she agreed, light dancing in her amber eyes. "But don't worry, you just caught her by surprise. Amna knows what she wants, but has a hard time going for it."

"And she wants this? Are you sure?"

"Trust me on this too, love." Eshi patted my arm. "She just needs to actually choose."

"And you," I asked, after a moment's hesitation. "Are you sure you want this?"

The hyenaling glowered at me. "I'm going to knife you if you ask me that again."

I chuckled and Eshi's expression softened. She leaned her head on my shoulder and let out a happy sigh. After a few moments spent chewing on my thoughts, I spoke again.

"This clan," I said after a few moments spent chewing on my thoughts. "We would, what, just all be together?"

"Mhm," she answered. "The strongest clans are tied by love."

"Love?" I asked, surprised. "I don't love Amna."

"Give her time."

I chewed on my lip, still struggling to understand. "Are all hyenaling clans like this?"

Her ear flicked against my cheek in a motionless shrug. "Several are, my mother had four different mates."

"Wait, so you want to be with other men?"

"No," Eshi said as if speaking to a child. "My mother was the center of her own circle. You're the center of mine, love."

"I... still have no idea what that means."

"Later, Naroh," she groaned, pushing herself off of me. "I'm tired, and your disgusting pants are giving me a headache."

"Yeah," I said, very deliberately not looking down at the filth staining me. "Sorry, let me go get the packs. Just... talk to Amna about all this first, okay?"

"Obviously," Eshi scowled.

"I'll get going then," I said, mollifying her with a quick kiss to the side of her head. Once on my feet, I nodded down to her still very naked breasts. "Do you want my tunic to cover up?"

"Absolutely not," she answered, giving the chunks of gore splattered over my stomach a pointed look. "I've got clean clothes in my pack."

"Fair enough. You'll be alright by yourself?"

"Yes, Naroh." Eshi rolled her eyes, though a smile pulled at the corner of her mouth. "Go!"

"Alright, alright," I chuckled, holding up my hands. "I'm going."

The steps of the ancient dais were wide and thick with dust. I was only a few paces beyond them when the sound of running footsteps made me pause. Amna burst into the sarcophagus chamber a few moments later with a glowstone clutched in one hand.

The elf was limping even more than before. Blood stained the front of her robe, and her headscarf was ripped. My heart lurched at the sight of her, only to have another wave of relief wash through me as her beautiful face broke into a wide smile.

"Naroh!" Amna cried, rushing forward. "You're alive!"

I laughed, holding my arms out to catch her as she launched herself at me. We tumbled to the floor together and I ended up on my back with her pressed atop me.

Then, before I could speak or think or do much of anything but stare into the open joy in Amna's face, she kissed me.

This time, I was the one who stiffened in surprise, and all I could do was gape up at her when she pulled away not long after.

"There," she said, satisfied. "That's what I should have done earlier."

"Amna, I—uh ..."

The elf laughed softly, a delighted flush coloring her cheeks. She smelled like sweat, blood, and singed cloth, but her body was so soft. Several curls of her midnight hair had escaped her headscarf to tickle my neck and face. Her eyes were on mine, the brown so warm and tender. "Thank all the spirits, you're still here. Are you hurt?"

For the second time in as many minutes, I struggled to speak past the lump forming in my throat. Amna had followed me into the darkness and had stayed to fight a battle she'd had no hope of winning. She was a wonder, and I knew that, just as with Eshi, I couldn't walk this path without her.

"I'm okay," I finally managed, slipping my palms onto her waist. "You're not hurt too badly? And what about Asu? The guardian?"

"I'm fine." Amna smiled and I felt the soft squish of her breasts as she shifted atop me. "The guardian collapsed before it could do too much damage, and the spirit disappeared along with the necromantic weave. Asu is alright too, though the saddle on his back is in rough shape, and he's bleeding from a few places."

"Good."

Then, without another moment's hesitation, I cupped her cheek with one hand and pulled her down into a long, slow kiss.

Her lips tasted warm, almondy, and sweet, and her tongue was quick and curious. My hand slid down her flank to join the other at her waist and the world faded around me as she melted into me.

Amna was an explorer; a spellsinger who danced with djinn beneath the desert stars. I lost myself in the feel of her, in the heat of her passion for life and mystery. Her lips tingled with the ethereal touch of her magic, and I could taste her boundless love of discovery in the soft caress of her tongue.

We parted after what felt like an eternity.

"Naroh," she murmured, her nose brushing against mine. "I'm sorry that I ran. I wanted to kiss you back, but I—"

"I caught you by surprise. I'm sorry about that, I..." The thought drifted away, my mind still struggling to emerge from the haze of her touch, taste, and scent. "Sorry, that kiss was so much better than anything I imagined."

"Oh?" Amna's dark eyes were bright. "Were you curious?"

I laughed. "Always."

Amna giggled as I pulled her down into another long, slow kiss. She sank atop me, and I felt my heart stretch and grow. Then, all at once, she stiffened. Her eyes flew open and she pulled away from me with a gasp. "Eshi! Is she— ?"

The hyenaling cackled loudly, interrupting her. Amna lifted her head and I craned my neck back to see Eshi leaning forward from the top of the dais, her naked chest quivering.

"I was wondering when you'd remember me," she said, grinning widely. "Although, I wouldn't be thinking of much else either if I was kissing Naroh like that."

"Eshi, you're bleeding!" Amna exclaimed, pushing herself off me. "And your breasts! What happened to you?"

The elf limped over to the hyenaling, fussing over the other woman while I pushed myself to my feet. I smiled to see them, a warm glow buzzing through my chest. Then, I turned to move through the dark tunnel towards the staircase and my good mood faded. I'd almost lost everything. We'd been lucky to survive this, lucky that this tunnel hadn't been trapped to oblivion.

Nabonassara had relied only on guardians to keep his tomb safe. Which, considering the power of that war-scorpion, hadn't been too bad a strategy.

I found all three packs fairly quickly, feeling my heart beat faster as I hurried back towards the central chamber. I'd bet everything I owned that we were the first divers to ever breach this tomb, and now that the stress of the moment was gone, my thoughts turned to what we might find buried here.

The location of Marduss's tomb? The secret that impossible necromancy? A cache of ancient knowledge or formulae? A wealth of gold? Artifacts, weapons, or stone tablets spelling out long-forgotten truths?

The possibilities were endless, and gods of fucking death, I couldn't wait to find out.

By the time I returned, Eshi and Amna were deep in conversation. I let their words wash over me as I climbed the dais and set the packs down beside them. My attention was on the sarcophagus, the ancient pharon's resting place, and the first thing I always examined when I entered a new tomb.

It was large and shaped out of a pale, gray stone. Thumb-sized holes were punched through the side to let the soul escape, while the lid was a heavy, unadorned slab of rock. It looked like it would be difficult to push open so, for the moment, I paid it no mind.

Images and hieroglyphics had also been carved into the sides of the sarcophagus. These would typically be moments from the deceased lamian's life, along with prayers and scenes from mythology. It was to show the Gods what sort of life the soul within had led and, curious about that myself, I crouched down to take a closer look.

What I found, instead, was a scene from the lamian conquest of Ashura.

It depicted a battle between the lamians and the elves. Time had worn away some of the details, but the edges were still sharp. I could clearly see the cloth-wrapped heads of the elves and the long, curved swords they held in both hands. Facing them was a legion of the dead with empty skulls and reaching hands.

I shifted to the side, moving my glowstone back along the ranks of the dead. Behind them were hyenaling dog-soldiers, armored in metal and wielding a variety of swords, axes, and spears. They were the guards and elite troops of the chariot-bound lamian generals were at the rear.

"Naroh?" Eshi said, poking me in the ribs. "Hey!"

I blinked, startled from my thoughts. Amna was kneeling behind the hyenaling, working to clean and wrap the wounds on her back. The cut along Eshi's stomach was already bound, though her breasts still floated naked and uncovered.

Both women were looking at me expectantly, their cheeks flushed and eyes bright. Eshi's face, however, quickly twisted into a scowl. "You didn't hear a word we said, did you?"

"Uh... sorry. What was it?"

Amna laughed and the hyenaling stared at me for a few moments before letting out a breath. "Never mind."

"What are you looking at?" the elf asked, her smile knowing. "Anything interesting?"

"Yeah... uh, it's strange. This scene shows the siege of the Broken Mountain." I turned back to the sarcophagus, brushing my fingers against the shape of the main lamian general. "Look, here's Ramesh the Great commanding the legions. This is his snake-headed scepter and he's got the Hooded Crown on his head."

"Why is that strange?" Amna said. "It was an important battle."

"Sure, but it happened centuries before Nabonassara took the throne. It's just strange that this is what he'd have carved on his sarcophagus."

"Maybe it's a clue?" Eshi said. "What happened in the battle?"

"Well, it was the last battle of the Ashuran Conquest. The swordmasters of the Broken Mountain were the last bastion of elven power after the city-states surrendered. They're also the ones who killed Marduss after he pulled down the walls of Uruq. Ramesh the Great led his army south through the Great Desert and laid siege to their mountain."

"He slaughtered us," Amna said. "When his army broke through, he had every single elf killed. Even the children."

"Fucking snakes," Eshi growled. "Why?"

"By wiping them out, Ramesh the Great both avenged his master and prevented the Order from becoming a rallying point for rebels," I said. "Of course, Nictossis III had to lay siege to the mountain again a few centuries later, but that was just against an army of escaped slaves."

"Alright." The hyenaling let out a breath, then her ears perked as she squinted at the sarcophagus. "But who's the lamian with the elves?"

"Lamian with the elves?" I frowned down at her. "What are you talking about?"

Eshi flicked her ears. "At the far end there, behind the army of elves. If you bring your glowstone over, you should be able to see him."

I stared at her for a moment and my heart, inexplicably, started to pound. A wave of tingling energy rolled through me as I turned from the women and moved along the side of the sarcophagus. I saw the Broken Mountain itself appear behind the lines of elven swordmasters, the landmark depicted as a great triangle with a notch cut into one side as if an angry god had struck it with an axe.

And there, standing in the center of the great mountain, was a lamian man.

I crouched down before the image, moving slowly, my eyes wide and heart wild. I recognized this lamian, despite the layers of cloth wrapped around his head. The scythe he held in one hand was unmistakable.

"It's Marduss," I said, hardly believing what my eyes were telling me. "Gods of fucking death, it's Marduss."

"What?!" Eshi and Amna both explained.

The elf hurried over to crouch down beside me, her eyes going wide as she brought her own glowstone close.

The hyenaling, for her part, kept speaking. "You just told me that those elves killed him."

"They did!" I said. "I don't—why is he alive here? He's got the headwrap on too and the elves... why's he on their side?"

"Marduss at the Broken Mountain," Amna said. "What does this mean?"

My mind was spinning, searching for something to latch onto. Marduss was the grand necrophant, the greatest necromancer to have ever lived, and the founder of the empire. He'd fought the elves. He'd conquered them. Yet, every clue, from the medallion to the elvish script carved into Nabonassara III's sarcophagus, tied Marduss and the elves together in ways that I couldn't imagine.

But that didn't mean that the lamian actually fought against his people, right?

"What does this mean?" Eshi echoed. "Naroh?"

"I don't—" I shook my head and let out a breath. "I don't know, but we have to find out."

"How?"

"By doing something dangerous." I stood and pulled Amna to her feet. She raised an eyebrow but looped an arm around mine and let me lead her back to Eshi. The hyenaling cocked her head to the side as I held my hand out to her, looking up into my sudden grin. "Up you get, matriarch. Our path isn't over."

Eshi snorted, though light danced within her eyes. "And where's this path taking our clan?"

"Across the desert," I said, flicking my gaze to Amna. My grin grew wider. "We're going to find the Broken Mountain."

The elf squeezed my arm, and laughter bubbled out from Eshi, a low cackle that made her naked breasts shiver.

The hyenaling grabbed my hand and let me pull her gently to her feet. "I'll be right beside you."

Epilogue

ISSIA SETTLED BACK ATOP her coils as the purple glow faded. The last of the magical latticework sank into the bones of her construct, and she let out a long breath.

It was finished.

The skeleton looked almost nothing like the hyenaling it had been in life. The bones were abnormally strong and thick. Each one had been stretched, lengthened, and warped, turning this hyenaling into a monstrous guardian.

Issia did not let her mind wander as she slithered around the corpse-laden bier, examining the jackal-headed construct from every angle. Perfection could not be rushed, and so she touched every bone with her fingers, shifting and turning them. The joints had been stitched together with gold wire, and the bones stretched and made to grow over every seam.

"Lift the leg," she ordered.

Her silent servitor obeyed, curling two of its four hands beneath the construct's thigh-thick tibia and lifting. With the leg so elevated, Issia could test its flexibility at the knee, ankle, and hip. Magic would, of course, be most of what held this construct together and propelled it forward, but the gold binding the bones would help enhance the construct's efficiency, and so was worth the extra work.

"Thank you, dear. Let's look at the next one."

The bones were heavy and unnaturally dense, and Issia herself would strain to keep the leg raised for any prolonged length of time. Her servitor, however, was more than capable, and she was able to take her time bending and twisting each joint. The arms took even longer, and Issia let out focused pulses of magic to test the golden shackles in between bending all ten clawed fingers.

A couple of hours later and she was getting close to declaring her work flawless.

With a flex of her tail and stomach, Issia leaned over the still motionless corpse. Golden locks of hair tumbled around her, and the scorpion pendant spilled out from between her large breasts as she bent to examine one section of rib.

"We did a good job with this, darling," she said, running a finger over the smooth, clean bone. "It all turned out quite lovely."

Her servitor didn't answer, but Issia liked to imagine she could feel the same sense of satisfaction thrumming through him. She settled back onto her ebony coils, humming to herself as she slithered to the head of the bier. Some of her good mood soured as she stared into the jackal's empty eye sockets. It was truly hideous, and yet, Issia could not deny feeling some bit of affection for the guardian she had created.

"Well, darling, have we forgotten anything?"

Issia tapped her lips in thought, her obsidian coils shifting and flexing beneath her. The preparations were complete, and after more than a month of work, this construct was ready. With one last pulse of magic and will, it would rise. Her eyes slid over the skeleton, searching one final time for anything she might have missed.

But, of course, there was nothing.

"It's perfect," she said, giving her immobile servitor a small smile. "Shall I kiss it to life, then?"

So speaking, Issia pressed her lips onto the tips of the fingers and touched the guardian's face. She brushed her fingers along the coarse, dead fur of its muzzle and beneath one empty eye. This, along with her habit of speaking to her drudge, was something she would never do in front of another. She did not need to touch the construct to raise it, and doing so in this way could not be described as anything other than foolishness.

Yet, Issia was proud of her work.

None who saw it could deny her mastery of the necromantic arts. And though this guardian would be as silent and unfeeling as all the others, it comforted her to feel some sort of fondness for the construct that would guard her body.

Then, just as she was about to push her magic into it, someone knocked on her door.

Issia lifted her head to stare at the portal on the other side of the room. Her heart, which had been beating a slow, steady rhythm, started to pound.

Sarach had returned.

"Go to the door," she ordered, letting her fingers slip from the guardian's face. "Open it on my command."

With a powerful flex of her tail, Issia hurried to the table beside her open balcony. The breeze through the opening was warm, and sunlight spilled in to puddle atop the pale, marble floor. She had a quick drink from the pitcher of water as her silent servitor found a place beside the door. Another flex of her coils brought her halfway into the beam of light, and she took a moment to look down at herself.

Today, Issia wore white.

The long, pale dress was low-cut and clung to her body's every sinuous curve. The silken material was cool against her skin and was belted to her waist with a loop of soft leather. She adjusted the thin straps over her shoulders and tugged the garment down to expose more of her ample chest. Gold shone around her arms, wrists, and neck, and Issia's honey-colored hair fell in thick waves. She was pleased with the way the light made her scales glow with obsidian depth, and the heat felt good on the exposed flesh of her arms and shoulders.

Satisfied with the way Sarach would find her, Issia reached up to tuck her scorpion pendant away. She normally kept it hidden between her breasts, but decided against it at the last moment.

"Come in," she called, settling atop her coils as her drudge opened the door.

Issia frowned as two hyenalings, instead of the single one she'd been expecting, stepped into her workshop. She recognized Sarach, of course, though both his armor and expression were worn and dusty from the road. The male beside him was one she'd never seen before. He wore a dirty robe, and his head was wrapped in a ragged piece of cloth. One of the ears poking out of it was notched and when Issia met his gaze, the hyenaling gave her a grin that stretched uncomfortably wide.

"Sarach," she said, her voice cold. With a flick of her will, the jackal-headed guardian that stood out in the hall entered and drew its twin swords. "You've brought a friend."

"Mistress," her guardsman said, crashing to his knees. "I've failed."

Issia stiffened. "What? Naroh isn't here?"

"No, mistress," Sarach said, bowing his head. "We followed the divers to the tomb in the canyon and confronted them not long after they emerged. I spoke with them for some time, but they refused to come."

"And why didn't you simply drag them here? A man and a single hyenaling should not have been a problem for a squad of house warriors."

"There was an elf with them, too, mistress. The three of them were wounded, but by the time we reached them, they had found their way back to the war-scorpion. It wouldn't let us near."

Failure was not a taste Issia was accustomed to, and it made her stomach roil. Her tail flexed, wanting nothing more than to squeeze, twist, and coil. The conversation with her father the day before, duty, marriage, her sister, and all of the things that she'd been careful not to think about came crashing through her mind. She struggled to maintain her perfect composure and to keep her features clear.

But Issia was a necrophant's daughter and heir to House Malash. Perfection was the mask she wore, and after several moments and one long sigh, it slipped back into place.

"And why," she asked, forcing her body to relax, "by all the gods of death and judgment, did you not confront them before they reached the scorpion?"

"The two mice were too much for my small-jawed friends," the strange hyenaling said. He was still on his feet and appeared unbothered by the jackal-headed horror looming behind him. "But you look hungry enough to swallow them whole."

“This is Kur,” Sarach said as she frowned. “He’s a priest.”

Issia’s flesh prickled, and this time, she wasn’t able to stop the rippling flex of her serpent’s coils. Hyenaling priests were dangerous and unpredictable, as reckless and elusive as they were insane. This man should not be taken lightly.

Yet, she was a necromancer in the heart of her domain, and she felt no fear. Rather, that same half-forgotten, predatory instinct stirred within her, recognizing a challenger.

“Sarach,” she said, not taking her eyes off the grinning priest. “While your decades of service to me might excuse the odd failure, this breach goes far beyond that. You will both die if you do not adequately explain yourself within the next two minutes.”

So, he did. Sarach began to speak, telling her of everything that had passed in the weeks he’d been away.

Issia let his words wash over her. Trusting her guardians, she turned to stare out into the sun-drenched world beyond her balcony. Without leaving her workshop, she let her eyes drift over the pyramid-shaped roofs of the nearest house necropolises and out into the city beyond.

Ikkad, and all that she could see would be hers one day.

This wasn’t new, of course. Ever since her power had manifested itself, Issia had known that the future of both the city and House Malash would one day rest atop her shoulders. It was a duty she had not once shied away from, and her earliest years had been spent learning all she would need to one day rule.

Not for the first time in her two and a half decades of life, Issia tried to picture herself in her father’s place. She imagined ascending to his seat in court, spending her days entertaining visitors and making peace between the city’s other bickering houses while ensuring her own scheming family members remained out of trouble. There would be parties and glittering balls, luxurious food, and all the wealth she could ever dream of. She’d have the power and influence to shape the empire itself, and a husband working beside her. The man would be a stranger, of course, and from a powerful family. He’d have his own goals and aspirations, but Issia would learn to handle him.

Besides, Ashura wasn't like many of the barbarous human kingdoms to the north, where power was passed only through the males of the familial line. Marriage would change nothing of her position. The necrophant's mantle was one of raw, necromantic power, and she had proven she could don it by chaining an entire legion, more than six thousand corpses, to her will.

No, Issia's future was guaranteed and appeared as blindingly perfect as the sun itself.

"So," she said, finally turning away from the open air. "This mongrel priest beat you to the divers, ruined your ambush, and caused you to fail the critically important task I asked of you. After which, not only did you decide against slitting his throat and leaving his bones for the vultures, you brought him into my private chambers. Did I understand all of that correctly, Sarach?"

The kneeling hyenaling did not look up from the floor. "Yes, mistress."

"I admit to having difficulty seeing the wisdom in all of this."

"I understand and ask for no forgiveness, mistress."

Issia shifted atop her coils, her anger rising despite her best efforts. "Tell me then, Sarach, after all this failure, is there even a single reason why I shouldn't execute the priest and have you stripped and thrown from the palace?"

"Because," Kur said, giving her another too-wide grin. "I know where the scorpion's going."

Issia remained silent, managing, at the last moment, to keep herself from snorting her disbelief.

"Our priests never lie, mistress," Sarach said from the floor. "And they know things. If Kur says he knows where it is, then he is telling the truth."

"Perhaps," she answered. "Or perhaps you've convinced yourself that this madman is your only chance at redemption."

The priest laughed, a high, grating cackle that made Issia's head throb. Her anger flared, and she was a moment from ordering her guardian to run him through when the hyenaling spoke.

"You've gotten hungry safely slithering around in your flawless cage." He grinned, his ears flicking above his dirty headwrap. "You gnaw and you chew, you bite and you swallow, but still your belly feels empty."

"Are those your final words, priest?" Issia said, ignoring the sudden pounding of her heart.

"No, no," Kur said, and somehow, impossibly, his grin widened. "But remember this if you do kill me, little serpent—sometimes, to fill yourself, all you need is that last, perfect bite."

Issia stared at the mad priest, her mind swirling beneath the perfect mask of her features. The words resonated within her, speaking to the hollowness in the pit of her stomach, to the feeling that something in her life was missing.

"Kill any of them that move," Issia ordered her construct before turning away.

The hyenaling's cackle followed her out onto her balcony. Sunlight enveloped her, the furnace heat of the afternoon pushing down on her and thickening the air. A rippling flex of her tail brought her to the balustrade. She leaned her palms onto the warm stone, and despite the smothering weight of the sun, Issia felt the storm within her ease.

Sweat prickled her scalp, and looking out over the city she would one day rule, she finally acknowledged the terrifying thought that had nibbled at the edges of her mind for as long as she could remember.

Issia wasn't happy.

She closed her eyes and bowed her head, shutting away the world that would soon demand so much of her attention. In this private darkness, she let herself consider the thought. It was such a frustrating thing, an ever-lurking distraction that had plagued her for years. Duty to her father and to her House were what truly mattered. Happiness wasn't important, and yet, like a missing tooth, the absence of it was hard to truly ignore.

Issia let out a long breath and opened her eyes. With her head bowed, the first thing that she saw was the golden, scorpion-shaped pendant resting atop her breasts. She reached up to cup it in one hand.

Her first real act of rebellion.

Not long after her fifteenth birthday, that empty, hollow misery had become unbearable. She'd felt herself start to crack and unravel at the edges. There had been a lamian from Murad visiting the Ziggurat, and, seeking him out, Issia had promised him half his weight in gold for the egg he carried. Her father had honored her bargain, though he'd been angrier than she'd ever seen him before. Issia spent close to the next year confined to her rooms, and despite the blow to her house's wealth and pride, she had never once regretted her action.

For Sin, the beautiful, black war-scorpion that had hatched from that egg had saved her life. In caring for her, Issia had been almost happy. She'd been able to throw herself back into her studies, grow her power, and build her mask of perfection.

Sin had allowed her to become the perfect daughter. Yet, now, the emptiness had grown too much for even a war-scorpion to fill.

"Priest," Issia called, her eyes not leaving her golden pendant. "Where is the white scorpion going?"

"Across the desert. To the Broken Mountain."

She felt her heart beat faster. There'd been several other smaller acts of rebellion over the years, things that she'd needed to do to keep herself sane. But this would be different. This would be so much more.

"One last bite," she murmured, tucking her pendant back between her breasts. "One last, perfect bite."

Naroh, she thought, seeing again the dark-eyed tomb diver. He had what she needed. She could be happy after this, she knew she could be. One last dereliction of duty, she told herself, and then she could fully dedicate herself to her father and house.

"Sarach!"

"Mistress?" She heard him respond.

"Get Sin's saddle ready. We're going to visit my sister."

The priests said that hunger was wicked, but surely, the gods would not begrudge her something as small as happiness? She clenched her fist and sent out a focused pulse of magic. Behind her, atop the stone bier, purple fire flared to life within two empty sockets.

No, she would have this. Issia would take it from Naroh, no matter how ready he was to give.

Rate and Review

Thank you so much for reading Tomb Divers. As a long-time fan of HaremLit I was eager to try my hand at it and I hope you enjoyed reading it as much as I did writing it.

If you've made it this far and would like to see more of my writing please take the time to rate and review this book. As a new indie author your feedback is the literal lifeblood of my career.

Naroh's story as well as any others I might write would not be possible without you.

About the Author

Robyn Bee is a writer who bumbles through life with all the grace of a honey-drunk bear. He is a lover of forest meadows, fantasy, history, and any sort of books that feature beautiful women and furious sword fights.

Expect stories of action, love, magic, and adventure; each one liberally sprinkled with spice.

Links to Explore

CHECK OUT THE LINKS below for more HaremLit and Romance for Men stories. Both communities are great and there are some truly talented writers there.

- https://linktr.ee/romanceformen
- https://discord.gg/6DgPaerTDU
- https://www.facebook.com/groups/monstergirlbooks
- https://www.facebook.com/groups/dukesofharem
- https://www.facebook.com/groups/haremlitbooks
- https://www.facebook.com/groups/1335086533800767
- https://www.facebook.com/groups/337959267036919

Printed in Dunstable, United Kingdom

65212540R00221